Louise Douglas is a copywriter. ~~~~~ ~~~~~ ~~~~~ ons and
lives in north Somerset with her partner. *The Secret by
the Lake* is her sixth novel. Her first novel, *The Love of My
Life*, was longlisted for both the Romantic Novel of the
Year Award and the Waverton Good Read Award, and
her third, *The Secrets Between Us*, was a Richard and Judy
Book Club pick.

Talk to her on Twitter @LouiseDouglas3 and visit her
website at www.louisedouglas.co.uk

WITHDRAWN

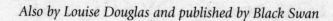

Also by Louise Douglas and published by Black Swan

The Secrets Between Us
In Her Shadow
Your Beautiful Lies

For more information on Louise Douglas and her
books, see her website at www.louisedouglas.co.uk

The Secret by the Lake

Louise Douglas

BLACK SWAN

TRANSWORLD PUBLISHERS
61–63 Uxbridge Road, London W5 5SA
www.transworldbooks.co.uk

Transworld is part of the Penguin Random House group of companies
whose addresses can be found at global.penguinrandomhouse.com

Penguin
Random House
UK

First published in Great Britain in 2015 by Black Swan
an imprint of TransworldPublishers

A CIP catalogue record for this book
is available from the British Library.

ISBN
9780552779272

Typeset in 11/14pt Giovanni Book by Falcon Oast Graphic Art Ltd.
Printed and bound by CPI Group (UK) Ltd, Croydon, CR0 4YY.

Penguin Random House is committed to a sustainable
future for our business, our readers and our planet. This book
is made from Forest Stewardship Council® certified paper.

MIX
Paper from
responsible sources
FSC® C018179

1 3 5 7 9 10 8 6 4 2

For my cousins: Julie, Mark, Richard, John, Paul, Sarah and Andrew, and their families, with all my love xxxxxxx

PROLOGUE

Blackwater, Somerset, July 1931

It was a beautiful thing, a heart-shaped pendant – a ruby surrounded by tiny diamonds, set within a gold clasp in the shape of two hands joined together – and dangling from a slender gold chain.

'It's more than a hundred years old,' Madam had explained some weeks earlier, 'and very precious. It's been in my family for generations.' Madam's jewellery, normally kept locked in the safe, had been laid out on a velvet cloth spread over the table in the dining room, along with her silver candlesticks, her Victorian tea-set and various other items of high value. They were making an inventory 'for insurance purposes', she had said, although that wasn't the real reason. The real reason was because she wanted to remind her young husband which side his bread was buttered.

The housemaid was holding a pen and notebook. *Ruby pendant*, she wrote under the column headlined: Description of item. 'Approximate value?' she asked the older woman.

'At least one hundred guineas.'

100 guineas, the girl wrote. The pendant lay on the ink-blue cloth beside its box. She could not properly see the colour of the stone. She reached out towards it; Madam immediately tapped her hand away.

'No, no, you're not to touch it, it's awfully delicate,' she snapped.

There were a great many things in the grand house called Fairlawn that the housemaid was considered too heavy-handed to touch.

Now that same girl sat on the trunk of a huge oak tree that had recently fallen into a grassy hollow at the side of the lake. In front of her the great expanse of water lay flat, echoing the light in the sky, shivering in the breeze and disturbed every now and then by fish rising to feed on myriad tiny flies that hovered inches from its surface. Sedge warblers were wading amongst the fringing reeds and the willows dipped their pale leaves down between the yellow iris to meet their own reflections. Cow parsley and nettles grew around the fallen branches of the tree, and pink and blue wild-flowers lay in scented drifts. The midges danced in their thousands.

The girl loved this cool, dappled place. She thought of it as somehow blessed.

The sun was bright in the clouds just above the horizon. It was growing late. She was waiting for her love. She looked about her, but all she could see were the trees and the lake; she listened, but all she heard was birdsong and the distant clopping of a horse crossing the dam at the end of the reservoir. Perhaps he was having trouble getting away. He often did.

She slipped her hand in the pocket of the ugly brown dress that Madam insisted she wear to work, took something out, glanced furtively around again, and then uncurled her fingers . . . and there was the ruby pendant, nestled in its delicate gold chain. She held the necklace up so that the diamonds caught the sunlight and fractured it into tiny splinters. Then she shut one eye and held the ruby close to the other, so that all she could see was the pure colour, and the way light cut through the blood-red interior of the stone. It was as if she were inside it, caught inside the jewel.

There was a sound to her right, the snap of a twig underfoot. She closed her fingers around the pendant and looked over her shoulder. It couldn't be him, he always whistled to let her know he was coming. She crouched down amongst the branches of the fallen tree, hiding behind its leaves and shadows. She peered through the greenery and her heart raced in despair when she saw who it was. The man was walking along the path that crossed behind the hollow. He stopped at the opening and stood for a moment with his hand raised to shield his eyes from the sun, looking out over the lake. He had taken off his jacket and was carrying it over his arm. The girl could see the braces pulled tight over his shoulders, the redness at the nape of his neck and its sinews, sweat glistening on his forehead, his thick, black hair.

She held her breath. She did not move. Her heart thumped inside her chest. He was so close she could see the black mole on his neck, the individual hairs of his

9

beard; she could smell him, even over the hot smell of the mud at the water's edge. If he took another step he would be upon her. She braced herself, prepared for the worst, but then she heard a voice in the distance calling him. He hesitated, but the call came again and this time he turned and went back the way he had come. She let out her breath and leaned back against the tree.

He must have seen her walking towards the lake and followed her. What if he had been watching her all along? What if he had seen her admiring the pendant? Could he have seen it? Might he have realized what it was?

'No,' she told herself. No, even if he had seen her sitting on the trunk, he would have been too far away to see what she was holding. He couldn't possibly have recognized the pendant.

He couldn't have.

Oh, but what if he had?

CHAPTER ONE

Les Aubépines, France, April 1961

It had been a glorious spring, warm enough to swim in April, and the day's damp towels were pegged on the washing-line in the garden behind the lovely old French farmhouse, the place where I'd spent my last ten summers with the Laurent family. Bicycles were stacked against the back wall, and tennis racquets and balls were heaped by the door. The air smelled of the settling dew, of the lovage and lavender that grew wild amongst the pine trees on the dunes, of summer's approach. The beach stretched pale, the waves frilled with silver as they tumbled and rolled on to the sand, and the sea beyond wrinkled and shifted, moonlight sliding over its surface like oil in a pan.

We were wrapped in cardigans, Viviane and I, sitting in the hollow of the dunes. The sand that had been warm earlier was cold now beneath our bare feet. The child was unusually quiet. She wrote her name in the sand with her finger and then took a handful and trickled it over the letters until the word disappeared.

She moved closer and rested her head on my shoulder. I put my arm around her and pulled her into me; we settled into the warmth of each other, as we always did, as we had done for all of her life. I had never felt such love for anyone, and I'd never felt such sadness either. I had always believed that I would never have to leave her. I thought we would be together, always.

'What time are you going tomorrow?' she asked.

'After breakfast.'

'I wish you weren't going.'

'Oh, Vivi, so do I.'

I couldn't tell Viviane how I was dreading the impending separation from her, and from her parents, Julia and Alain. I could not explain that I didn't know how I would muster the strength to tear myself away from the family I had loved so deeply for ten years, ever since Vivi was a baby. Instead I rested my cheek against the top of her head and breathed in the salty smell of her hair, committing the moment to memory so it would be there when I needed it later, when I was alone.

'*Why* do you have to go?' Viviane whispered.

'I've told you, sweetheart. My grandmother is ill and my father needs me at home; there isn't anyone else to help him.'

'And what about me? What will happen to me?'

'Oh my darling, you'll carry on growing up and you will become cleverer and better and stronger. Your dear mother and father will look after you. And I'll write to you and you'll write to me and it will be almost as if we were still together – you'll see, it will be almost the same.'

12

'It won't be the same at all.' Viviane picked up a twig and dug the point of it into the sand. She concentrated on this for a moment and then added: 'At least I'll still have Emily. Emily wouldn't leave me.'

I smiled and ran my hand the length of her back. 'I thought *you* had left *her*,' I said. 'I thought you'd decided you were too big for imaginary friends now that you're almost ten.'

Viviane shrugged. She flicked sand into the air with the point of the twig.

There had been a time, not so long ago, when I'd had to lay a place for Emily at the table, when Julia, Alain and I had to be careful where we walked in case we accidentally stepped on Emily's toes, when, at bedtimes, I was obliged to read a story to Emily and kiss her good-night, along with Viviane. Lately, though, her name had hardly been mentioned and Viviane was less inclined to wander off alone, her hand holding an invisible hand, her lips moving as she carried on both sides of a two-way conversation. Once or twice I'd been surprised and amused to catch myself feeling sorry for the imaginary friend whose place in Viviane's affections was being superseded by tennis lessons and new friendships, a passion for music. That evening, I was actually relieved to hear that Emily was still part of Vivi's life. At least she would have Emily's company when I was gone.

I kissed her head.

'It's late now, darling, and it's getting cold. We ought to go in. Your mummy will be wondering where we are.'

I pushed myself to my feet, held out my hands to pull Viviane up, and then dusted the sand from my shorts. Viviane stood and wrapped her arms around my waist.

'Oh Amy, please don't go!' she said.

The night was still and lovely. The sky was full of stars, the Milky Way draped across the firmament so there seemed almost more light than darkness. Moon shadows stretched long and low across the sand, the wind breathed amongst the pine trees, the needles whispered. I looked for one last time towards the sea and I took hold of Viviane's hand and I felt as if my heart was breaking.

CHAPTER TWO

Two days later, I arrived back at the family home, a steelworker's two-up two-down in Sheffield, the house my grandmother shared with her son, my father, and her black Labrador dog, Bess. Nothing much had changed in all the years I'd been away. I tried not to notice how dark and cramped and uncomfortable it all was and threw myself into the task of caring for Granny.

She and I had never been close and my genuine, heartfelt pity for her was tempered by knowing what I'd given up in order to come home to care for her. When I was a child, she had rarely shown me affection, even when I'd desperately needed it. And now she needed me and I'd had to leave the family I loved with all my heart to come back to her.

I had been nine years old and the war was still raging when my beautiful mother, the mother I adored, kissed me for the last time, told me she was going out to buy cigarettes, tied her headscarf beneath her chin, buttoned up the fox-fur collar of her coat, left and never returned. That night I cried for her. The next day I knelt on the bed to look out of the front window, waiting for her to turn the corner and come down the street, all clippy in her heels with her skirt-hem swinging, but she did not appear. I asked the neighbours but nobody had seen her. I couldn't understand why neither my father nor my grandmother was concerned about her whereabouts. What if a bomb had fallen close to where she was? What if she was trapped, somewhere, in the rubble, and nobody was looking for her? I couldn't understand why they didn't miss her as much as I did.

Dad ignored my tears and my questions. Granny was made of sterner stuff.

'Be quiet,' she said as I sat sobbing at the tea-table, 'or I'll give you something to really cry about.'

'Oh please, Granny,' I begged, 'please make my mummy come home.'

'It would be best if you didn't think about her,' Granny said – which was, I suppose, a gentle way of letting me know that my mother was gone for good.

A few days – maybe a fortnight – after my mother had left, we moved into Granny's house, Dad and I, and a new family moved into ours. Dad continued to refuse to talk about my mother at all and Granny frowned upon any public mention, forever after referring to her absent daughter-in-law as 'that piece'. My mother was demoted from the centre of my universe to someone so peripheral she could not even be named. I wrote her name, Daisy, in the dust on the floorboards, I scratched it into the window ledge, I picked a hundred daisies and made her name out of flowers. I tried to bring her back to me by force of will. It didn't work.

My father left my upbringing to his mother as he had previously left it to his wife. He spent his nights at his important war work in the foundry and his days, when he was not sleeping, tending to his pigeons, or racing them, all the time with an expression on his face that implied he had expected little from life, and had not been disappointed.

I learned early on to keep my love for my mother, and my anxiety, to myself. I don't think I was a particularly difficult child. I did my best to please my grandmother, until the day it dawned on me that perhaps such a thing was impossible. After that, I simply stayed out of her way as much as I could. I left school and home at fifteen, paying my way through nanny college by taking cleaning and waitressing jobs in the evenings and at weekends. As soon as I qualified, I moved to France to live with the Laurents – Viviane, Julia and Alain. Julia had been a professional ballet dancer, but had injured her hip badly in a fall. Pregnancy and childbirth had debilitated her further. She needed somebody to help her care for her baby daughter and fortunately, from all the candidates who applied for the role, she chose me. I was officially an employee but I felt, from the start, like one of the family. I'd come to understand what it meant to receive affection, to be trusted. I had found myself cared for and valued, and for the first time since my mother went away, I felt I belonged. In return, I'd given my heart and soul to the Laurents. I would have done anything for them; anything.

But my grandmother was dying and there was nobody else to look after her; I had no choice but to return to

Sheffield in the spring of 1961 and it was difficult. Twelve years had elapsed since I'd last lived at home. It wasn't easy to adjust to being back in the cramped old house, walking the old streets with the dog, seeing the old faces, but I did my best. The harder I worked, the less time there was to think about what I had left behind. And I tried not to think about France and the Laurents, really I tried, because I could hardly bear the anguish of missing them when I did.

I nursed Granny as kindly and patiently as I could, and somewhere amongst the spoonfuls of warm broth I held to her lips and the cool flannels I used to soothe her forehead, the two of us achieved a kind of peace. I made her as comfortable as I could and did my best to alleviate her loneliness and fear. I tried to talk to her. I wanted to forge a bond with her, but she was so frail it seemed unkind to speak of anything of consequence. The past had been painful for us both and I didn't want to dredge up bad memories in her last days. So I chatted instead of mundane things: the weather, the buildings they were knocking down in the city centre, the flowers I'd picked from the allotment and put in a vase on the window ledge. Granny blinked at me through milky, pale blue eyes. I couldn't be sure if she heard me or not, or if she understood. Often, she drifted off to sleep while I was talking; she rarely said a word to me, pointing if she wanted me to pass something to her. Yet she watched me and I sensed that she was glad I was there.

One afternoon, she asked for a drink of ginger wine. 'We don't have any, I'm afraid,' I told her. 'I didn't even know you liked it. Shall I pour you a glass of sherry instead?'

'Please,' she whispered. 'I have a craving for ginger wine.'

'All right,' I said. 'Not to worry, Granny. I'll go out and get you some.'

I went next door and asked the neighbour, Mrs Botham, to sit with my grandmother while I was out and Mrs Botham wiped her hands on her apron and said it would be no bother at all.

I hurried down to the Black Horse. The landlord knew my father and by the time we'd exchanged a few words and I'd hastened back to the house, my grandmother had slipped away.

'She went ever so peacefully,' Mrs Botham said. Her eyes were puffy and her nostrils were red. 'One minute she was telling me how good you'd been with her and the next she was gone.'

'I should have been with her,' I said.

'I reckon she sent you out on purpose because she knew her time had come and wanted to spare you the ordeal,' said Mrs Botham. She took hold of my hand and squeezed it. 'Your granny was right proud of you, Amy. She might not have said it to your face, but she was.'

I thought it was kind of her to say that, but I didn't really believe her.

After Granny's funeral, I found myself lonelier than ever, drifting. My father hardly spoke to me. His routine had not changed in all the years I'd been away: he worked, he slept, he saw to his birds. And the pigeons still cooed in their loft out the back, calling to him. I looked through the kitchen window while I was washing the dishes and saw him cradling his favourite up to his cheek, stroking the soft feathers on the back of its head with his knuckle, his lips moving close as he whispered endearments through the blue wisps of his cigarette smoke. I bit back my hurt as I wondered, as I had done many times before, what it was about me that made it impossible for my father to treat me with a fraction of the tenderness he showed to his birds. The same thing, I supposed, that had driven my mother to leave me without a word of explanation, without a backwards glance. I took the bottle of ginger wine from the pantry shelf, and poured myself a drink.

I wrote to Alain and Julia asking if I could return to them. Julia wrote back to say that Alain's old aunt Audrine had moved in to help with Viviane, in my absence. 'It's clear that she was terribly lonely before she came to us, so I can't ask her to leave,' Julia wrote. 'I'm so sorry, dear Amy, but we'll do everything we can to help you find another job.' And they did. They put me in touch with an old friend of theirs, the manager of St Theresa's, a children's home on the other side of Sheffield. Bridget Adams was looking for a level-headed young woman to work as a matron to the younger children. It was a live-in position. I wrote a letter of application enclosing a reference written by Alain, and received one by return informing me I had been appointed to the post. It would be helpful if I could take up the role at the earliest opportunity.

That evening I made my father liver and onions for his tea before he went off to work the night shift at the foundry. When he'd finished eating, I cleared away his plate and told him I would be moving out. His surprise caught me offguard.

'I thought you'd be stopping awhile,' he said. He took his cigarettes out of his waistcoat pocket and tapped one from the packet, avoiding my eye.

'If you need me, Dad, if you want me to stay, then I will,' I said.

He put the cigarette between his lips, and I passed him the matchbox. A memory assaulted me: he and I sorting cigarette cards after we'd moved into Granny's house. We were arranging the cards on a board that Dad would eventually frame and hang on the wall of the bedroom we shared, me sleeping in the bed at night, him during the day. I remembered us sitting together, head to head, at the kitchen table, close to the stove where it was warmest. I recalled the smell of his hair oil and the warmth of his body, the myriad tiny burn scabs on his forearms beneath the covering of black hairs, the feel of the cards, stiff between my fingers, each one a mini-masterpiece.

'Which one's your favourite, Birdie?' he had asked. He always used to call me 'Birdie'.

'That one!' I pointed to Loretta Young. I grinned and swung my legs beneath the table.

'That's my favourite too,' my father had replied, bumping his shoulder companionably against mine, and I'd been so proud that we shared the same opinion.

Now he struck the match, narrowing his eyes as he drew the flame to the end of the cigarette.

'What about the dog?' he asked, without looking at me. 'I don't have the time for her. What'll happen to her?'

'I'll take her with me,' I said, 'they said that I could.'

He said: 'Right.'

I tried once more, for the sake of the memory, to restore the connection between us. 'I don't want you to be lonely here on your own, Dad, after I've left. I'll be able to pop back at weekends. I can still do your washing and shopping if you'd like me to.'

'There'll be no need for that,' my father said. 'I can manage.' And he flicked the match into the sink, stood up and went outside, through the back door into the yard. I heard him calling to the pigeons. 'Come on, my beauties, where are you? Where are you, eh?'

I watched him for a moment, but my eyes were stinging. I went upstairs to pack.

CHAPTER THREE

I had been at the children's home for four months and the summer of 1961 was turning into autumn. My work was often exhausting and the hours were long. The home was under-staffed and under-funded. It relied on charitable donations for everything other than the absolute basics, and the children were dressed in hand-me-downs and had few toys and no books. The staff did their best with what they had. I was terribly fond of the children in my care; some of them, poor dears, had been through so much in their lives already. Although we had very little to work with, we still managed to have fun. We were forever organizing games of rounders or French cricket, activities of which the children never seemed to tire. It was so different to how my life had been when I worked for the Laurents – I'd never had to deal with nits, or worms, or scabies before, let alone malnourished children, children who had had polio or rickets, children who had never learned to eat with a knife and fork. It was different and sometimes it was very difficult, but I loved the work. I loved the small progresses that were made every day. There was nothing more rewarding than the moment when a traumatized child finally held her hand out to me, or when a teenager beaten black and blue by his stepfather gave a belly laugh for the first time.

I still missed the Laurents dreadfully, but I exchanged letters with Julia every week and Viviane always wrote a few lines for me too, while Alain sometimes enclosed a postcard. The three of them had, by that time, moved from the beach house at Les Aubépines back to the Paris apartment where they always spent the winter months. I knew the family, their homes and their routines so very well that it was easy for me to imagine what they were doing, which restaurants they were frequenting, how they were spending their days. They had invited me to come for Christmas, but I wanted to help give the children in the home the best Christmas possible so we'd agreed, instead, that I would fly out to Paris in the New Year when I had arranged a few days off.

I was really looking forward to my holiday, saving up for my plane ticket and planning the gifts I would give to Julia and Alain and the places I would go to with Viviane – the parks and museums, the markets at the side of the Seine, her favourite cafés. I imagined the two of us walking together as we used to, she swinging my hand in her mittened one, our breaths cloudy in the freezing air and beautiful Paris with its long avenues, its elegant, blond stonework, the bridge where we liked to stand and watch the boats chugging along the river with Notre Dame behind us, the smell of coffee and frying crêpe batter, the tall houses with their curlicued balconies, the pretty lights in the shops, the music and the seasonal decorations: I could hardly wait.

Then the letter came.

I recognized Julia's handwriting, but was distracted that morning because the education inspector was due to visit St Theresa's and I was anxious that everything should be just right. It didn't register with me that the letter was inside an ordinary envelope and not written, as all the others had been, on blue airmail paper. I didn't notice the British stamp. I simply tore the envelope open and took out the single sheet of paper folded inside. The writing, normally bold and confident, was spidery and faint. I took a deep breath, and I read:

Dear Amy,

I don't know how to begin to write this letter to you because I know it will hurt you. I don't want to do that, but I have to tell you here and now because there's no other way.

Alain is dead.

How can he be gone? How can Alain be gone and the world still keep turning? You know he was my love, my life, my reason for living. He was my everything.

But Amy, he is gone.

I have no husband. Viviane has no father. There is no money, no choice but to return to England, to my parents' old cottage in Blackwater, the place where I grew up. And that's where we are, Amy, here in Somerset, in limbo. We are falling apart. I need you, Viviane needs you. I am struggling to cope with my own grief, I cannot cope with hers as well.

*You know us better than anyone. Please come back to
us. Please come and help us. We cannot manage
without you.*

Yours always, in love and sorrow,
Julia

Bridget, the manageress of the children's home, was
shocked to hear of Alain's death, but could not have
been more kind. She told me that of course I must go to
Julia and Viviane, at once. She kissed me and assured
me that she, unlike Julia, would manage without me. I
promised to return one day. I said goodbye to the
children, although it was terribly hard, and explained
why I had to go. The little ones cried when they heard
that the dog, Bess, would be leaving with me and I had
to promise that I wouldn't let her forget them. And then
I packed my bag and I left, again. I felt like a leaf being
blown about by the wind, incapable of taking charge of
my destiny, but reacting, all the time, to circumstance,
running from one crisis to another.

After a seemingly endless journey, I was the only person
who alighted the train at Blackwater, a small remote
stop – the end of the line. I had been travelling for most
of the day with Bess for company and I was bone tired,
overwhelmed by the need to be with Julia and Viviane,
to look after them and help them, and an equally strong
fear of how I would find them and how they would be.
   I was sad too, for myself, in my own right. I had loved
Alain for the man that he was, a campaigning journalist

with a heart the size of the sun whose every working moment was driven by integrity, and the search for truth and justice. My sorrow weighed me down, adding to the burden of regret I'd felt after my grandmother's death.

I stepped off the train, heaving my bag behind me. The train driver walked past me, bade me goodnight and disappeared into the darkness. I followed him down the platform lit only by a single, dim yellow lamp, and out of a gate on to a lane that only went one way. It was eerily quiet and the isolation of the place was unsettling. There was something in the atmosphere that I did not recognize at first – a heavy silence, a chill in the air. I walked along the lane, spooked by the hooting of an owl hunting in the woodland beyond, and my own footsteps, Bess walking close to my heel.

After a short while, the lane rose sharply uphill before opening out on to another road and here the temperature dropped a couple of degrees. It was then I recognized what had been causing the strange coldness, the muffling quiet. I found myself standing on a dam that crossed one end of a long, wide lake – a reservoir. The lake was stretched before me, dark and immense, a vaporous mist floating like steam above its surface. I could not see the moon as it was hidden by clouds, but its silvery brightness permeated the mist and the water beneath it – and all of it together, the light in the darkness and the smell of the water, the space . . . made me feel odd, as if I were in a dream. As if I were not myself, but somebody else altogether.

CHAPTER FOUR

I followed Julia's directions and walked uphill, past a grand house set behind walls and gates, taking the road that led up to the village, before turning into the lane where she had lived, as a child, and where she now lived again. The clouds had uncovered the moon and I could clearly see Reservoir Cottage, one of a pair of semi-detached houses standing alone on a rise of land. Behind, in the valley, the moonlight shimmered on the water and upon the ghostly mist, and I had a strong sensation that the lake was calling to me. My eyes were drawn to it and it was hard to look away. I gazed at it for a moment longer, then looked back to the cottage.

It was the mirror image of its adjoining neighbour with a gable over the top front window and a garage to one side. The front garden was overgrown and unkempt. I pushed open a small wooden gate almost hidden beneath the fingery black fronds of an overhanging yew and walked down the path. Logs were stacked haphazardly by the garage, and ivy crept over the path and the walls, up the trunks of the trees. Bess held back, reluctant to approach the house. She growled anxiously.

'Don't be silly,' I told her, 'there's nothing to be afraid of here.'

I knocked at the door. When nobody came to let me in, I turned the handle and pushed the door open. A light bulb swung slowly on the end of a wire beneath a yellowing lampshade, casting shadows over a narrow wooden staircase with lines of paint on either side and a bare strip in the centre of each step where a carpet had once lain. I could hear a clock ticking somewhere in the house, but apart from that it was silent.

'Hello!' I called. 'Is anyone there?'

There was movement in a room to my left; a door creaked open and Viviane emerged from the shadows. She was pale and thin, the spirit gone from her, but the moment I saw her dear face, my heart leaped. She ran to me, her arms outstretched like a baby's, tears spilling from her eyes.

'Oh Vivi!' I whispered. 'Oh my darling!'

I held the child in my arms, rocking her against me, holding her as tightly as I could. She was taller than she'd been the last time I saw her, and her hair had been cut into a bob, which made her seem older, but she was still the same, still my own, dear Viviane, my beloved girl. We clung on to one another.

'You came back,' she sobbed.

'Oh sweetheart, of course I came! I came as soon as I found out what had happened. My poor girl, you poor, dear thing.'

I held on to Viviane, held her close and smoothed her

29

hair and the side of her face, and I breathed in the scent of her while her tears soaked into my coat. I whispered, 'Shhh,' and, 'There, there,' and, 'It's all right, darling, I'm here now. I'm here,' until her crying subsided. Then I dried her cheeks with my handkerchief and kissed her face. Eventually she calmed enough to give me a brave little smile. The smile grew stronger when I told her that Bess would be part of the family now too. There was no sign of Julia. By then, I had been inside the house for a good five minutes and Vivi had been crying all that time, yet her mother had not come looking for her.

'Where is Mummy, sweetheart?' I asked. 'Is she sleeping?'

Viviane wound the handkerchief around her fingers. 'No, she's in the back room.'

'What about your great-aunt Audrine?' I asked. 'Where is she?'

'She didn't want to come to England. We left her behind in France.'

'Oh. OK. Will you take me to see Mummy?'

Viviane nodded.

I followed her down the hallway and into a narrow, dark room, lit only by the dull glow of an old-fashioned standard lamp. Julia was sitting in a chair in the middle of the room, rocking it slowly backwards and forwards, the runners grating a mournful rhythm on the floorboards. A blanket was wrapped over her knees and a shawl around her shoulders. Her face was strangely shadowed, but expressionless; so still it might have been made of stone. Bundled on her knees was Alain's favourite sweater, the cream cotton Fair Isle he always wore draped over his shoulders. Her walking stick lay on the floor beside her.

Viviane hesitated at the doorway, holding on to Bess's collar. I walked slowly towards Julia. She did not look up to me. She did not stop rocking. She gave no indication that she knew I was there. I stood in front of her and then I crouched down so that my eyes were on a level with hers. She finally looked at me and the sadness I saw in her face was so all-encompassing that I had to fight back my own, reciprocal tears.

I took her hand.

'Julia, dear Julia,' I said softly. 'I'm here now to help. I'm here for as long as you want me to be here.'

Julia held on to my hand, as if there were nothing else left in the world that she could hold, as if every other hand she had tried to hold had let her go.

'He's gone,' she whispered.

'Darling, I know.'

'Do you know how he died?'

I shook my head.

'The police shot him.'

'The police?'

'He was in a café with a group of Algerians and was caught up in a raid. They shot him and now they've frozen his assets pending an investigation. We have no money, Amy.'

'We'll manage.'

'The apartment in Paris is gone and the house on the coast. This is all that is left. If I hadn't inherited this cottage, I don't know what we would have done.'

'I thought the cottage was tenanted.'

'It was supposed to be,' Julia said. 'The agents do their best, but the tenants never stay. I suppose we were lucky the place was empty when we needed it.'

I reached over to kiss Julia's cheek. Her skin was cold and soft.

'We'll be all right, I promise.'

'I can't pay you,' she said. 'I have nothing to give you.'

'It doesn't matter. That's not important. I'm not here to work for you, but because I love you both.'

'Oh, Amy!'

I smoothed Julia's cheek with my hand.

I said: 'When you feel stronger, you can tell me what you want me to do. But for the time being, I'll take care of everything. You mustn't worry about a thing. We are together, the three of us. We will be all right.' Even as I said them, the words sounded hollow.

CHAPTER FIVE

Leaving Julia in her rocking chair, I set to looking around the house with Vivi leading me by the hand. The cottage was Victorian and, although it was large, the passageways were narrow with awkward angles and there was an over-abundance of cornicing and dark paintwork. The rooms were of a reasonable size, high-ceilinged, but they weren't beautiful rooms; there was far too much wood and the decor was dated. The carpets that had once covered the hall and stairs had been lifted, but in the living room there was an ancient rug that did not quite meet the walls. It must have been of good quality originally, but the fussy pattern was morbid and unpleasant. On the wall opposite the door was a large mirror and a painting of Jesus on the Cross in a home-made frame. There was a second picture in the living room, a framed piece of fabric worked in cross-stitch. The words inside the sampler read: *For the living know that they will die, but the dead know nothing and the memory of them is forgotten. Ecclesiastes 9:5*. The work was dated 1928.

I stood in front of it, holding Viviane's hand. It was a

miserable thing, the stitching untidy, done without care.

'Did Mummy make this?' I asked.

Viviane shook her head. 'It was Mummy's sister. She had to do it as a punishment.'

'I didn't know Mummy had a sister.'

'She died a long time ago.'

'Oh, how sad!' I glanced at Vivi. She wasn't looking at me, she was watching Bess who was lying beside us, all dog-eyed melancholy, with her chin on her paws.

'So will you show me where I can sleep?' I asked, trying to sound a little more cheerful.

Viviane nodded and took me upstairs. The landing floorboards creaked beneath our feet. A daddy-long-legs bumped at the landing window, up and down against the dirty glass, the colour faded from the old curtains and dust on the ledge. I caught a glimpse of the lake beyond: its clean, silvery stillness took my breath away.

I had a quick look around. The master bedroom was at the back, overlooking the garden and the lake. The bed was strewn with Julia's clothes and the dressing table with her cosmetics and creams, but the pretty little pots and bottles did nothing to alleviate its gloom, the shadows in the corners or the domination of a huge wardrobe that loomed from the wall opposite the bed.

Viviane's was a much smaller but well-proportioned room beside it, with a single bed and a wardrobe taking up most of the space.

'This used to be Mummy's bedroom when she was a little girl. There's a bigger bedroom at the front,' said

Viviane. 'But I wanted to be next door to Mummy.'

'Of course you did.'

I was drawn, again, to the window. The moon was higher in the sky now and sketchy clouds were drifting by like waifs. The back garden sloped downhill. There was a largish outbuilding, some kind of shed, silhouetted black against the perimeter fence, and beyond the fence was a large field leading down to the reservoir, with its fringe of trees. I could just make out the lights of the big house that I'd passed on my way up, and the line of the road on top of the dam. On the other side of the lake, in the distance, were a number of single-storey buildings bunched together, lights shining brightly from some of the windows.

'What is that place?' I asked Viviane.

'Mummy said it used to be an asylum but now it's a nursing home for old people. The man from next door lives there.'

'You've met him?'

'No, his wife told us. She's popped round a few times. Come on, we haven't finished.'

The bathroom was at the side of the house and at the front were two more doors. The first opened into a box room, empty save for an ugly, metal-framed bed and a small chest of drawers. Viviane looked up at me.

'You can sleep here,' she said, an apology in her voice. Both of us were thinking of the beautiful bedroom we had shared in the Paris apartment, with its floor-to-ceiling windows, its linen curtains, the gorgeously deep beds, the chandelier, the woollen rugs so thick that our feet sank into them, and everything smelling of the lemony wax polish the cleaner used on the wood and the fresh, scented flowers that always, somehow, seemed to be in the silver vases.

'This will be perfect,' I said as cheerily as I could. I smiled, to show that I meant it, and put my bag on the narrow bed.

We went back out on to the landing. The other door was closed and there was a key in the lock. A small wooden plaque had been slotted into the woodwork. It was a plain oval with eight letters inscribed on it in black: *Caroline*. Around the plaque were marks, as if someone had tried, but failed, to gouge it out.

I looked at the plaque, and then at Viviane. She was picking at her nails.

'Was this Mummy's sister's room?' I asked.

Vivi nodded.

'Shall we look inside?'

Vivi shrugged.

I turned the key and reached for the door handle. As my fingers drew close I felt repulsed as if I were reaching out to touch something long-dead. Viviane was watching me now and I sensed that she understood what I was feeling, that she had felt it too.

'We think there are mice in there,' she said quietly. 'We hear them sometimes.'

'Mice are nothing to be afraid of,' I said. I turned the handle and pushed and, with a groan, the door scraped open.

I pressed the light switch and, in the centre of the room, a weak bulb flickered. The room was icy cold.

Superficially, it was like the other rooms in the

cottage, plain and square. The door was panelled, with a dark, Bakelite handle, and the skirting boards were deep and bevelled. But this room was different in that it was wallpapered beneath the picture rail rather than painted. The paper was an unpleasant yellow colour, narrow vertical stripes with a yellow-brown design twisting up through the columns between the stripes. Cobwebs hovered in the corners. Caroline's old room seemed unloved. It must have been empty for years.

'Let's go down again,' Vivi whispered. She pulled at my arm.

'Yes,' I said. 'Let's.'

That first evening, I made the best dinner I could from what little there was in the pantry cupboard and the three of us ate together at the kitchen table. Julia looked down into her soup as it cooled but I never saw her raise the spoon to her lips. We sat in silence, the only sounds the quiet clink of cutlery on crockery and the ticking of the clock. When it chimed the half-hour, we all flinched.

Afterwards, Vivi and I took the dog out for a short walk. A light shone from behind the closed curtains of the front window of the house next door. I glimpsed a movement behind the curtains; somebody was watching us.

'Who lives there?' I asked Vivi.

'Mrs Croucher. The doctor's wife.'

'So the old man in the nursing home used to be a doctor?'

Vivi nodded. 'Yep.'

'Is his wife nice?'

'She made some jam tarts and did some shopping for us.'

'That was kind.'

'Mmm,' said Vivi.

We walked on down the lane. Bess sniffed at the bottom of the hedgerows. The moon cast a good light but in the shadows it was very dark. I kept looking to my left, over towards the lake – almost completely hidden now by the mist that had become more substantial and lay over the water like a mask. I pulled up the collar on my coat. Viviane's hand reached out and found mine. Her fingers were cold.

'I've missed you so much,' she said.

'My darling girl, I've missed you too.'

'I'm so glad you've come back.' Viviane paused for a heartbeat. Then she added: 'And Caroline says she's glad too.'

'Caroline?'

Vivi indicated the empty space beside her. 'I left Emily in Paris. Caroline is my new friend.'

CHAPTER SIX

I told myself that I would feel better in the morning, when I'd had a chance to give the box room a good clean and make it my own, but that first night was interminable. The mattress was thin and lumpy; it smelled of damp, and every time I turned, the metal bedframe rattled. I was cold and uncomfortable, but what kept me awake was more than that.

The desolation of the cottage, the quiet outside and the reservoir lying beyond like something waiting, ate into me. I was exhausted but wide awake. I'd brought the dog up to my room, pretending it was for Bess's sake but really because I craved the company. My mind kept drifting back to Les Aubépines, the house by the sea. It was a big house, much larger than this one, but I'd never felt lonely or afraid there. Everything about that house had been warm and sunny and welcoming. I remembered how we used to spend our summers in the garden, or on the beach. Whole days were spent in the sunshine: picnics on the beach, collecting shells with Vivi, building sandcastles and then going back to the house hungry and a little sunburned, my skin taut with salt and sand, to prepare the evening meal while the Laurents showered and changed. They were such happy times. I had thought they would last for ever.

I had been so wrong.

I pulled the blanket over my shoulder and made a pillow of my arms. Cold came up through the floorboards and deathwatch beetles knocked in the woodwork. Each time sleep crept close, I imagined a footstep or a whisper on the landing. My mind played tricks on me. Once I thought I heard Viviane cry out and I left my bed to check but she was fast asleep.

Julia had swallowed a sleeping tablet with a large glass of gin earlier and the snoring from her bedroom, combined with Bess's breathing, made a lullaby. Eventually I did drift into unconsciousness but once the immediate tiredness had been assuaged, there was nothing to anchor me in sleep. Towards dawn, something disturbed me. I opened my eyes but could see nothing but the weird shadows of the branches of the trees in the front garden waving on the ceiling. I experienced a panicky discomfort; for several moments I did not know where I was or why I was there. Then I remembered and with each heartbeat I felt wider awake until I reached a point where I knew it was hopeless trying to sleep again. I uncurled myself, slipped my legs out of the bed, and rose carefully to my feet.

'Come on,' I whispered to the dog.

I walked slowly down the stairs, keeping one hand against the wall, trying not to make a sound. The wood was cold beneath the soles of my bare feet. I went into the kitchen and switched on the light. The gin bottle was on the counter. I took an upturned glass from the drainer, rinsed it under the cold tap, set it down beside the bottle, unscrewed the cap and half-filled the glass. I took a mouthful. The burn in my throat and stomach was scorching but comforting. I drank some more. Then I picked up the glass and took it into the front living room. Bess followed like a shadow.

I tucked myself up on the sofa. Bess jumped up and lay beside me with her chin on my thigh. She sighed. I stroked her head, gently pulled her silky ears. I drank another mouthful of gin. Jesus looked down reproachfully from the wall.

'Sorry,' I said to Him. 'But You haven't been much help to this family so far, have You?'

My eyes drifted to the sampler. Why make a child work on that particular Bible verse? Weren't there hundreds of beautiful, positive words to choose from, more appropriate passages even for a child who was being punished? Words that might have taught her something good about life? Caroline must have *hated* sewing that sampler, I thought. Every stitch must have pained her. Her anger and frustration were clear in the untidiness of the work. I wondered if she had sewed it here in this room, perhaps sitting where I was sitting now. I tried to imagine her, tried to bring her to life. And then . . .

It began with a chill that raced through me, completely unexpectedly, starting in my core and then pumping in a single heartbeat through every vein and capillary in my body, making the hairs on my arms stand on end. For a moment I could not identify the source of the fear, and then I noticed that Bess was looking up towards the ceiling and I heard a sound, a dull shuffling above.

Something was moving in the empty bedroom.

Bess growled, a low, warning growl, and the hackles rolled up along her back and her ears were low and flat against her head.

'Shhh,' I whispered. 'Shhh.'

Above us, something dragged, or was dragged, across the floor, terribly slowly.

I held my breath. My blood ran to ice. I was rigid, looking up to the ceiling, listening to whatever it was moving across the floor – and then suddenly the noise stopped, directly above me. For a moment there was silence, and then a loud thump, like something being dropped.

Oh God!

I listened, but there was only silence now, and in a way that was worse.

No mouse had made those sounds, no rat or squirrel.

I stayed absolutely still, hardly daring to breathe, my hand on the dog's collar. Time went by and I became colder and colder but still I did not move. I stayed where I was until the moon had disappeared and the sun was rising over the reservoir. I stayed until the sky had turned the blue-white colour of milk and the first birds were singing in the trees. Only then, at last, did I dare to creep from the room and go back up the stairs.

The door to the empty bedroom beside mine had been closed when I came downstairs, the key turned in the lock. Now it was slightly ajar. I hurried past, back into my own room, keeping hold of Bess the whole time. I shut the door and pushed the chest of drawers up against it. And then I got back into the bed and I pulled the sheets up to my face and lay there with my arms around Bess, so grateful for her company, while Bess stared at the door and growled low in her throat.

CHAPTER SEVEN

A few days passed. Still Reservoir Cottage did not feel like a home. At least there were a few provisions in the pantry, provided by Mrs Croucher. The kindly neighbour had also arranged for deliveries of milk, bread and coal and even had the telephone reconnected, at her own expense, in case of emergency. I couldn't do anything about the old-fashioned furniture or the dark paintwork, but I spread the few pretty things Julia and Viviane had brought with them around the cottage to soften its austerity. I draped one of Julia's gauzy scarves over the picture of the Crucifixion and I hung Viviane's bright blue duffel coat on the rail at the bottom of the stairs, beside my brown one. I paired our shoes up by the front door. I tried to impose some of the Laurents' personality on the house, but I had little to work with and the house had a strong and stubborn personality of its own. Cleaning, I thought, might help. The cottage was not dirty exactly, but there was a peculiar thin and greasy layer of brown dust over everything. As soon as a surface was polished, it seemed to become dusty again.

Viviane was keen to be involved with whatever I was

doing. I suspected that before my arrival the poor child had done little more than drift around the house, lonely and sad and too afraid of disturbing or upsetting her mother to do anything that drew attention to her own unhappiness. We found an old vacuum cleaner in the cupboard under the stairs. It was a huge unwieldy thing that probably dated back to the 1940s, but we located a spare bag and managed to fit it into the machine. I gave Viviane the job of cleaning up the dust and she was content to do this until Julia complained that the noise was giving her a headache.

We went out into the garden so that Julia could rest undisturbed. The day was bright and windy. The trees dipped and swayed; starlings swooped in a sky that was one minute grey and threatening and the next sunny and blue, its character always reflected back by the lake that lay below it. We found an ancient metal swing and the remains of a bench that had collapsed, and an old chicken-house that was falling in on itself. At the bottom of the garden, by the fence, was the large brick shed that I'd seen from Vivi's bedroom window. Planks had been hammered over its window and the door was bolted shut, the bolt held in place by a thick padlock fastened to a chain. I tried but I couldn't shift the chain or the door at all.

The fencing at the bottom of the garden was rotten, but there was a gate at the far end that opened out into the field that led down to the lake. On the other side of the fence, in the field, was an old, abandoned settee.

'We could sit on this and watch the sun go down over the lake,' I suggested.

'It's hideous.'

'It's a settee and there's a view.' I smiled at her, then added, 'Why do you keep looking over your shoulder, Vivi?'

'She's watching us.'

'Who is?'

'Mrs Croucher from next door. She's peeping out from behind her curtains. She's always spying on us.'

'Us? But I've only just arrived.'

'Me and Caroline, I mean.'

'Oh.'

'Caroline says she's obsessed.'

'I expect she's just lonely.' I looked over my own shoulder and saw the shape of the old woman at her back-room window, very still. 'It *is* a bit unnerving, though, her standing there like that.'

'Caroline says she wants to know everything about us.'

I laughed at this. 'Your new friend Caroline has an awful lot to say for herself, Vivi.'

I tried to make it into a joke, but even I could hear the hint of anxiety in my voice and I knew Viviane was intuitive enough to hear it too. I found it difficult to even say the name *Caroline* in a light-hearted way, knowing that it was also the name of Julia's dead sister.

Viviane shrugged and kicked at a rock in the soil. 'Caroline knows everything,' she said quietly.

'Oh she does, does she?' I raised my eyebrows high, and tipped my head to one side so that Vivi would know where this conversation was heading. 'Does she know that Mrs Croucher is just a harmless old woman

46

with too much time on her hands? Hmm? And does she know that I'm going to chase you, and when I catch you I'm going to tickle you until you beg for mercy?' I wriggled my fingers towards Vivi and the child squealed and ran away, and for a while the two of us laughed and chased one another like we used to do on the beach in France, with the dog, relieved that we were at last having some fun, barking at our heels.

CHAPTER EIGHT

The following Saturday, I put Bess on the lead and Vivi and I walked together along the footpath that curled up through the woodland making a shortcut to Blackwater village. There wasn't much to it: a couple of pubs, a small general store, a Post Office, a few shops and a doctor's surgery.

The village hall was beside the shop. The door was open and inside, women were preparing for a craft sale. We could see trestle tables covered with home-made toys, knitted and sewn items, and jars of preserves, cakes and pies.

Viviane gazed inside wistfully.

'Can we come and have a look later?' she asked.

I thought of the money saved in the Post Office account I'd opened when I started work. And my father had given me two pounds before I left Sheffield. I didn't know how long it would have to last, but I could spare a few pence to give to Vivi.

'Yes, of course we can.' I squeezed her hand.

Viviane smiled. 'Do you remember, Amy, how Papa always liked going to the flea markets in Paris?'

'I remember. And he was forever buying second-hand books from the stalls by the river.'

'Oh yes! Mummy used to pretend she was so cross.' Viviane put her hands on her hips and adopted her mother's exasperated expression and tone. '"If you bring any more filthy old books into my nice, clean apartment, Alain Laurent, I swear I'm going to throw them all into the Seine! And you'll be going in with them!"'

I laughed and then we stopped together, struck, at the same time, by the church that had suddenly loomed into view before us. It stood alone on a ledge of land above the reservoir, as if it were gazing out over the water, watching.

'I wish Papa was buried here so I could go and put flowers on his grave,' Viviane said wistfully. 'He must be so lonely in the cemetery in Paris all on his own.'

'You could go up to the church to sit and think about him. It doesn't really matter where he's buried. It's being close to him in your heart that counts.'

'Caroline says it *does* matter.'

I pulled the girl closer and kissed the top of her head. When I spoke, I spoke calmly but firmly.

'Caroline doesn't really know everything, Vivi.'

'She knows all about being dead.'

Viviane spoke easily, in a matter-of-fact tone of voice. I was certain she had not intended the words to shock, nor was she trying to be deliberately provocative. She had responded naturally to my observation, as naturally as if we had been talking about something everyday. I did not know how to react. I told myself: *It is good that we address this now, straight away, so there is no room for ambivalence or confusion later.*

When I next spoke, I made sure my voice was relaxed, as if this were a perfectly normal conversation.

'Caroline's not dead, Vivi,' I said quietly. 'She's a made-up person, a made-up friend. She's not alive like we are, because she exists only in your mind. That's not at all the same as being dead.'

'She's not made up, not like Emily was,' Vivi replied. 'She's real. Her name is Caroline Cummings and she used to live where we live now. She used to be Mummy's sister but she's been dead for years and years.'

'Sweetheart, that's not true.'

'I'm not telling lies.'

'I didn't say that you were. All I meant was that—'

'Caroline said you wouldn't believe me. She told me I wouldn't be allowed to be friends with her once you knew who she was.' Viviane pulled away from me. She went on ahead, walking quickly with her head down, rebellious in her stance.

'Oh Vivi, don't be like that,' I called but she ignored me. She called to Bess and then ran even further ahead, putting enough distance between us to make communication impossible, and only then did she slow her footsteps to a walk.

I followed her down towards the lake, turning the exchange over in my mind. *Don't make too much of it*, I told myself. *Don't make this into something bigger than it really is.* Vivi had always been an imaginative child. She was dealing with an immense grief. No wonder some things were becoming twisted in her mind. Perhaps making dead-Aunt-Caroline into a new imaginary friend was Vivi's way of exploring death in a way that was manageable to the child, and less frightening to her, less overwhelming. This was the obvious, rational explanation. And if this was the case, then it was nothing to be worried about; this phase would pass in its time, as Vivi's grief became less intense.

We walked down to the narrow strip of woodland at the water's edge. A path led through the trees, eventually opening into a grassy hollow bisected by the ancient trunk of a huge tree that must have fallen decades earlier. Moss had grown up over the old wood, and the lake behind was the colour of pewter, shiny and still. The hollow was full of fallen leaves and smelled of damp, of fungi and decay. The reeds in the shallows were dying too. Vivi picked up a stick to use as a switch, climbed up on to the trunk and walked along it, holding her arms out for balance. Her lips were moving. She was talking to Caroline. I watched her as she moved; she was such a graceful child, like her mother, and I was proud of her and sorry for her at the same time. She put her head to one side, pretending to listen to something Caroline was saying, then she looked over her shoulder, at me. I had the uncomfortable feeling that I was the subject of whatever conversation was going on between the two of them.

'Come on,' I called. 'Your mummy will be wondering where we are.'

She jumped down and we headed back up the hill. We were crossing the fields when a mucky old jeep towing a rickety metal trailer bounced across the grass towards us and drew up alongside. A swarthy-faced man in a tweed cap leaned out of the passenger window.

'You there! Put that dog on a lead,' he said gruffly.

Viviane and Bess looked at me anxiously. I was in no mood to be spoken to so rudely.

'Why should I put her on a lead?' I asked. 'She's not doing any harm. There's no livestock in this field.'

'You're on my land, Aldridge land.'

I straightened my back. 'There's a footpath sign on the other side of that stile clearly pointing in this direction. This is a public right of way.'

'I don't give a damn about that. This is my land and if I see that dog running loose, I'll shoot it.'

Viviane stiffened in alarm.

'You'll do no such thing,' I said, outraged.

'I'll do as I please!'

Beside the man, in the driver's seat, was a younger man with a narrow face. He was hunch-shouldered, forearms on the steering wheel, staring straight ahead through the windscreen.

'Leave it, please, Father,' he said.

The older man ignored him. He scowled at me. 'Where are you from? I don't recognize you.'

'We're living in Reservoir Cottage – not that it's any of your business.'

'You're renting the place?'

'The house belongs to Viviane's mother, Julia. Her parents used to live there.'

'Hello,' said Viviane.

The young man leaned around his father and touched his forelock as a greeting. Viviane grinned.

The older man was frowning. 'Julia Cummings?' he asked.

'She's Julia Laurent now, but yes, the same Julia.'

'You're telling me Julia bloody Cummings is back living in Blackwater?'

'Please don't use language like that in front of Viviane.'

'My papa was killed,' Viviane said. 'We didn't have anywhere else to go. Do you know my mother?'

The man looked away. 'Just get off my land,' he said. 'Stay off it, you hear me? If I see that dog running loose, there'll be trouble. Come on, Danny.'

The younger man winked at Vivi, then put the vehicle into gear and it began to pull away, up the hill, lurching over the ruts. We watched it go, puffing black smoke from its exhaust.

'What a rude man,' Viviane said.

'He was. We'll have to try and avoid him from now on.'

'He doesn't like the Cummings family very much, does he?'

'Not on his land anyway.'

'"This is *my* land!"' Vivi said, parodying the man. '"My *bloody* land!"' She stuck out her chest and puffed out her cheeks. '"Get off my land, you dirty Cummingses! Go on! Be gone with you! Or I'll . . . I'll shoot the lot of you! I'll have your heads mounted and hung on my wall!"'

'Stop it!' I said, but I was so relieved to see a glimpse

of the old, naughty Viviane that I could have kissed rude Mr Aldridge for bringing her back to me.

We carried on together up the hill, all awkwardness – and Caroline – forgotten. I followed the progress of the vehicle as it turned into the lane above the field, trailing clumps of mud. I lost sight of it behind the trees, but a few moments later it appeared again. It was heading downhill towards the lake.

CHAPTER NINE

I used some of my precious cash to buy an expensive bottle of high-strength cleaning fluid in the hope it might obliterate whatever it was that was producing the unpleasant smell that permeated the walls of the cottage. I started by clearing out the cupboard beneath the stairs. As I worked, I day dreamed, remembering my last summer at Les Aubépines. There was a pool at the back of the house and, in my mind, I could see Julia, in her white swimsuit, lying on a lounger, one leg bent at the knee to ease the pain in her hip, a paperback in her hand. Beside her was Alain, not relaxing, but sitting astride his lounger with his portable typewriter between his knees, a cigarette burning between his lips and his fingers hammering at the keys. And there was Viviane running towards the pool; diving in. I remembered the glitter of sunlight on displaced water, Vivi surfacing, smiling, splashing towards the ladder at the shallow end, blinking furiously, her hair sleek, like a seal. The memories were so real to me. I still could not fully accept that those happy times would never return. I was grateful for our innocence back then, for not knowing what the future had in store.

I pulled myself back to the present, to the boxes of candles and old newspapers stacked in the cupboard. At the very back, I found a certificate, an award presented to the child Julia for her neat handwriting. Beneath was a tiny, old-fashioned photograph of a young couple standing outside Reservoir Cottage. The man was buttoned up in a home-made suit. He was pale with receding hair and round, wire-framed spectacles. The woman was looking down at the baby in her arms and a small child stood beside her. I held the picture up to the light. The older child was as dark as Julia was fair. Her hair was in ribbons and she was beaming at the camera, a toothy, open smile. She looked a delightful, happy little thing. 'Is that you, Caroline?' I murmured, and at that very moment the bulb in the hall began to flicker. It continued for some moments and the back-room door swung open and Julia came out, leaning heavily on her stick.

'What's wrong with the lights?' she asked.

'I don't know.'

Julia sighed and turned the light off at the switch. Nothing happened for a moment, then the bulb glowed brightly, so brightly it hurt my eyes, then it burned itself out with a pop. It was still light outside, but the hallway was plunged into a gloom so dense it was startling. I blinked to clear the glare from my eyes.

'Damn!' said Julia. 'The bloody electrics. The whole house needs rewiring – nothing's been done to it in decades.' She hunched over her stick. She looked terribly tired. 'I tried to persuade Mother to have it modernized

56

but she wouldn't hear of it. She said she liked it the way it was, as if anyone could like being as uncomfortable as this. God, I need a drink.'

I followed Julia into the kitchen. She pressed the switch to turn on the kitchen light, but nothing happened.

'The fuse has blown,' she said. 'The box is in the cupboard there, on the wall. Can you have a look, Amy?'

'Yes, of course.' I still had the photograph in my hand. 'Look what I found. Is that you and your parents and your sister?' Julia glanced at the picture and nodded. I put it down on the table. 'Caroline looks very sweet,' I said. Julia said nothing.

'You never speak of her,' I went on, trying to coax her to talk.

'No.' She frowned. 'We weren't close.' She pulled out a chair and sat down, gazing out of the window down towards the lake. The light fell on to her face, showing up the lines and the dark shadows around her eyes. She pushed back her hair and for a moment I glimpsed the young Julia, the beautiful ballet dancer who had captured Alain's heart. That woman didn't belong here. She belonged in France with her husband. She ought to be living her old life, drinking wine with her friends, talking into the early hours, having fun.

I turned from her, opened the cupboard door and found the fuse box draped in dusty cobwebs.

'Vivi told me your sister died,' I prompted gently.

'Yes,' Julia said. Her voice was quiet.

'A long time ago?'

'She was seventeen.'

'How old were you?'

'Eleven, twelve. A little older than Vivi is now.'

'How awful for you.'

'It wasn't awful because I wasn't here when she died.'

'No?'

'I used to spend the summer holidays with my aunt in Weston-super-Mare. I missed Caroline's death altogether. Even the funeral.'

'What happened to her? Was she ill?'

Julia shook back her hair and smiled at me weakly.

'It was a fever. Have you found the blown fuse, dear?'

'Yes, it's here.'

'Can you mend it?'

'I'm sure I can.'

I took a knife from the drawer and sat down opposite Julia. I used the point of the knife to unfasten the screw that held the burned fuse in its casing.

Julia picked up the twist of fuse wire and played with it, turning it between her fingers.

'When Alain died, I knew it was important for me to be a better mother to Viviane than my mother was to me,' she said suddenly.

I looked up at her.

'Oh, I don't mean Mother was unkind or cruel or anything like that. It was just that she was so distant after Caroline's death. She shut herself away and she never let me come close again.'

'It must have been terribly hard for her, losing a daughter so young.'

58

'Yes,' Julia said. 'Yes, she took it all very badly.'

I gave a sympathetic smile.

'She wasn't here when my aunt brought me back from Weston that summer. She had gone to stay with friends, to recover from the shock.'

'So who looked after you? Your father?'

'No, I went to stay next door with the Crouchers. They were terribly good to me.'

I put the old fuse on the table and picked up the new one. Julia passed me the wire.

'Back then, Dr Croucher used to run his surgery from the cottage next door,' she said. 'Mrs Croucher let me help her with the dispensing. She called me "Nurse Cummings"! And the doctor showed me all his instruments and explained what they did. I was allowed to practise using the stethoscope on him.'

I smiled and wound the wire around the casing.

'Mother came back eventually, but she was different. She packed me off to ballet school as soon as she could. It was as if she could hardly wait to be rid of me.'

'I'm sure that's not true.'

'That's what it felt like. Once I was at school, I rarely came home. Mother always had some reason why I couldn't be here for the holidays so I stayed at school or with friends. She'd come to visit me every now and then, but it wasn't the same.'

'No?'

'No. I was so glad to leave school. And then, of course, I joined the company and I was dancing, travelling round Europe, which was marvellous and exciting and a long way from here, and then I met Alain and I was living a different life and this all seemed so far away. It didn't belong to me.' She looked up at me. 'You must have wondered, Amy, when you were working for us, why I never took Vivi to visit her English grandmother.'

I didn't reply. I had privately speculated, of course, on the reasons for the rift between Julia and her mother – her father was long dead by then – but she had never spoken of them and I had not liked to ask.

'I didn't visit my mother because she wanted me to stay away,' Julia said. 'She didn't want me to bring Viviane here.'

She was speaking quietly but I could hear the bitterness and hurt in her voice.

'Why didn't she?' I asked.

'Because she was ashamed. Because of Caroline. She didn't want Vivi to be tainted.'

I waited for her to explain but she said nothing more on the subject of her sister. Instead she said: 'The only time I returned was for Mother's funeral.'

'Yes. I remember.'

It had been three years earlier, during a particularly unpleasant winter. Julia and Alain had returned to Blackwater for the burial. I'd stayed in Paris with Viviane.

Julia sighed. 'I never thought, not for a single moment, that I would end up living back in Blackwater.'

'This is only temporary.'

'I hope so.' Julia watched as I cut off the end of the wire. She worked at a scratch in the fibre of the wood of the kitchen table-top with her thumbnail. 'Have you fixed it?'

'I think so.' I stood and slotted the fuse back in the box.

'Ready?' I asked. Julia nodded. I lifted the main switch and the kitchen light flickered and then began to glow more brightly.

'Well done,' Julia said, but she did not smile. She reached across the table, took hold of my hand, raised it to her lips and kissed it. Then she said: 'I have such a headache, dear, I think I'll go upstairs and lie down for a while. Would you be an angel and bring me up a cup of tea and an aspirin?'

'Of course,' I said.

I helped her to her feet, and Julia leaned on me as we made our way up the stairs. When we reached the landing, I glanced towards the empty bedroom. The door was open a few inches. There seemed to be an unfathomable loneliness behind it.

CHAPTER TEN

The next day, the temperature dropped suddenly. A cold wind whipped around the cottage, leaves blew along the path and gathered in the corners. The loose gutter above the empty bedroom banged repeatedly, like somebody trying to get in. Down in the valley the surface of the lake was unhappy, roughed up. A mist of spray was forming over the dam where the water was throwing itself against the wall with a violence I had not seen before. It was deeply unsettling.

I went to the shops, and by the time I returned, my hands were red and raw. I filled the scuttle and spent an age kneeling at the front living-room grate, lighting rolled-up sheets of newspaper, burning my fingers on match after match as I tried to make the fire take. Julia sat behind me on the couch. She was playing with her glasses, turning them over between her fingers.

'While you were out,' she said, 'I spoke to Mrs Croucher.'

'Oh yes?'

'She says there's a lovely new school in the next village along. It's called Hailswood, and by coincidence

62

I used to go to school with the headmaster, Eric Leeson, when he was a boy. Mrs Croucher says she's certain he'd take Vivi and withhold the fees for a few months, until I can afford to pay. She's going to ask the doctor to make the arrangements.'

'That sounds ideal.'

'It does, doesn't it? They're apparently very keen on encouraging the arts, music and sports at Hailswood; they even have their own choir. And it's a small school, so it won't be too overwhelming for Vivi.'

I poked at the damp coal. 'It'll be good for her to make some real friends,' I said.

Julia reached across the armchair and put her hand on my shoulder. 'As opposed to pretend ones, you mean?'

'Well, yes.' I glanced at Julia. 'She's told you about her new imaginary friend?'

Julia nodded. 'Caroline.'

'Don't you think it's a bit odd? The name, I mean?'

'It can't be coincidence. It must have been the name on the plaque on the bedroom door that inspired Vivi.'

'That's what I thought too.' I was trying to gauge if Julia minded this appropriation of her sister's name. Julia was looking down at her glasses, rubbing at a scratch on one of the lenses with the pad of her thumb.

'Vivi does seem to be spending a great deal of time with Caroline at present,' she said. 'We thought she'd grown out of the whole imaginary friend phase. We hadn't heard anything of Emily for months. Alain used to tease her about it and she was embarrassed. She used to say: "I'm too big for such nonsense now."'

I took hold of Julia's hands. 'I have to tell you, Julia, I've asked Vivi about it and she told me that imaginary Caroline and your sister Caroline are one and the same. The two have become confused in her mind.'

'Oh!' said Julia.

Behind my back, the flames flickered in the grate. I could hear the moisture hissing in the coal, the smoke being sucked up the chimney. And outside, the wind rattled the drainpipes and howled mournfully in the eaves. The loose gutter banged on the wall. I could feel Julia's tension, the tremble of anxiety in her cold hands.

'I don't like the sound of that,' she said. 'No, I don't like the sound of that at all. It's one thing having an active imagination, but talking to somebody who you know is dead is something else altogether.'

I tried to keep my voice relaxed when I spoke. 'It's important that we don't make this into more than it is. We must be gentle with Vivi. She's hurting. She needs time to recover from the shock of losing her father – and talking to Caroline, no matter who she thinks Caroline is, is obviously her way of dealing with her grief. If it's helping her, then I can't see how it can be such a terrible thing.'

'But Amy, this can't be normal – it can't be healthy! Don't you think it's an awfully morbid thing for Vivi to be doing? At her age, she should be playing with her skipping rope and reading storybooks, not communing with the dead. She shouldn't even be thinking about such things. This is awful!'

'Julia, please . . . if you overreact or come down too heavily on Vivi, you'll only frighten her or make her feel that she's done something wrong. She might start hiding it from us, or telling lies. As long as we keep an eye on it, and make sure it doesn't evolve into anything more . . . well, sinister . . . then it will be fine. I'm sure this phase will pass soon enough, just as all the other phases have passed.'

'Oh, I hope you're right.' Julia let go of my hand and reached for her tumbler. Ice clinked against the glass. She took a drink, swallowed, swirled the gin around the ice cubes then suddenly burst out: 'No. No, it's *not* all right. The thing is, Amy, it's more complicated than you realize. My sister, Caroline, well . . . she was a troubled girl who led a short, difficult life. She was the kind of person who made other people unhappy.' Julia drained her glass. 'I know this is an unkind thing to say about my own sister, but if Caroline were still alive, I wouldn't want my daughter going anywhere near her.'

I was shocked by this, although I did not show it. Instead I said, with all the conviction I could muster: 'But Vivi's not *really* talking to Caroline. She's merely fitting your sister's existence on to her imaginary friend, as if she were fitting clothes on to a paper doll. Don't you see, it's better that she does this than suppress her grief and hide it away. That merely saves up the pain for the future.'

'How can you be sure that this is what Vivi's doing?'

'I can't be absolutely sure but I read a great deal about child psychology during my training and this sounds exactly like the kind of thing that might happen in these circumstances.'

Julia was unconvinced. 'Well, perhaps you're right,' she said. 'I still don't like it one bit.'

I squeezed her hand. 'If all goes to plan, Vivi will be starting at her new school soon. There'll be lots of distractions. Why don't we wait and see what happens then?'

'It's about all we can do. I have no other ideas and not a great many options.' Julia smiled ruefully. 'Would you be a darling and go and top up my drink, Amy? My hip's killing me. You might want to fetch some more kindling too. It doesn't look as if that fire's taking.'

She was right. The pyramid I'd made of newspaper and sticks had collapsed and now the coals were merely steaming in the grate.

I poked at the coal. 'The chimney doesn't seem to be drawing properly,' I said.

'That fire's always been awkward, ever since Father bricked up the fireplace in Caroline's room,' Julia said.

'Why did he brick it up?'

'Oh . . . After Caroline died, my mother was convinced she could still hear her voice in the bedroom. Father said it was the wind in the chimney. Dr Croucher helped him seal the opening. We've had problems lighting fires in this room ever since.'

CHAPTER ELEVEN

Mrs Croucher was as good as her word and did exactly what she'd promised Julia she would do. She went to the nursing home, Sunnyvale, and spoke to her husband, who telephoned the headmaster of Hailswood School and the relevant arrangements were soon made. Viviane was to start the following week. There was little time to prepare but I took her into Bristol on the bus to buy her uniform.

It was an adventure and a joy to be away from the cottage and amongst crowds of people, to have the distraction of shops with brightly lit windows full of Christmas decorations, and kiosks on the streets selling roast chestnuts and hot potatoes, and jolly carollers singing on the podium in the middle of the shopping centre. Viviane enjoyed it too. Her eyes were bright and there was colour in her cheeks. We walked the cold pavements, weaving in and out of the shoppers, dodging the crammed buses. Vivi walked close beside me, so close that nobody could come between us. She slipped her hand into mine, and I held her tightly.

We went into the shoe shop first. Viviane's feet were

measured, and we bought some brown lace-up school shoes. Vivi complained they were ugly and she had a point, they were clumpy things, but they were practical and they met Hailswood's specifications. After that we bought the green tunic, grey cardigan, a pair of white blouses and a tie. The regulation coat was terribly expensive, so instead we bought a woven badge and then found a cheaper grey coat in British Home Stores that the badge could be sewed on to; it would do. We also purchased a games bag, a pair of shorts, an aertex shirt and a school hat.

When we returned to Blackwater and were walking along the lane, we saw a man in the front garden of Mrs Croucher's cottage. He was chopping wood and stacking the logs to one side of the porch. He had taken off his jumper and tied it around his waist by the sleeves. He must have felt my eyes on him because he turned and I recognized him at once as the son of the ill-tempered man who'd been in the jeep in the field. He stood up, took off his gauntlet, and wiped his forehead with his wrist.

'Hello,' I said.

'Hello.'

'Go on inside,' I told Viviane. 'Show Mummy what we've bought.'

Vivi gave me a look that indicated she'd rather stay outside and see what happened next but I gave her a little push and she complied. I walked across to the wall at the front of Mrs Croucher's cottage.

'I'm Amy,' I said.

'Daniel.' He smiled. I smiled back. I tucked my hair

behind my ear. He held out his hand and I looked at it stupidly for a moment before I realized what he meant by it; I then took it, and shook it, feeling his fingers around mine. We held hands for a moment longer than was necessary. Then I stepped back, self-conscious and lost for words.

'We met before, down in the field,' I said eventually.

'Yes, I remember. My father wasn't in the best of moods.'

'No, he certainly wasn't.'

'I'm sorry about that. It was nothing to do with you, not exactly. There's no love lost between the Aldridges and the Cummings family.'

'Really? How terribly melodramatic. Why?'

'Julia hasn't told you?'

'No.'

Daniel looked away. He hesitated for a moment and then he said: 'It's traditional. There's not much to do out here in the country. We have to make our own entertainment.'

'Oh. I see.'

'Anyway,' he went on, changing the subject, 'how do you like Blackwater? It's not too quiet for you?'

'I'm growing used to it.'

'You're not seeing it at its best. In springtime it's beautiful.'

'Yes, I'm sure it is.'

'You should see the birds on the lake.'

'I'd love to.'

'Will you still be here in the springtime?'

'I'm not sure.'

'If you are, then you'll see what I mean.'

'Yes.'

We smiled at one another and then there was one of those silences that happen when two people don't want to stop talking to one another, but neither can think of anything to say. Then I remembered something.

'Am I allowed to ask you for help?' I asked. 'Is it permitted under the terms of the family feud?'

'I daresay we could come to some arrangement.'

'Good,' I said. 'In that case, some animal or other is getting into one of the upstairs bedrooms in the cottage. It disturbs us and Julia's nerves aren't good. I don't know what to do about it.'

Daniel gave me an uncertain smile. He looked up at the cottage.

'It's probably squirrels,' he said. 'They build their nests for winter round about this time of year.'

'I hope that's all it is,' I said, and then I felt foolish, because of course it would be squirrels. What else could it possibly be? 'Would you take a look for us?'

He hesitated again, and then seemed to come to some resolution in his mind. 'Of course,' he said. 'I'll have a look in the loft. Chances are that's where they're coming in. I'll finish off here and then I'll be over.'

'Thank you.'

I nodded, and then I turned on my heel and went into the cottage. Vivi was in the back room with Julia, describing the dresses she had seen in the department store in Bristol. Neither of them noticed me. I ran upstairs into my room and wished the light bulb was brighter as I hastily drew on eyeliner and dabbed on a little lipstick. I nipped into Julia's room to puff *Memoire Cherie* on to my wrists and throat. Then I smoothed my hair with my hands and trotted downstairs again. I popped my head round the door to the back room.

'Daniel Aldridge is doing some work next door. He's going to check the roof for holes,' I said.

Julia looked up. 'Daniel Aldridge?'

'Yes.'

'He's coming in here?'

'Yes. It's OK, you don't have to do anything. He's just going to look into the loft.'

Julia put her fingers to her forehead. 'Amy, I wish you wouldn't do things like that without asking me. We don't need anybody to look in our loft.'

'He'll only be a few minutes. I'll shut the door if you like. You don't have to talk to him.'

'All right,' she said. 'You do that.' She closed her eyes and rubbed her brow with her fingers. 'I don't want to see him.'

She then turned her attention back to Vivi. I closed the door before I left the room.

When Daniel came, I showed him upstairs. There was a drop-down ladder tucked into the hatch on the landing and I held the torch and watched as his legs and feet disappeared through the hole into the darkness. I passed the torch up to him and heard him moving around.

'The only living things up here are spiders,' he called down. 'I can't see any daylight at all. There's nowhere obvious that anything is getting in.'

I did not know if I should be relieved or disappointed

by this news. I waited until Daniel dropped down again through the hatch. His hair was garlanded with cobwebs. He handed me an old leather satchel. It felt icy cold. 'I found this hidden away behind the chimney stack,' he said. He shook his head and dust drifted around him and floated in the air. 'As far as I can tell, nobody's been up there for years. I'll have a look outside, see if there are any holes in the brickwork. Where are you hearing the noises?'

'In there.' I indicated the empty bedroom. Daniel went as far as the door, reached out his hand to open it, and then paused. I couldn't be sure if he had sensed something strange, as I had, or if it was reading the name on the plaque that had stopped him.

'I don't need to go in,' he said and his voice was slightly different, slightly cold.

'Is something wrong?' I asked.

'No, no.'

He turned around and went back downstairs. I followed him outside, holding the satchel close, and stood at the foot of the ladder propped against the wall while he climbed up to look for holes in the brickwork, pulling away fingers of ivy and poking at wood that hadn't been painted for years.

'It seems pretty solid,' he said. 'I can't see how anything could be getting in.'

'Well, thanks for looking.'

He came down and stood beside me in the front garden, making a fuss of Bess.

'Maybe whatever it was has been and gone,' he said, 'but if you have any more problems, you can always give me a call.' He passed me a card and our fingers touched. The gesture was so innocent that any intimacy I felt must have been imagined. Still I felt myself blush. 'That's my number and the one above is my father's,' said Daniel. 'If you can't reach me, leave a message with him, and I'll get back to you.'

'OK.'

'Only if you do that, it's probably best if you don't say who you are. Say you're calling about the squirrels and I'll know it's you.'

'All right.'

We walked together to the jeep. He opened the door and climbed inside. 'It was nice to meet you properly,' he said.

'You too.'

'I daresay I'll see you about the village.'

'I expect you will.'

I watched as he leaned forward over the steering wheel, pulled out the throttle, started the engine.

Oh please, I thought, say something else. Don't just drive away – make it so that there is something more between us.

Daniel put the vehicle into reverse and turned it carefully. I stood and watched, holding Bess's collar. When the jeep was pointing in the correct direction, he wound down the window and leaned out. 'Amy?'

'Yes?'

'Perhaps we could go for a drink one evening.'

'Yes, that's a good idea.'

'OK. Will you call me?'

'Yes.'

I watched as he drove away down the lane, relieved and happy that he had reached out to me, that there was potential for us ahead. But as the vehicle disappeared I felt a rush of loneliness so cold it was as if the temperature of the very air had dropped a couple of degrees. With a heavy heart, I turned back to the cottage. There was the lake beyond, fading to black in response to the gloaming sky, shadows creeping over its surface and God knows what beneath, weaving through weed that drifted like hair, coiling through the coming darkness.

CHAPTER TWELVE

I went up into my room and sat on the bed, holding the satchel. The leather was stiff and dark, mummified almost, although in the creases I could see the pale fawn colour it had once been. The letters *CC* had been neatly incised into the front flap, perhaps with the point of a compass. They stood out darker than the rest of the leather, black where the dust had engrained itself. I followed the twin curls of the letters with the tip of my finger, imagining the young Caroline sitting in the room beside mine, making her mark. I wondered how it was the satchel had found its way into the loft. Daniel said it had been hidden. What had he meant by that?

'Did you put it there, Caroline?' I whispered. 'Did you put it there out of sight in the hope that one day it would be found?'

I didn't expect to hear a reply, of course, but still the silence that hung in the room was deafening. I had the sensation of being watched, of something waiting.

I forced stiff leather straps through the buckles that

secured the flap and opened the satchel. A spider scuttled from the darkness inside, long legs fingering. I cried out, jumped away and watched as the spider, followed by its shadow, disappeared down the side of the bed. I pushed the satchel a couple of times to see if anything else was inside and when nothing emerged, I lifted it by its corners and tipped the rest of its contents on to the bed.

There were ancient pencils, an eraser so old and dry it was crumbling, a sketchpad and a school exercise book. On the front, in elaborate, old-fashioned handwriting was the name *Caroline Anne Cummings* and above it a stamp saying *Blackwater Village School*. I flicked through. The book was full of exercises marked and commented upon in red ink. *Not good enough. Where is the rest of your work? A poor and lazy attempt. See me. Stay behind. Detention. Slipper.*

Slipper?

Oh, that was how it was in many schools, not just then but now, I knew that. There were, and probably always would be, teachers who believed that children could be bullied into learning, punished into submission. I found it barbaric that anyone of the slightest intelligence could believe that fragile young minds could be improved by such treatment; it was as mad as thinking seedlings would do better thrown out on rough ground at the mercy of the elements than they would being nurtured in a warm greenhouse.

'Poor old you,' I murmured to the child Caroline, whose worst crime appeared to have been failing to understand long division.

Next, I looked through the sketchpad and it was obvious that art was where Caroline's talent lay. There were drawings of the lake, individual water birds and animals, sheep grazing, a duck surrounded by ripples of water, pheasants, a sleeping dog. Caroline had returned several times to the same place, a view over the lake that was framed by the leaves of trees, as if she were looking at it through a picture window. The view was vaguely familiar to me. I too had seen the lake from that spot – it was the hollow with the fallen tree. Caroline had captured some of the moods of the water in the texture of its surface; a moorhen amongst the reeds on a peaceful day; spray caught in the wind above waves shaped like bared teeth on a different occasion. She had drawn for her own pleasure. These pictures might never have been seen by anyone else. This thought unsettled me. I alone was connected to her through time, through the pencil-marks on the paper, through that outlook over the water.

Something else lay on the bed: a Swan Vesta matchbox. I laid down the sketchpad and picked up the box, pressed open the cardboard drawer. Inside was a piece of lint, browned by age, and wrapped inside the lint was treasure: a gold chain, very fine, with a golden pendant – a heart-shaped ruby surrounded by little diamonds set into the gold. The gems were framed by a pair of clasped hands joined at the top of the heart.

I held the necklace up to the light. I closed one eye and, with the other, stared into the ruby. I had never seen anything so beautiful. I lost myself in its colour.

'Oh Caroline,' I said in awe. 'This is lovely. Where did you get this?'

I listened but still there was no answer, no sound at all.

CHAPTER THIRTEEN

That night, I could not sleep – and it wasn't only because I was worried about the spider crawling up to seek me out. My dreams were disturbed and when I woke, I heard whispers from the empty bedroom. I imagined the window open, a draught blowing through, moon shadows dancing on the walls. I closed my eyes and I saw the colour red, the inside of the ruby; I saw a dark stain spreading slowly across the floorboards in the empty bedroom. I saw the shape of a young girl standing by the window . . . and then the girl turned slowly to confront me and her face was white and glassy like ice and her eyes were dark as death. She held out one hand towards me and as I watched, the flesh fell from her like ash and her hair floated away like dandelion seed. All that was left was the darkness where she had been; she was described by her absence and I woke with a scream in my throat. Cold and shaky, I at last dropped into a patchy, shallow unconsciousness and was woken almost at once by Viviane, who had come creeping into my room. I was so pleased to see her. I lifted the covers and she slipped into the bed beside me. Her feet, on my legs, were icy and her teeth were chattering. I held her close.

'What is it, darling?' I whispered. 'What's the matter?'

'It's Caroline,' Vivi said. 'She doesn't want me to sleep.'

'What do you mean by that? Why doesn't she want you to sleep?'

'Because when I'm sleeping, she is all alone. She's been so lonely for so long. She keeps saying: "Don't leave me, Vivi."'

I kissed her head. 'How about if I tell you a story, like I used to when you were a little girl?'

Viviane said: 'Mmm.' I felt her relax in my arms. 'Tell us about the Pigeon Princess,' she breathed. 'Caroline would like that very much.'

This sounded to me more like the imaginary friend of the past – dear, non-existent Emily – who articulated Vivi's hopes and dreams, who said, through Viviane, the things that Viviane herself did not want to say. I told myself to relax. The child's breath was hot and damp, a shaky vibrato against my clavicle. I smoothed her hair. We had curled up together, like this, a thousand times.

'Once upon a time,' I began, 'there was a little pigeon who lived in a hole in the factory wall . . .'

The next day, the anxiety about Vivi's imaginary friend returned. I told myself it was the simple fact that I was overtired that distorted my thinking and my reasoning. If I weren't so exhausted, then I'd be able to rationalize the situation. But I was tired, and I couldn't seem to think straight. I went outside for some fresh air and glanced at the lake, amenable that morning – pastel-blue and white, a flock of white birds feeding at its edges. I walked around the garden three times with Bess, trying to think of a good reason not to telephone Daniel Aldridge – it was too soon, he would think me neurotic, I didn't know him well enough to confide in him – but I knew in my heart that none of these reasons was valid. I went inside and I called him. He sounded pleased to hear from me but we were both tongue-tied. We tried, and failed, to make small talk. He offered to take me out for a drink, to the pictures, even to the dancehall in Weston-super-Mare, but I was not in the mood for dancing. I asked if, instead, we could go for a drive.

'I need someone to listen to me,' I told him, 'to tell me if I'm going crazy.'

'I'm told I am a very good listener.'

'Then you are the man I need.'

He came as soon as he could, picked me up in the jeep and we drove though the Mendip lanes, across the top of the hills, bare and yellow now for winter, patches of grey striated rock breaking the dying grass and acres of dead bracken and the tough little wild goats grazing the cliffs above the gorge. We parked at the top of a long, winding lane, and gazed out at the sky and the clouds and the colours of the sunlight on the fields, the drystone walls. From this vantage we could only see a small section of the lake, a tiny, distant line of blue amongst the browns and greys. Up here, woolly cattle turned their backs to the wind and the jeep rocked, buffeted by gusts. A goshawk perched on a fence-post and stared at the undergrowth. I imagined the little creatures running through the limp grass below, the voles and mice careering through their tiny tunnels, their feet pitter-pattering above the frozen ground, their minute little hearts pumping away. I pulled my coat tight about me and I looked through the window while I told Daniel about Vivi and about her imaginary friends, first Emily and now Caroline – the aunt who had died as a teenager brought back to life. Daniel was very quiet as he listened. He was looking out of the window and hardly seemed to be breathing.

'I know a little about psychology,' I said, 'and I'm aware that imaginary friends, like toys, are a device children use to play out scenarios that frighten or confuse them. So it might be that Vivi is using Caroline as a kind of basket into which she can transfer her anxiety about losing her father.'

'That seems logical,' Daniel said.

'It doesn't *feel* right, though. I'm worried I should be doing something – that if I don't, something awful will happen.'

'Something awful has already happened. Her father has died. That's what's at the root of all this.'

'I know. But . . . you'll think I'm being stupid, Daniel, but Julia has told me things about the real Caroline.'

He stiffened. 'What things?'

'Well, she's intimated more than actually said. But I know Caroline was a difficult person, that she had few friends. Julia changes when she speaks of her. She has no affection for her. I suspect things were very bad between the two of them.'

'Oh.'

'Yes. And even though I know it's not really dead Caroline talking to Vivi, if Vivi finds out or even senses some of her mother's feelings, I fear she may start to incorporate them into her imaginary conversations. She may start to give imaginary Caroline the attributes of the real Caroline. She's only ten, Daniel. I can't bear the thought of her being tainted by all this.'

Daniel pressed the palms of his hands against the steering wheel and stretched his arms. 'Would you like a drink?'

I smiled. 'You brought something to drink?'

He took a hip flask from the pocket in the side of the car door and passed it to me.

'You'll have to drink straight from the flask, I'm afraid.'

'What is it?'

'Apple brandy. It cures everything from blocked drains to broken hearts, or so my father tells me.'

I took a sip, and the heat went to my cheeks at once. I drank some more, then wiped my lips and returned the flask to Daniel. 'Lovely!' I said.

He took a drink and considered his words. Eventually he said: 'I think the less fuss you make of this, the quicker it will pass.' He turned his face from me, looked out of the window again. 'I'll tell you something about me,' he said. 'It's something that's difficult for me to talk about. My mother died when I was a baby.'

'Oh Daniel, how terrible! I'm sorry, I didn't know.'

'You don't need to be sorry; how could you have known? Obviously it didn't affect me at the time. I was less than a week old. I didn't know any different. But when I was old enough to understand something of what death meant, it used to haunt me.' He looked down at his hand, scratched at a scab at the base of his finger. 'I was there when she died, physically there. And I used to think that somehow it was my fault.'

'You were a few days old. How could you be to blame?'

'I know, I know, it's irrational. But a child's mind isn't rational.'

'No, I don't suppose it is.'

He picked at the scab. Any moment now, it would begin to bleed. I couldn't bear it. I covered his hand with mine. Still he wouldn't look at me.

'I thought about my mother so much, that she started to become real to me. I knew other people couldn't see her, I knew *they* thought she was dead, but I really believed she was with me.'

'How do you mean?'

'If I was lonely, she would take my hand; if I was afraid, she'd wrap herself around me and make me feel safe. At night, as I was falling asleep, I'd hear her whisper in my ear.'

'What did she say?'

'That she loved me, that she was sorry she'd let me go but that she'd always be there with me; that even when I was sleeping she was watching over me. I can still hear her voice in my mind.'

He took another drink from the flask. I watched his throat move as he swallowed.

'My father couldn't bear it. It used to drive him mad. But the more he tried to stop me being with her, the more I wanted to be with her. We fought all the time.'

'What happened?'

'Father hired a psychiatrist who recommended I be sent to boarding school. He believed cold showers, discipline and a rigorous exercise regime would sort me out.'

'Oh. And did they?'

'They taught me to keep my secrets to myself.'

I put one hand on Daniel's arm. He was still staring through the window. 'My father thought he was acting in my best interests,' he said. 'Suffice to say, that was the last time I confided anything to him.'

'Perhaps you bringing your mother back to life, so to speak, was your way of compensating for the guilt you felt over her death,' I suggested.

'Yes, I thought of that too. I blamed myself for her dying, and the only way to put it right was to make her live again.'

I followed his eyes. The hawk was hunting now, flying low and concentrated over the dead heather and gorse, tipping and dodging the gusts of wind. In the distance, I glimpsed the white bob-tail of a running deer.

'All I'm trying to say is that children's minds don't work the same as ours,' he said. 'You don't know what Viviane is feeling and she probably can't tell you, or is afraid to.'

'What should I do then?' I asked. 'How can I help her?'

'Keep talking to her. Talk about her father. Don't force her to hide her feelings. Try to make her understand that death is a natural process, even when it is brought about through violence. Being less afraid of it helped me. It brought me a kind of peace.'

I looked at Daniel's face, still in profile. It was a beautiful face and, despite being so new, it was becoming very dear to me.

He turned and smiled at me. 'There,' he said. 'You know everything there is to know about me now.'

'Not everything.'

'The most important thing. Does it change your opinion of me?'

'Not at all,' I said.

I wished that he would kiss me and when he made no move to do so, I, emboldened by the apple brandy, kissed him instead. And it was lovely.

He asked for my number before we parted and he found an old pencil in his bag and I wrote the number on a scrap of paper. He told me he would call me soon.

CHAPTER FOURTEEN

I didn't mention any of that conversation to Julia. I didn't even tell her that I'd spoken to Daniel Aldridge but I did tell her that I was thinking of taking Vivi up to the churchyard to put some flowers on her grandparents' grave. I said I thought it might help to demystify death and be a starting point for conversations about Alain.

'Vivi needs to be encouraged to talk about her feelings,' I said, with some confidence.

Julia was unconvinced. She did not want to accompany us because the cold weather was exacerbating the pain in her hip and she said she could not even contemplate the walk uphill. However, she did not oppose the idea. I suggested the outing casually to Viviane who thought it over for a while, and then agreed.

We cut some holly and ivy for the grave, took the dog with us and walked in silence through the woods past a line of silver birch where little spade-shaped leaves of pale green and yellow were fallen like confetti and heaped wetly around the feet of the trunks. Viviane peeled a strip of bark the colour of mother-of-pearl and then broke it into smaller pieces which she dropped behind her, as if she were a child in a story who might need to find her way home. I tried a couple of times to persuade her to talk about her father, but she would not humour me.

When we reached the churchyard, I hooked Bess's lead over the gatepost and Viviane and I wandered in, through nettles browned and dead, all caught with threads of spider silk that shimmered in the grey light. The ground was hard beneath our feet. Beyond, the lake shone green and glassy, perfectly still save for where the waterbirds rippled at its edges, frilling the surface.

Caroline must have known this path; she must have seen the lake in all its myriad moods, and Daniel's mother must have done so too. All the people who came and went to the church, who were born and lived and died in Blackwater – they must have felt what I was feeling now; they must have known their time would be measured but the lake would remain, changing all the time but always there.

I looked back. Viviane was trailing behind me with her hands in the pocket of her duffel coat.

I went back to her. 'It's all right, sweetheart,' I said. 'Really it is. There's nothing to fear in graveyards. See how peaceful it is here? Listen – how quiet it is. How calm. It will be the same where your papa lies.'

'It's not the same,' Vivi said. 'Where he is, there are buildings all around, and traffic and people cutting through the pathways to get to the station. People go into the cemetery to eat their lunch. They walk their dogs and meet their girlfriends and do business and have arguments. It's not quiet at all. And don't,' she said angrily, 'tell me next that that's good because Papa didn't like being on his own. Don't keep trying to say things to make it better because nothing can make it better!'

I reached out to take her hand but she stalked past me, went ahead around some ancient, tilting headstones. I looked up towards the church tower and then felt dizzy, as if there was too much oxygen in my blood. The tower loomed above me and for a moment the ground seemed to shift and tilt. I felt a rush of panic. Viviane had stopped ahead of me. She was staring down at a grave. I walked over to where she stood. The headstone, plain and modest, marked the final resting-place of Julia's parents, *Beinon Cummings, loving husband of Cora and father of Julia. Also Cora, his devoted wife.* An urn full of carnations sat in the centre of the chippings. I crouched down to place the holly and ivy on the grave.

Viviane ran her finger around the letters carved into the stone.

'Who put the flowers on the grave?' she asked.

'I've seen Mrs Croucher walking this way with flowers in her basket.'

'Do you think anyone is putting flowers on Papa's grave?'

'Of course! He has so many friends.'

'Had,' said Vivi. 'He *had* friends. When he was alive.' She picked a flower out of the urn and pulled the petals out one by one. I didn't ask her to stop. 'Why isn't Caroline's name on the headstone?'

'I don't know, sweetheart.'

Julia would know, but it wasn't the kind of thing I could ask her at present.

I moved away from Viviane, reading other inscriptions. There was the grave of Thomas Sale, killed in Normandy in the Second World War, and brothers Harry and Jack Burridge who had lost their lives in the First. Mary, Violet and Herbert Jamieson, aged two, three and six had been taken by the angels within three weeks of one another in 1867. I found a cluster of Aldridge gravestones, far grander than the others and in more prominent positions – look-at-me graves with urns and railings and statuary, even an angel with an outstretched arm holding a rose. I wasn't thinking about where I was going, but I found myself on the far side of the church, in its shadow, out of the sun, where the ground was frozen amongst the brambles and the weeds. That was where I found Caroline's grave, alone and almost hidden.

Her gravestone was a small, plain one, set away from the others. There was no stone urn, no marble slab or monument or memorial. Just the headstone amongst the frost-blackened weeds and brambles with the name Caroline Anne Cummings and the dates of her birth, in April 1914, and her death, aged seventeen, on the last day of August 1931.

A single yellow rose lay on the grave, the edges of its petals frilled with pink. The rose was fading but it was not dead, despite the frost on the ground and the cold on this side of the church. Somebody had been to visit Caroline that morning, somebody had brought her the flower.

A cloud moved over the face of the sun and Bess, at the gate, suddenly began to bark, a throaty, warning bark. I could see neither the dog, nor Viviane.

'Vivi!' I called. 'Where are you?' I pushed myself up and began to stumble back around the church. There was no path and the icy ground was uneven, lumpy with ancient, unmarked graves and rabbit holes, brambles that caught around my ankles. 'Vivi!'

She came slowly round the corner, looking terribly sad and small and vulnerable.

'What's wrong?' she asked.

I felt foolish. 'Nothing,' I said. 'Nothing.'

I put my arm around Vivi's shoulder and led her back towards the footpath and the sunlight and Bess. I held her very close, keeping up a stream of reassurances and endearments, wishing that love alone was enough to make the child less sad and confused. I told her that nobody ever really dies, because they live on in the memories and hearts of all the people who loved them.

'What about people who aren't loved?' Vivi asked. 'What about them?'

I looked at her hopelessly. I did not know how to answer that. Viviane pressed the heels of her hands into her eyes, trying to push the tears back.

By this time we had returned to the grave of Cora and Beinon Cummings. The flowers that had been so carefully arranged had been taken out of the little metal urn, torn into pieces, and scattered about the grave. The holly and ivy was kicked and scattered.

Viviane looked at me through her tears and I did not have the heart to tell her off.

We walked to the gate, unhooked Bess's lead and walked out into the fields where sheep were grazing the sparse winter grass and tiny grey moths fluttered amongst the arms of the old apple trees, bare of leaves now but heavy with boulders of black mistletoe in their crooks and frost-silvered on one side. Beside me, Viviane was pale and broken, a lost and frightened little girl in mourning for her father. I held on to her. I was determined that I would not let her suffer. I would rescue her from her loneliness and bring her back to the place where she knew she was safe and loved. I would help her come to terms with Alain's death. I would hold on to her, I would not let her drift away.

And the lake shone green and still as it had shone when Caroline had been alive, and the robin sang on the bough and everything was peaceful and quiet.

CHAPTER FIFTEEN

On the morning of Viviane's first day at Hailswood School, I walked with her to the place where the bus would pick her up. Viviane looked very young in her new uniform, the dark green tunic and the long grey socks held up with elastic garters, the clumpy brown shoes, the coat, the hat. Everything was too big for her. She seemed to me about six years old and I was terribly worried about letting her go off somewhere new, where she knew nobody, on her own. I held tightly to her hand and kept up a steady stream of cheerful conversation so that neither of us would have the chance to dwell on the hours that lay ahead.

It was early, still. The sun was only just rising over the hill on the far side of the lake, the sky was a pearly dazzle of pink and yellow. At the top of the other side of the valley, farm buildings and trees stood silhouetted against the colours of the sky and frosted fields as white as if they'd been sprinkled with sugar. In the distance, the odd car and lorry wound their way up the shoulder of the hill, on the road to Bristol. The lake looked beautiful and mysterious that morning, like a film star glimpsed at a distance; like a memory of my mother, lips painted into a red cupid's bow framing little white teeth that were smiling above a fox-collared coat, waving as she walked to the shop to buy her cigarettes. I wanted to stare at the lake but I kept losing sight of it as we walked, as it disappeared behind the walls of a house, or a copse of trees . . . and each time it came again into view it seemed to have changed colour and shape and texture, just like the memory of my mother.

I waited with Viviane until the bus came trundling around the corner, watched hot-eyed as she climbed on board and found a seat by the window, pale and brave and stoic. I touched my fingers to my lips and blew her a kiss as the bus bumped away, puffing out clouds of exhaust smoke.

When it was gone, I felt as lonely as I had ever felt in my life. I walked on up to the village, tied Bess outside the stores and went inside, in to the smell of ham and cheese and cabbage leaves. Our neighbour, Mrs Croucher, was already there. I knew she had been a great support to Julia before my arrival at the cottage. We'd exchanged pleasantries before, but this was the first time the two of us had talked at any length. The old woman was pleased to hear that Vivi was starting at Hailswood. She also asked about Julia.

'I never see her out and about,' she said quietly, so she wouldn't be overheard. 'I don't believe she's left that house since the day she arrived.'

'She's finding life very difficult without Alain.'

'Of course she is, the poor dear.'

'I wish I knew what to do,' I said.

'I'll have a word with my husband. He'll know. He attended to the bereaved during the war, you know.'

The old woman paused to cough into her handkerchief. 'Excuse me,' she said, 'I have a terrible weak chest.' She leaned over, struggling to breathe, and then, when she had recovered, continued: 'Oh yes, and afterwards we received so many letters telling us what an enormous help he had been.'

'That would be awfully kind of you. Would your husband mind? He's in the nursing home, isn't he?'

'Yes, dear, but he's perfectly well. His body's not what it was but there's nothing wrong with his brain.'

Her face was soft and sad. 'I don't like to think of poor dear Julia suffering,' she said. 'Dr Croucher and I were never blessed with children but if we had been, we'd have wanted a child exactly like Julia. We couldn't have loved her more if she'd been our own daughter.'

She paid the shopkeeper, took her change and began to pack her shopping trolley. When it was full, she tipped it on to its wheels and dragged it towards the door. 'I'll ask my husband about Julia,' she called. 'Remember, if there's anything else we can do to help, you know where to find us.'

I thanked her and told her I would pull the trolley back to her cottage for her. As we left the shop, she asked, 'Does Robert Aldridge know that Julia's back?'

'Daniel's father? Yes, he knows.'

'Ah,' said Mrs Croucher. 'Good. That's all right then.'

CHAPTER SIXTEEN

Viviane finished her first week at the new school and it had been a success. She slept in on Saturday and mooched around in the morning in her dressing gown with a sweater over it, her hair flattened where she had slept on it.

Meanwhile, the cold front passed over and behind it came the rain. The colours of the lake dulled and softened, they became brown, green, black. Fallen leaves were thick on the ground, like a new layer of time laying itself down, being absorbed back into the earth. I thought of all the leaves that had fallen in the lake. I imagined them floating down through the depths, lying on the bed, the old valley floor, hiding whatever was down there, covering it over, layer upon layer, year upon year.

I had not seen Daniel for a week or so. I called his number several times, but nobody ever answered and I did not have the courage to leave a message with his father. Once or twice I saw the jeep in the distance, and I waved to it, but it never came near to me. I thought perhaps I had misconstrued the warmth I'd felt between us, the desire that was in that first kiss we shared. I thought about it so often that the memory became distorted. I couldn't be sure of anything.

I wanted to talk to Julia about Daniel, but I couldn't. She had too much on her mind already and it would have seemed selfish to talk about my fledgling love when hers was already over.

Julia was not sleeping well. She said it was the pain in her hip that disturbed her but also she was anxious, worried about money. She talked about putting the cottage up for sale, there being nothing else available to sell. She had left everything of value in France. She blamed herself for not thinking ahead. In the aftermath of Alain's death, she had been so consumed by emotion she had forgotten the practicalities of life, a carelessness that was completely understandable but, in her eyes, foolish because we still had to eat. She berated herself for not thinking to pack at least some jewellery, a few first-edition books, or pieces of antique silver. I almost ran up to my room to find the pendant, to show it to her. I was certain it had value and it would be an item we could sell, but something made me hold back. I didn't feel ready to show it to Julia yet. I didn't want to explain how I had come by it. Nor did I want to remind Julia of her sister, not when any mention of Caroline caused such obvious pain.

It would have been cruel. Julia was not herself. Before Alain's death, she had been a happy, vivacious, attractive woman who cared about her appearance, who had an endless appetite for company and conversation and laughter.

Now she complained most days of a headache. She was gaunt and drawn; her face was ashy and lined and the dye was growing out of her hair so the roots were white around her skull, making her seem much older than she had looked before. I gave her aspirin and water and asked what else I could do to help her. She wanted nothing, she said, but solitude. She went outside most days, for a little fresh air, and watched as Vivi and I tidied the front garden as best we could. But she refused to walk to the village with me and only once or twice did she hobble down the lane to meet her daughter off the school bus.

The weather was inclement but still I took Viviane and Bess out so that Julia should have her peace. Vivi, at least, was more cheerful – full of stories about her new school.

There was no library in Blackwater, it was too small. There was no café either, nowhere we could go to meet people – and even if there had been, I wasn't sure if I would have gone. I was beginning to notice a reservation amongst the villagers. I'd thought at first that their reticence, their unwillingness to chat, was because I was a newcomer to the area. But by this time my face must have become familiar yet still I found it difficult to strike up conversation. It was all right until I said that I worked for Julia – and then the shutters came down. Perhaps, I thought, people were made uncomfortable by knowing that Julia had so recently lost her husband. Perhaps they didn't know what to say.

So Vivi and I kept our own counsel. We walked through the fields. The heavily-trafficked areas around the gates had been churned by the feet of cattle into pools of mud that clagged our boots. We stepped past or over the worst of it, Viviane trailing behind me, switching sticks. We walked the path around the reservoir as far as we could go without trespassing on the land belonging to the nursing home. I kept an eye out for Daniel, hoping I might see him, but there was no sign.

One day, when Julia's headache was so bad she felt she could not leave her bed, Vivi and I walked down to the reservoir. We leaned over the wall at the near end of the dam where the overflow splashed 10 feet down into a wide spillway, a solid stone canal the width of a main road, and was carried away rushing and tumbling and foaming, fierce and angry.

'Where does the water go?' Viviane asked.

I held tightly to the back of her coat. 'I suppose it must end up in the sea.'

'But how does it get there?'

'Through tunnels and underground pipes.'

'What would happen to you if you fell in? Would you be able to swim to the sea?'

'Oh Vivi, I don't know! You'd be washed into the tunnels and you'd drown, I suppose. Don't let's talk about it.'

Vivi leaned further over the wall, so far that the soles of her wellington boots were no longer touching the ground. I held even more tightly to her coat.

'What shall we talk about then?' she shouted down into the water below.

'I'll tell you a story.'

'Not another pigeon one.'

'There are pigeons involved.'

'I bet I know it already.'

'You probably do.'

When she had jumped back down, I told her about the girl who lived in a house in Sheffield with her mother who smelled like toffee and her father who smelled of pigeons and her grandmother who smelled of vinegar. And how the girl was blissfully happy until one day her mother went to the shops to buy cigarettes and never came back.

'Was the mother dead?' Vivi asked.

'No.'

'Why didn't she come back?'

'I don't know.'

'That's sad.'

'But there's a happy ending. Because when the girl grew up, she became a nanny and she went to live with the most perfect family *ever*.'

'Did they live in France?'

'Yes, they did.'

'Were they called the Laurents?'

'Yes!'

'And did they have the best and most beautiful daughter in the whole wide world?'

'That's uncanny! How did you guess?'

'I'm just a genius,' said Viviane.

'You certainly are.'

Vivi grinned. She put her hand into mine.

Back at the cottage, Julia was still in bed, in the dark, so tired she could barely open her eyes. There was a sour smell to the room. I sat beside her and tried to encourage her to drink some tea but she was too lethargic even for that. I felt the first stirrings of panic. Julia had had nothing but aspirin all day. I called the doctor, who arrived in due course. He was young, no older than me, and he smelled clean, of carbolic soap and hair oil. He went upstairs, spoke to Julia for a while and then he came back down and wrote a prescription.

'Sleeping tablets,' he said. 'These are stronger than the ones she already has, so they should help her.'

'Thank you, Doctor.'

'You must be sure she doesn't take them on an empty stomach.'

'But she's hardly eating anything at the moment.'

'Can't you tempt her with some of her favourite foods?'

Peaches from the tree trained up the wall of Les Aubépines? Fresh bread from the boulangerie in the village? The garlicky cold cuts she preferred from the Paris charcuterie, the little sugared pastries, the apricots, the unsalted butter so yellow and fresh, the lemons, the sparkling rosé wine, the cheese that smelled like drains but tasted like heaven? How could I tempt her with what little I could afford to buy from the village stores?

'I'll do my best,' I said.

The doctor took his coat from the stand by the front door and put it on. He looked around him and I swear I saw him shudder.

'It's dreadfully cold in this house,' he said. 'Perhaps

Mrs Laurent would feel more inclined to get up if you made the place a little more cheerful.'

I bit my tongue. I wanted to reply sarcastically that such a thought had never occurred to me but I held back. It didn't do to be rude to doctors.

He left and eventually Julia did dress and come downstairs, very slowly, sideways, holding on to the banister. But I had to go and fill the prescription because she would not leave the cottage. All she wanted to do was sit rocking in her chair in the back room, remembering Alain. His sweater was always on her lap or nearby. Sometimes she held it to her face, as if she could inhale the essence of her lost husband from the wool.

CHAPTER SEVENTEEN

Julia remained in this lethargic state for a few days so I was relieved when I came into the cottage one morning the following week after taking Vivi to the bus stop and heard her moving about in the back room.

'Hello!' I called. As I put my bag down by the front door, I noticed the thin layer of dust that lay on the banister, even though I'd polished it the day before. The dust depressed me. It felt sometimes as if the cottage hated me, as if it was deliberately, truculently, opposing all my efforts to civilize it and make it more homely.

I went to find Julia.

She was silhouetted in the light from the window behind but she turned to face me.

'You'll think I'm losing my mind, Amy,' she said.

I laughed. 'Of course I won't.'

'But you will.' Julia looked about her. She fingered the crucifix around her neck. Then she said: 'I know this sounds ridiculous, I know it's crazy, but after you left this morning I came down and I was sitting in my chair, thinking about Alain, and I . . . oh! I heard my sister Caroline's voice. I heard it clear as a bell.'

I crossed the room and I took hold of her hand, and stroked it.

'Julia, darling, you know that can't be right. You're exhausted and you're enervated and . . .'

'There was a name she used to call me, Goody Two Shoes. I had completely forgotten about it. It's been years and years since I've heard anyone use that term, but this morning I heard it again.'

I lifted Julia's hand close to my cheek. 'Julia . . . if Caroline *was* here, if she had the chance to talk to you, don't you think she would have said something more significant? Out of all the thousands of words she could have used, why those ones?'

'To let me know it was her. Because it could only be her. Because nobody else ever called me Goody Two Shoes ever, in all my life, only her.'

'Julia . . .'

'It would be just like Caroline to say something unkind.'

'Come on, Julia, it wasn't Caroline. It was in your mind.'

'Don't look at me like that, Amy.' She took away her hand, went to the window and leaned on the ledge, staring out. 'I know what I heard.'

'It's not that I don't believe you, but don't you think that perhaps you spend too much time alone in this house? Perhaps we should make an effort and go out together.'

Bess was whining by the door, her tail tight between

105

her legs. I stood and went to the door, opened it for her and the dog crept nervously into the hall, a low growl in her throat.

'If we went to the village club one evening, for example,' I continued, 'maybe you'd see some of your old friends.'

'I don't have friends here,' Julia said.

'There must be people you know.'

'I went away to ballet school aged eleven, remember, and I've hardly been back since.'

'But the club would be nice. I've looked at the programme – they've got all sorts, a quiz, a flower-arranging demonstration and somebody giving a talk about the history of witchcraft in Somerset. That might be fun.'

'Fun?' Julia gave a cold laugh. 'I don't think so.'

From the hallway Bess growled.

'In fact,' Julia said, 'there's probably nothing on this earth I'd least rather do.'

Bess started to bark, a panicky, high-pitched bark.

'What's wrong with her?' Julia asked.

'I don't know. Bess! Shhh!'

'I know you mean well, Amy, but I don't want to see anyone from the village,' Julia said. 'Oh for goodness' sake, make the dog be quiet!'

'Bess! Stop it!' As I turned towards the door I thought I glimpsed, reflected in the mirror on the wall, a person standing a little way up the stairs – a slight, female figure with one hand on the banister.

'Vivi?' I called. 'Is that you?'

I went into the hall and looked up the stairs. I couldn't see anyone and I thought whoever it was must be crouching against the wall, hidden in the shadow of the banisters.

'Vivi?'

I ran to the foot of the stairs and almost tripped over Bess who was cowering below them, growling. I looked up.

Nobody was there.

CHAPTER EIGHTEEN

I crouched down beside the dog and smoothed her ears. I said: 'Shh, Bess, shh, it's all right.' She was trembling. I was trying to calm myself at least as much as the dog. My heart was racing and I had that nauseous, dizzy feeling that precedes a faint.

'Is it Vivi?' Julia called. 'Did she come home early?'

'No, no,' I replied, 'it was only a draught. I hadn't closed the door properly.'

I opened and shut the door again so that Julia would hear it slam. I leaned against it and closed my eyes, counted to three, opened them and looked again. There was nobody on the stairs, there never had been. It must have been a shadow I saw in the mirror, or a smear of dust on the surface of the glass. It must have been a trick of the light. It was nothing. I took off my coat, hung it up, and picked up the bag that I'd left by the door.

'Come into the kitchen, Julia,' I called. 'I'll make some tea.'

The kitchen was the brightest room in the house and the least claustrophobic. It was where I felt most at ease.

I laid out two cups and saucers but my hands were shaking so badly that the crockery jumped and rattled. I put my palms down flat on the counter, leaned forward and tried to steady myself.

Julia came limping into the room. She had draped Alain's sweater about her shoulders, the arms tied in a knot around her neck.

'I'm sorry,' she said, 'I didn't mean to snap at you just now.'

'It's OK.'

'It's just . . . oh, it's more complicated than you realize. I don't like being here, Amy. I don't like remembering, I don't want to see old faces. I just want to be away from here.'

'I understand.'

'You're so patient with me.' She put her hand against my cheek. 'Are you all right? You're pale, Amy, pale as milk.'

'I do feel a bit strange.'

'Then sit down. I'll see to the tea.'

She propped her walking stick against the counter and filled the kettle from the tap. I looked through the window. The sky was a papery white. Julia followed my eyes.

'Not long until Christmas,' she said. 'God, I'll be glad when it's over.'

I thought of all the plans I had made for the holiday, the party I was going to organize for the children in the home, and then my trip to Paris. I'd been so looking forward to Christmas that year.

'I used to love this time of year when I was a child,'

Julia said. 'I wouldn't have believed you if you'd told me there'd be a time when I would dread Christmas.'

'What did you like about it?'

'Everything! But mostly the anticipation, the preparations, you know?' She smiled, remembering, and touched the hollow of her neck, stroking it with the pad of her finger. 'Mother and I used to spend hours in this room making puddings. She gave them as gifts every year.'

'What about Caroline?' I asked tentatively. 'Did she help?'

'Caroline? No.' Julia lit the gas and put the kettle on the hob. 'My sister wasn't one for helping.'

I waited but she didn't say any more.

'Did you hate her?' I asked quietly.

'I didn't hate her – I don't hate her.'

'You never speak of her with any affection,' I pressed.

'Don't I?' Julia feigned surprise then brushed it away. 'No, I don't. Perhaps I do hate her. But I didn't always.'

'So what changed?'

'She did.'

'Was it adolescence?'

'More than that. She used to be such a kind girl. She was lovely with me. We did everything together and I adored her. Oh, she was everything to me, Amy . . .' She trailed off, lost in thought, and her face softened as she remembered. She smiled for an instant but then the shadow that always seemed to come when she spoke of Caroline returned. 'Then her whole personality changed. It happened very quickly. Suddenly she couldn't stand having me anywhere near her. Mother said it was jealousy.' She turned away from me, towards the window, and the brightness outside was reflected on to her face. 'I was a pretty little girl, the sort of child adults liked. I got all the attention, all the compliments, and the more I was praised, the more I courted that praise – and the more Caroline distanced herself from me. I *was* Goody Two Shoes. I could do no wrong in my mother's eyes and that must have been difficult for Caroline, but she was partly to blame for the disparity between us. She never seemed to grasp the fact that if she simply did as she was told, if she told the truth, if she wasn't so rude and unpleasant to my parents and their friends and neighbours, then she wouldn't be in trouble all the time.'

Julia gazed into the eyes of her reflection in the windowpane.

'She did some terrible things, Amy. People said she was wicked. They said she had bad blood inside her, a bad heart.'

'Those are cruel things to say.'

'But if you knew what she did, how she treated people! And in the end, she proved them right. She . . . well, perhaps it wasn't all her fault. Perhaps she couldn't help herself. Someone should have realized that she wasn't right; something was wrong with her mind. She couldn't control her emotions. That was it. She was out of control.'

The girl who had drawn the lake in her sketchpad hadn't been out of control. The girl I imagined sitting down by the fallen tree looking out over the water was not someone wild and wicked. The disparity was so great, the difference between my imagined perception of Caroline and the version Julia was describing.

Are you sure? I wanted to ask. *Was she really so bad?*

Julia was still speaking. 'And after she died, I know this sounds awfully heartless, but I was relieved, even though I didn't know the half of what she'd done back then. I don't mean I wanted her to die, at least I don't think I did, but there was so much anger in the cottage when she was around, so many arguments. She made my father so angry and my mother so unhappy. When I came back from Weston that summer and she was gone, the quiet was a relief. Nobody shouting, or crying; nobody making threats, no punishments, no ugly words or tantrums, no slamming doors. My father and Dr Croucher had taken everything out of Caroline's room. They'd even papered over the walls. There was nothing of Caroline left. Mother was so terribly sad, and she felt as if the whole village was judging her and she never really recovered, but the sadness was easier to bear than the unhappiness that preceded it. Did you bring the milk in, dear?'

'It's in the pantry. I'll get it.' I glanced at Julia. She was calmer now, less agitated. 'Why did your mother say she felt judged?'

'Oh . . . because of what Caroline did.' I passed her the milk and she picked at the foil lid. 'The bluetits have been at the cream again.'

One good thing about Viviane being at school was that during the days, at least, she was oblivious to her mother's depressed condition. She came home in the afternoons happy and tired and full of anecdotes about her day. Her cheeks were flushed and her hair was untidy, her socks around her ankles. She had an endless stream of tales to tell about the other girls, their lives and friendships and families. That afternoon we chatted as she sat at the kitchen table wolfing down cheese sandwiches.

'Mr Leeson,' she said, 'that's the headmaster . . .'

'I know.'

'Well, he wants me to practise singing so that I can be in the choir, although it means going to choir practice after school sometimes. But I don't mind that. It sounds fun and you can have your tea at school if you want. Once you're in the choir you can go to all different places on the minibus. In the summer they even go to France on a singing tour. Imagine that! I could end up going back to France with my English friends! What if we went to Paris?'

'That would be wonderful.'

'Mmm.' Viviane nodded and smiled. 'Polly Mathieson, that's another girl in the choir, has her own pony. He's called Bertie and he's an Exmoor and she says I can go and ride him one day. She says I can go to Pony Club with her even without my own pony. Although maybe Mummy will buy me one. Do you think she will, Amy?'

'One day perhaps. She can't afford ponies at the moment, darling.'

'Oh. Well, never mind. I can learn to ride on Bertie while I'm waiting.'

'That's the spirit. And the teachers are being nice to you?'

'Mmm! Especially Mr Leeson. He said he will keep a special eye on me and that I am to go to him if I have any problems. He told me Dr Croucher wants to be kept informed of my progress.'

'I'm glad he's looking after you.'

Viviane giggled. 'Oh he is! They all are. I am an important new addition to the team.'

CHAPTER NINETEEN

Christmas was on its way. The village shop windows had been decorated with cotton-wool snow and tinsel, and several of the houses had Christmas trees twinkling in their windows. In the countryside, too, winter was settling itself. The nights were closing in, squeezing the daylight into so few hours that I was forced to spend more and more time inside the cottage. But I walked whenever I could, enjoying the country-side, the lingering colour-changes of the moorlands and the fields, the freeze and thaw of the ground under-foot, the berries on the bushes, the birds gorging themselves as they prepared for the worst months of winter. The summer's foliage was dead now, dis-appearing back into the peat.

Most of all, I spent time thinking about Daniel and watching the lake.

The more I came to know it, the more I was drawn to it and the more I realized how complex it was, some-thing organic and living, sometimes capricious, sometimes shy.

Its mood was different every day. It could change in

the time it took a cloud to move across the sun, from a tranquil blue to a fractious, wind-tossed pewter. Some mornings it was still and ghostly white, mist hanging above it in pale drifts like exhaled breaths, and the water beneath as quiet as if it were sleeping. Other times it was the colour of lichen, its surface shivering like the pelt of an animal, and then I imagined it lying in wait, as if it might suddenly leap out of the valley and gallop across the Mendip Hills like some mythical monster. Occasionally it was red and inky and hot, a lake that belonged to a different country or a different planet. Always it was beautiful. Always it seemed to me that it was hiding something; that there was some truth about it that I did not see, or understand. I tried to listen, but I could not hear its whispers.

I walked Bess down the lake track so often and came to know it so well that I could close my eyes and picture the ruts and puddles on the pathway and the nature of the different trees that lined it, the shape of their empty twigs and the knots of their roots, the smell of fox and badger, leaf-rot, rabbit and mud. We walked down to the hollow by the lake and if it was not too damp, I sat on the ancient trunk and watched the birds on the water. I imagined Caroline sitting where I sat with her sketchpad, beneath the same trees, seeing the same water, feeling the same cold air. I put my hand on to the trunk, thinking of Caroline's hand, three decades earlier, in the same place. Perhaps this was the only place where she felt calm and peaceful. Perhaps it was the only place where she wasn't out of control. I closed my eyes and tried to conjure up some sense of her, and

I wondered if, when she sat down there sketching, perhaps she had some sense of me. The only thing that separated the two of us was time.

Despite everything Julia had said, I could not be afraid of the Caroline who used to sketch in the hollow by the lake.

Sometimes I walked up the hill, instead of down, and I found my way on to the Mendips, on to Burrington Ham and Blackdown Moor, where wild ponies grazed doe-eyed amongst the gorse and buzzards hunted over brown swathes of dried bracken. Bess pricked her ears and sniffed the air; deer, pretty and delicate with their white bustles, watched from stunted blackthorn glades and the skylarks rose from their invisible nests, a creamy flash of underwing, a call as fresh as apple.

From the top of Blackdown, I could see Blackwater lake spread out in full, tapering at the far end. When I walked the other way, to the west, I could see Glastonbury Tor rising up from the Somerset flatlands, silvered where water had settled on the fields. The black firs of Rowberrow Warren arched down towards the lower hills and in the distance was the Severn Estuary and South Wales. Sometimes I could even make out the ferry cutting the water that divided England from Wales, its smoke trailing. They were going to build a bridge across the estuary, but I couldn't see how, the distance was too far. I liked to walk the lonely top paths where I had a bird's-eye view, where the wind ruffled and gusted through twiggy heather bushes and where, at the end of the short days, clouds of field sparrows shoaled in their hundreds, flying together, myriad tiny wings beating like distant hoofbeats. Although most of the land was boggy, some paths ran with water, like streams.

I was there one day, waiting for Bess to find her ball which was lost in the dead bracken, when a rangy tricolour collie with one blue eye and one brown wandered up and drank from the pool at my feet. Bess came closer and growled at the dog.

'Leave her,' I said, but Bess's hackles were up and her ears were down. I said, 'Come on,' and began to walk away but I was too late – the dogs were already at one another in a tangle of teeth and fur and yelping. I stepped into the pool to try to grab Bess's collar, but the collie's owner was there and he said: 'Enough!'

It was Daniel.

The dogs circled uneasily and then moved apart. I was breathless, my heart pounding. It had been weeks since I last saw him, since I had kissed him, and I was tongue-tied. I blushed at the memory of my previous brazenness.

'I thought they were going to kill one another,' I said.

'It was nothing,' Daniel said. 'They didn't mean anything by it.' He held out his hand and I took it. He pulled me out of the water.

'Hello again,' I said. I smoothed my hair, brushed myself down.

'Hello.'

'How are you?'

'Happy to see you again,' he said.

'I'm happy to see you too.'

'Are your feet wet?'

'Yes.'

Daniel offered me his arm and I held it for balance while I took off my boot and emptied the water from it. I was standing with the boot upturned in my hand when Daniel said: 'Look.'

Far away, a bird made a curve in the sky, and then returned, describing a graceful S shape.

Daniel held his binoculars to his eyes, adjusted them. 'Here,' he said, and he passed them to me. I dropped the boot and put my foot down on the wet grass. I held the binoculars to my eyes but could see nothing but a fast-moving blur of sky and moor. He helped me, guiding my hand gently until the lenses found the bird. It moved so quickly that I struggled at first to follow it, and then, when I found the knack, I was dizzy with the speed and soar of it.

'Oh!' I said. 'What is it?'

'A harrier. You don't see them up here often.'

'I've seen hunting birds before.'

'Buzzards or kestrels maybe; sparrowhawks, even a goshawk. Most likely not a harrier.'

I passed the binoculars back to him, hopped back into the boot. Daniel was looking at the bird again. His green jumper and old brown jacket with a broken zip made him seem like part of the landscape. The two dogs, having put their differences behind them, were sniffing the edges of the path together.

'You didn't call me,' I said quietly.

'I couldn't get through on the number you gave me. During the day it was always engaged. In the evenings there was no answer.'

'But we are always there.'

'Honestly, Amy, I tried so many times I know it off by heart.'

He told me the number I had given him and I recognized it at once.

'That's my father's number,' I said. 'I gave you my father's number in Sheffield.' I laughed, embarrassed and also relieved. 'He takes the phone off the hook during the days, while he's sleeping, and he goes out to work in the evenings. I'm so sorry, Daniel. I can't have been thinking straight when I wrote it down.'

'It's OK.' We walked on for a moment or two. 'Why didn't *you* call *me*?' he asked.

'I thought you didn't want to speak to me.'

'How could you think that?'

'I don't know. I just did.'

He gave me a little push with his shoulder.

'Idiot,' he said.

I pushed him back. 'Idiot yourself.'

We smiled at one another and began to walk companionably close together, our shoulders and arms bumping from time to time, smiling from time to time.

'You like birds, do you, Daniel?' I asked.

'Very much.'

'But I've heard shooting on the Aldridge land.'

'They're shooting pheasants that were bred to be shot.'

'Still killing birds.'

'But the money raised is used to protect the habitat of the wild birds. My father has many faults but he cares a great deal for the conservation of wildlife.'

'That's something in his favour at least.'

'He's not so very bad, you know.'

'Hmm,' I said.

We walked together along the path, me skirting around the pools of water, Daniel walking through them. I picked up Bess's ball and threw it for the dogs to chase.

'So how is Viviane?' Daniel asked.

'Better now she's started school.'

'Is the imaginary companion still around?'

'Yes. I'm keeping an eye on it, like you said, but trying not to worry too much.'

'Good,' said Daniel. Then, 'Are you busy on Friday evening?'

'This Friday? I'll have to consult my social calendar to be sure, but off the top of my head, no, I don't think so.'

'Then come to the pub. I'll buy you a drink.'

'OK. I'd like that.'

We had reached a crossroads in the path, by the Beacon Batch Trig Point that marked the highest point in the Mendips and the ancient, Stone Age barrows built on the brow of the hill. The wind blew the clouds towards us and my hair whipped across my face. I gathered it in my hands, holding it back. My face was freezing.

'The rain's coming,' Daniel said. 'You want to get yourself back down to the village.'

In the valley down below, the lake was dark grey and angry, little spitty waves fighting on the surface.

121

'Aren't you coming?' I asked.

'I left the jeep on the other side of the moor.' He held out his hand and I took it. He leaned over, and this time he kissed me so deeply that I could hardly bear to let him go.

'I'll see you on Friday,' he said.

'OK.'

'Don't forget.'

'I won't.'

'The Hare. I'll be in the Hare.'

'OK.' I waved and then I set off down the rocky slope with Bess at my side. My socks were squelching inside my boots but there was a lightness in my heart. I felt the happiest I had felt in months.

CHAPTER TWENTY

The next day, an extravagant bouquet of flowers arrived at Reservoir Cottage from Bruno Rolland, the editor of Alain's newspaper. There was a note. Bruno wanted to come over to England to talk to Julia.

Julia looked at me over the top of the bouquet, pollen dusting her chin. The flowers had seemed so bright when the florist gave them to me at the front door, but as soon as they were inside the cottage, in the darkness of the hallway, their colours had seemed to fade and they had become sad and weary. The oppressiveness of the place even affected them.

'I don't want to see Bruno,' she said.

'Isn't he one of Alain's oldest friends? Mightn't he be able to help you?'

'He's not coming out of friendship. He wants to take Alain's notebooks and no doubt he'll use whatever he can find in them to achieve his own political ends.'

'He thinks there's evidence in the notebooks?'

'Certainly.'

'Then why not give them to Bruno? That way, the instigators of the shooting may be brought to justice.'

'Not like this. Not by giving all Alain's work away. He didn't die to make his publishers rich. I won't let them hijack his work.' Julia pressed the bouquet back into my arms. 'Do something with these, will you? All they will do is die. Already they're dying. Take them away.'

I held the flowers to my face and the printed paper wrapped around them crackled and the tail of the ribbon bow was silky against my wrist. I took them into the kitchen. Julia was right, there was a smell of decay about the out-of-season roses and freesias; the petals were already soft, the leaves already wilting. The dustbin was kept at the side of the cottage. I opened the back door and I saw Mrs Croucher, dressed for the weather in a coat, headscarf and boots, opening the gate at the bottom of her garden. I called out to her, and the old woman turned. I ran down the garden. 'Would you like these flowers, Mrs Croucher? Julia's not in the mood for them.'

I held the bouquet over the wire fence so she could see them properly.

'They're very pretty,' Mrs Croucher said, 'and they must have cost a fortune.' She looked at the flowers, considered. 'I could take them down to the nursing home, I'm sure they'd be grateful, only that's a big bunch for me to carry all that way. I'd struggle with them, dear, because of my chest. I had tuberculosis when I was a child and I've never been right since.'

'Are you going there now?'

'Yes.'

'Hold on then, I'll fetch my coat and walk with you.'

That's what I did. We walked together down to the

reservoir, passed the spillway, crossed the dam and turned right beneath an archway made of wrought iron with a sign that read *Sunnyvale: First-class Residential Nursing Care for Gentlefolk*. The gates beneath the archway were open and beyond was a drive leading to the main building.

'It looks very nice,' I said.

'You wouldn't believe it was once a lunatic asylum, would you?' said Mrs Croucher. 'They treat the residents like royalty these days. It's more like a hotel than a nursing home.'

I gave her the flowers. 'I'll leave you here,' I said. 'Tell your husband that Julia sends her love.'

'Won't you come and meet him?'

I hesitated, but she insisted and so I followed her inside.

Sunnyvale's entrance area was laid out like the reception of a country hotel, with a wooden desk, bookshelves and easy chairs. It had been lavishly decorated for Christmas with a real tree hung with gold and red baubles and fairy lights, and cards fastened to the beams.

I gave the flowers to the nurse at the reception desk who admired them and then directed us to the day room at the end of a lushly carpeted corridor. It was a light and airy room, well-furnished. Mrs Croucher led me towards a well-built, bearded man in a wheelchair. He was talking to an elderly man wearing a dog collar beneath a shabby black suit – the vicar.

The two men were deep in conversation although they stopped when they saw us. Mrs Croucher

125

introduced me to her husband, then to the vicar, Reverend Pettigrew, and also to his daughter, Susan, a lumpy, middle-aged woman in a housecoat, who was hovering nearby. Susan, I was told, worked in Sunnyvale as a cleaner. Mrs Croucher leaned close to my ear. 'Susan's not quite the full shilling,' she whispered. Susan may not have heard this, but she certainly guessed the meaning. Her cheeks coloured. I was terribly embarrassed for her but thought the kindest thing I could do was pretend I hadn't noticed.

'Well,' said the vicar, rubbing his hands, 'I'd best make a move. People to do, things to see!'

'Don't go on my account,' said Mrs Croucher. 'I'm always glad to see my husband's friends haven't forgotten him.' She smiled at me in a conspiratorial way. 'They still play cards twice a week, these boys, and I have more than a suspicion that whisky is involved!'

The doctor spoke for the first time. 'Perhaps you could show the vicar out, dear,' he said to his wife. 'I'd like to have a quick word with this young lady.'

They went, eventually, and when they and Susan were gone, the room seemed to fall quiet. The other residents went back to their crosswords, their books and their knitting. The doctor beckoned me closer, took my hand and raised it to his lips, barely touching my skin. The old-fashioned courtesy and the intimacy of the gesture caught me somewhat off-guard. I could feel the touch of his lips long after he had let go of my hand.

'It's a pleasure to meet you, Amy. I've heard so much about you,' he said. 'My good lady wife keeps me

126

informed of the comings and goings at Reservoir Cottage. Shall we go into the dining room? It's more private and this is a sensitive matter.'

He picked up the old-fashioned black doctor's bag at his side and laid it across his knees, then wheeled himself out of the room. I followed, unsure as to what he wanted to talk about. The other residents did not seem to be watching us, but still I sensed that they were. I fixed my gaze on the back of the doctor's head. He still had a full head of white hair, with a strong curl. It was neatly and expertly trimmed at the nape. The backs of his ears curved pink, dotted with age spots and moles.

The dining room was grand, filled with tables with cloths on, already laid for lunch; sprigs of holly and ivy had been placed on the window ledges and draped above a massive fireplace. A wireless was playing beyond. I could hear the muffled strains of Bing Crosby singing 'White Christmas'.

'Shut the door, please,' the doctor said. I did as he asked. He indicated that I should sit down and I pulled out a chair and sat with my hands on my lap and my feet together, side by side, feeling as if I were somehow being assessed. The doctor's gaze was friendly but direct. He was the kind of man who, I imagined, wouldn't miss much – a reader of people. I had a niggling worry that someone might have seen Viviane tearing up the flowers on the Cummingses' grave and had told the vicar, and that the vicar might have told the doctor and *that* was what he wanted to talk to me about. I was beginning to understand how things worked in this village and was certain that very little went unnoticed.

'Nothing to worry about,' said the doctor. He cleared his throat. 'I'll come straight to the point, my dear. I'm concerned about Julia.'

'Julia?'

'Yes.'

'Well,' I paused, 'it's good of you to be concerned. Thank you.'

We looked at one another for a moment. He was waiting for me to say something else. Did he want me to tell him that Julia was falling apart? That she was hearing voices? That I was desperately concerned too?

The silence was becoming uncomfortable when the doctor steepled his fingers and said: 'My wife tells me that Julia never leaves Reservoir Cottage, nor does she talk to anyone outside the house. She says that Julia makes no effort to look after herself and neglects her appearance. In addition, she is losing weight and looks tired all the time. Is that right?'

'She's had a terrible time but she's a strong woman,' I said. 'She'll come through this.'

'With all due respect, you're hardly qualified to be a judge of that,' the doctor said kindly, and he sat a little straighter, made himself a little larger. He was a large man anyway. No matter how I straightened my spine, I felt small by comparison. He smiled at me over his fingers. 'It's commendable that you don't want to be disloyal to Julia. I understand. But *you* need to understand the possible ramifications of allowing the situation to slide. The longer Julia carries on like this, the more she is at risk.'

'At risk? Of what, exactly?'

The doctor paused, as if for dramatic effect. He knew he had my attention now. He unclasped his hands and stroked his beard, with his thumb and forefinger. 'My dear girl, I don't want to alarm you, but someone like Julia, bereaved, isolated and lonely . . . how can I put this . . . ? Someone like her might well harm themselves.'

'Julia would never do anything of the kind.'

'You're forgetting, my dear, that I know Julia well. I know the history of her family.' He leaned forward in his chair and lowered his voice, almost to a whisper. 'Julia's sister, Caroline, had severe mental problems. Did you know that?'

'Well, Julia intimated . . .'

'And her mother, Cora, once attempted suicide.'

I must have gasped at this revelation because the doctor's face relaxed a little, gratified by my reaction.

'Cora hanged herself in Caroline's bedroom,' he said. 'Fortunately her husband reached her in time and managed to cut her down, but she was never the same afterwards. She spent several months in the asylum, in this very building, before she was strong enough to return home, and then only under my strict supervision. She had to take medication for her nerves for the rest of her life.'

'Julia told me her mother went to stay with friends after Caroline died.'

'Because that's what we told Julia. She was only a child herself then and we didn't want to frighten her. Everyone in the village did everything they could to protect little Julia.'

129

Of course they did. That's exactly what would have happened.

The doctor spoke again, still in that same low, husky whisper. 'The female Cummingses have a predisposition towards mental fragility,' he said. 'You understand, Amy? Julia is vulnerable and she seems to be following the precise trajectory of her mother's decline. Frankly, without intervention, I fear the worst.'

'So what do you think should be done?'

The doctor sat back. His face was etched with pity. 'Caring for somebody as fragile as Julia is too much for one person. It's too much responsibility. She needs to be amongst people who know her well. People who could share the looking-after of her. Her husband's family perhaps?'

Alain's parents and siblings, an affluent, charming and argumentative family who lived near Toulouse, would, I was certain, have already offered to take Julia and Viviane into their home but Julia must have declined their invitation. She had never felt comfortable with them. She referred to them, collectively, as 'the Torrents' – 'posh', she said, and 'too noisy'.

'I'll talk to her,' I said. 'She's been thinking, anyway, about putting the cottage up for sale.'

'Good,' said the doctor. 'Well, that's something.'

There was a moment's silence, which was, I realized, my signal to leave.

I stood up. 'Thank you, Doctor, for your concern and your kindness,' I said. 'And also thank you for helping arrange for Viviane to go to Hailswood. Thank you for everything you've done for us.'

'It's my pleasure,' he said. 'My pleasure.'

CHAPTER TWENTY-ONE

The light was on in the kitchen and Julia was sitting at the table. I saw her as I approached the cottage through the garden. I went in through the back door, crossed the room and kissed her cheek. She took off her glasses and rubbed the bridge of her nose, where they had pinched. 'What was that for?' she asked.

'I'm pleased to see you, that's all. What are you reading?'

'One of Alain's notebooks.' Julia laid the glasses down on the table. 'I was thinking, while you were out, about Alain, and his death, and making it relevant. I don't need to talk to Bruno. I can transcribe Alain's notes myself. His shorthand is atrocious but I can try to make sense of it and then perhaps I could finish his work for him.'

'That's a wonderful idea!'

I shrugged off my coat and hung it by the door, pulled out a chair and sat beside Julia. Her blouse was done up on the wrong buttons, and I could see the strap of her bra, dirty and grey through the gape in the neckline. Julia smelled warm and sour, like yoghurt. These small vulnerabilities made me feel very tenderly towards her, the woman who had always been so careful of her appearance, so immaculate in her dress, so kind to me.

She put one hand gently on my arm.

'Where have you been?' she asked me.

'I walked down to Sunnyvale with Mrs Croucher and met the doctor. He obviously cares for you a great deal.'

'The old darling! Is he still taking care of himself? Still dapper?'

'Oh yes.'

'He's the best-dressed man I've ever known. My father always said he was the epitome of a gentleman.'

'He's certainly very personable.'

'He always wore a suit, even when he was lancing a boil or cutting out an infected tick. His shoes were always polished. He had very clean fingernails. And do you know what he used to do, Amy, to make himself less frightening to children? He used to wear coloured socks and he always had a handkerchief folded in the front pocket of his suit to match his socks. It was a joke for his young patients. Whenever we saw him, my mother used to say: "What colour handkerchief will the doctor be wearing today?" And we tried to catch him out but his socks and his handkerchief always matched. He took great care of that. He was always so gentle with children.'

Julia's smile suddenly faded. 'Caroline never found it funny, though.'

'No?'

'No.' She shook her head. 'She used to sabotage the socks.'

I laughed. 'How did she do that?'

'She was so naughty! Mrs Croucher used to do the washing every Monday and she'd hang the coloured socks and hankies out to dry on the clothes-line, all paired up, seven sets of each, one for every day of the week. Caroline used to sneak over the fence and mix them up: a red sock next to a blue one, or else she'd turn alternate socks over so they were pegged at the ankle instead of the toe. Sometimes she stole a handkerchief. We'd hide behind the hedge and watch Mrs Croucher come out and we'd see the confusion on her face when she unpegged the mismatched pairs. And Caroline would be watching with a kind of glee but I was terrified – *terrified* – that Mrs Croucher would realize what was happening and that Caroline would be in the most awful trouble. The fear made the whole thing funnier. I used to have to stuff my cardigan sleeve into my mouth to stop myself shrieking with laughter.'

Her face had softened at the memory. She looked younger. I could see behind the mask of middle age the pixie-faced child who used to hide with her sister.

'Why were you so afraid that Caroline would be in trouble?' I asked. 'Mixing up the laundry is hardly a capital offence.'

Julia winced at that phrase, but recovered quickly.

'I didn't want there to be any more upset. Caroline had already caused a dreadful stink for the doctor.'

'Goodness. What did she do?'

Julia pushed her hair back from her face and clasped her hands on the table in front of her.

'I haven't thought of it in years. Perhaps if I tell

you, you'll understand more what Caroline was like.'

I nodded encouragement and she continued. 'It was crazy. Completely and utterly crazy. She made this stupid accusation . . . it was just ridiculous. I never understood *why* she did it but then I never understood the half of why Caroline did what she did.' She sighed. 'My father had a pocket-watch that had been passed down through his family. It was his pride and joy and one day it went missing. Mother and I searched the house, searched high and low, but we couldn't find it. Father was in a terrible state. While we were hunting for the watch, Caroline took it upon herself to walk all the way to Chew Magna. She went into the police station there and told the officer behind the desk that Dr Croucher had stolen her father's watch. She said she'd seen him take it and hide it in his black bag.'

'No! What happened?'

'The police officer drove Caroline back to Blackwater. He parked the car outside the cottage here – you can imagine the commotion that caused – then he came in and told our parents what Caroline had said. I was sent next door to fetch the doctor and ask him to bring his bag round to our house, which he did. Everyone was in the kitchen, right here at this table, my mother and father, the police officer and Dr Croucher. Caroline was standing where you are now. I was watching her. Her eyes were bright and her cheeks were flushed. She seemed . . . oh . . . excited. The police officer asked Dr Croucher to open the bag and empty it. He took everything out, one item at a time, all his instruments and bottles and jars, and he laid them on the table. It seemed to take for ever. It was excruciating. And Caroline . . . Well, as soon as the bag was opened, the excitement disappeared. As each item came out of the bag she became paler. I thought she might cry, or faint. By the time the bag was empty, it was as if she had shrunk down inside herself, become a shadow of the girl she'd been earlier.'

'So the watch wasn't in the bag?'

'Of course it wasn't.'

'But it sounds as if Caroline really believed the doctor had taken it?'

'She knew perfectly well that he hadn't. Once everyone had left, Father asked her directly, he said: "Do you know where my pocket-watch is?" and she said: "It's in my satchel," and he looked and it was.'

'Why would she do that? What did she possibly have to gain from hiding the watch in her satchel and then accusing Dr Croucher of its theft?'

'Attention? Notoriety? You're the one who's studied Psychology – you tell me. Everything Caroline said was a lie. She had a compulsion to lie. I don't know *why*, perhaps these days it would be recognized as some kind of condition.' Julia sighed. 'Anyway, Father took off his belt and he beat her. He said he would beat the badness out of her.'

'Oh dear.'

'Oh dear indeed. It was awful. Father was weeping as he hit her.' Julia covered her face with her hands and shuddered. 'And Mother was begging him to stop but he said he didn't know what else to do. He said it was for her own good. I was upstairs in my room. I had my

136

hands over my ears but I could still hear. Father was weeping and Mother was pleading and Caroline . . . I don't know what Caroline was doing. She didn't cry out; she didn't make a sound. Oh God.' Julia trailed her fingers through her hair. 'Dr Croucher was terribly good about it, you know. He consoled my parents, told them that he didn't hold them responsible, that young teenage girls were prone to fantasies and that nobody should make too much of it and so on and so forth – but of course they were still hideously embarrassed.'

'And after that you were afraid of something similar happening again?'

'Yes, I was. I can only have been eight or nine years old but I was concerned about my sister. I didn't know why she was behaving as she was, but these battles she insisted on fighting were battles she could never win.' Julia reached out for my hand. 'Do you see, Amy, how difficult it is to talk about Caroline? Are you beginning to understand how troubled she was?'

'Yes,' I said. 'Yes, I am.'

Later, when I was alone, I took Caroline's satchel out from under my bed, and I removed the gold pendant from the matchbox. I held it in the palm of my hand, the light shining through the ruby making pinpricks of red like spots of blood on my skin. It was such a lovely thing. I closed my eyes and I tried, once again, to make myself feel as Caroline must have felt when she held it in her hand.

'Caroline,' I whispered, 'were you going to blame the doctor for this one, too?'

CHAPTER TWENTY-TWO

Viviane came home from school humming 'Once in Royal David's City'. Her eyes were alive and happy but when she looked about the cottage, the joy drained from her face.

'It's so miserable in here. We need to get ready for Christmas,' she declared, shrugging off her coat and hanging it up. She looked about her again; I followed her eyes and sympathized. There was nothing joyful in the hallway of Reservoir Cottage, nothing bright or cheerful at all. Julia looked too and I knew what she was thinking; I could read her thoughts by the expression on her face.

'Oh darling,' she said gently, 'not this year. Let's let Christmas pass us by this year. We have nothing to celebrate.'

And no money to celebrate with.

Vivi's face was a picture of consternation. 'But we must have a proper Christmas, Mummy. We must – it's our tradition! And Papa would be mortified if he thought we were letting things slip.'

Julia laughed. 'Mortified? Since when have you used the word "mortified"?'

'Everyone says "mortified" at school, Mummy,' Viviane said primly. She turned to me. 'Remember what Christmas was like in France, Amy?'

'Oh, yes.'

The lavishness of those French Christmases! The lights, the candles, the greenery, the food, the wine, the parties. The apartment in Paris was red, green and gold, gifts piled beneath the tree, people coming and going, beautiful people, little girls in bows and barrettes come to play with Viviane, and adults dressed up to the nines, those glamorous women in their heels and silks and stoles, the men in their suits, the cigarettes and perfume and hair oil, the conversation, the seduction, the dancing. And we'd all come from that to this chilly, dark cottage, not one single decoration, not one single card. Was it really only a year that had passed? Paris felt, to me, like a lifetime ago. I looked at Vivi's urgent little face and I thought: She's right. We should make an effort for Christmas.

I turned to Julia and I could see that she was thinking the same.

'There were some trimmings,' she said, 'a few bits and pieces – fir cones that Caroline and I painted when we were children. We used to keep them in the loft.'

'The loft's empty now. Where else might they be?'

'The shed?' Viviane suggested.

'The shed's not been used for thirty years.'

'I'll go and have a look anyway,' Viviane cried. She pulled her boots back on, grabbed her coat and ran outside, calling to Bess. I followed her into the kitchen and stood at the back door watching as she skipped down to the bottom of the garden, the dog following.

Julia stood beside me, leaning on her stick.

'She won't get it open,' she said. 'After Father died my mother and I tried. We couldn't find the key to the padlock and the window is so well sealed it's bombproof.'

Julia filled a glass with water from the tap, took a sip, then held it in her hand, gazing out. 'I used to play in that shed. It used to be my hideaway.'

'Did your father build it?'

'No, it belonged to the reservoir superintendent, who lived here before we did. There's a plaque inside that says *Bristol Water Company*. Father used to show it to people who came asking about the history of the lake. He never used it. He kept his tools in the garage so he turned the shed into a playhouse for me. Mother trained a climbing rose up around the door and I put a rug in there, a little table, cushions, blankets and curtains at the window. I cut out pictures from magazines to decorate the walls. It was where I went when I was lonely or unhappy. I loved it. I had tea parties for my toys. It was my favourite place until . . .'

Her voice fell away. I looked at her. Her eyes were full of sadness. She smiled at me.

'I feel as if I'm always telling tales on her.'

'Caroline?'

'Yes, Caroline.'

'What did she do this time?'

'She set fire to the shed. It wasn't long after the pocket-watch incident. Father used to store petrol in the garage. One day, Caroline came home from work and she took a can, went into the shed and doused everything that was inside, with petrol. I was next door with Dr Croucher – I had earache, I think. We heard my mother's screams. He ran out to see what was going on, but before he could stop her, Caroline lit a match and threw it into the shed and she stood there and watched it burn, all my toys, the blankets, everything.'

Julia finished the water and put the empty glass back in the sink. Outside, Viviane tugged at the shed door handle, rattled it and then, frustrated, kicked it. She put her hands in the pockets of her coat and walked around the building, looking for weaknesses.

'It was a proper blazing fire,' Julia said. 'Dr Croucher and my father tried to put it out, but Caroline had been thorough. Nothing inside could be saved. The structure was sound but all the toys and furnishings were ruined. Mrs Croucher wouldn't let me go outside. We watched from her kitchen window. I was crying. She had her arms around my waist and her chin on my shoulder and she was rocking me. "There, there," she was saying, "never mind." Father was scuttling around like a lunatic, trying to douse the flames with spadefuls of soil and Dr Croucher was helping but they couldn't do anything really. In the end they gave up and waited for the fire to burn itself out. Caroline was just standing there, where Vivi is now, watching. I could see her face – it was glowing in the light of the flames and sometimes the smoke blew towards her and she'd disappear for a moment. I couldn't understand her. I could not, for the life of me, work out why she would do such a thing.' Julia sighed and crossed her arms about herself. 'I never played in the shed again. Father sealed up the window and put a padlock on the door. I don't believe anyone has been inside since.'

'Where did she work?'

'Hmm?'

'You said Caroline had come home from work.'

'Oh yes. Yes. She used to be a housemaid for the Aldridges. She stayed there during the week but came home at weekends.'

'Daniel's parents?'

'Yes.'

Viviane came back into the kitchen, her cheeks rosy with cold.

'No luck, Vivi?' I asked.

'I can't make it budge at all.'

'The decorations wouldn't be in there anyway,' Julia said. 'My mother wasn't much of a one for Christmas. She must have thrown them away.'

Viviane didn't say anything else, but I could feel her disappointment. Somehow or other, I promised myself, I'd find a way to decorate the cottage for Christmas.

That evening, Julia took a sleeping pill and went to bed early. I sat downstairs, in the back room beneath the master bedroom because I couldn't bear to sit alone in the living room, beneath the empty bedroom, even though the living room was the only warm place, the only room with a fire. I wrapped myself up in jumpers and a scarf with socks over my stockings and tried to read my book, but my mind wouldn't settle. Instead, I started to make a list of the things I needed to buy before Christmas, substituting cheaper alternatives for expensive items, but my heart wasn't in that task either.

I was sick of potato and onion soup; I was cold and I was bored and I was lonely.

I decided to telephone Daniel. We would see each other tomorrow evening anyway, in the pub, but if he was free, perhaps he would drive up and come to sit with me and talk for a while. Perhaps he would bring some of his father's apple brandy. I went into the living room, doing my best to avoid eye contact with Jesus on the wall, and dialled Daniel's number, but there was no answer. My disappointment was crushing. I stood beside the telephone table with the receiver in my hand, the darkness of the room gathered around me, the only sound the pattering of raindrops on the window and the wind, desolate, in the chimney. There was nobody else I could call. My father would be at work by now, the Sheffield house would be empty. I would try Daniel's number again.

I held the receiver to my ear. Now there was no dial tone. I jabbed the cradle a few times with my finger but still nothing. I depressed the cradle one last time and something changed: now I could hear a voice on the line through the earpiece. It had the otherworldly, disconnected sound of a call being made a long way away: a crossed line.

I tried to disconnect the other call, but I couldn't. The woman – it was a female voice – was still there. The tone and pitch of her voice had become higher and more urgent; she sounded distressed. I put the handset back in the cradle and wandered around the room, pacing its four walls. I did not want to talk to the woman, but what if she was in serious trouble? What if nobody else could hear her?

I picked up the phone again.

'Is someone there?' the voice called. 'Are you there? Can you hear me?'

'Hello?' I replied. 'Hello?'

'They're watching,' the woman called, distant as if she were on the other side of the world.

'Who is watching?'

'They pretend they're not looking but they're watching all the time.'

'Who is this?' I asked. 'What's your name? Where are you?'

'They're still there!' the woman cried. 'They never went away.'

The line, suddenly, went dead.

CHAPTER TWENTY-THREE

Friday began as a miserable day. The sky was surly, with the early darkness that presages the worst of winter, and the storm that had set in the day before had not blown itself out. Rain came down in torrents, shrouding the valley and the reservoir, drumming relentlessly on roofs and windows, whipped about by a fractious wind. The cottage felt more isolated than ever. When the coalman came, creaking in his oilskins and dragging his sacks to the bunker at the back of the cottage, he said some of the lower lanes were already flooded, that the old Bristol Road was impassable.

I wrapped up well and walked through the wind to the village store where I used the dregs of my money to buy an exercise book for Julia to transcribe Alain's notes, and some glue, a tube of glitter, cardboard and cotton wool. None of this cost much, but it was money that could have been used for food and the extravagance made me feel guilty. Before I went into the cottage, I knocked on Mrs Croucher's door and explained that I would be going out for a couple of hours that evening.

'Would you mind coming round to sit with Julia and Viviane while I'm out?' I asked.

Mrs Croucher's face lit up with pleasure. 'Oh, there's nothing I'd like more,' she said. 'I'll make a fruit cake and we can play cards. Perhaps little Viviane could join in?'

'I'm sure she'd love that,' I said. In my mind I was thanking God for the gift of Mrs Croucher's cake, a treat that wouldn't cost us a penny. It was so long since I'd tasted something rich and sweet that my stomach almost growled with anticipation.

Inside Reservoir Cottage, Julia was in a restless mood, pacing the kitchen with a letter in her hand, her face tensed into a frown.

'It's from the bank in France,' she said, slapping the letter down on to the kitchen table. 'They say I'll have to go to court to challenge the legality of freezing Alain's assets. It could take months, years even, to sort it out. And it will cost money to hire the lawyers I'll need and I *have* no money. I am stuck, Amy. What am I to do?'

I put down the shopping bag, and took hold of Julia's cold hands.

'We'll be OK.'

'We won't be OK. We can't survive on fresh air. What will we eat? How will we manage? We can't expect the school to keep educating Viviane for free. We can't pay the telephone bill or the rates. I can't even pay the coalman. What are we going to do?'

'I could find paid work in Bristol perhaps, something to see us through.'

'Amy, you are a sweetheart, but I can't ask you to do that. You, work to support Vivi and me, when you're already doing so much for us out of the goodness of your heart? No.' She let go of my hands and paced the room. 'What we must do is sell the cottage, as quickly as we can. We'll need to tidy it up a bit, decorate the empty bedroom. The wallpaper in that room is hideous. We'll strip the wallpaper, Amy, you and I, and then we'll put up something new. Something bright and modern. There are a few tools and paintbrushes in the garage. Let's see what we can find.'

We found what we needed, a metal bucket and a wallpaper scraper. As I rinsed off the dust and cobwebs at the kitchen sink, I could hear Julia in the living room, talking on the telephone.

'Yes, I understand,' she said. 'I know winter's not a good time to sell.'

I took an old cloth from the cupboard under the sink and carried the bucket upstairs, slopping water on the bare floorboards. Bess padded after me. The storm had set in now, closing around the cottage. I unlocked the door into the empty bedroom and pushed it open with my foot. The room was gloomy and icy cold and it still had its strange, pervasive smell, not mice, not damp but something old and organic, something unhealthy.

Perhaps it still smelled of Caroline's death.

No, I told myself firmly. *Don't be so silly.*

I set the bucket on the floor, went into Viviane's room, fetched her transistor radio and set it up on the window ledge. Bess stood at the door whining.

'Come on,' I called, patting my knees. 'Come on in, Bess,' but the dog wouldn't move.

I switched on the radio, pulled out the aerial and found some music playing – 'Walk Right Back', a cheerful song that I liked. Satisfied, I crossed to the chimney wall and began scoring lines in the dark yellow wallpaper with the blade of the scraper. Then I dipped the cloth in the bucket and slapped water on to the paper, working it into the slashes I'd made, trying not to think how the colour of the yellow paper reminded me of diseased skin, and how the cuts were like wounds. As I did this, the music coming from the radio faded, to be replaced by a buzzing, static hum.

Annoyed, I dropped the cloth back into the bucket and returned to the radio. As soon as I picked it up, the song returned. Pleased it was working, I set it down again and got back to work with the scraper, chipping away at the cuts in the paper and then working more water underneath, trying to drench the backing paper so that it would come easily away from the wall. But within moments, the radio reverted to the hum. This time I could hear voices in the fog of sound. More specifically, I could hear a female voice, a distressed whisper fading in and out of the distortion. The voice was horribly familiar. It sounded like the voice I'd heard on the crossed line of the telephone.

You are being ridiculous, I told myself. I dried my hands and went back to the radio. I picked it up and moved the dial with my thumb, and the noise became louder and quieter as the transistor moved through the air-waves, picking up voices and sounds, all distorted, all crackled but I couldn't seem to lose the voice in the static. No matter which wavelength I turned to, I could hear the woman's voice coming through. I tried to turn the radio off, but I couldn't. I turned it over and prised the cover to the battery compartment off with my thumb. I took out the batteries but there must have been some vestigial energy stored in the radio because the static was still there, and the voice amongst it.

In the end, I threw the radio into the bucket of water where the sound gurgled and died as it sank to the bottom. I stared at it, staring back at me, the odd bubble freeing itself and rising to the surface.

'Damn!' I said. Why had I done that? Why had I been so stupid?

I left the room. Bess lay waiting on the landing, her chin on her paws, watching me with wise eyes. I pulled the door shut behind me and the two of us went back down the stairs.

Julia was rocking in her chair in the back room, cradling Alain's sweater. I leaned against the wall with my eyes closed until I had composed myself.

'Amy?' Julia called. 'Is that you?'

'I'm making tea,' I replied. 'Would you like some?'

'The estate agent said it's too close to Christmas to put the cottage up for sale,' Julia replied. 'He said he'll come and put a board up on the twenty-seventh. Apparently the market's not good at the moment.'

'No?' I stood at the doorway to the room.

'No. He said it might take a while. After that, I called the bank. I spoke to the manager and asked for a loan.'

'What did he say?'

'That he would never lend money to a woman without a husband no matter what the circumstances.'

'Oh, Julia.'

She looked to me and smiled sadly.

'It's as if all my worth as a person was taken by the same bullet that shot Alain.' She stroked Alain's sweater, absentmindedly, as if it were a cat. 'We shall have to make every effort to sell the cottage as quickly as we can. It's our only option. You're very pale, Amy dear. Did you make a start on the wallpaper?'

'I started, yes, but I didn't get much done. I'll carry on later.'

CHAPTER TWENTY-FOUR

Viviane had arranged to bring a friend back with her from school that evening – Kitty Dowler, a rosy-faced child who lived in a farm up on the hills. She smelled of sweat and dogs, and her tunic was frayed at the hem but she was a cheerful girl not in the least put off by the darkness of the cottage, or its suffocating coldness.

'Come on,' she said to Viviane when she had been introduced to Julia and given a glass of milk and some bread and margarine. 'Let's go upstairs.' Her accent was broad Somerset.

'Stay out of the empty bedroom, Vivi,' I said. 'I've started to strip the walls. I don't want you touching anything.'

'OK.'

I smiled at Kitty. 'I'm glad your mother didn't mind you coming to stay tonight.'

'I don't have a mother. She died in childbirth,' Kitty said in a matter-of-fact voice.

'Oh! I'm sorry.'

'It's OK. I have two older brothers and a dad. And

they were all glad that I was coming here because they can go out to play skittles.'

'That's good! Listen, girls, while I'm out this evening, Mrs Croucher's coming round. She's baking a cake and you can play cards with her and Mummy. That'll be fun, won't it?'

The children nodded.

'I won't be late back,' I said. 'You'll be OK, won't you?'

Viviane pulled a scornful face. 'We're not babies. We'll be *fine*!' she said.

The Hare was a small, dark pub. It was busy, with an overflow of clientele – farmers, most of them – standing outside despite the cold. Their breath made puffy clouds about them, and the smoke from their cigarettes was blue and thin amongst all the thicker, grey exhaled breaths. The rain had stopped but the wind still gusted, sending an empty cigarette packet somersaulting down the road. I made my way inside, through a narrow porch lined with posters and fliers. The public area was a tiny room with a sloping ceiling, crooked floorboards and a cavernous fireplace. It was warm and noisy and crowded; the men's voices were loud, they filled the space with their elbows and bellies, their rolled-up sleeves and burly shoulders, their individual pewter pint jars gripped in their hands reflecting the flames of the fire. I looked around but I could not see Daniel. I excused my way through the men, looking for him, and then I heard a few notes of a guitar and then a male voice. The voice was raw and dear to me. I squeezed through the crowd and at last I saw him. He was perched on a stool in a corner curled over a battered old guitar with his hair falling all over his face. He was singing a song about missed opportunities.

I watched and listened and my heart felt as if it were swelling inside me. I watched his face, the way he kept his eyes down, looking towards the guitar. I watched the way his lips moved and his fingers strummed the strings, how tenderly he held the guitar. I watched him and I felt something I had not felt for a man before. It was a longing to be close to him, a craving to be held and played the same way he held the guitar . . . but it was more than that. Daniel moved me. He was a good man. I wanted, more than anything, for him to be happy. I wanted to look after him, to care for him and protect him, to be the one who made him happy.

I wished the song would never end, but when it did, the drinkers clapped and cheered. Daniel nodded his thanks then leaned down to pick up his tankard and took a long drink. He kept his head low but I saw that the flesh around his right eye was swollen and the eye narrowed to a slit.

'Danny's old man's been at him again,' someone muttered and someone else replied: 'He stopped him beating ten bales out of some kid he caught trapping birds on the lake.' I turned towards the voices to hear more, and while I was not looking, Daniel picked up his guitar and disappeared into the back of the pub. I tried to follow but the pub was busy and by the time I had squeezed through to the spot where he had been, there was no sign of him. I asked but nobody knew where he was. Had he forgotten that we had arranged to meet? Had he changed his mind?

I went outside, but I couldn't see the jeep. And I couldn't bear to go back into the pub again, to endure the sympathy or the scorn of the drinkers if it turned out that I had been stood up. I decided I would go back to the cottage, to the company of women and a slice of Mrs Croucher's cake.

The air was bitterly cold and damp and smelled of woodsmoke. I followed a footpath down an alleyway that ran past the backs of a jumble of cottages and out-buildings until I reached the crossroads where I could either follow the path or divert back to the road. The path would be quicker but it would mean cutting across the churchyard in the dark.

I set off at once, without giving my imagination time to get to work, walking quickly, hearing the rhythm of my own footsteps, the in and out of the air in my lungs, my heartbeat. I passed the last few houses in the village, light shining around the edges of the curtains and the flicker of Christmas lights in the windows. The lake, down below, was wide and quiet, like something sleeping, something old and knowing. I could not see, from this distance, but I imagined how full it must be after so much rainfall, and how the excess would be gushing over the overflow into the spillway, thousands of gallons of ice-cold water rushing back to the sea. I thought of all those cold, dark tunnels that carried the water away, all those secret passageways, the power of all that water.

I reached the churchyard, took a deep breath and

went through the lych-gate. It was perhaps forty paces to the other side.

I counted to seven, and then I broke into a trot as I went into the shadow of the great church tower, out of the moonlight. I was blinded by the dark, immersed in it as if it were something solid. I had to slow down; I couldn't see two feet in front of my face. I held out my hands, feeling my way through, counting my footsteps, nineteen, twenty, twenty-one . . . Then from the darkness, I heard footsteps behind me. I quickened my pace until I was running, and then I stumbled on something and fell on to the grass.

The footsteps grew closer; I could hear panting, and a voice.

'Amy, it's OK, it's me, Daniel!'

I turned and he was there, behind me. He helped me to my feet and I held on to him.

'I'm sorry,' he said. 'I didn't mean to frighten you. Are you all right?'

'I'm fine.'

'Are you sure?'

'Yes, yes, I'm fine.' I was embarrassed now by my show of panic. 'Sorry,' I said, 'to make such a fuss of nothing.'

'I shouldn't have come up behind you like that but I didn't see you until the last minute. I always come this way. I know it like the back of my hand.'

'I know – I know it's stupid. I just . . . oh, what an idiot I am!'

I put my face into the shoulder of Daniel's jacket, and the feeling I had felt before in the pub returned, only now it was me being protected by him. Alone I had been vulnerable, with him I was inviolate. He put his arm around my shoulder and we walked on slowly together.

'My mother's grave is here,' he said.

'Yes, I noticed it before. What happened to her, Daniel, if you don't mind me asking?'

'You haven't heard?'

'I hardly speak to anyone. Only the shopkeepers and Mrs Croucher.'

'Well, she drowned. In the lake.'

'This lake? Blackwater?'

'Yes.'

I looked over towards the moonlit lake flattening the valley below, so smooth and quiet, so large and, from this distance, so still. How deceptive it was. It seemed benevolent and gentle, but beneath the surface the water was moving. It was forming currents, shifting and sliding, deep streams of water weaving past one another like sinews, travelling from the river inlet towards the spillway, water twisting and twining like huge, invisible eels trying to find their way back to the sea.

And Daniel's mother had drowned in that water.

'Oh Daniel, I'm so sorry. Being here, living so near to the lake must remind you of her all the time.'

'My father likes to take a boat out, and he sits there alone and thinks of my mother.'

'That's romantic.'

'He likes to feel close to her. He still loves her so very much. I don't believe he will ever stop loving her.'

I didn't want to have a reason to dislike Mr Aldridge any the less, but this revelation caused me to feel a pang of sympathy in my heart.

We reached the gate on the far side of the churchyard, went through it, and walked away from the darkness together, our bodies touching in a way that was both comforting and companionable. 'I heard you singing,' I said. 'You're very good.'

'I wasn't sure if it would be your kind of thing.'

I held on to his arm. 'Well, it is. And you are my kind of thing, Daniel Aldridge.'

I sensed that this pleased him. 'Is it too late to buy you a drink?' he asked. 'We're only two minutes away from the Lake Inn.'

'No,' I said. 'It's not too late.'

The Lake Inn was not like the Hare, it had been done up to appeal to the kind of people who drove out to Blackwater on Sundays for the view: flock wallpaper, stuffed fish in glass cases on the walls, fishing rods strung on the ceiling, horse brasses nailed to the beams and silk flowers in coloured glass vases on the tables. That evening, the Blackwater Horticultural Society had taken over one side of the bar for their Christmas social and a dozen elderly men and women in paper hats were arguing gleefully about the best time to plant Hellebore. I sat on a bench by the window, feeling the draught on my back while Daniel went to the bar. He returned with two pints of cider, pulled up the stool opposite and sat with his elbows on his knees and his head held low so the wound to his eye was less obvious. I wondered if I was supposed to avoid talking about this for the rest of the evening, or if it would be impolite to ask about it already knowing, as I did, the cause.

Instead, I steered the conversation round to the wild birds Daniel loved, and he told me about the lapwing and golden plover that only came to the Mendip Hills in the winter months, about the hunting birds – the hen harrier and the merlin – and birds with names like the words of poetry: fieldfare, siskin, whinchat, nightjar, ring ouzel and brambling. I finished my drink and he bought me another. I drank, felt pleasantly soft and dizzy.

'Who taught you about the birds?' I asked.

'My father. They're his passion. That's how he met my mother. They were both down at the lake at the same time. He was in pursuit of the very rare Lesser Scaup and instead he found her. He lent her his binoculars.'

'That's a sweet story.'

Daniel took a drink. 'Nobody sees that side of him. People don't realize how much he loved her. I've heard it said that my parents' marriage was one of convenience, that Jean Debeger wanted a young husband with prospects to save her from spinsterhood and that Robert Aldridge needed a wife with money to save the estate from bankruptcy. They say it was no more than a business arrangement between a young, impecunious man and a wealthy, middle-aged woman. But if they saw how much my father still pines for the woman he lost, then they wouldn't talk like that.' He put the glass back on to the beer mat. 'I don't remember her, of course. I only know her through what he tells me.'

In that respect, I was luckier than Daniel. I thought

of my own mother smiling as she leaned to kiss me, the fur collar of her coat, her red lips. Her hair was swept back from her head, a blonde wave. She was wearing gold earrings. I wondered, for the briefest moment, if she was happy, then put her from my mind.

'Will you have another drink?' Daniel asked.

'I'd like to, but I'd better get back. Vivi has a friend staying over and Mrs Croucher is keeping Julia company so I can't be late.'

'Half an hour won't hurt.'

'I don't like to leave Julia on her own. The doctor told me it's not good for her.'

'Perhaps she wants to be on her own.'

'Even if she does, Dr Croucher said I'm not to leave her.'

Daniel said: 'When animals are hurt, what they do as a rule is find somewhere quiet and dark and private, and they lay low until their wounds are healed.'

'Time doesn't seem to have helped your father.'

'He dwells on the cards life has dealt him and the drink fills him with self-pity. I'm sure Julia isn't like that. Give her the space to mend herself and things will soon begin to get better.'

'Do you think so?'

'Yes.' He placed his hand over mine. 'Do you really have to go?'

'I'm afraid so.'

'Then I'll come with you. I'll walk you home.'

He helped me into my coat, and we left the warmth of the pub and set off once again, into the night. Daniel took my hand and put it in the pocket of his jacket. He held it warm inside his own hand. I wished all of me would fit into that pocket.

'When will I see you again?' he asked as we walked.

'Whenever you like.'

'On Christmas Eve my father always hosts a party for the village before the midnight mass. It's tradition. Do you know the house – Fairlawn?'

'The big one by the lake?'

'That's the one. Everyone will be there. If you were to come down, I could slip away and meet you outside. I could show you where I live.'

'You mean I can't come to the party?'

'I'm afraid you can't.'

'I don't suppose I would be welcome in your father's house.'

'Never mind my father. This is my invitation to you. I want you to myself. I want to show you my home.'

'All right.'

'Wait by the pillars outside Fairlawn at eight o'clock. I'll come and find you.'

'By the pillars?'

'Do you mind? It won't always be like this.'

'I don't mind.' I smiled.

We walked on until we reached the cottages. The lights wound round a small, artificial tree were twinkling in the window of the Crouchers' cottage, but Reservoir Cottage was as dark and self-contained as always.

'Don't you celebrate Christmas?' Daniel asked.

'We couldn't find any decorations.'

'That's a shame. But then old Mrs Cummings wasn't much of a one for Christmas.'

'You knew her?'

'Not really. She hardly ever left the cottage but when I was up here doing jobs for the Crouchers, she used to watch me from the windows. I would wave to her and she would wave back.'

There was a movement inside Reservoir Cottage. We watched as a figure came to the living-room window, reached up and drew first one curtain, then the other.

I tried not to look at the window of the empty bed-room above. I was afraid I might see something there.

Instead I turned to Daniel and slipped my arms around his neck. I kissed his mouth, taking care not to touch the sore part of his face. He kissed me back. It was even lovelier than before and the feeling inside me grew and became stronger. I welcomed it. I think I knew already then what it was, and that it was part of me now, and that it would never go away.

CHAPTER TWENTY-FIVE

The next morning, it being a Saturday and there being no school, we had a cup of tea and what was left of Mrs Croucher's fruit cake for breakfast. Then I cleared the kitchen table and sat with Viviane and Kitty making paperchains and decorations. By lunchtime the kitchen was strewn with paper and glitter and paint and glue, and a cheerful, festive mood had descended on the cottage. One of Kitty's brothers arrived to pick her up before lunch. I went to meet him at the door, and he said: 'Have you seen this? It looks like the Spirit of Christmas Present has been to visit!'

Viviane pushed past me and I followed her out. Leaning against the wall was a Christmas tree already set in a metal pail and lavishly decorated with ribboned bows and an elaborate string of coloured fairy lights. There was also a huge bunch of mistletoe, and a wreath of holly and ivy.

'Did you bring these?' Viviane asked Kitty's brother.

'Did I heck! They were there when I got here. Looks like Father Christmas came early to you.'

'It must have been Daniel,' I said, and I could not hide my smile.

Kitty's brother helped us bring the decorations in and set them up in the living room. The lights, when they were plugged in, twinkled beautifully. Even Julia smiled and held her hands together over her heart, the pale skin of her face reflecting patches of red and green and yellow. 'Lovely,' she said. 'Perfectly lovely!'

Kitty's brother invited Viviane to come back to the farm for the afternoon, promising to return her to Reservoir Cottage before dark. She was eager to go and I thought of the food she would be fed there, and was pleased to send her away. The young people disappeared and the cottage was quiet again.

Julia sighed. 'We ought to unplug the lights to save the electricity,' she said.

'They use barely anything,' I said, thinking that a few extra pence on the bill would make little difference to our situation. Julia shrugged. She pulled Alain's sweater on over her dress and returned to his notebook. I went back upstairs, back to the wallpaper in the empty bedroom. I felt better that day, after spending time with Daniel, and I was determined not to allow myself to be spooked by my own imagination.

I left the door open and Bess lay on the landing as I chipped away at the paper. It was hard work. Mr Cummings and Dr Croucher had not pasted, but glued the paper to the wall in places; that was why it was so difficult to remove. The glue and the wet paper stank and the patch of exposed distemper beneath the paper grew terribly slowly like a wound that was not healing, but expanding – green-coloured flesh uncovered beneath peeling skin.

CHAPTER TWENTY-SIX

Viviane was up early on Sunday. I heard her footsteps on the stairs. Bess turned a circle on my bed, sighed and lay warm in the hollow of my legs. I snuggled further under the blankets where it was cosy and tried to fall back to sleep but I couldn't. Instead I thought of my Daniel and his kindness and his easy ways, but that was no comfort to me because the spectre of his mother's death and his father's violence cast shadows over my thoughts.

Daniel should have left his father, I thought. He should have gone away from Blackwater, far away, and made a new life for himself. I had found the strength to leave my father, and he wasn't a cruel man; his only vice was his bitterness, his refusal to forgive my mother for not loving him enough to stay.

But that wasn't her fault. You can't make yourself love a person, any more than you can make that person love you. Love is not a matter of choice.

Thinking of my father was making me feel guilty. I had posted him a Christmas card, but that was all I'd done. I turned over. Bess grumbled and turned too.

Those of us who are bound by love, not by responsibility, are the lucky ones, I thought and I remembered the children in the home where I'd worked for such a short time, the little ones who were entirely alone, and that thought almost broke my heart.

After a while, weary with sleeplessness, I climbed out of bed and went downstairs, my mood lifted by the smell of pine resin coming from the living room. I plugged in the fairy lights – because their cheerfulness outshone the gloom, no matter how hard the gloom fought back – and went into the kitchen. Viviane was already there, sitting at the table making more decorations.

'Good morning,' I said. Viviane did not look up from the paper angel she was making.

I lifted the kettle to test its weight. 'How about a drink?' I asked. 'Cup of tea?'

'No, thanks,' said Viviane.

I sat opposite the child with my chin in my hands, while I waited for the kettle to boil. Vivi had lined up the angels and was painting faces on them with care and precision.

'They're beautiful,' I said.

'I'm making them for Kitty's dad. He said nobody ever makes angels for pig farmers.'

'That's sad.'

'Mmm. He said just because he smells like you-know-what, it doesn't mean he can't appreciate something pretty.'

'He sounds a nice man.'

'He is.' Vivi looked up then. 'Oh Amy, I miss Papa so much.'

'I know you do, darling.'

'Everything was better when he was alive.'

'I know.'

Viviane sucked her lower lip, then dipped her brush into the little pool of red in the lid of her paint box. 'Remember the decorations we used to have in the apartment in France? It used to take us a whole day to put them up, and you would make a jug of hot chocolate to keep us going. Remember the glass birds with the real feathers in their tails that we clipped on to the blinds?'

'I remember.'

'And those baubles Mummy bought from the shop in the Champs Elysées? If you held them up to your eye and looked through them towards the light, you could see hundreds of different colours like magic. What happened to those baubles, Amy? Who has them now?'

'I don't know.'

Viviane dipped the brush in a jam jar half-full of water and twirled it round to clean the bristles. A smudge of red paint drifted in the water. I reached out and ran my fingers along the back of her wrist.

'Next year you can start again, Vivi. You can start a new collection of decorations.'

'They won't be the same, though, will they?'

'No, they won't be the same but that doesn't mean they'll be worse, just different, that's all.'

'Why do things have to change?'

'I don't know, my darling.' I took hold of the child's hand and I kissed it.

Viviane paused. 'Amy?'

'Yes?'

'Do you believe in hell?'

I took a deep breath. 'I don't know. I don't think so.'

'So even if you did something really bad, even if you for example killed someone, you wouldn't go to hell?'

'I'm not planning on killing anyone.' I laughed. 'Why do you ask?'

'In the Bible it says that people who do bad things go to hell.'

'Not everything in the Bible is true.'

Vivi shrugged. She was concentrating very hard on her painting. There was something about her demeanour that made me uneasy.

'Is there anything you want to talk to me about, Vivi?' I asked. 'Has someone said something to upset you?'

She still did not look up but she shook her head. I decided not to press her.

I took my tea upstairs and returned to work in the empty bedroom. The stripped area seemed to have grown smaller while I was absent, as if the wallpaper was alive and was trying to repair the damage I had inflicted. Already it seemed an endless task and one I half-wished I had never begun. There was something repulsive about the wallpaper, something more than the bilious colour, the sickly pattern. Perhaps it was the awful smell of the decades-old glue, perhaps it was its obstinacy. Perhaps it was something else altogether.

CHAPTER TWENTY-SEVEN

There had been no mention of Viviane's imaginary friend for a while. Caroline had not disturbed Vivi's sleep; all her talk was of the new friends she had made at school and nothing out of the ordinary had happened in the house. I had stopped worrying so much about Viviane and Julia and I was so buoyed by my feelings for Daniel that I was less anxious at home. Superficially at least, things were improving inside the cottage. Then, just a few days before Christmas, the mirror broke.

It was a Tuesday, a better day, a bright, sunshiny day. I had already walked the dog and was upstairs changing when the telephone rang. Julia picked up the receiver in the living room and I could hear that she was speaking to the estate agent. Suddenly there was a crash and Julia screamed.

I ran down the stairs. Julia was standing on the rug in the centre of the dark wooden floorboards with the receiver still in her hand, and all around her were shards of glass. Fragments glinted, reflecting the colours of the fairy lights. The big, convex mirror that had hung above the fireplace had fallen out of its fancy, sunburst frame, hit the edge of the hearth as it fell, and exploded. The frame, empty now, was still on the wall, with nothing inside it. Anxious bleats were coming from the telephone.

'Don't move, Julia,' I said. 'Keep still.'

Julia was as white as a ghost. She dropped the receiver. It bounced once and then lay on the floor beneath the table, on the end of its cord. She was staring at the mirror frame in horror.

I pulled on my shoes and pushed the dog back, away from the broken glass. I then went into the living room, glass crunching beneath my soles, and picked up the telephone receiver. 'Mrs Laurent will call you back presently,' I said and I replaced the receiver into its cradle.

Julia raised a shaky finger and pointed at the place where the mirror had been. 'I saw Caroline,' she said.

'It must have been a trick of the light,' I said gently.

'It wasn't. I saw her as clearly as anything. It was as if she was watching me through the mirror!'

'It was your own reflection distorted in some way, that's all it was, honestly. Here are your shoes. Put them on, darling.'

'My mother stood in front of that mirror every morning,' Julia said. 'She used to stand there and put her lipstick on, like this.' She pursed her lips and mimed the act of drawing on lipstick. Then she turned to me. 'And I was thinking about that. I was on the telephone, thinking about my mother putting on her lipstick and when I looked up, there was Caroline, looking out of the mirror.'

'You can't have seen Caroline—'

'I know! I know I can't have, but I did! Oh Amy, what's happening to me? Am I going completely mad? First I hear her voice, then I see her face in the mirror!'

'It's because you're here and you're thinking about her, that's all.'

Julia crouched with difficulty to gather up the pieces of broken glass.

'Please don't do that,' I begged, 'you'll cut yourself. Leave it to me.'

'It was my mother's mirror and now it's broken. If we collect all the shards, we can take them to a restorer!'

'You can't repair a broken mirror, Julia. Some things just can't be put back to how they were.'

'Everything I care about is broken!' Julia cried. She clenched her fingers over the fragments and at once blood began to seep from her hand.

I dropped to my knees, put my arms around her and held her. 'Let go of the pieces,' I pleaded. 'Let them go, Julia. Don't hurt your hands for nothing.'

'I saw Caroline,' Julia whispered. 'She was watching me.'

This time, I didn't contradict her. I gently forced her fingers open, took the bloodied shards from her and then held her, rocking her as if she were a baby. As I did so, I had the sensation of something moving past, a draught. I glanced over my shoulder and I saw the feathery strands of the tinsel on the tree lift and waft like hair in the wind.

CHAPTER TWENTY-EIGHT

I heard the creaking of the chains of the swing, rhythmic as a heartbeat, reminiscent of the creaking of the floorboards in the back room beneath the runners of Julia's rocking chair. I looked through the window and saw Viviane in the garden, in her school clothes, sitting on the swing in the gloaming. She had taken off her coat and hooked it over the black branch of one of the overgrown apple trees and she was lying back with her legs stretched out, her body almost a straight line, as the swing swung backwards and forwards and back again.

I went outside. The fishing boats were out on the lake, their lamps spots of light in the blackness of the valley. The air smelled of dead leaves and woodsmoke, of damp and of winter. In the house, the light shone dully through the back-room window out into the garden. I couldn't see Julia but I knew she was there. The thought of what else was inside the house was like a chill settling on my shoulders.

Viviane swung and I went over to the shed. I tried the door once again, as if it might have somehow freed itself from the padlock. It would not budge, so I went to the window and put my fingers beneath the wood hammered over it and pulled at the planks, trying to prise one loose, but all I did was make my fingers sore. I leaned back against the shed wall and imagined it being filled with fire. I imagined the child Julia watching from next door's window as her beloved hideaway went up in smoke, Mrs Croucher whispering comforting words into her hair. I imagined Julia's father and Dr Croucher frantically throwing spadefuls of soil into the shed, trying to extinguish the flames. I imagined what Caroline must have felt like, standing a little apart, watching, feeling the heat of the fire, every now and then being engulfed by the smoke. Why had she done that? Was she so jealous of her little sister that she was compelled to destroy the child's sanctuary?

What had happened to her afterwards, I wondered. Another beating, or something worse?

I listened to the creaking of swing chains around the metal pole at the top of the frame and the rhythm became a phrase in my mind: *They're watching, they're watching, they're watching.* The words became louder and louder in my mind until I could bear them no longer. I crossed the garden and took hold of the chain, pulling the swing to a halt. 'Come on, sweetheart,' I said to Viviane. 'It's raining. Come inside now.'

Viviane looked at me and her eyes were confused, as if I had just woken her from a deep sleep.

'Come on, Vivi, you're getting wet,' I said. 'You'll catch your death out here.' I glanced around me. The night was closing in; it was already too dark to see the shape of the lake, and although nothing was different in the garden, I was afraid that something might be hiding behind the hedge, or watching from the edges of the field beyond. 'Come on,' I said again. 'Let's go indoors.'

Viviane pushed the ground with her feet, twisting the chain away from me. I let go and she set to swinging again.

'Caroline said I don't always have to do what you say,' she said.

I sighed. 'Why are you being like this, Viviane? It's not like you.'

She did not look at me. She stretched out her arms and tipped back her head and looked instead up at the sky, at the rain that was falling down on her. I felt the rain fall cold on my head and I wiped the drops away from my eyes. I didn't know what to do.

I stood and watched for another moment, and then I said quietly, 'OK. You do as you wish, but I'm going in. I'll see you when you're ready.' Then I told Bess to stay with Vivi. On my way back to the house, I picked up Viviane's rain-soaked coat and I had a good look around, to make sure nobody was lurking; nobody was watching her. As I walked away from Vivi, I thought I heard her say something.

I stopped and looked round. 'What was that?'

'Nothing,' Viviane said.

But I had heard the words. I had heard them as clear as anything.

Goody Two Shoes.

CHAPTER TWENTY-NINE

I told Julia I was going to go out for a couple of hours, to celebrate Christmas Eve with Daniel Aldridge.

'At Fairlawn? With Robert Aldridge?' Julia asked.

I did not want to tell her the truth, that Daniel was going to sneak away from the party to meet me in the darkness of the garden. So instead I said cheerfully: 'Why not?'

'Does Robert know you live with me?'

I perched on the arm of the settee beside her and took her hand. 'Yes.'

'Then don't go, Amy. Robert won't welcome you into his house.'

'Daniel told me the whole village was invited. And anyway, Mr Aldridge could hardly make a scene at his own party on Christmas Eve in front of all his guests.'

'If he'd had enough to drink he could.'

'What does he have against your family?'

Julia said nothing.

'Is it something to do with Caroline?'

Julia nodded. She looked down. A tear spilled out of

her eye and dropped on to the back of her hand. 'Oh Julia,' I asked, 'what did she do?'

The clock ticked and a cloud shadowed her face but then she shook it off.

'I wasn't here,' she said. 'I was in Weston. They kept it all from me. I didn't find out until years later.' She sniffed and wiped her nose. 'Oh, let's not talk of that now, not at Christmas. She wasn't all bad, my sister, you know. She had a good side too.'

'Then tell me about that.'

'Her good side? Hmm. Well, she was very good at drawing, although sadly most of her drawings were in the shed when she set fire to its contents. And when she wasn't telling me to go away and leave her alone, she was sometimes quite kind. She used to take me down to the lake. We had a secret place, a hollow with a fallen tree. We used to spend hours down there together. We'd swim and then we'd lie out in the sunshine to dry off and she'd tell me her stories. And she sang. She had a lovely voice.' She smiled and then she was silent for a moment. 'Blackbird,' she whispered, 'bye bye.' Another tear made its way down her cheek and she brushed it away with her fingers.

I looked at the lights on the Christmas tree, their reflection in the black window glass. I had a sudden feeling of being watched, that uncomfortable 'hairs standing up on the back of the neck' sensation.

'I won't go out,' I said. 'I won't leave you on your own this evening.'

Julia squeezed my hand. 'Amy, darling, all I want to do is have this first Christmas without Alain over and

176

done with. You go and meet your sweetheart. Borrow one of my dresses, if you like – take anything you want from the wardrobe and have a good time, and promise me that you won't worry about me and Vivi. We'll be fine on our own for a few hours.'

'Are you sure?'

'Of course I am.'

I kissed Julia's cheek, then I ran upstairs. I changed quickly, in my cold bedroom, then I went into Viviane's room to say goodbye. The girl was lying on her bed asleep, her head resting on one outstretched arm. A book lay face down on the floor beside the bed – *Rebecca*. Her eyes were swollen and the skin of her cheeks was tearstained. I covered her over gently with a blanket, and then I leaned down to kiss her.

'Sleep tight, sweetheart,' I murmured, then left the room quietly, pulling the door to and switching off the light before I went.

CHAPTER THIRTY

The night was cold and silvery, perfect for Christmas Eve. Even the lake was in the spirit, its surface black and smooth, reflecting the moon and the stars beautifully; it was innocent that night, pure, holding its breath. I was thinking about Julia and Caroline, the older sister taking the younger one to swim in the lake, and I was so wrapped up in these thoughts that I almost bumped into the back of Mrs Croucher, who was ahead of me walking down the lane.

'Hello, Amy,' she said. 'Don't you look a picture!' She wheezed dreadfully. 'You're not going to the Christmas party at Fairlawn, are you?'

'No . . . I'm going to meet somebody,' I said.

'Oh yes? A young man? I like to see the young folk enjoying themselves,' she said with a smile. 'Who is he? Anyone I know?'

'It's a secret,' I replied with a wink. Then, to change the subject, I asked, 'What about you? Are you heading for Fairlawn?'

'No, dear. I'm on my way down to Sunnyvale. The vicar holds an early mass for those who can't make it up to the church. It suits me better – I can be in my bed before midnight.' She was wracked, then, by an alarming spasm of coughing that doubled her over. I patted her back and tried to support her. She leaned against me.

'Mrs Croucher,' I asked, 'are you all right? Can I do anything for you?'

'Oh goodness,' she said, as she straightened, 'my chest! This cold weather will be the death of me.'

'Poor you,' I said. 'Are you sure you're up to walking all the way down the hill?'

'I'll be all right,' she said. 'Perhaps someone will give me a lift home afterwards.'

'If not, you must stay there,' I said. 'Here, take my arm. Let me help you.'

We walked on down the hill together. Candles flickered in the windows and the air was still with the special quietness of Christmas Eve. I no longer felt sad. My heart was beating with anticipation; every step I took closer to Fairlawn was a step closer to my darling. I said goodbye to Mrs Croucher at the fork in the road at the side of the lake, and hurried along towards Fairlawn. The entrance to the house was marked by two grand stone pillars topped by recumbent lions on either side of the drive. I looked at my watch. Even though I'd walked so slowly with Mrs Croucher, I was still a little early. I kept to the shadows and followed a smart family group through the open gates and up wide stone steps that led to a large front door. The door was open and inside I could see a girl in a pinafore and waitress headband taking coats while another handed out glasses of sherry. The first girl was flushed and nervous. She seemed young and out of her depth, desperate not to put a foot wrong. Caroline had once worked here, in this house, I remembered. Was that how she had been too?

The light from inside the house was like a beacon shining in the dark night. Behind the girl, in the hallway, a huge Christmas tree stood beside a grand staircase and a fire was burning in an enormous hearth strewn with holly and ivy and glowing with candles. The tricolour collie was lying in front of the fire together with two cocker spaniels. It all looked beautiful and welcoming. I felt a twinge of sadness that I could not go and join the celebrations, that I was excluded because of the actions of someone I had never met, and who had died before I was even born. I slipped back into the shadows, and waited by the pillar. Daniel found me there a few moments later. He kissed my cheek.

'Come on,' he said, 'it's not far.'

In a moment we were at the back of the house, quite alone and following a path that bisected the lawn to a gate that opened on to a dark bridle-path. I could smell the lake. I could feel the weight of all that water close by and the air was a degree or two cooler. The water changed the atmosphere as if the lake had a personality and it affected the mood of the valley around it, and the longer I was in Blackwater the more sensitive I became to the lake and its power.

'Christ, it's cold,' said Daniel. 'There's a chance of a white Christmas yet.'

'Oh, I hope so. Does the lake ever freeze over?'

'When it's cold enough, yes.'

'We could go skating.'

'We could.'

'I used to take Vivi every year in Paris. We both loved it so much.'

'Then you'd better pray for a cold winter.'

I held on to Daniel's arm as he led me to another gate into the garden of a small lodge almost at the water's edge. I'd seen the lodge before, and knew it was where Daniel lived, but I'd never been so close to it before. Three steps led up to a green door, lit by a lamp. Daniel took a key from his pocket, unlocked the door and switched on the light.

'If ever you need me and I'm not here, there's a spare key on the ledge above the door,' he said. 'Come in.'

He stood back and I stepped into a long room with a living area at one end and a bed at the other. There were two doors – a kitchen and bathroom, I assumed. The walls were decorated with paintings of birds and pencil sketches and coloured drawings. Daniel turned on a small lamp, with a peach-coloured shade that cast a rosy glow, and then knelt to light the gas fire. While he was doing that I looked at the pictures.

'These are incredible.'

'Drawing birds is all I'm any good at. And shepherding.'

'And looking after your father.'

'That too. They're all rather niche activities but somebody has to do them,' he said, laughing. 'Sit down, Amy. Make yourself at home.'

'Thank you.'

Daniel held out his hands as the flame flickered

along the run of the fire. Then he stood and took off his coat. I followed the pictures to the far end of the room and sat on the bed, a soft double bed covered with coloured blankets and cushions. I unbuttoned my coat and took off my shoes, then I lay back on the bed and stretched my arms above my head. I knew what was going to happen and I felt very happy about it – happier, certainly, than I had ever felt with anyone I'd been to bed with before.

'It's so nice and warm in here,' I said.

'I'm glad you like it.'

'And the bed is lovely.'

'It's old. I'm afraid the springs are given to creaking.'

'It's much nicer than my bed in Reservoir Cottage.'

He walked over to the bed and sat beside me. The mattress tipped me towards him. He reached out his hand and touched me just beneath the lobe of my ear. Then his fingers followed my jaw and my neck, down to the hollow of my clavicle. He leaned down and kissed me. 'What's your bed like there?' he whispered.

'It's lonely,' I said.

Daniel lay down beside me. He put his hand on my stomach, between my blouse and the waistband of Julia's yellow silk skirt. One finger found its way beneath the elastic of my suspender belt. I shivered.

'Your hand is *freezing*,' I said. And then, because I didn't wish there to be any room for doubt about what I wanted, I added, 'It would probably be warmer if we took off our clothes and got under the covers.'

'Yes,' Daniel said. 'It probably would. You go first.'

The mattress was so giving, already it felt like a friend

to me. The flickering flames of the fire and the faint, whooshing sound of the gas in the pipes made the room cosy and welcoming. I undressed quickly and when I was naked I pulled back the covers and I slid underneath them. Only then did I look at Daniel, who was gazing at me with an expression of joy that was open and honest and adoring; it made my heart beat with such affection for him. I was given to him, I thought. We were meant to be together. It was so lucky that we had found one another.

'I've thought about bringing you here a thousand times,' he said, 'and I thought I'd worked out every possible way the visit might play out, every word we might say to one another and every action we might take before you agreed, or didn't agree, to get into my bed. I never thought for one second it would be as easy as this.'

'I've never seen the point of making things difficult simply for the sake of propriety,' I said.

'Propriety is a very over-rated virtue in my opinion.'

'Mine too.' I pulled the patchwork coverlet up to my chin. 'Stop talking, Daniel Aldridge, and take off your clothes.'

Daniel did as I asked. He was more beautiful unclothed than he was dressed. He climbed into the bed beside me, put his hand on the side of my face, and then slid it down my neck, my shoulder, my breast so that I could feel my heartbeat reflected back to me from the palm of his hand. I could feel the heat of him. I reached my hand down and he bit his lip and closed his eyes, as if in exquisite pain.

'Oh!' he groaned.

'Say something,' I whispered.

He leaned down and he kissed me on the mouth. I kissed him back.

'If you keep doing what you're doing, I don't know where this will end,' Daniel mumbled. He put his face into my hair. He was breathing heavily.

'I know where it will end,' I told him.

And after that we were all hands and legs and mouths and skin, we were hot and excited and urgent and we fitted together. And afterwards as we lay wrapped in each other's arms, breathless and shy and full of an incredulous happiness, hardly believing that such an amazing, unlikely bliss was possible, I said to Daniel: 'This is the best part,' and he replied: 'All of it is the best part.'

We did not talk any more; our bodies wanted to come together again and it was less rushed this time, more deliberate, more tender. Afterwards Daniel kissed my face and stroked my cheek with the back of his fingers. 'I don't believe this,' he said. 'I don't believe *you*. You are absolutely perfect.'

'That's what I think of you too,' I told him.

We could not stop ourselves from smiling.

'I'm afraid your gloriousness made me completely forget my manners,' Daniel murmured into my hair. 'Would you like something to drink, my darling?'

'Yes, please.'

'Then stay right where you are. Please. Don't move. Don't go anywhere.'

He stumbled out of the bed. I watched through the

open doorway as he went into a small kitchen. I smiled as I watched his naked back amble across the room and then the curve of his shoulders as he crouched to open the refrigerator door. Outside, the church bells were ringing, calling the villagers to mass, and although Reservoir Cottage was not far away, it was far enough for me to feel as if I had left my life and my troubles behind, in a different world, and I didn't want to go back to it. I wanted to stay where I was.

CHAPTER THIRTY-ONE

Daniel took a bottle from the fridge, prised the lid free on the corner of the kitchen window ledge and caught the froth that spilled out in his mouth. He came back to the bed and passed the bottle to me.

'It's cider,' he said. 'We make it ourselves. There's a press in the old stables at Fairlawn.'

I took a swig. 'It's very good. Do you sell it?'

'We give a barrel to the pub once in a while. Mostly my father drinks it. That and the apple brandy.'

I took another drink then passed the bottle back to Daniel and rested my head on his shoulder. 'Do you have any pictures of you growing up in Fairlawn?'

'Why?'

'Because I want to know all about you.'

'I'll tell you anything you want to know.'

'I need pictures. I bet you were a really cute little boy.'

'I wasn't.'

'Show me.'

Daniel sighed in the exaggerated manner of one who is pretending to do something under duress, leaned under the bed and came back up with a photograph album. We sat together, propped up by pillows, passing the bottle between us and looking at the pictures. At the front of the album were old images of various members of the Aldridge family, the men in moustaches, the women in pale linen, and of the house under construction, before the reservoir was flooded. At that time, the land behind Fairlawn was nothing more than a shallow valley – marshland that must have been a haven for wildlife.

'When I see a reservoir, I always imagine a drowned village beneath it,' I told him. 'I think of a ghostly church bell clanging beneath the water, presaging doom, and abandoned possessions floating through the rooms of submerged cottages.'

'Nothing so romantic,' Daniel said. 'Most of the reservoir is not even very deep; only the area by the dam drops below forty feet. If there were a church anywhere in the lake, you'd see its spire and most likely its roof.'

'Which I suppose would be a hazard for the fishing boats.'

'Indeed.'

'Who's this, the lady in the hat?'

'My mother.'

I looked back in time, into the face of a slender woman in brogues and a tweed skirt-suit, wearing a trilby at a jaunty angle. There was a ribbon around the crown of the hat, and a couple of feathers tucked into the ribbon. The woman's eyes were in shadow, but her lips were dark against her skin, and her hair was so pale it seemed white in the photograph. She was holding a cigarette, in a holder, between her fingers. She looked poised and confident, a strong woman.

'She's very striking. Was the picture taken at Fairlawn?'

'No, I don't know where that was. It looks like some shooting party or other. And that's her with my father on their wedding day at the church.'

'Oh, it's so glamorous! All those flowers and that's such an exquisite dress. I wouldn't have recognized your father. He looks so young and handsome. The moustache suits him so!'

'He was fifteen years younger than my mother and quite the charmer in those days, by all accounts.'

'He looks very like you.'

'Everyone says the likeness is strong. This one here, that's the only picture I have of the three of us together. It was taken the day after I was born.'

'You were born at Fairlawn?'

'I suppose I must have been. We're all in the garden, under the chestnut tree.'

'Your mother looks so well and so happy.'

'She'd waited a long time for me.'

'But you were worth waiting for.'

'Of course.'

Daniel kissed my shoulder then he reached over and turned the page.

'That's my favourite picture of my mother.'

'By the reservoir?'

'Yes, she's standing on the dam, between the pumping station and the spillway. She used to sit on the grass bank and look out over the water. It's the best place for birdwatching because you can see the whole lake. I go there often myself. There's never anyone else there.'

'Why ever not?'

'Because it's the only part of the reservoir that's dangerous. Everywhere else the ground slopes away shallowly beneath the water. There, it's like a cliff.'

'Is that where she drowned?' I asked gently.

Daniel nodded. Then he took the photograph album and closed it. He leaned down and put the album back under the bed. I wondered if I had asked too many questions but he sat again, kissed me and wound my hair around his wrist.

'I hate to do this,' he said, 'but I'll have to be back at Fairlawn in time to walk with Father up to midnight mass or else he'll come looking for me. He likes us to attend these village events together, to put on a united front. You could stay here, if you like. You could wait for me.'

I shook my head. 'I have to get back to the cottage. I need to be there when Viviane wakes in the morning.'

'It would be nice if you were here when I wake in the morning.'

'Another time, maybe.'

We got out of the bed and dressed quickly and quietly; the mood had changed. Now I felt awkward and a little embarrassed being naked in front of Daniel, pulling on my underwear, reaching behind my back to fasten my bra, conscious of the way the suspender belt pinched into the flesh of my stomach. I hoped I had not been too forward. I hoped he would not regret what we had done.

I went into the small bathroom, dropped the two used johnnies into the little bin, washed my hands and face and borrowed Daniel's comb to tidy my hair. The make-up I'd put on earlier was smudged; I looked tired and vulnerable and I felt, suddenly, lonely and hopeless. I did not want to walk up that hill alone, back to that miserable cottage, back to that narrow little bed and the empty bedroom next door to mine, to all that unhappiness. I did not want to have to be strong for Julia and Vivi, to struggle to do my best to turn what meagre food we had into something that approximated to a Christmas dinner, to spend the next day jollying the pair of them along. I did not want to think of Caroline dying in the room next door to mine.

I put the comb down and leaned on the basin and gazed at my bedraggled reflection.

Stop this, I told myself. *Self-pity is neither attractive nor useful.*

My eyes filled with tears.

I sat down on the edge of the bath and pressed my hands into my eyes.

'Amy?' Daniel called, after several minutes had passed. 'Are you OK?'

'Yes,' I replied. 'I'm coming.'

I didn't look him in the eye as he helped me into my coat and I slipped on my shoes. He opened the door for me and led me outside, and now the air was stinging cold and a fog was spreading out from the lake, creeping around the lodge, insinuating white strands of dampness through the skeleton branches of the trees, hiding the ground. I rubbed my hands together to keep them warm while Daniel sat on the step and tied the laces on his boots. I was watching him and he was looking down at his feet and neither of us noticed Mr Aldridge coming through the fog, not until he was upon us. He was a big man, tall and broad, yet he had crept up quietly, soft-footed – or maybe I was just too lost in my thoughts to hear him. I started when I saw him, and then I composed myself. I would not be intimidated by the man.

'Hello, Mr Aldridge,' I said, to alert Daniel to his father's presence.

Mr Aldridge came up close to me, too close, so I could smell the heat of him and he said: 'What's going on here? Having your own little party, are you, Daniel?' He swayed on his feet and his words were slurred as if his tongue was too big for his mouth.

'I asked Daniel to show me where he lived,' I said.

'You asked him to show you where he lived, did you? And what else did he show you, eh?'

'Father, please.'

Mr Aldridge leaned towards me. His breath reeked of cigars and faintly of something rotten. I did not give any ground. I tried to see beyond the fleshy face, the watery eyes, I tried to see back to the good-looking, proud man I had viewed in the photograph. I reminded myself that it was grief that had turned Mr Aldridge into the pathetic bully he was now and I couldn't hate him, I couldn't, not when I could see Daniel so clearly in his features, not when he had the same eyes as his son, the same jawline, the same cowlick on his forehead.

I didn't hate him, but I didn't like him, not at all. Not

when he was so rude, so aggressive, not when he hit and hurt his son.

The feeling was mutual. He didn't like me one bit either. He jabbed his finger towards me. 'I'm warning you to stay away from my son,' he snarled. 'I don't want gold-diggers like you sniffing around him.'

'Don't talk to Amy like that,' Daniel said.

'I'll talk to her any way I want. I know that you and your employer don't have two pennies to rub together,' he said to me. 'I've heard how you're always setting up tabs, asking for credit. I know the child's education is being given gratis, out of pity.' He turned to his son. 'Why do you think this girl's interested in you, Danny, eh? What do you think it is? Do you really think it's your good looks that attract her? Your charisma? Your personality?'

'I won't have you talking like that,' Daniel replied calmly.

'It's all right, Daniel,' I said. 'It doesn't bother me. I'm going now anyway.'

'Wait,' he said. 'I'll walk you back.'

'What about mass?' Mr Aldridge slurred. 'It's almost time for mass!'

'I'll meet you at the church,' Daniel said. He took hold of my arm and we walked briskly back to the footpath, heading uphill, Robert Aldridge's curses ringing in our ears. 'I'm sorry,' Daniel said. 'Father's had too much to drink and it makes him emotional. He doesn't mean any of it. Please slow down.'

'I don't know why you make excuses for him.'

'He's not all bad. You've only seen the worst of him.'

'Is there a good side to him?'

The walk uphill was steep, and even after we climbed above the fog, the air was cold in our lungs and talking was difficult. When we turned into the lane towards Reservoir Cottage, the church bells stopped ringing and the silence was overwhelming. Daniel took me in his arms. I held back for a moment and then pressed myself against him. I did not want to be separated from him.

'You'd better go,' I said, because the prospect of goodbye distressed me so badly that I had to have it over and done with. 'Go to mass. Let me get back to Julia.'

Daniel tried to kiss me but I turned away. I couldn't bear this.

'Happy Christmas, darling Amy,' Daniel said.

'Please go. You're going to be late.'

I did not watch him walk away. I never wanted to watch him leave me again.

CHAPTER THIRTY-TWO

The previous Christmas, I had spent with the Laurent family in Paris. Viviane had woken early and brought her stocking into my bedroom. She had climbed into the bed beside me as she had done every year since she could climb out of the cot herself, switched on the lamp and, slowly and methodically, had taken everything out of the stocking and laid it on the coverlet. There was always a coin and an orange, always a handful of sweets, and a bauble in a box, one for every year that Viviane had been born, bought from the special shop on the Champs Elysées. Viviane always saved the bauble to open last. First she opened the little presents. That year there had been a woollen hat (hand-knitted by me), a diamanté hair clip in the shape of a butterfly, a snowglobe with two children building a snowman inside, a box of coloured pencils and a French storybook, a small jigsaw and a miniature pram for her doll's house, together with a tiny baby doll.

We had stayed in bed together until dawn, when I washed and dressed and padded through the beautiful apartment to the tiny kitchen, where I made coffee and eggs benedict and laid out a tray for Julia and Alain's breakfast. I took the tray into the couple's bedroom, left it on the table by the window as directed, wished them both *Joyeux Noel* and returned to the kitchen to start preparing the vegetables for the Christmas lunch.

Friends had come over for the lunch and it had been a lavish meal that lasted from noon until dusk, but in the late afternoon I took Viviane out, just the two of us, and we went ice-skating in the Tuileries, holding hands, falling over, laughing as we skated amongst the others on the lake that afternoon in a Paris silver with cold, the pavements glowing in the pools of gold made by the streetlights. I loved that city. I had felt the blade of my skates cutting into the ice, I heard the scoring as I moved forward, the air icy against my face, and I turned to look at Viviane – and she was laughing, her cheeks rosy, her nose red and her eyes bright. The raspberry-coloured hat I'd knitted for her was pulled down low over her ears.

We wandered back to the *7th arrondissement* after dark, back along the beautiful, wide streets, beneath the Christmas lights and the city all aglow; we took the lift up to the top floor, went back into the apartment. The table had been cleared of the plates and cutlery but Alain and Julia and their friends were still sitting around it, eating bread and cold meat, drinking Pastis now, chins in their hands, listening to music on the record player. They had lit candles around the room and they were merry and loud, arguing about politics, about de Gaulle 'the great asparagus'. They looked up and greeted me and Vivi when we came in and then they carried on talking. After I'd washed up, and put Vivi to bed, I'd gone and sat with them. I had never felt happier.

Nobody could have predicted how drastically things would have changed in one year. That Christmas in Reservoir Cottage, Julia and I filled a stocking for Viviane who, bless her heart, did her best to look surprised and pleased with the meagre gifts we'd scratched together. We ate potatoes, mince and onion for lunch. Julia drank gin from the time she woke until the moment she fell asleep on the settee after lunch, and Vivi and I walked down to the lake and threw pebbles into the water, each one a wish for the coming year.

I think we were all glad when it was over.

But nothing was better afterwards. In fact, everything was about to become a great deal worse.

CHAPTER THIRTY-THREE

After Christmas, the house went on the market, the weather became bleaker and so did Julia's despair. She had no appetite, no enthusiasm for anything, and nothing Vivi or I said or did seemed to make any difference. All she wanted to do was sit quietly on her own, deciphering the shorthand in Alain's notebooks – or pretending that was what she was doing. Often she simply sat and rocked with the sweater on her lap. She had become very sensitive to noise and did not like to be disturbed by Bess, by Viviane, by anyone.

Viviane herself was growing quieter and more intro-verted with every day that passed. I phoned her class teacher, who assured me that Vivi seemed happy enough when she was at school, but when she came home she spent hours alone in her bedroom, her lips moving as she carried on long, intense conversations with the imaginary friend who was not there. She had fallen out with Kitty over something Kitty had said to her. She would not tell me what it was. This troubled me, because if Vivi was trying to protect me from knowing what had been said, then it must have been something really bad.

There was some happiness in my life because Daniel was in my life. The happy times were like bright, scented bubbles of pleasure in a bath full of cold, dirty water. They could not compensate for the fact that I was desperately worried about both Julia and Viviane, and about our lack of money. Daniel would have helped us, of course he would, but how could I ask to borrow money after all his father had said about me? When Mr Aldridge was convinced my heart was set not on Daniel, but on the contents of his bank account? How could I casually say, 'Any chance you could lend me fifty pounds, darling, just to keep the wolf from the door?' I knew I couldn't.

Everything depended on Julia selling the cottage.

A week went by and nobody came to look at it. Julia said she would not let the estate agent know how desperate she was but then I heard her pleading with him on the phone. He told her again that it was the wrong time of year to sell, nobody wanted to move immediately after Christmas, and that to generate interest he needed to advertise the cottage in the local newspaper. For this he would need photographs of both the interior and exterior. Julia urged me to hurry up with the stripping of the wallpaper so that the empty bedroom could be decorated. She couldn't show the room to anyone who came to view the property, not with its half-stripped walls. Because it was proving such an arduous task, she joined in herself to help, despite the pain in her hip and her exhaustion. And it was Julia who found the drawing on the wall.

I'd been to the village store to negotiate yet another

tab with the shopkeeper, which I promised to pay off at the end of the month. The shopkeeper had seen the For Sale sign outside the cottage and understood our predicament. Fortunately, she was a kindly woman, a relative newcomer to the village who, I think, understood how I felt, being an outsider. She had agreed to keep supplying us with the basics for the next few weeks and even slipped a small bar of chocolate into my pocket, 'for the little'un', as I left. My gratitude knew no bounds.

As I walked back to the cottage, my mind was drawn to the ruby pendant. That had to be worth a small fortune. I knew that really, it wasn't mine to sell, but Caroline – if it ever had belonged to her – certainly had no use for it any more, and in many ways, it would be a relief to be rid of the thing. Nobody knew about it, it had been lost for at least thirty years, forgotten in its matchbox in the satchel in the loft. If Daniel hadn't gone up to look for holes in the roof it could well have stayed lost for many more years. If it didn't belong to Caroline, but had been – heaven forbid – stolen by her, then drawing attention to it would only open up scars that were barely healed. I couldn't bring myself to show it to Julia, proof of yet another of Caroline's wrong-doings, and although selling it would be morally wrong, keeping it seemed almost worse. It was like a guilty secret eating away at the back of my mind. I could sell it. I *should* sell it. Putting food on our plates was more important than any niggling scruples I might have.

I had more or less made up my mind by the time I was back. I let myself into the cottage through the front door and leaned down to unhook Bess's lead.

'Amy?' Julia called. 'Is that you? Come up here quickly!'

I kicked off my boots and trotted up the stairs in my socks. Julia was standing at the door to the empty bedroom, and the light was behind her so her face was in shadow.

'What is it?'

Julia leaned on her stick with one hand, and with the other, took hold of my hand. Hers was cold as ice. She led me into the room, the stick tapping on the floorboards, and we stood in front of the wall to the left of the chimney breast, a patch of the exposed wall about the size of a dinner plate stripped of its paper.

'Look,' she whispered.

I was already looking.

On the wall was a crude depiction of a man hanging from a beam, like a drawing from a game of Hangman – only this dead man was characterized by his tongue hanging from his mouth, by the awful lolling of his head and by the girl standing with her hands on her hips staring up at him, smiling. The image had been drawn so furiously that the tip of the pencil had scored holes in the plaster. I covered my mouth with my hands. It was horrible.

'That's the reason for the wallpaper,' Julia said. 'They wanted to cover up the drawing.'

'No wonder.' I shuddered.

'It's Dr Croucher,' Julia said.

'How can you tell?'

'I just can. It has the look of him when he was younger.'

I felt cold suddenly – uneasy. I sensed a movement on the skin of my neck, as if somebody had breathed into my collar. I turned and nobody was there – but as I turned, the necklace I was wearing broke. The tiny beads bounced and scattered on the floor, disappearing between the cracks in the floorboards. I dropped at once to my hands and knees to gather up as many as I could and Julia crouched down to help. Our heads were close together, the ends of Julia's hair skimming the top of my hands.

'I'll scrub it off,' I said, panting as I gathered the beads. 'I'll go at it with the wire brush.'

'We have to do it now, Amy. At once! Vivi mustn't see it. Bloody Caroline! She won't leave me alone. Still spreading misery, still causing pain.'

'What are you talking about?'

Julia and I looked up. Viviane was standing at the door in her grey socks and her olive-green school tunic, the grey cardigan, the brown ribbon that had held back her hair loose now, falling beside her face. She had not stepped into the room, and so she was only half-lit, and in that mid-way gloom she seemed as ephemeral as a whisper.

'What aren't I allowed to see?' she asked.

I stood up and backed towards the wall, to hide the drawing behind my body. 'Nothing,' I said.

'Why aren't you at school?' Julia asked.

'We've got choir practice in the church. We came home early to get ready. I told you.'

'I'm sure you didn't, Vivi.'

Viviane came further into the room. I backed closer to the wall, until I was almost leaning against it.

'You were talking about Caroline?' said Vivi.

'No.'

'Yes, you were. Why? What's she done?'

'Nothing.'

'She has done something. You just said she had. You said "Bloody Caroline".'

'It's not your business, Vivi.'

'What did she do?'

'It was a long time ago and it's not important now, sweetheart,' I said. 'Let's go and find you a snack.'

'You said she was spreading misery and causing pain. How do you know that? How do you know what she was trying to do?'

'I was her sister,' Julia said. 'I was close to her.'

'No, you weren't!' Viviane said. 'You were Goody Two Shoes so busy running round in circles trying to please all the grown-ups and be a good little girl that you never noticed Caroline. You had no idea about her life!'

'Vivi, stop it now,' I said.

'You weren't there, Vivi, you know nothing about any of it,' said Julia.

'I *do* know – I *do*! Caroline was trying to protect you, Mummy!'

'She was trying to protect me? Caroline didn't *protect*, Vivi, Caroline *damaged*. She hurt people. She stole and she lied and she—' Julia stopped herself. Her face was white but her cheeks were flushed. 'She did some terrible things,' she finished.

'No,' Vivi cried, 'she didn't! You're not listening!'

'I don't want to hear any more.'

'You didn't listen then and you're not listening now!'

'Get out of here, Vivi!' Julia said. 'You don't know what you're talking about.'

I stepped forward and tried to hold Vivi but she shook my hands off and leaned towards her mother, crying and shouting at the same time.

'You're a bitch!' she screamed. 'No wonder Papa preferred to go to meet the Algerians than be at home with you! No wonder he'd rather be *dead*!'

Julia raised her hand and slapped her daughter's face. She hit her so hard that Vivi stumbled and the noise was absolutely shocking. It seemed to bounce from the walls of that awful room. For a moment Vivi was still, crouched on the floor holding one hand to her cheek. Then she pushed herself up and ran from the room. We heard her feet thumping down the stairs and seconds afterwards, the slam of the back door.

'Christ!' said Julia. 'Oh Christ, what have I done? I've never laid a finger on her before! What's happening to me, Amy?'

'She'll be OK,' I said as calmly as I could, trying to stop my voice from shaking.

'I'm turning into a monster!'

'You're not. I'll go after her. I'll take her up to the church for her choir practice and after that it'll all be forgotten.'

'Oh, I don't think so. She's old enough now to resent me for that for ever.'

'It was one slap, Julia, delivered in the heat of the moment. You mustn't make too much of it.'

Julia covered her face with her hands. 'Everything is so horrid today, the cold, this room, that terrible drawing, Vivi's mood . . . oh God, and me. What is to become of me, Amy? Where will this all end?'

'You're a good mother, Julia,' I said. 'Vivi pushed you too far, that's all. You're only human. It'll be all right. You'll get through this. You will.'

'Not without Alain. I can't do it without him.'

'You will have to,' I said – and then I went down after Viviane.

CHAPTER THIRTY-FOUR

I walked around the churchyard while I waited for Vivi to come out of choir practice. I could hear the singing inside the church and the sound was magical, Viviane's voice following the descant tune above the others. My mother, before she left, once took me on an outing to a model village. I had especially loved the church because when I knelt down beside it and put my ear close to the little building, I could hear organ music coming from inside, and singing. I found it miraculous.

'But who were the little people singing inside the church, Mum?' I had asked for ages afterwards. 'Who *were* they?'

I knew who was inside the church at Blackwater – Viviane and eleven other girls from Hailswood School, most of them older than her, some of them experienced and talented singers. When I'd walked up to the church with Vivi an hour earlier, the girl had been subdued and yet proud. The slap had humiliated her but at the same time her anger had solidified from something vague and amorphous into a nugget of pure rage.

I sincerely hoped the singing would put her in a better

mood and in some way compensate for the argument earlier.

I went to the Aldridge section of the graveyard and looked for Daniel's mother's grave. It was the most ostentatious of them all, the one with the angel with the outstretched arm. The headstone informed me that she had died only three days before Caroline. It commemorated the final resting-place of Jean Matilda Aldridge: *A wonderful and loving wife to Robert and mother to Daniel, taken from us so tragically, on August 28th 1931, gone but never forgotten and always remembered in our hearts with the very greatest affection, respect and devotion.*

Too much, I thought. Too many words. It was almost as if Robert, if it was he who had composed the inscription, had been trying to compensate for something. Was it grief that made him so verbose, or regret maybe?

I walked on round to the back of the church, to where Caroline was buried. Her grave was as dark, inconspicuous and overgrown as before, but somebody had placed a pot of snowdrops on it. I felt a shiver of pity for the flowers, which would never survive in this cold, dark place, and for Caroline. She and Jean Aldridge had died so close together in this small village and had been treated so very differently. I tugged at the ivy fingering its way over the modest little stone, then jumped at the sound of a throat being cleared behind me. I turned guiltily, feeling altogether as if I'd been caught doing something I shouldn't have been doing.

It was the vicar. 'I'm sorry,' he said, 'I didn't mean to alarm you. I just wondered if I could be of any help?'

I'd met him before, briefly, in Sunnyvale. Reverend Pettigrew was a small, slope-shouldered man in his dog collar and shabby suit, the shoulders speckled with dandruff. He was rubbing his hands together against the cold. There was a dewdrop on the end of his nose, which was red and bulbous. Just behind him was the woman who had been cleaning in the nursing home – Susan, his daughter. She was buttoned into an old coat that was too small for her and pinched around the arms and waist. It looked too worn out and thin to be keeping her the least bit warm. She seemed so cold and miserable that I had a strong urge to take her indoors and make her a hot drink.

I stood up. 'I'm waiting to meet one of the children rehearsing inside the church.'

'Ah yes,' said the vicar, 'the choir are practising for their performance at Sunnyvale. I'm looking forward to that. As patron of the nursing home, I generally act as compère at those sorts of dos.' He held on to the lapels of his jacket and swelled with self-importance. I smiled as if I were impressed and he continued: 'We spotted you looking at Jean Aldridge's grave just now. I was curious as to your interest. You're too young to have known either Jean or Caroline Cummings.'

'I work for Julia, Caroline's sister.'

'Ah, of course you do.'

'And it seems strange to me that they died within three days of one another but were buried so differently.'

The vicar shook his head. 'They died in the same week, certainly, but that was all they had in common.'

'Oh?'

'Jean was a wonderful woman,' said the vicar. 'She went through so much and then to have her life snuffed out like that when she'd finally fulfilled her dream of becoming a mother as well as a wife . . . well, it was a tragedy. An absolute tragedy.'

Saint Jean, I thought, and then I was annoyed with myself for feeling unkindly towards someone I had never met, my darling Daniel's mother. The vicar was right – it *was* a tragedy for a woman to die within days of the birth of her one and only child.

The vicar fished in his pocket, produced a crumpled handkerchief and blew his nose.

Behind him, Susan clutched the handle of a shopping bag with her plump hands. Her nails were bitten to the quick. She was looking at the ground.

'But Caroline's death was tragic too,' I said. 'She was only seventeen when she lost her life.'

The vicar gave a kind of snort.

'It was completely different,' he said.

'How was it different?' I asked. I couldn't help but feel defensive of Caroline; she was not my family but I knew about her now. I felt as if she belonged to me.

'Sadly, there are some people whose lives are best forgotten. Caroline was one of those.' The vicar sniffed. 'She had very few friends, and I'm afraid she turned everyone against her.'

'I was her friend,' Susan said quietly. 'I liked her.'

'I know *you* did,' the vicar said bitterly, 'but *you're* not like most people.' He rubbed his nose with his handkerchief and then addressed me again. 'Caroline was troubled,' he said, 'very troubled. Hasn't Julia told you about her?'

'A little.'

'Well then, I'll show you something.' He took hold of my elbow. I did not like the feeling of his hand touching me but felt it would have been an over-reaction to snatch my arm away, so I acquiesced, walking beside him back around to the other side of the church, the sun-facing side with the path running past it and the village looking towards it. Susan shuffled behind us.

The vicar stopped. He pointed up towards the church.

'You see that window, the one that's different to the others?'

'The one that isn't stained glass?'

'Exactly. It used to be a stained-glass depiction of *The Sermon on the Mount*. It dated back to the sixteenth century and had been saved from an earlier church and reinstated here. The reason it's not an invaluable stained-glass window now is because young Caroline threw a stone through the original. The church was full of people at the time.'

I looked up at the window. The last of the sun shone down through the cold, cold air and I looked up and I felt dizzy. From inside the church, the pianist played and Viviane's voice rang through the glass, clear as a bell: *Ave Maria*.

The vicar continued: 'The stone smashed right through the window and the glass rained down on the congregation. Caroline wasn't even fourteen, she was still a child, but already she had such evil inside her.'

'Evil?' I gave a small, disbelieving laugh. 'That's rather strong, isn't it?'

'Evil,' the vicar repeated firmly.

And then for an instant, the briefest instant, no more than the time it took for my heart to beat twice, I felt a fury, rage like I'd never felt before. I imagined I heard an organ playing inside the church, not the tinkly piano that was accompanying the school choir but a thunderous, pitching organ bellowing out discordant notes, and the village voices were singing together, voices lumbering after the organ, straining for the tune, and I was outside, excluded, and I felt angry and hurt and utterly humiliated. I looked around and there was a rock, a good-sized rock, and I bent down to pick up the rock and it felt good and heavy in my hand.

I wanted to break that window. I wanted to shatter that pretty glass. I wanted to show those people inside the church that I counted, that I existed, that I mattered.

And I breathed in and the anger and the humiliation were gone and I was myself again. The air was still cold and bright and the vicar was still talking. He was describing the damage caused by the rock, how the people inside the church had rushed outside, shocked and deeply upset that the beautiful and ancient window had been broken.

'I came out of the church and Caroline was standing there, right where you are now, staring up at the window,' the vicar said, 'and do you know what she did when I remonstrated with her? She laughed at me! Can you imagine such wickedness? She *laughed*!'

I thought of the drawing on the wall, the man swinging, the tongue lolling. Caroline had hated the doctor. Had she hated the vicar too?

Susan put her thumbnail into her mouth and chewed at the cuticle. Her upper lip was dark with whiskers.

The vicar rocked on his heels. The tone of his voice changed as he moved on to the next part of the story. 'Mr and Mrs Cummings were devastated, of course, but they couldn't afford to pay for a replacement window so Dr Croucher put up the money. Caroline told me if we replaced the window with more stained glass, she would break it again. That was the kind of girl she was. We didn't want to risk bringing further embarrassment to her dear mother and father. So we left the window plain, as it is now.'

'You could have replaced the stained glass after she died.'

'We tried,' said the vicar, 'but the lead framework had twisted and we couldn't get the glass to fit. So that plain window will always serve as a reminder to the village of a wicked act and a wicked young woman. And the one beside it, the one that depicts *The Virgin and Child*, that's the one that dear Jean's parents, Sir George and Lady Debeger, dedicated in memory of their poor deceased daughter. It seems ironic that the two should be side by side.'

'Why ironic?' I asked.

'Because of what Caroline did to Jean.'

'What did she do?'

The vicar caught his breath. He glanced at his daughter. Then he took his handkerchief out of his pocket once more and blew his nose again. Inside the church, the song reached a crescendo, an extended, beautiful, musical *Amen*.

'Come on, Susan,' the vicar said, 'they're finishing now. You need to get in and lay out the Bibles ready for Prayer Group.'

'You didn't tell me what Caroline did to Jean Aldridge!' I called but either he did not hear, or he pretended not to.

He walked away from me, along the path, and Susan shuffled after him, pausing only to look over her shoulder and send me a glance of sadness.

I waited by the church door for Viviane as a gaggle of chattering schoolgirls came out of the church. Vivi was the last out, walking with a tall, thin, dark-haired man, lanky in his suit. He acknowledged me with a wide, personable smile but Vivi stiffened when she saw me. The man put his hand on her shoulder and guided her towards me.

'Hi,' I said, with a smile. 'I was listening outside. That sounded wonderful, Vivi.'

'Young Viviane here has a real talent,' said the man. He held out his hand. 'Eric Leeson,' he said, 'headmaster and choirmaster.'

I took his hand. 'I'm Amy.'

'I know exactly who you are. My good friend Dr Croucher has told me all about you.'

'Have you been all right, Vivi?' I asked.

There was an awkward pause. Viviane stared at her feet.

'She's been fine,' said Mr Leeson. 'She was a tiny bit

tearful earlier but we went into the vestry and had a little chat, and you're OK now, aren't you, Viviane? You're our star performer. You're not going to let a little family spat get in the way of your singing, are you?'

Vivi shook her head. She leaned a little closer to him. He squeezed her shoulder. I felt terribly awkward. I didn't know if I should explain or apologize. I did not know what Vivi had said to Mr Leeson; she may have exaggerated the argument, or played down her own role in instigating the slap. And yet the last thing I wanted to do was cause her more embarrassment or pain.

'Come on then,' I said. I held out my hand to Viviane, but she did not take it. Instead she pushed past me and made her way alone, down the path.

I moved to follow her but Mr Leeson said quietly, 'Leave her – let her be. Give her a little space. She's a good girl and she's strong. She's going to be fine.'

'Thank you,' I said, 'for all you're doing to help her.'

'Oh, it's my pleasure,' said Mr Leeson. He adjusted his tie. 'Really, it's the least I can do.'

CHAPTER THIRTY-FIVE

The very next day Daniel called, saying he wanted to see me. He said his father would be out all day and suggested I walked down to Fairlawn. I left Julia scrubbing at the drawing in the empty bedroom with a wire brush and some Vim scouring powder and walked down the hill. Daniel met me on the lane. He was bundled in his outdoor clothes, looking like something organic that had grown up out of the fields and the woods and the countryside. He held out his hands to me; they were filthy but I took them anyway.

'I've been out with the sheep,' he said.

'I never would have guessed!'

He laughed. 'Do I smell agricultural?'

'A little. It's OK. I don't mind that smell.'

'Really?'

'On you I don't mind it.' I smiled.

'I'd forgotten,' Daniel said, 'how very much I like you.'

'I like you very much too,' I said, 'and I think I always will.'

He coloured a little and I felt my cheeks heat in

empathy. 'Come on,' he said, 'I'll give you the grand tour of the Aldridge pile.'

'Where's your father?'

'Out on the lake.'

'You're sure he won't come back?'

'I'm sure.'

'If he found me in the house he'd suspect me of filching the family silver.'

'I'll check your pockets before you leave,' Daniel said. I thought if he knew how dire Julia's financial situation really was, he would not joke about it. He led me towards the house. Dead black leaves were blowing across the lawns, bunching at the feet of the tree trunks. There was a wheelbarrow on the pathway, a rake propped up against the wall, but no lights were on inside the house. It gave the impression of being empty.

I followed Daniel inside. The hallway had been stripped of its Christmas decorations and the fire was no longer burning, but huge radiators kept the place warm and it was light. The furnishings were grand but past their best and it felt a comfortable, lived-in house. Coats were piled on a rack, with boots lined up beneath on sheets of muddy newspaper. Unopened mail lay on a table beneath a mirror hung at an angle, a stack of ornithological books piled beside it.

Daniel pulled the door shut and then he took hold of me and kissed me. His hands were inside my coat. I was bright with desire but I pulled away. Not here, I thought, not here.

'You *are* going to show me around, aren't you?' I asked.

215

'If that's what you want.'

Daniel sat on a chair by the table and took off his boots. I wandered over to the wall and studied an oil painting of a cocker spaniel with limpid brown eyes. The tricolour collie was about my legs, a whisper of a dog, her claws clicking on the floor. Daniel put his boots on the newspaper, stood up in his thick grey working socks and took off his coat.

'Would you like coffee?' he asked.

I nodded and followed him into a large kitchen, grand but untidy. A crate was crammed with empty bottles by the back door and washing was drying over a rack suspended above a huge old Aga. It was men's washing: corduroy trousers and cotton shirts, socks and underpants, a sweater with frayed cuffs. Mr Aldridge's laundry. These intimate items made me feel uncomfortable. I bit at a nail while Daniel filled the kettle.

The lake was framed by the window. A few boats, tiny from this distance, were bobbing on the water.

'Is your father in one of those boats?'

'Yes.'

'What is he fishing for?'

'Trout, but it's not the fish that's the attraction,' Daniel said, 'not where my father's concerned. His hook won't even be wet. He'll be sitting on the boat as usual, listening to the water slap against the side, drinking whisky and thinking about my mother. The angling's just an excuse. Sugar?'

'Please. Four teaspoons.'

'Four?'

'Five if you have plenty of sugar.'

Daniel glanced at me. 'I have a sweet tooth,' I said, not wanting to admit I hadn't been able to afford to take sugar in my coffee for months.

'OK,' he said. He obligingly stirred in several heaped spoonfuls of sugar and passed me the mug.

'Would you like something to eat?' he asked.

'No, I'm fine.'

'Are you sure?'

'Well, I could possibly manage something.'

'Toast?'

'If you're having some.'

He made several rounds of toast and politely looked out of the window as I spread as much butter and jam as I could on to mine and then wolfed the slices down, wiping the delicious grease from my lips with the back of my hand.

He waited until I had finished and then he took my plate from me and kissed me. 'I like to see a girl with an appetite,' he said.

'You're with the right girl then,' I said.

We drank our coffee and then he took me into a large, light sitting room with tall windows framed by faded yellow- and rose-coloured curtains, tatty old sofas, dog blankets, bookcases. It was the sort of room that would make me want to stay inside it for ever, curled up with a book. There was a grand fireplace with the remains of a fire, a pile of ash and a half-burned log, in the grate.

'I want to show you something,' Daniel said. He led me to an alcove, tucked away at the back of the room, and drew back a curtain. Behind was a portrait of a woman, painted in the naive style that was so popular in the late 1920s. 'This is my mother, Jean Aldridge.'

I stood in front of the picture and looked at it closely. The painting, full of colour as it was, was more revealing about Jean's personality than the photographs Daniel had shown me before. Jean was slender, like Daniel, blonde and small-featured, with a neat mouth and pale-lashed eyes. In this picture, she was wearing a watery-green sweater and a blue glass necklace and holding a ginger cat in her arms. She was standing in the garden at Fairlawn with an apple tree to one side, a pear tree to the other and the lake behind her. The trees were full of birds. She was not quite smiling.

She had been through so much and she finally had what she'd always wanted.

'Father had that painted for my mother for her fortieth birthday,' Daniel said, 'a year before I was born. She didn't like it apparently. She thought it made her look old.'

'She doesn't look old.'

'She was sensitive about the age difference between herself and my father.'

'I'm sure she had no need to be. She's very beautiful. Why is the painting hidden away?'

'Father can't bear to look at it. He doesn't like to be reminded of her.'

'Oh dear.'

I reached out and took hold of Daniel's hand. It was

unnerving to stare into the eyes of his mother, knowing that she would be dead within two years of this picture being painted and knowing that she did not know this. It felt intrusive. I looked away.

'It's such a shame,' I said, 'that she never got to know you.'

'I was with her, you know, when it happened,' Daniel said.

'You said that you were. So how come . . . I mean . . . why didn't you drown too?'

'She'd parked my pram on the dam while she went down to the water's edge with her binoculars.'

'And she slipped and fell in?'

Daniel did not answer this. He drew the curtain over the picture and walked back into the main part of the room. His shoulders were hunched.

'I'm sorry,' I said. 'That was dreadful of me to ask about your mother so bluntly.'

'I don't like to talk of it.'

'No, of course you don't. I'm so sorry, Daniel. Can you forgive me?'

'Let's change the subject?'

'Yes, let's do that. Tell me about this picture.' I pointed to a small, framed drawing, depicting a dark-faced duck, surrounded by ripples of water. 'It's cute. What is it?'

'It's a very rare Lesser Scaup, the bird that brought my parents together.'

'I don't think I've ever seen one of those before.'

'Well, you wouldn't have, would you? They're very rare.'

I laughed and then leaned in to look at the duck.

219

'Your father must have loved your mother very much.'

'He would have done anything for her,' Daniel said. 'Anything. When he gets drunk he tells me he'd give up everything he has – the house, the land, his money – for just one more day with her, another chance to hold her. He says he has never known another woman like her, someone so honest and courageous and loyal. He says he doesn't know how his heart can continue beating without her around. He's telling the truth. You can see it in his eyes.'

His voice was quiet and low. I glanced towards him and saw that his face had become sad. I did not know what to say to console him so instead I wandered across the room to the large, mullioned window. The view beyond was peaceful, the lake lying in the valley and the hills above, the birds flying over, the skeleton trees drawn on to the hillside and the grass behind them a dull, wintry yellow.

I looked across the water and I let my mind drift alongside Mr Aldridge's boat. I thought of him bobbing on the little waves and watching the light on the water and thinking of the woman he loved. I felt sorry for the man. Because if she had been everything to him, and she was gone, then what was left?

Daniel's hand was on my shoulder. I reached up and covered it with mine.

Daniel kissed each of my knuckles in turn. 'Would you like to see the rest of the house?' he asked.

'Yes, please.'

I followed him up the stairs, up three half-flights to a

grand landing. At the top was a large board with a crest on it, like a coat-of-arms with a brightly coloured, symbolized animal at each point of a compass in the middle. A painted banner beneath read: *Blackwater Village Club.*

'That's all that's left of the original village club,' Daniel said. 'It used to be on the land where the doctors' surgery is now.'

'What happened to it?'

'It was bombed in the war. And afterwards they built the new hall.'

'Oh, right. What are these animals?'

'They're supposed to represent the cornerstones of a balanced community. The lion is for leadership, the ape is for education, the lamb is for religion and the gryphon is for caring and health.'

'That's a lamb? It's hideous.'

'It's in the heraldic tradition of a lamb.'

'Hmm,' I said. 'So why does your father have this monstrosity hanging on his landing?'

'Out of respect for my mother's family. When the club was running there were always four committee members, all equal and each representing a key element of the village. My maternal grandfather was the area MP so he took the lion's role.'

'I see,' I said. 'And was Dr Croucher the caring gryphon?'

'Yes. Reverend Pettigrew was the lamb, obviously, and the village school's headmaster was the ape. He died in the war.'

'What about your grandfather?'

'He's passed away too. The village club committee was disbanded after the war.'

'The vicar and the doctor are still friends. I've seen them at Sunnyvale.'

'They go back a long way, the two old codgers.'

I took hold of his hand, relieved that the mood had, at last, lightened. 'So tell me, young Mr Aldridge, which of these hundreds of rooms used to be your old bedroom?'

'There are only eight bedrooms, Amy, you do exaggerate. It's the last door down there, on the left.'

'Who slept in all the others?'

'My father and mother had separate rooms and another had been converted into a nursery for the baby – me – when I came along. This one here was her sewing room and then there are three guest rooms. They're quite impressive.'

'And this one?'

'That's only a small room. It's of no interest.'

'Can't I look?'

He took a breath. 'Really, there's nothing in there.'

I turned the handle and opened the door anyway. I stepped inside. The room was cold and obviously rarely used; it had the closed-off atmosphere of a place that has been abandoned. There was a bedframe, some stacked-up furniture covered over with a dustsheet, a couple of suitcases. The paintwork was brown and dull and the room lacked all the charm and cosiness of the rest of the house. I shivered and wrapped my arms around me.

'Who slept here?' I asked Daniel.

'The maid,' Daniel said. He had not come into the room.

The maid. That had been Caroline.

I walked across the room to the window, my heels clicking on the floorboards, and looked out at the view of the lake beyond. I had that strange feeling of losing myself, of slipping, for a heartbeat, into Caroline's skin. I turned, to check that everything was as it had been and that I had not gone back in time, and there was Daniel, silhouetted in the doorframe, watching me. With the light behind him like that, with the glare of the sunlight in my eyes, he could have been somebody else; he could have been his father.

Everywhere I go, I thought, Caroline has already been. Everything I see, she has already seen.

There was a single picture hung on the wall in the room – an old Victorian photograph, sepia-coloured, with the borders faded away. A man and a woman were posing beside a window, a large aspidistra in a pot on a plant-stand beside them. The woman was seated, wearing a long dress with a nipped-in waist and a full skirt; the man stood behind her, one hand on her shoulder.

'Who are they?' I asked. My voice was thin in the dusty air of this closed-off room.

'Those are my maternal grandparents,' Daniel said. 'That's the Right Honourable George Debeger MP and his wife, Lady Matilda.'

'They look very grand.'

'They were.'

I stepped closer to the photograph. I stared at the

necklace around the woman's throat. I knew it well. It was a narrow gold chain with a heart-shaped pendant – a ruby surrounded by diamonds – and the gems were framed by a pair of clasped hands, joined at the top of the heart.

CHAPTER THIRTY-SIX

When I returned to the cottage that evening, pleasantly weary after an afternoon's lovemaking in the lodge, I looked up and saw that the light was on in the empty bedroom and somebody was moving around in there. I found Julia writing at the table in the back room.

'Vivi's in the empty room,' I told her.

'It's all right. I've cleaned away the drawing. There's nothing in there she can't see.'

'Is she OK?' I asked.

'She's quiet. Will you have a talk with her, Amy? She doesn't seem to want to talk to me.'

I said that I would and went into the kitchen to make a start on supper. Before I had so much as emptied the vegetables into the sink, there was a scream from upstairs. Julia and I bumped into one another in the hallway in our rush to see what was wrong. I helped her up the stairs, both of us going as fast as we could and Bess trailing behind.

Viviane was standing in the empty bedroom pointing to a cup on the mantelpiece. 'The cup just moved!' she said.

We peered at the cup. Very slowly, almost imperceptibly, it rocked on its base. I glanced at Julia to see if she had seen it too and I could tell from her pallor that she had.

'My God!' she breathed. She clasped her hands together and held them to her lips.

Then Vivi cried: 'Stop it, Mummy! Make it stop.'

'Amy,' Julia whispered, 'you pick it up.'

I reached out my hand to still the cup but I could not bear to touch it. The three of us stared, horrified but fascinated, as the cup revolved desperately slowly on the rim of its base, making a soft, scraping sound as the china grated against the tiled surface of the mantelpiece.

'It's Caroline,' Viviane told us. 'She's here!'

'No, no, darling, of course she isn't,' Julia said but her voice was shaky and to my ears her words lacked conviction.

'But what if it *is* her? What if she's come back?' Vivi's voice was rising. I put my arm around her and the child pressed her face into my side.

As Julia looked around desperately for something she could use to stop the cup, I felt Vivi release her grip on me. Her knees buckled beneath her, and I caught her at the exact same moment the cup fell from the mantelpiece and broke on the floor.

'Vivi!' Julia cried. 'Oh my darling, my darling!'

We carried her across the landing into my bedroom and laid her down on the bed. Julia sat beside her and rubbed her daughter's cold hands until the colour seeped slowly back into Vivi's cheeks and her eyelids flickered.

The moment she came out of the faint, she began to cry. Tears tumbled from her eyes, one after the other as they had done when she was a tiny child, inconsolable over some perceived injustice.

'There, there,' Julia crooned, 'my poor baby. Just let the tears come. You'll feel better after a little cry.'

Viviane spoke through her sobs. 'It was her,' she said. 'It was Caroline. *She* was moving the cup!'

'No, darling, no. It was a draught that was coming through a crack in the brickwork of the chimney, or—'

'It was her! I know it was. She said she'd do something to prove that she's still here.'

Julia glanced at me for help. I stroked Viviane's hand. 'Vivi, it's really important that we don't let our imaginations get the better of us. Strange things – things we can't easily explain – sometimes happen. That's just life.'

'I know what happened, Mummy.' Viviane sat up and wiped her cheeks, calmer now. 'I heard you talking about me with Mrs Croucher. I heard you both saying horrible things about Caroline and you said you didn't like me having her as my friend and I didn't want you to be upset so I stopped talking about her and you thought she'd gone away and that I'd forgotten her. But I hadn't forgotten, I was only pretending and she never went away. She's been here all the time. She's here now.'

Viviane looked from her mother to me, and back again; her face was tense and urgent.

'What did you hear us say?' Julia asked. There was a strange tone to her voice.

'I heard you say . . .' Vivi glanced from her mother to

me, and then down at her hands '. . . that Caroline was wicked and that she should have been locked away when she was a child.'

'You shouldn't have been listening, Vivi.'

'I'm sorry, Mummy, but I couldn't help it. I knew you were sad and I wanted to listen so that I could try to help make you better.'

Julia kissed her daughter's forehead. 'You are a dear child.'

Viviane looked up again. Her eyes were wide and sincere. 'You do believe me, don't you?' she asked. 'You have to believe me or else Caroline will find another way to show you that she's here. She won't go away, you know. She's not going anywhere.'

Later, when Viviane was back in her own room with the door closed and Julia was downstairs working on Alain's notes, I unlocked the door, switched on the light and went into the empty bedroom. I felt tense and prickly and frightened but I made myself stand in the centre of the room. I listened . . . but I heard nothing.

'Caroline,' I said softly, 'if you *are* here, prove it to me. No vague signs, no half-heard whispers, nothing that is open to misinterpretation. Show yourself to me.'

I waited.

I listened to the rapid pulsing of my own heartbeat but nothing happened.

Nothing was different.

The shadow of a spider, scuttling up one side of the wall, made me jump – but that was all.

The room, with its half-stripped wall like a wound

too diseased to heal, its bare boards still littered with broken china, the scratched stain where the drawing had been, felt cold and empty but nothing more sinister than that.

I realized I'd been holding my breath. I exhaled, and the room was so cold that my breath made a little cloud.

'There's nothing here,' I said out loud. 'There never has been.' *It's an empty bedroom that used to belong to a troubled young girl. We are projecting our own terrors into this room. Anything we feel in here is coming from us.*

I knew about poltergeists. I'd read of hauntings in the pages of the popular Sunday newspapers that my grandmother favoured. I recalled they tended to be prevalent in homes where there was a child on the cusp of puberty, a child with some kind of energy that he or she could not disperse in any other way but psychically. Ten-year-old Viviane, robbed of her father, uprooted and alone, fitted the template perfectly. The ghost was not without, but within.

CHAPTER THIRTY-SEVEN

We pretended that the cup incident – as Julia referred to it – had never happened. Julia and I were brisk and businesslike with Vivi, and with each other, the following morning. We chivvied one another along with bravado, pretending that all was well in the cottage. I was anxious to get Vivi out of there, on to the school bus. The moment she was on board, Kitty Dowler started talking to her, their falling-out obviously forgotten, and a couple of other girls leaned forward to chat and Viviane stopped being a frightened, confused, bereaved little girl and became a normal child with normal friends. I waved goodbye but she wasn't even looking. I went back to the cottage. Julia had been on the phone to the estate agent.

'He's terribly discouraging,' she said. 'Nobody wants to buy older houses any more. Apparently they all want the new ones, with central heating and fitted kitchens and picture windows. His exact words were: "Imagine the opposite of your cottage, and that's what people are looking for these days."'

'Oh dear.' I bit my lip and made a sympathetic face.

'They're building some new houses just along the valley at Bishop Sutton and those are selling like hot cakes.'

'But those won't have the character of this place.'

'People don't want character, Amy. They want convenience.' Julia sighed. 'He's going to come and take photographs. We have to finish decorating that bloody room.'

'OK, I'll go back to it.'

'Only be a darling and light the fire first. My hands are so cold I can't even turn the pages of the notebook.'

I was laying the fire when I found the advert in the *Mendip Times* newspaper. It was a small ad lost amongst myriad larger advertisements in the *Services Offered* pages. Most of them offered log-cutting, drain-clearing or mole-catching services. This one was from a psychic medium.

Her name was Violet-Anne Dando, and beneath the name and a telephone number was the simple message: *For more than 20 years I have been offering considerate friendship and advice to those wishing to contact departed loved ones. Visits can be arranged in the comfort of your own home, for your convenience. Quieting the restless a speciality.*

It was comforting to know that so many people, even in this sparsely populated part of the country, had restless spirits that required professional quieting. We weren't the only ones to be affected in this way.

I rolled up the sheet of newspaper into a paper stick, then I unrolled it. I tore off the corner with the advert and tucked the scrap of paper behind the clock on the mantelpiece. I felt cross with myself even as I did this, and slightly embarrassed, but it was a comfort to know the telephone number was there if the situation ever became so desperate that we didn't know who else to turn to.

I laid wood and then coal on top of the paper. Something was niggling away in my mind. I had the power to help Julia and Viviane. The potential solution to all their problems lay in a matchbox in a satchel under my bed. I'd thought about selling the pendant a million times and couldn't decide if it was the right thing to do, or not. There would be no harm or compromise of morality in having it valued, I thought. It might be worth less than I imagined, in which case there would be no point in selling it, but my instinct was that it was worth a small fortune, certainly enough to enable Julia and Vivi to move into pleasant, rented accommodation for a few months while they waited for the cottage to sell. If the piece was valuable, and I were to sell it, I'd have to take it far away from Blackwater, away from anyone who might recognize it or know of its provenance. First, I needed to find out what it was worth. Then I'd make the decision.

Thinking of the pendant always made me uneasy, and it was worse now that I knew for certain that it had belonged to Mrs Aldridge's mother who had, presumably, given it to her daughter Jean. Perhaps I should talk to Daniel. Perhaps I should just be honest with him. I could explain how it had come into my possession – it was he who had found the satchel, after all – and then tell him the truth about how desperately cash-strapped we were. But there were two problems with this. Firstly, I didn't want Daniel to think – ever – that I was after his money. And secondly, although Daniel would be sympathetic, of that I was certain, his father was a different kettle of fish. There was a very real danger that if he knew the pendant had been in the Cummingses' possession for all these years, he would make as much trouble for the family as he could. Was it possible to bring a posthumous conviction? Could a fine or punishment be conferred on Caroline's surviving relatives? I did not know and dared not risk it.

I lit the fire for Julia, then went upstairs and began, once again, the thankless task of chipping away at the wallpaper in the empty room. It was frustrating, cold, miserable work. The glue seemed to get everywhere, as did the tiny fragments of the vile paper. The skin on my hands was dry and raw, and I felt as if I smelled of glue, as if the taste of it was in my mouth all the time. Julia and I had been working at the paper for weeks now and we were still nowhere near finished. How much easier it would be if we could simply hire a professional to come and do the job. Somebody who knew what they were doing would have the paper off and the room repainted within a day or two. And if that were to happen, then the estate agent could come and take his pictures and the advert could go in the newspaper and people would come and look at the cottage and everything would be fine. How much would it cost to hire a man in to do the work? Three or four pounds maybe? That wasn't really a lot.

I went downstairs, made sandwiches, put two on a plate and took the plate into Julia. She was sitting at the dining-room table reading back through the notes she had made.

'Ham and mustard,' I said, putting the plate down beside her.

'Ham? Can we afford ham?'

The butcher had given me a couple of slices for free but I didn't want Julia to know that we were, by that point, surviving on little more than the kind-heartedness of the shopkeepers. 'They were selling it off cheap,' I said.

Julia took off her glasses and rubbed the place between her eyes. 'I do so miss French bread,' she said. Then she smiled and reached out her hand to me. 'The bread you bake is wonderful, dear, I didn't mean that it wasn't, but sometimes I long for bread I can break between my hands, bread with a brown crust and the dough inside light as air and still warm. I could kill for a fresh baguette, some creamy yellow butter and a good slice of Brie to go with it – and some of those juicy grapes straight from the vine that grew at the back of Les Aubépines . . .' Her voice drifted off.

My mouth watered at the thought of those sweet black grapes. I went back into the kitchen, considered my options while I tidied up, then put on my coat.

'I'm going out for an hour,' I called to Julia.

She did not answer.

The rain was coming down in sheets. The grass was sodden, silver-puddled; it was slippery beneath the soles of my boots. The day was drawing away, light tucking itself behind the clouds shadowing the sky. I walked down the garden, past the pile of rotting timber, past the locked-up shed that had been Julia's father's pride and joy. I went through the rickety old gate at the bottom of the garden and into the field behind, and I stood beside the old sofa by the fence where there was a little shelter from the rain. I pulled the hood of my coat as far forward as it would go and I made myself small and I gazed out into the greyness. The lake was disappearing behind the rain. There were no boats on the water that evening, no patient, sou'westered fishermen drenched on the banks with their keep nets and bait boxes; there were no birds, no walkers, no deer, nothing but greyness as far as the eye could see and, on the other side of the lake, the distant sprawl of the Sunnyvale Nursing Home.

I took a deep breath and headed down towards it.

I found Dr Croucher in his wheelchair in Sunnyvale's day room reading the newspaper. He dominated the room. The other residents were smaller than him, more silvery, not nearly so well-groomed and somehow less substantial. He gave no indication of having noticed me come into the room but I was certain he knew I was there. I went to stand beside him and he continued to read. I said: 'Excuse me, Doctor,' and only then did he look up.

He folded the newspaper methodically and laid it down on the table beside him. He took off his glasses and put them on top of the paper.

'Amy,' he said. 'How nice to see you again. Sit down.

Would you like a drink? The girl will get us one,' and he looked towards Susan Pettigrew who was spoonfeeding soup into the mouth of a trembling old lady.

'No, I don't want anything, thank you,' I said.

The doctor stroked his beard. 'Well,' he said, 'you've walked all the way down here and you're soaked to the skin. It must be something important. What can I do for you?'

I spoke quietly. 'I was wondering if you could lend me ten pounds.'

'Ahh,' said the doctor. He said nothing else until the silence between us had become uncomfortable. 'Ten pounds? Why do you need that kind of money?'

'To have one of the rooms in Reservoir Cottage redecorated. It's not for my benefit, you understand, but so that Julia can sell the cottage as quickly as possible.'

'Does she know you've come to see me?'

'No. She would be mortified. And there's no reason for her to know. I'll make up some excuse for having come by the money and pay to get the work done myself. As soon as the cottage is sold, Julia will pay me what she owes me and I'll give the money straight back to you.'

The doctor was silent for a moment but I knew, in my bones, that he was pleased that I had come to him. He enjoyed the power it gave him, the fact that he now knew we needed help, that we were desperate.

He decided to milk it.

He steepled his fingers, rested his chin on the tips and gazed at me. 'Why did you come to me?' he asked.

If he wanted to be flattered, I would oblige. I gave him a shy smile.

'Because I know you're a good man and that you care about Julia,' I said. 'And also because I knew you'd appreciate *why* the particular room I'm talking about needs attention. You helped Mr Cummings attend to it in the past. Julia and I had started stripping the paper and we realized too late why it had been glued so firmly in place.'

Now the doctor's eyes widened and the colour drained from his cheeks. He cleared his throat and straightened his tie.

'You're talking about Caroline's bedroom?'

'Yes.'

The doctor nodded and fidgeted for a moment, brushing dust from his knee, polishing the handle of his wheelchair with the palm of his hand.

'What, exactly, have you exposed?' he asked.

'We've only cleared the wall to the left of the fireplace. There's a drawing, do you remember?' I leaned closer. '*A hanging man,*' I whispered. 'We scrubbed it away but now the wall is a mess. We can't paint over it as it is, we can't do anything until the rest of the wallpaper is removed, and oh, Doctor, it's taking so long to do it ourselves.'

'Yes,' he said. 'I see. And of course I'll help. Let me think for a moment. Obviously this needs attending to quickly. Why not leave it with me? I'll find somebody to replaster and paint the room, somebody you can trust not to say anything about what is hidden beneath the paper, and I'll be responsible for paying them. I'll need a day or two. When that is done, I'll call you.'

'No, you can't telephone. Julia will almost certainly

answer and then she'll know we're in cahoots. Couldn't Mrs Croucher bring a message to me?'

He paused. 'Mrs Croucher doesn't know about Caroline's graffiti. It's best she's not involved.'

'Then how will I know what's happening?'

'Come back the day after tomorrow. I should have everything in place by then.'

'All right.' I nodded. 'It's terribly kind of you, Doctor.'

'No, it's the least I can do. I'm glad to help Julia in any way I can. Dear God.' He rubbed the space above his nose with the back of his thumb. 'You shouldn't have to be worrying about such things and neither should Julia. Beinon and I should have done the job properly the first time around.' He looked genuinely upset.

'I'm sorry,' I said. 'I really didn't mean to distress you.'

The doctor waved away my concern. 'You don't have to worry about me,' he said, 'you just take care of Julia. Lock up that room. Don't let her or the child inside.'

'Are there more drawings?' I asked.

'There are. Wicked drawings. You will do as I say, won't you?'

'Yes, of course. I'll make sure nobody goes into the room. Thank you so much for your help.'

'No need to thank me.' He shifted in his chair and took something out of his jacket pocket – a wallet. He extracted a five-pound note and held it out. 'It's for you,' he said.

I shook my head. 'I can't take that.'

'Take it,' the doctor said. 'Buy yourself something nice. Treat the little girl if you wish.'

238

'Really, I can't accept this.'

'Take it,' the doctor said, and his voice had an authority that forbade any further protestation. 'Go on. Spend it on food if you must, whatever you like. Only make sure,' he said, 'that the poor dear child is kept away from that terrible room.'

CHAPTER THIRTY-EIGHT

I folded the five-pound note and put it in my bag. Already I was planning what I would do with it. Fish and chips, I thought. I would buy us all a fish and chip supper, with mushy peas, gravy, salt, vinegar – as much as we could eat. And cake. I'd pay off my bills at the shops and then I'd buy the ingredients for a cake, and I'd make a great big cherry cake with vanilla butter icing on top and a whole pot of blackcurrant jam in the middle. I would buy a tin of Nescafé coffee – we hadn't had any at Reservoir Cottage since before Christmas – and a bottle of lemonade. I would buy chocolate and fresh bread, a pound of butter and a joint of meat. I'd make a roast dinner tomorrow, we'd have carrots and parsnips and cauliflower cheese, gravy and stuffing, a whole tray of Yorkshire puddings.

I was headed back to the reception desk at Sunnyvale, my stomach growling with anticipation as I planned the meals we would eat, when I felt a gentle tapping on my shoulder. I turned to see Susan Pettigrew. I was so lost in my thoughts that I didn't register who it was for a moment and perhaps when I said, 'Hello,' I sounded a little off-hand.

Whether or not I put her off, Susan didn't say anything. She merely stood close to me, looking terrified.

'Did you want to talk to me, dear?' I asked.

Susan's eyes flickered around nervously. She nodded.

'What did you want to talk about?'

Susan came up very close to me, and whispered: 'Caroline.'

'All right.' I smiled. 'I'd be happy to hear what you have to say.'

Susan looked around her again. The receptionist, at the front desk, was only a few feet away but she was speaking on the telephone, not looking at us. Susan held one hand up to her mouth, to mask her lips, and she muttered: 'She wasn't evil.' She shook her head to emphasize this. 'She wasn't even bad.' Her eyes at once reddened and so did her cheeks. 'She was my friend.'

'Oh Susan, I know she was.'

Susan blinked and tears caught on her lashes. 'She was my only friend,' she said. Her shoulders were hunched and her head held low as if she were trying to make herself as small as possible. Tears were running down her downy cheeks.

'Come and sit with me by the fire for a while, dear, and we can talk,' I said gently.

'It's not allowed.'

'Surely we can have a few minutes.'

'No. I'm not allowed. I'm not presentable.' She fidgeted up her sleeve for a handkerchief. I passed her mine. She took it and dabbed at her eyes, mumbling, 'They said Caroline did it on purpose, but she never; it was an accident.'

'What was an accident, dear?'

'Mrs Aldridge going under the water.'

'Oh!'

The receptionist heard my gasp and looked up. She saw Susan's distress. I put one arm around Susan and turned her, so our backs were towards the reception desk.

'I don't understand,' I whispered. 'I know Mrs Aldridge drowned in the lake, but what does that have to do with Caroline?'

Susan's voice was urgent now. She twisted the handkerchief furiously between her hands. 'She never meant to hurt her! It was an accident!'

The receptionist put down the telephone receiver, stood up and began to walk towards us.

'Susan! Come on, dear, leave our visitor alone,' she called. 'What will Matron say if she finds out you've been a nuisance?'

'It was an accident!' Susan repeated fiercely. 'She wasn't supposed to go in the lake!'

The receptionist had reached us. She took hold of Susan's arm. 'Sorry,' she said to me. 'She gets herself into a bit of a tizz sometimes, don't you, dear?'

'I was telling her about Caroline!' Susan said.

The woman rolled her eyes. 'Caroline, Caroline! It's always Caroline! Now's not the time or place, is it, dear? We've talked about this before, haven't we? Come on now. Don't make me get cross.'

She hurried Susan away, back along the corridor, ignoring my protestations. I was afraid of making things worse for Susan but that was no excuse really; I should have done more to help her. I watched her go, then I buttoned my coat and left the building, the money safe in my bag.

I walked up the hill feeling as if I were carrying a weight on my shoulders. Susan's words went round and round in my mind. I told myself I should be feeling better about everything; the doctor had agreed to sort out the redecorating of the empty bedroom and we would all eat well that evening. I didn't feel better though; I felt more unsettled than ever.

CHAPTER THIRTY-NINE

I told Julia that I had found the five-pound note in the lining of my suitcase. We all celebrated this serendipitous find by dancing, hand in hand, around the kitchen table. After that I went to the Lake Inn and bought three fish suppers to take away and two bottles of beer and one of lemonade, and Julia, Vivi and I ate like queens, queens who enjoyed sucking every last morsel of salty grease from their fingers. We fed the fish skins to the dog. And after that, happily sated, I arranged to meet Daniel for a drink. I was full of food and sleepy but he didn't seem to mind that I was quiet.

It was so easy to be myself with him; there were no secrets of the heart that I would hide from him. We sat in the pub and talked of this and that, but it was enough for me that we were simply there, together, as if that was how we always had been and always would be.

When I was with him, it felt as if everything was falling perfectly into place. I already knew that soon, there would never be a morning when I didn't wake up, or a night when I did not fall asleep beside Daniel, and that that was how my life had always been meant to be.

He was my way forward. He was my future. With him, there would be no uncertainty; with him I would be secure and happy. I did not doubt him, not for one second.

We had a lovely, peaceful evening and afterwards we spent a while together in the car steaming up the windows, and only after that did Daniel drop me off at the end of the lane. I kissed him goodbye and walked alone towards Reservoir Cottage. As I drew closer, I could see the lights were still on, even though it was gone midnight. I began to run back towards the house, praying that nothing bad had happened.

Viviane was waiting for me in the hallway in her nightdress and slippers. She threw her arms around me and pressed her head against my shoulder.

'What is it?' I asked. 'Darling, what's wrong?'

Julia wandered out from the back room, leaning on her stick, a glass in her free hand, looking terribly tired. Vivi looked up towards her mother.

'Amy, dear, while you were out there was a telephone call,' Julia said. 'It was a neighbour of your father's – a Mrs Botham.'

'Is it my father? What's happened to him?'

'Now don't panic, he's all right but he's in hospital. You need to go back to Sheffield. That's it, sit down. Let Vivi hold your hand, take the glass. Now listen, sweetheart, it might not be as serious as it sounds but the doctors think it's his heart and they're taking every precaution. Drink the gin, it'll do you good. Vivi has been round to Mrs Croucher's to borrow a copy of the train timetable. You can go back to Yorkshire in the morning. We've booked a taxi to pick you up at seven. All the arrangements have been made. You don't need to worry about anything.'

But I can't leave you, I thought. How can I leave you both alone?

I dropped my head into my hands. There was barely enough food in the cupboards to last the week and although I had money now, I knew Julia wouldn't go to the shop to spend it. There were God knows what horrors hidden behind the wallpaper in the empty bedroom and, if I went away, I would miss my appointment with Dr Croucher – which would delay the redecoration of the room. How could I possibly leave Julia and Viviane? How could I?

'I can't go,' I said.

'But you must, dear.'

'There's no benefit in me going,' I said. 'It will make no difference to Dad if I'm there or if I'm not and you need me here.'

I looked at Julia, held her eyes. I had once told her that my father cared more for his pigeons than for me and she had laughed, but not unkindly. 'Birds are not complicated,' she had said, 'but daughters are. Perhaps he doesn't know *how* to love you.'

'You must go,' Julia said, more firmly. 'If, heaven forbid, your father takes a turn for the worse, and you aren't there for him, you will never forgive yourself. And I will never forgive myself either.'

'But how will you manage?'

'We'll be all right,' Julia said. 'God willing you'll only

be gone a few days and we can cope for that time. Mrs Croucher is next door if we need anything, and we have the telephone.'

I turned to Viviane. 'And you'll be up in time to catch the bus to school each morning?'

'Yes, of course.'

'And you'll remember your choir practices? Because it's not long until the concert now.'

'Yes! It's not like Mr Leeson would let me forget.'

'Go upstairs and pack yourself a little bag, Amy dear,' Julia said gently, 'then you must try and get some sleep.'

I did as she said. By that time, the others had gone to bed and the house was quiet. The door to the empty bedroom was closed and locked, as it had been when I went out, but I had a compulsion to look inside. I turned the key, pushed the door open, switched on the light and went in. The room seemed to contract away from me, like a sea-creature closing itself back inside its shell. I had a sense of its withdrawing and I reached out to steady myself against the doorframe in case the floor beneath my feet disappeared. Strips of half-peeled wallpaper hung around the chimney breast, like lacerated skin. The patch of wall that we had scrubbed, where the drawing had been, was dark and bad-tempered, a filthy plaster slapped over a wound.

I became suddenly tearful. I left the room, locked the door, took the key and put it in my coat pocket. Then I finished packing – only a few things, I didn't intend to be away for long. At the last moment, when I was almost done, I pulled Caroline's satchel out from under the bed, unfastened the buckles, opened it up and took out the gold necklace that had once belonged to Daniel's grandmother. I dangled the chain over my fingers, watched the pendant swinging, the way the ruby caught the light; it was exquisite.

It belonged to the Aldridges. It was part of Daniel's inheritance, and more than that, part of his family history. Already it was a secret, a barrier between the two of us. I had not directly lied about it, but not telling was a kind of dishonesty; it tainted our relationship.

I wished I'd never set eyes on the thing.

CHAPTER FORTY

At Bristol's Temple Meads station the next morning, I called Daniel from a telephone box to let him know what was happening, assured him that I would be fine and that I would miss him. He said he wanted to come with me; I told him that was absolutely not necessary. I promised to call again that evening. Then I treated myself to a cup of tea and a slice of buttered toast. I sat in the café at a table between shafts of sunlight falling through the high glass roof and shared my breakfast with Bess, who I had brought with me at the last moment, at Julia's insistence. She was worried about keeping the dog at Reservoir Cottage when I was not there to look after her. How would she be exercised, Julia had asked, while I was away? Where would she sleep? I looked down at Bess, who sat beside my knee, looking up at me. I smoothed her ear, soft as silk.

'I'm glad you're here,' I told her.

Bess thumped her tail. I offered her the last of the toast and she took it very gently from my fingers. It felt as if the dog and I were isolated in our own little bubble of aloneness. All around, people in coats and scarves and hats were going about their ordinary daily business. They were reading newspapers, talking to one another, blowing on their fingers, holding tightly to their brief-cases, looking down the tracks to see if trains were coming, checking their watches. For weeks my world had been confined to the lake, the hills, to the village of Blackwater. I no longer felt that I belonged in this big, hectic outside world. I had become disconnected.

The train was busy, but the guard helped me find a seat by the window where Bess could sleep between my feet. As the train rolled north, I rested my chin on my hand and stared out of the window, watching my reflection superimposed over the bleak, wintry countryside. I let myself drift into an almost-sleep in which my father's pinched face moved through my mind and disappeared as quickly and smoothly as the winter countryside. I let myself dream, for a while, about Daniel.

My father's next-door neighbour, Eileen Botham, was waiting on the platform at Sheffield, bleached hair set in a severe permanent wave protected by a headscarf decorated with black and white Scottie dogs tied beneath her chin. She waved when she spotted me and headed across the platform. I was enclosed in a bony hug, a cloud of Max Factor.

'Hello, my pet, how are you?' Mrs Botham asked.

'I'm fine,' I said.

Mrs Botham patted Bess's head. 'It's nice to see your Granny's doggie again,' she said.

I didn't bother to reply.

I had prepared myself for being alone in Sheffield. I hadn't counted on the company of Mrs Botham, a widow who, as my grandmother never tired of pointing out, was no better than she should be. She had a reputation, according to Granny, for being a gossip and a busybody. It was probably true, but I had been reluctantly grateful to Mrs Botham when she volunteered to make the sandwiches for the wake after my grandmother's funeral and then handed them round. She'd helped me tidy up afterwards too. She was nice enough but she was just a bit *much*.

It suddenly occurred to me that perhaps Mrs Botham and my father were more than neighbours to one another. I glanced at the woman sideways.

No, surely not. She could hardly be less like my mother if she tried.

'It was good of you to let me know about my father, Mrs Botham,' I said.

'There's no need to stand on ceremony. You're to call me Eileen. After all, I've known you since you were knee-high. You used to play in my yard. Do you remember?'

'No.'

'Well, you did. You were a shy little thing but very polite.' Mrs Botham took hold of my arm, and we walked towards the exit together.

'How is my father?'

'He's being stoic. There's not many as survives a heart attack, but he did. He's on painkillers and he'll be in hospital for a couple of days. After that, he's to come

251

home and rest. The doctors said we should treat it as a shot across the bows.'

We?

'Where is he?'

'He's in the General and he's in good hands. He's been told he's to stop smoking.'

'Dad will never stop smoking.'

'Oh, he will if I have anything to do with it!'

I glanced at Mrs Botham again. This time, the older woman noticed the look and she flushed. She cleared her throat. 'I've been keeping an eye on him,' she said. 'Somebody has to.'

'Yes,' I agreed. 'Absolutely.'

We had reached a small patch of grass outside the station. Bess sniffed it suspiciously and then, satisfied at last that it was safe, circled three times and squatted, holding her tail out straight behind her with a self-conscious expression on her face. Once done she looked at me expectantly and I told her she was a clever girl.

'Can I see my father now?' I asked Mrs Botham.

'No, pet. They're very strict with the visiting hours. And you must be tired. We'll go home and get us something to eat and then we'll be ready to see him in the morning.'

Back at the house that had once belonged to my grandmother I sat at the table squashed into one end of the kitchen and politely drank the tea and ate the pie and chips Mrs Botham had warmed for me while she took Bess outside and saw to the pigeons. The kitchen was tiny and old but it was warmer and more comfortable than I remembered. Mrs Botham had clearly been at work. Some home comforts had been introduced. After I'd eaten, I washed the dishes. The water was piping hot, delivered directly from a newly installed boiler, and the towel I used to dry my hands was soft and fluffy and smelled of flowers. Granny's towels had been uniformly hard and stiff and smelled of old washing-up.

Before she left me that evening, Mrs Botham asked if there was anything else I wanted, hesitated as if unsure as to whether or not she should kiss me, saw the expression on my face, decided against the kiss, and bade me goodnight. I waited until I heard her footsteps going up her own stairs, through the wall that separated the two houses, and then I telephoned Reservoir Cottage. Julia answered at once. She said everything was fine. Mrs Croucher had brought round a lamb stew and a treacle tart for their supper, Vivi was doing her homework and – dropping her voice – there'd been no mention of *you know who*. We spoke for a few minutes, then Julia, anxious about running up my father's telephone bill, urged me to end the call.

'We'll speak again tomorrow,' she promised.

After that, I called Daniel. We talked about my father, my journey, Daniel's day, and then I told him about Mrs Botham.

'She's taken over,' I said. 'She's still living next door – well, at least while I'm here she is – but she's as good as moved in. Her pinny is hung on the hook in the kitchen, there's a bar of lavender soap in the privy, there's even a pair of her slippers by the front door.'

'At least they're not under the bed.'

'Oh don't!'

Daniel laughed. 'Isn't it a good thing that she's so involved?'

'How is it good?'

'Because you know somebody is looking after your father, that he's not lonely, that he has somebody else in his life besides you, someone he can talk to.'

'He's not the kind of person who needs other people.'

'Everybody needs other people,' Daniel replied.

'But not her.'

'Wasn't it Mrs Botham who called the ambulance when your father had the heart attack?'

'Yes.'

'And didn't she go with him to the hospital?'

'Yes.'

'And did she wait with him while he was examined? Did she talk to the doctors? Did she find out what was going on?'

'All right,' I said. 'I see your point.'

He was right. When the doctors said my father must stay in hospital for a few days, it was Mrs Botham who caught the bus home, packed up his pyjamas, his toothbrush and his cigarettes, and then caught another bus back to the hospital to deliver them to him. It was she who caught a third bus back to his house after that, who went to the trouble of finding the Reservoir Cottage telephone number and leaving a message for me. And she must have spoken to Julia a second time, some time during the day just passed, to find out which train she should meet at the station after she had prepared a meal for me and made up the bed.

I sighed, leaned my head against the wall and closed my eyes.

'I wish you were here with me, Daniel. You make me a better person.'

'There is not a single thing wrong with you as you are,' he said.

When I went to bed, I found Mrs Botham had put a hot water bottle between the sheets. There was a note on the bedside table.

Sleep well, pet. Anything you need, just knock on the wall. Yours, Eileen.

I fell asleep counting the cigarette cards in their frames that were hung on the bedroom walls, Loretta Young smiling down at me with her knowing, ageless smile.

CHAPTER FORTY-ONE

When I woke the next morning it was already light. The bedroom door was open and Bess was gone. I put on my father's dressing gown and went downstairs. The dog was in the kitchen lapping scrambled eggs from a bowl on the floor. She wagged her tail between her legs when I came into the room but did not stop eating.

Mrs Botham looked up from the stove; her eyes were anxious.

'I hope you don't mind me giving the doggie her breakfast.'

'Of course not. It's very good of you.'

'Sit yourself down, Amy, the kettle's on.'

Now Daniel had made me look at things from a different point of view, I realized it was very relaxing to be told what to do. It was nice that somebody else was up first to light the fire and heat the water; it made a pleasant change for somebody else to be in charge.

Mrs Botham put a plate of egg on toast on the table in front of me. 'I'm ever so glad you came,' she said. 'Your father said he wasn't sure you'd come but

I knew you would. He misses you terribly, you know.'

'He has a funny way of showing it.'

'It's not your father's way to say how he's feeling out loud,' Mrs Botham said. 'It doesn't mean that he's not feeling anything.'

'He talks to the pigeons.'

'And you know why that is. It's because he knows they're not going to run away and leave him. They always come back. There's a reason why they're called homing pigeons, you know. There's a reason why he's so fond of them.'

In due course, we caught the bus back into town, queued up at the hospital entrance with the other visitors, and then trooped into the men's ward. My father had the bed closest to the door. He was sleeping when we arrived. He lay on his back with his mouth open, his head making a dent in the centre of the pillow and his hands crossed tidily on top of the overblanket. I stood helplessly beside him, trying to reconcile how he was now with how he always had been before.

'You mustn't worry, Amy,' Mrs Botham said. 'He's going to be fine.'

She moved the ashtray on the table at the side of the bed to make room for the cake tin she'd brought. Then she took off her gloves, perched on the side of the bed and patted Dad's hand.

'Don,' she whispered. 'Don, wake up, you've got a visitor.'

My father's eyes flickered open, he gave a little panicked snort, remembered where he was and said,

'Oh,' in a disappointed tone of voice, as if he had hoped to find himself back at home. Then his eyes fell on me. He blinked, and reached out for his spectacles. Mrs Botham passed them to him, and he put them on. He hitched himself up the pillows, squinting into the light.

'Birdie?' he asked quietly. 'Is that you?'

'Yep,' I said.

'You came home?'

'Just like a pigeon.'

Mrs Botham went off to find a doctor. It was kind of her to give us some time alone together. Mostly we were quiet. There didn't seem to be the need for either of us to say anything and for the first time in my life I realized this was not a bad thing. When the bell rang to signify the end of visiting hours, I stood reluctantly and kissed my father's cheek.

'I'll be back tomorrow,' I said.

'There's no need.'

'I'll be back anyway.'

The afternoon was bitterly cold, wind washing the rain off the moors, sending it sideways into the streets, down the rooftops, over the areas of the city, devastated by the war, that were being cleared to build new roads and flats, great swathes of rubble heaped behind hoardings. Mrs Botham and I sat side by side on the bus, sharing a bag of Mintoes as the windows steamed over.

'When we get back,' said Mrs Botham, speaking awkwardly around the sweet in her mouth, 'you wrap up warm and take that dog for a quick walk and I'll make us some dinner. Would you fancy some chips?'

It would be the third day running that I had eaten chips. I said that I would fancy them very much.

'You'll stay and eat them with me, won't you?' I asked.

Mrs Botham said that she would.

That evening, the two of us sat together and worked on a jigsaw puzzle that Mrs Botham had given my father as a Christmas present. I found myself so engrossed that it was gone eight o'clock by the time I remembered to call Reservoir Cottage. The phone rang out, but nobody answered.

I pressed my fingers down on the cradle and redialled, but the same thing happened again.

Mrs Botham looked up from the jigsaw. 'Perhaps they've popped out for a breath of fresh air,' she said. I didn't want to burden her with my worries so I smiled and agreed that perhaps they had. Mrs Botham wasn't to know that Julia never popped out for anything now.

I didn't sleep well that night. I was safe and warm in my lovely bed with the hot water bottle and the ironed sheets, but my heart couldn't settle. It kept returning to Reservoir Cottage, rattling around those cold, dark rooms, searching for whatever it was that had kept Julia and Vivi from answering the telephone.

The next day, at the hospital, my father seemed brighter. He was sitting up when we arrived, his hair had been combed and there was a little colour in his cheeks. Mrs Botham made her excuses and scurried off again, and I poured Dad a glass of lemon barley water. He asked for his cigarettes. I picked up the packet, and then put it down again. I said: 'Really, Dad,

259

you must stop. Smoking is no good for your heart.'

'I didn't know you cared about my heart,' he said.

I took hold of his hand and I raised it to my lips. I kissed the back of it, the dry skin, scarred by a thousand small burns.

When Mrs Botham and I got back that evening, I called Reservoir Cottage every hour, on the hour, but nobody answered the telephone.

I sat at the table in the kitchen while Mrs Botham worked on the jigsaw in the front room and I wondered if I should call Daniel and ask him to drive up to the cottage to check that everything was all right. Each time I was on the point of telephoning, I talked myself out of it. What could he do? Julia would be alarmed if he turned up on the doorstep out of the blue – she hadn't been at all happy when I'd invited him in to look in the loft. Most likely, there was nothing wrong. If I sent him to investigate, it would look as if I didn't trust Julia, and she might end up being rude to him. Perhaps my absence had forced her to leave the cottage. Maybe she'd snapped out of her inertia and taken Vivi into Weston-super-Mare to the pictures. Maybe they'd gone down to the village club or for a walk, or perhaps they were eating with Mrs Croucher. The fact that they weren't answering the phone didn't mean that anything was wrong.

I was up early the next morning. At eight o'clock, the time when Viviane should have been getting ready to leave for school, I telephoned Reservoir Cottage again, and again there was no answer. I called the operator and asked her to see if there was a fault on the line. She checked and said there wasn't. I put my coat on over my father's dressing gown and paced up and down the scrubland at the end of the road while Bess sniffed at the feet of the privet hedges and the night's darkness faded over the moors, bleached away by a cold dawn. The key to the empty bedroom was in my coat pocket. I turned it over between my fingers. My mind spun the different threads of my anxiety together; I couldn't think logically.

When Mrs Botham came, I tried to explain but it was difficult because she didn't know all that had happened before; she had no understanding of the context of my fear.

'I shouldn't worry, pet,' she said. 'If anything bad had happened, you'd have heard by now. Somebody would have contacted you.'

But would they? What if something *really* awful had happened and Viviane and Julia were in the cottage and nobody realized they were there? Mrs Croucher might notice if something was wrong, but she might not. She was used to not seeing Julia. Not seeing Julia was normal to Mrs Croucher.

'I have to go back to Somerset,' I said.

Mrs Botham looked up from the frying pan.

'I'm sorry,' I said. 'Really I am. But I daren't leave it any longer. I have to go back. Viviane needs me and Julia doesn't have anyone else.'

The fat in the pan spat. Mrs Botham moved two rashers of bacon around with her fork. There were two rosy circles in the middle of her cheeks.

'What about your dad?' she asked.

I went over to her and put my arms about her waist. 'Eileen,' I said, 'he's the lucky one. He has you.'

In the end, I left the dog with Mrs Botham. They both seemed pleased with that part of the arrangement at least. Mrs Botham said she'd be glad of the company and that Bess would give her a reason to get out of the house. Bess herself was already becoming accustomed to the superior quality of the food she was being fed here, and was in no hurry to go back to vegetable scraps.

I didn't want to leave her though. I didn't want to go back to Reservoir Cottage on my own, without her.

'She'll be all right,' Mrs Botham said. 'And you'll be back before you know it, won't you, to pick her up?'

CHAPTER FORTY-TWO

And soon enough there I was again, outside Reservoir Cottage, more fearful about what I would find than I had been the first time. I put my bag down and pushed the front door. It swung open. The inside of the cottage was in darkness. The air was cold – no fire had been lit, and there was a strange, rotten, damp-hair smell. It was too quiet – I couldn't hear a thing. I stepped inside and switched on the hall light, wishing Bess was with me. I wished it more than anything.

'Hello!' I called, but the word seemed to disappear the moment it left my lips. Nobody answered. I left the door open behind me as I moved forward, looking into the downstairs rooms, turning on the lights as I went. All the rooms were empty. I hesitated at the foot of the stairs, one hand on the wooden acorn at the end of the banister as I looked up into the darkness above me. 'Hello!' I called again. 'Julia! Vivi!'

Again, nobody answered.

The silence was unbearable. In the back room the clock ticked. Outside, somewhere, a fox screamed.

I put one foot on the first step of the stairs, took hold

of the banister, tried to summon the courage to move up. My heart was beating so hard that it hurt. I wished I was not alone. I was terrified of what I might find at the top of the stairs but I was compelled to go and look.

Slowly, one step after another, I ascended. When the board creaked on the third step from the top, I cried out in fear.

Stupid, I said under my breath, *you're being really stupid*, but I couldn't contain my fear or pretend that it was not real.

I finally reached the top of the stairs. I switched on the landing light, leaned forward and pushed open the door to the master bedroom. It squeaked on its hinges. The light from the landing fell into the room and there was Julia, lying on top of the bed, her arms and legs and hair spread all about her and Alain's notebook beside her, flattened open. I could not tell if she was alive or dead.

I was hardly breathing myself.

I stepped forward, the boards giving beneath my feet. I reached out tentatively, lifted Julia's wrist, *Oh God, let her be OK*. Her skin was icy cold, but I could feel a pulse.

I laid Julia's arm down and sat on the edge of the bed. I shook her shoulders gently.

'Julia? Wake up!'

She groaned.

'Julia, darling, it's me, Amy. Did you take a pill, dear? Did you take a sleeping tablet?'

Julia sighed and turned her head. 'So tired,' she whispered. Her breath was sour and it smelled of gin.

'What about Vivi? Where is she? Is she all right?'

But Julia wouldn't say anything else; she was deeply asleep, unconscious.

I looked around for Julia's pill bottle, but couldn't see it. I tried to calm myself. I needed to be calm; panicking wouldn't help. I had to find Vivi. I covered Julia over with her blankets and left the room. I pushed open the door to Viviane's room; it swung back slowly. The room was empty.

I had known it would be.

I knew where she was.

I put my hand down into my coat pocket. The key was still there. Slowly, fearfully, I went towards the empty bedroom. The door was ajar. I pushed and it creaked as it swung open. The room was in darkness but moonlight came through the window and I could see that someone had been tearing at the wallpaper.

I stepped forward. In the eerie blue half-light, I made out words scrawled down the side of the wall.

I hate Jean Aldridge. I wish she was dead.

I didn't want to look at the wall but I was drawn to it as if somebody was holding my hand and leading me towards it.

I hate Jean Aldridge I hate Jean Aldridge I hate Jean Aldridge I hate Jean Aldridge, repeated a hundred times perhaps, filling up the whole side of the wall. It was weird and frightening, and because the four words had been written so many times it was as if they had lost their individual meaning and become something else: a curse.

'Amy?'

I turned and I saw Viviane. Swollen-eyed, limp-haired, in creased and soiled clothes, she was like an urchin in a storybook, a filthy sprite. She came out of the darkness of the room towards me, slowly, stiffly, and I took her in my arms; she held on to me, like the frightened child she was. She was so very small. The top of her head smelled of salt and sweat and dirt; it smelled of misery. I cradled her, rocked her, stroked her hair. She was limp in my arms and I was gripped by a sudden fear that the door would shut and the two of us would be trapped inside with God knows what else. I could not let that happen.

I pulled Vivi towards the door. 'Let's go and get you warm.'

'No,' she said, resisting, 'I must stay here. I have to finish.'

'Finish what, darling?'

'Taking the paper off the wall. Caroline said I had to.'

'But you're allowed a break. Caroline won't mind if you have a little rest.'

'No, I have to stay here, where she can find me!' The child's voice was desperate, tearful. 'She said that I must!'

'Caroline doesn't want you to make yourself ill, Vivi, really she doesn't. Come with me.' I moved her towards the door, slowly, slowly. The child was a deadweight in my arms. At the threshold, Viviane turned back.

'She wants you to see what she wrote.'

'I've seen it.'

'She hated Jean Aldridge.'

'I know.'

266

'She wanted Jean Aldridge to die.'

'Come on, Viviane, come downstairs.'

'She deserved to die.'

I closed my eyes. I thought: I can't deal with this. I don't know how to. I don't know what to do.

I kissed Vivi's forehead. 'Sweetheart, you mustn't talk like that. What would Papa say if he heard you saying such things?'

The mention of her father seemed to bring Viviane back to her senses. She allowed me to help her out of the room. I pulled the door shut behind us and took her down the stairs and into the kitchen. I closed the front door, drew the curtains in the front room then put on the kettle. I turned my back to Viviane, so the child should not see the tiredness and shock in my eyes. I waited until the immediate wave of despair had passed, found some strength from somewhere, sat down at the table, took hold of Viviane's hands and turned them over. The nails were torn and filthy and there were bruises on the ends of her fingers and scratches on her palms.

'Vivi, why? Why did you do this to yourself?'

'Caroline said I had to get the paper off the wall before *he* covered it up for good,' Vivi said. She sounded exhausted, close to tears.

'He?'

'Yes! He's going to have it covered up and then nobody will know.'

I didn't know how Vivi could have heard about the doctor's offer to organize the redecoration of the room. Had I mentioned it inadvertently? Had I let something slip?

I laid her hands down on the table and fetched a bowl of warm water and a clean cloth. I began to wash her fingers, as gently as I could.

'Your poor hands are so sore. Has your mummy seen that writing?'

Viviane shook her head. She blinked rapidly, fighting back tears, and then she wiped her nose with the back of her hand.

'Mummy's been sleeping.'

'All this time?'

'I gave her some pills.'

'You gave Mummy sleeping pills? Oh Vivi, why did you do that?'

'She wouldn't let me go into Caroline's room. She said I mustn't but I had to.'

'How many pills did you give her?'

'Three.'

'You're sure? It's important, Vivi. You're certain you gave her three pills, no more than that?'

'Three yesterday and three today.'

'Did you put them in a drink?'

Viviane looked up towards the ceiling.

'Listen,' she said.

'I can't hear anything.'

'Listen.'

And there it was, the faintest sound from upstairs, a scratching sound, like something sharp being scored into plaster.

I stood up and pulled the door shut, slammed it. I leaned against it.

'It's her,' Vivi said in a tired, sad voice. 'It's Caroline.'

'No, it's not. Maybe there's a twig caught in the gutter or something.'

Vivi sighed. 'What must she do to make you believe in her?'

I thought, I must be calm, I must be rational. I was dealing with a troubled little girl who had got everything out of proportion in her mind, that was all. There was nothing to fear. Panicking would make everything worse.

I looked at Vivi, in front of me at the table, small, pale, filthy, her hair wild. Her chin was in her hand, her eyes were wide and dark, deeply shadowed, her lips pale and faintly blue against her skin.

Vivi was gazing at me with such sincerity that it almost broke my heart. She truly believed that Caroline was real.

I can't let this go on any longer, I thought. I have to do something.

But what? What can I do?

I remembered the advert I'd torn from the paper: Violet-Anne Dando, the woman who quieted restless souls. At the time, I hadn't thought I would ever really call her. I hadn't actually believed that we might need a medium, or a spiritualist or whatever she was.

Now, crazy as it seemed, I thought she might be the only person on earth who could help us.

CHAPTER FORTY-THREE

As that awful evening wore on, so the scratching noise in the empty bedroom grew louder, as if something inside was growing increasingly frustrated. The longer it went on, the harder it was for me to persuade myself that it was the wind, or a small animal, or some aberration in the plumbing of the cottage. The sound was under my skin, it ate into me. If it went on much longer, I was certain it would drive me mad. I couldn't bear it, it was like a thought going round and round in my mind, a thought I couldn't expel. The educated, sensible, logical part of me knew there must be a rational explanation for the noise; the scared, exhausted, emotional side insisted it was not caused by any natural phenomenon. I was so overwrought that even the simplest decision was difficult. Whatever I did to ameliorate the situation would also have an opposite effect that might make things even worse. I felt I ought to call for an emergency ambulance for Julia, but then I would have to explain how she had come to be drugged. If the authorities found out that her own daughter was responsible, wouldn't they be likely to insist Vivi was taken to Borstal, or whatever it was they did with disturbed children? If that were to happen, it would be the end of the Laurents. Julia would never forgive me and Vivi would risk being traumatized for the rest of her life. And any involvement of third parties, any unravelling of the events that had led us to this point would mean revealing the secrets of the empty bedroom. The cottage would never be sold. The whole village would know what had been going on. What harm would that do to Julia? To Viviane?

I kept telling myself that I only had to get through the night. In the morning, God willing, Julia would wake up and the two of us could decide what to do for the best for Vivi. I had to find a way to get through the night.

I didn't want to be upstairs, but there was no way to bring Julia down so after I'd given her something to eat I took Viviane with me into the master bedroom. I pushed the chest of drawers up against the door and when Vivi asked why, I told her it was because of the wind.

'I don't want that door blowing open during the night,' I said. I am certain Vivi did not believe me for a moment.

The two of us squeezed into the bed with Julia, Vivi in the middle and me at the far edge. The sheets were damp and cold and smelled of sour milk. I lay on my back, wide awake, with my eyes open, praying that Vivi would fall asleep. She could hardly have slept at all in the last two days. Surely her body would give in soon?

But Vivi would not sleep. She lay beside me, stiff and

rigid, and her breathing was not rhythmic or slumbering and I could sense her tensing every time the scratching noise in the empty bedroom stopped, and then started again. The night was deeper, the hour was lonelier, but it seemed to me that the noise was angrier now, and more demanding. Julia's gentle snoring did nothing to soothe either me or Viviane.

'I need to go to Caroline,' Viviane whispered.

'No,' I said. 'You're staying here with me.'

'But she needs me!'

'Caroline can manage without you for one night.'

Vivi began to sob beside me.

'What is it now?' I asked, my temper as fractured as my nerves. I struggled to keep the frustration from my voice.

Vivi sniffed. 'Caroline says I should have given you sleeping pills too.'

I was a heartbeat away from shouting at the child, scolding her, telling her to stop being so ridiculous, to snap out of it. Vivi must know, somewhere in her mind, that Caroline was a fantasy she herself had created. I blamed myself for not acting more decisively. Perhaps I had made things worse by allowing Vivi to perpetuate the myth of the imaginary friend. What if, by not discouraging it more firmly, I had effectively held open the gate for Vivi to walk forward into severe psychological illness? I had thought Caroline was a strategy for the child to cope with her father's death. What if I had been wrong? What if Julia had been right about the dangers of allowing Viviane to talk with Caroline?

She was only ten years old and she had drugged her

own mother. She was claiming to have befriended a teenage girl who had died thirty years earlier. Dear God, Julia had been right, there was nothing healthy about that. In that dark, lonely room, I wrung out my anxieties, twisting every last drop of potential damage from them, and all the while the noises coming from the empty bedroom grew louder until, at last, there was a bang like a gunshot from the other side of the bedroom door. I felt it in my bones; it vibrated the walls of the cottage. Vivi, beside me, jumped physically – even Julia stirred and murmured: 'What's that?'

I couldn't bear to be in the cottage another moment.

'That's enough,' I said to Vivi. 'We're going.'

Vivi sat up at once. 'Where are we going? I can't go anywhere. I can't leave her!'

'Just for tonight, Vivi, just for one night. Come on.'

'No, Amy, I can't!'

I ignored Viviane's pleas. I climbed out of the bed, went to the door and pushed the chest of drawers out of the way. Vivi fidgeted behind me, staying close, whimpering.

'Wait here,' I told her.

I went into Vivi's room, grabbed her school clothes and stuffed them into a bag. I then went back out on to the landing, keeping my eyes averted from the door to the empty bedroom, and returned to the master bedroom. Julia was back soundly asleep. I put my head down close to hers and whispered, 'I'll be back in the morning, dear Julia. I promise I'll be back.' I placed her walking stick on the bed beside her, so that it was to hand, in case she should need it.

Vivi stood beside the bed, looking very small and scared. My heart filled, once again, with pity for the child. I took her hand. 'Come on, sweetheart,' I said. 'Let's get out of here.'

We left the cottage quickly, leaving the lights on inside, and hurried hand in hand through the winter night, through a fog so dense it was like rain. The wet air muffled our footsteps. Nobody was driving; nobody was out. The lake was obscured, the lights of Sunnyvale had been extinguished; the hooting of an owl was distorted.

The bag was heavy, the handles digging into my palm. I swapped hands. We turned and walked down the hill towards the lake.

Viviane was quiet now, she hadn't said a word since we left the cottage. I squeezed her hand. 'When it's foggy like this,' I said, 'it's like being invisible. Nobody can see us, nobody knows we're here.'

'So nobody would know if something bad happened to us.'

'Nothing bad is going to happen.'

Vivi was shivering. 'What about Mummy?'

'She's sound asleep, darling. No harm can come to her.'

'What if she wakes and we're not there?'

'She won't wake before morning.'

Vivi gave a sob. 'It's my fault.'

I stopped and put my arms around the child. 'No, no, darling, it's not your fault. You shouldn't have been left on your own like that. I shouldn't have left you both.'

'What if Mummy dies?'

'She won't die! Of course she won't. She just needs to sleep until the pills have worn off. Oh Vivi, darling, don't cry. Mummy will be fine, I promise you. We'll all be fine.'

We continued forward. The fog grew heavier the closer we came to the water, until it was so wet and heavy that it condensed on our skin and our hair like dew. We walked past the entrance to Fairlawn House, past the two lions on their columns. I glanced up at them, gazing down at us so fierce and ancient – and that was when I nearly lost my nerve.

'Nearly there,' I said cheerfully. 'Just a bit further.'

We disturbed a couple of ducks roosting on the verges of the pathway that led to the lodge. They quacked noisily as they ran from us and we heard the double splash as they escaped into the lake. I climbed the steps, knocked on the door, waited and knocked again, but Daniel did not come. So I stood on tiptoe, patted my hand along the ledge at the top and, thank goodness, found the spare key. I opened the door.

'Hello!' I called softly, but there was no answer and the lodge was in darkness.

'Come on,' I said and I led Viviane inside, closed the door. 'We can stay here for tonight. You can have a good rest.'

Daniel had drawn the curtains inside the lodge before he went out. I crossed to the bed and turned on the small lamp. The room was filled with a soft light, and with colour. I knelt and turned on the gas fire. Warmth billowed out. I held out my hands, felt the heat blow away the damp of the fog, and with it went my fear. I felt safe here. We would both be safe.

Viviane sat on the edge of the bed, yawned extravagantly and then kicked off her shoes and burrowed beneath the covers like a little mouse. By the time I reached her, she was already asleep, breathing deeply through parted lips, as if she were inhaling sleep, grabbing hold of it. Her lashes flickered against her cheeks. I tucked the sheets in around her shoulders, kissed her. Then I wandered over to the window. Where was Daniel? It was so late. What was he doing? I looked out through the curtains but I couldn't see anything; all that was out there was darkness, and although I knew the lake was there in all its still immensity, it was hidden by the fog. Anything could have been beyond the window, anything at all.

CHAPTER FORTY-FOUR

I woke suddenly the next morning. I opened my eyes and remembered where I was. The gas fire was turned down low, but the flames were still flickering, casting an orange light. Outside was still dark, the sun had not yet begun its ascent over the lake.

I was warm and comfortable in the big, soft bed but somebody in the room was snoring. I sat up and rubbed my eyes. Daniel was asleep on the rug by the fire, curled beneath mismatched blankets, his coat folded for a pillow, his socked feet sticking out of the end and one thin forearm extended at an angle. The sight of him filled me with tenderness. I had not heard him come in. He had made no attempt to wake me.

I went quietly into the bathroom and turned on the taps. The water was hot and the bath filled quickly. I shook out a towel and hung it over the radiator, then went to wake Viviane, my finger over my lips. When she saw Daniel, Viviane stared at him for a moment then asked, 'Is he your boyfriend?'

'Yes,' I said, although 'boyfriend' seemed too childish a word for whatever it was that was between us. 'Now go and wash yourself. Hurry. You're not to miss the school bus this morning.'

I waited while Viviane bathed and then I helped her dry and dress. She looked pale and poorly, but I thought the best I could do for her was to act as if everything was normal and stick to our routine. And it seemed to be what Vivi wanted too, because she made no protest about going to school.

Daniel was still sleeping when we left. Before we took the road up to the village, we walked down to the lake's edge. A white winter sun had burned away most of the fog; now, only drifts of mist hung above the water. A flock of white birds swept over the surface, and everything was white and silver and bright. I thought of Caroline again. She must have stood here too on mornings like this and looked out over the water. Did she imagine what it must be like to be a bird, to have the freedom to fly away, to leave?

Sometimes, I thought, I loved gazing out over the lake. Sometimes it was nothing more than an expanse of water, a mirror to the sky, a beautiful, benevolent waterscape and – oh! – those reflected greys and whites were so lovely that morning. I could have watched them for ever.

Vivi pulled at my sleeve. 'Come on,' she said, 'or I'll miss the bus.'

We walked up the hill. At the top, we looked back at the wisping haze floating over the lake, reflecting a strange and magical light. The windows of the Sunnyvale Nursing Home caught the early pink sunlight on the far side of the lake.

278

Vivi held tight to my hand, her fingers clutching mine through the wool of our gloves. She swung her arm. We smiled at one another.

The bakery was open and I had money in my purse. I bought a hot sausage roll for Viviane's breakfast and tucked a cheese salad sandwich and a bag of crisps into her satchel for later. When the bus came, Vivi climbed on board and was immediately gathered up by her friends. She found an empty seat by the window, raised her hand and pressed it against the glass, and I raised mine and pressed it against the other side of the window until the bus pulled away.

I turned to walk back to Reservoir Cottage. I hadn't gone far when I heard footsteps behind me and turned to see Daniel, hunched against the cold. He was jogging to catch up, his breath fogging around his face. He kissed my cheek and then smiled.

'Hi,' he said.

'Hi.'

'Are you OK?'

'I'm fine. I'm sorry we gatecrashed your place last night.'

'It was nice to get back and see you there in my bed.' His hands were in the pockets of his jacket. I linked my arm through his. 'What happened?' he asked.

'It's a long, complicated story.' I looked at the ground. 'I have to get back to the cottage. Julia's on her own and I'm worried about her. Can I call you later?'

'We could go and check on her together.'

'We could, but . . .' I knew that Julia was embarrassed, or worse, by the rift between the Cummings family and

279

the Aldridges. I did not fully understand it, not yet, but I was certain she would not be happy to wake in her vulnerable state to find Daniel in the cottage.

'And if she's all right, you can make me a cup of tea and tell me about your father,' he continued.

I shook my head. 'I'm sorry, Dan, but not right now. I need to talk to Julia alone.'

The words came out a little more harshly than I had meant them to. 'I'm sorry,' I said again. 'It's not that I don't want to talk to you.'

Daniel shrugged. 'No problem,' he said, and he turned and jogged away again, back down the lane.

CHAPTER FORTY-FIVE

The postman saluted as he cycled past and the grocer's van was delivering to one of the tucked-away houses. The sun was burning through but the lawns and rooftops still had a damp twinkle. Sparrows and pigeons were making a feast of the few remaining berries on the hedges in the garden and behind was the lake, pale blue now, a lovely soft colour. I watched a boat make its way slowly to the centre of the reservoir and then stop and I wondered if it was Mr Aldridge, gone out to be alone and to think of his lost love.

I looked up to the front of Reservoir Cottage and glimpsed a movement in my bedroom window. Was it Julia? I couldn't be sure it wasn't the reflection of a bird or a drifting leaf. As I stood there, gathering the energy to go inside, the front door of the adjoining cottage opened and Mrs Croucher stood on the doorstep, hunched and bedraggled in her housecoat and slippers. She coughed horribly into her hand, almost doubling over as the spasm wracked her lungs. I went to her at once.

'Oh gosh, Mrs Croucher, you don't look well. Can I help you?'

'I caught a chill, dear,' Mrs Croucher replied hoarsely. 'I'm feeling a bit under the weather. You've been away.'

'Yes.'

'There were noises in the nights – all night. I couldn't sleep.'

'What noises, Mrs Croucher?'

'Footsteps in your house. People going up and down the stairs.'

'I'm sorry you were disturbed, but I'm back now and—'

'It went on all night. Footsteps and bumping and banging, doors slamming. And in the end it was so bad that I thought there must be intruders in your cottage. So I picked up my fire poker and I went to look through the front-room window. I crept through the garden, up to the house and I was there, close to the glass, looking in – and then suddenly this face came looming out of the darkness. It came right up to the other side of the glass – and it was the girl's face! I almost fell over. I was so shocked. I thought it was *her*!'

'Who?'

'Caroline!' She coughed again, bent over, struggling to breathe. I put my arm around her.

'Please go back inside,' I said. 'It's so cold out here. Come on, let me see you in.'

The old lady allowed me to help her back inside her home, but was still talking, touching her neck, quivering with anxiety.

'She was making a face, you see, an ugly face, pulling back her lips and her eyes all wide. She was trying to scare me.'

'Oh, I'm sure she wasn't.'

'So I came back here,' Mrs Croucher said. 'I locked the doors and I went back to my bed but every time I closed my eyes I saw her face again. I saw her staring.'

'Well, you were tired,' I said. 'And it was dark, and you were upset. No wonder your mind played a trick on you. I'm so sorry you had to have all that worry.'

I ushered the old lady into the living room, lit the gas fire and persuaded her to sit beside it with a shawl around her shoulders while I put the kettle on to boil and telephoned the doctor's surgery. The doctor promised to come at once. I took a cup of tea and honey into Mrs Croucher and sat beside her rubbing her frail hands, trying to warm her up. Her chest wheezed terribly each time she inhaled and her eyes were red and watery, her skin an awful dun colour.

'The noises next door . . .' she said again.

'Oh, please don't get upset!' I begged. 'It won't happen again.'

'It sounded like they were moving things about.'

'It was just Viviane.'

'There were footsteps up and down the stairs.'

'Children can be so noisy.'

'It reminded me, you see. It reminded me of the night Caroline died.'

The old woman dropped the words into the air, into the cold air of the room where her husband used to hold his surgeries, and they hung there as if they were something physical, something real. Something important.

'The night Caroline died?' I repeated softly.

'Yes.'

'Why did it remind you of that night?'

'Because of the noises. The footsteps on the stairs. I heard them bringing her body down. I heard them bumping against the wall.'

I wanted to press my hands over my ears. I didn't want to hear any more, but Mrs Croucher kept talking.

'She'd been ill since they brought her back from the lake,' she said. 'She was getting worse. My husband told me that she was going to die, that it wouldn't be long. He was sitting with her. It had been quiet all evening.'

She was taking tiny little breaths, and the phlegm crackled in her lungs; her voice was weak and feeble, but she wanted to tell me about that night and I had no option but to hear her out.

'I went round to see if I could do anything to help, but Beinon – Mr Cummings – answered the door and he said they could manage. I asked how Caroline was and he shook his head. He just shook his head. And I said, "Thank goodness little Julia's not here," and he said: "Yes, that's the one thing we can be grateful for." Then he closed the door and I came back here, and I did some knitting and then I went up to bed. And I didn't expect to sleep, because you can't sleep, can you, not when you know that a person is dying next door, but I did – and then I was woken in the middle of the night and it was my husband, shaking me. "Wake up," he was saying. "Wake up, Olive! I've brought Cora round and I need you to look after her." I said: "Has Caroline passed?" and he said she had. So I came downstairs and I sat here, in the living room, with Cora. She was quiet.

She was like a statue. She just sat there, she wouldn't say anything, just sat there she did, gouging her nails into the backs of her hands, making them bleed. I couldn't leave her. I couldn't do anything. And we could hear the footsteps on the stairs next door.'

She paused to cough, and it was a terrible fit, the worst so far. As soon as she could draw breath she wiped her lips with her handkerchief and continued.

'So many footsteps. Firstly it was Beinon and my husband clearing up the room, up and down they went and we could hear their voices, just the murmur of them, and then the undertakers came and we could hear them clomping up the stairs in their boots, and then we heard the sound of them coming down again, with the body.'

She closed her eyes, and I heard the noises with her, the undertakers carrying Caroline down the stairs, her shoulders and feet bumping against the wall and her mother sitting here with Mrs Croucher, knowing what was happening, seeing it all in her mind's eye, her elder daughter wrapped in a shroud being manhandled down the narrow staircase.

'It must have been awful,' I said.

'And I looked at Cora's hands and they were bleeding. She'd made her own hands bleed. And I asked her to stop hurting herself and she looked at me as if she did not understand. She just stared at me as if she couldn't even see me. Her eyes were open but she, Cora, wasn't behind them any more. The woman I'd known, my neighbour, was gone. It was the start of her breakdown.'

'Grief does terrible things to people.'

'It wasn't because of the grief.' Mrs Croucher paused, hesitating. 'At least, not only because of that. It was because of what Caroline had done to Jean Aldridge three days earlier.'

'What had she done?' I asked, although I thought I knew the answer already.

'She pushed her into the lake,' said Mrs Croucher. 'She murdered her. Mrs Pettigrew, the vicar's wife, was walking back from the asylum. She saw it all.'

Mrs Croucher's hands settled on her lap. They picked at the hem of her housecoat. Her chest gurgled and wheezed.

'If that's what happened, why wasn't Caroline arrested?' I asked.

'We kept the whole business to ourselves,' she said. 'Nobody outside the village knew. We kept it from the children. If the police had been involved, Caroline would have been tried for murder and she'd have hung – and imagine the shame that would have brought to Blackwater. And what would it have done to poor Cora and Beinon, to little Julia? Nobody wanted that. The village committee decided to put Caroline in the asylum. She could stay there for the rest of her life, out of the way.'

'But she didn't go to the asylum?'

'No. She had a fever so they brought her home.'

'To die?'

'Yes. They brought her home to die. And it was all too much for Cora, one thing after the other – a murder and then a death – it was too much. She was sitting there, where you're sitting, and we could hear the footsteps on the stairs when they came to collect the body. We heard the undertakers struggling down the stairs. And oh, dear God, when you were away, all through the night all I could hear was the bumping and the banging, the footsteps – and all I could think of was Cora's face that night. It took me back there. It took me right back.'

Our elderly neighbour covered her face with her hands and wept. I put my arm around her. I felt the old skin and bones tremble beneath my touch. I felt the rattle in her chest.

CHAPTER FORTY-SIX

When the doctor came, I left Mrs Croucher with him and went back into Reservoir Cottage. I opened the curtains and turned off the lights, checked that the door to the empty bedroom was still locked then woke Julia, who was still drifting in her narcotic slumber.

I explained what had happened to her as gently as I could and then comforted her when, woozy and slow, she struggled to understand why her daughter would wish to drug her. I ran a bath and helped her into the water. While she soaked and warmed her aching bones, I took a bucket of bleach and a scrubbing brush into the empty bedroom.

'This is the end of it,' I said, not so much addressing Caroline as the bedroom, its walls, the hideous, glued-on paper. 'I've had enough of all of it.'

And I had. I was tired, I was sad and I was angry: with Vivi, with Caroline and with myself. Nobody, I thought, came out of the story I had just heard in a good light. I set to cleaning the writing off the walls with a vigour I hadn't felt before. '"I hate Jean Aldridge",' I muttered bitterly. 'Couldn't you at least have come up with something a bit more original, Caroline? Hmm?' And then I remembered that these words had been scrawled by a murderer, a teenage killer – a seventeen year old with a heart as black as sin. I shuddered. I could not bear to touch the letters, but kept the brush between my fingers and the wall.

Caroline must have written the words before she drowned Jean Aldridge. The writing was evidence of the hatred in her head. The killing was not a spur-of-the-moment crime, not something that happened in a flash of anger. Caroline had wished Jean dead. And of course this was what Dr Croucher hadn't wanted Cora or Julia to see; this was what he wanted to protect them from. This was why he and Beinon Cummings had glued paper over the walls of Caroline's bedroom immediately after her death, while little Julia was still on holiday. This explained everything.

I worked furiously and heard Julia release the water from the bath at the same time as I heard a car engine draw up outside. I crossed to the window and looked out. The local doctor's car was still parked outside Mrs Croucher's cottage and a second vehicle had pulled up behind. Painted on to the side of the vehicle were the words: *Mendip House Sales*.

A lanky, balding man climbed out of the driver's side and picked up a briefcase from the footwell. With him was a younger man, with a camera and a tripod. I was paralysed, torn between a desire to keep them out of the house, and an equally strong impulse to beg them to do whatever they could to sell the property as fast as possible. Both men looked up at the same moment and saw me standing at the window. I stepped back at once into the shadows, but it was too late: they knew I was there.

'Oh, bloody hell!' I said. I looked at the wall, the half-bleached writing. It would have to wait.

Julia was still in the bathroom. I locked the door to the empty bedroom, ran downstairs and met the men at the door with an approximation of a smile.

'We've come to take measurements and photographs,' the estate agent explained unnecessarily. He was dapper in a well-cut suit, shiny shoes, a fashionable, bootstring tie. His assistant was a shorter, stouter young man with soft, wavy hair and a rosy complexion.

'I'm afraid now is not a good time,' I said.

'We made the appointment with Mrs Laurent.'

'You'll have to come a different day.'

Julia hobbled down the stairs behind me, damp-haired, bleary-eyed and bath-soft, wearing a peach-silk dressing gown tied at the waist and a pair of Viviane's black rubber plimsolls. She was moving painfully slowly with her stick.

'Who is it?' she asked, peering over my shoulder. 'Oh, Mr Hardcastle! I thought you were coming on Thursday?'

'This is Thursday.'

Julia looked at me, confused.

'You've been asleep a long time,' I said gently.

She turned to the men again. 'I'm not feeling well and the place is a mess. Could you come back another day?'

'It's such good weather for photographs,' the assistant said, 'and the forecast isn't good for the next few days. Could we at least do the outside shots?'

Julia's hand was on my shoulder. She gave a little squeeze and whispered to me, 'Would you mind terribly showing them round, dear?'

'Of course not,' I said. My teeth were gritted.

I put on my coat and trailed back out into the cold again. I showed the estate agents the outside of the cottage, the front garden, tidy now, and the small garage, the coal-bunker, the wood-store, the long, narrow back garden and the brick shed. The agent stood with his hand shielding his eyes staring at the lake, and the lake, placid, pale, gave nothing of its nature away.

'You can't put a price on a view like this,' he said. 'People will pay good money for this kind of view. Take a photograph of the lake, Bob.' He looked considerably more cheerful than he had done earlier. Then, while his assistant set up the tripod, he turned to the shed.

'Mrs Laurent never mentioned this. It's a good-size outbuilding, solid. People like this kind of thing.' He tugged at the door. 'Can you open it?'

'We can't find the key.'

'It's a good selling-point, but not in its present condition. You'll need to clean it out and reinstate the window. Can you do that?'

'Yes, we can sort that out.'

'Good, good.' The estate agent rubbed his hands together. 'Things are looking up. We could market this cottage as being ideal for the small businessman, the entrepreneur. The new houses in Bishop Sutton have tiny gardens, no outbuildings. They can't compete with this. Take a picture of the shed next, Bob,' he said.

CHAPTER FORTY-SEVEN

The men worked quickly and had finished within the half-hour. Bob wound the film out of the camera and tucked the roll into his pocket. Mr Hardcastle shook my hand and made me promise to call as soon as the interior was ready to be photographed. As they were reversing their car out of the lane, an ambulance came bumping down in the other direction. It stopped outside Mrs Croucher's cottage. I called to Julia and we went outside to see the old lady being carried from her home into the ambulance, swaddled from her feet to her chin in blankets, and with an oxygen mask over her nose and mouth. The young doctor was with her.

'How is she?' Julia asked.

'It's pneumonia,' the doctor said, 'and she's dehydrated. We need to get her into hospital as quickly as possible.'

'Oh, you poor dear,' Julia said. She leaned over the stretcher and laid her hand gently on Mrs Croucher's forehead. 'Now you're not to worry, Olive. We'll let your husband know where you are and we'll keep an eye on the cottage for you. You concentrate on getting better.'

Mrs Croucher looked back at her with such tenderness. Julia smiled. 'Everything's going to be all right,' she promised. 'You'll see.'

Mrs Croucher closed her eyes and the ambulancemen placed her stretcher inside the vehicle. We watched the ambulance reverse carefully out of the lane, then Julia wrapped her arms around herself and shivered. 'I do hope she'll be all right,' she said.

We went back into the cottage. Julia sat at the kitchen table.

'Would you like something to eat?' I asked her.

She shook her head. 'I don't think I could keep anything down. I feel awfully sick. What a dreadful day this is turning into.'

'Would you like to lie down, dear? Shall I bring your pillows and blankets down and make you a bed on the sofa?'

'I've been lying down for too long. Thursday? It's Thursday already? I missed Wednesday altogether. I slept through it. Dear God.'

She was trying to make light of what had happened, but neither of us smiled.

'I sat with Mrs Croucher this morning while we waited for the doctor,' I said.

'Oh yes?'

'She was in a bad way. She . . . she told me about Caroline,' I said.

Julia looked up sharply. 'What about her?'

'That she killed Mrs Aldridge.'

'Oh.'

We were silent for a moment. Only the clock ticked.

Julia was gazing out of the window. Her cheeks were deeply flushed. I thought: There, it is out in the open at last.

I took a deep breath. I said: 'Now I understand why everything is as it is. I understand why you didn't want Vivi to go to the village school. I understand why Mr Aldridge hates the Cummings family and why you didn't want to talk to Daniel. I understand why he wouldn't say anything to me about his mother's death, why he always shied away from the subject. I can understand his reticence – it was out of consideration for you. But why didn't you tell me, Julia? Didn't you trust me?'

Julia sighed. 'Oh Amy, darling, it was nothing to do with trust. Why would I tell you something like that? I don't like to talk about it – I don't like even to think about it. I wish my mother had never brought me in on the secret.' She reached over for my hand. 'It was thirty years ago, a generation ago. I was a child when it happened. Most people my age don't know; the doctor and the vicar – those who did know – kept it quiet. It's only the old ones who remember. And now Mrs Pettigrew is gone, my mother and father are gone, Sir George and Lady Debeger are gone. In another decade, almost everyone who knew about it will be dead and it will be over, forgotten. Nobody at all will know that Caroline Cummings was a murderer. The less we talk about it, the less we remember, the sooner it will be finished with. The important thing – the main thing, Amy – is that Viviane doesn't find out about this. She must never know. She mustn't.'

'No,' I agreed.

'You won't say anything?'

'Oh Julia, no, of course I won't. I'll never breathe a word of it.'

I left her downstairs and went back up to the empty bedroom. I rolled up my sleeves and set to work, scrubbing away at the awful writing. I'd barely been at it for ten minutes when I was interrupted, once again, by a hammering at the front door. I looked down, and saw the vicar with a thickset man I did not recognize.

Oh for goodness' sake, I thought, what now?

I threw the brush into the bucket, went downstairs and opened the door.

'Yes,' I said brightly. 'What can I do for you?'

'Hello, Amy,' said the vicar. 'How are you?' He smiled a wide smile and he rubbed his hands together. A gust of wind lifted a strand of hair from the top of his head and then laid it down again.

He is one of those who knows, I thought. His wife witnessed the murder. Every time he passes this cottage, every time he speaks to me, he must be remembering what happened.

'Who is it?' Julia called from the back room.

'Nobody,' I called back.

I could not bring myself to smile at the vicar. 'I don't mean to be rude, but I'm rather busy,' I said. I indicated my apron, my tied-back hair, the tiny scraps of paper stuck to my stockings and forearms.

'It seems we came along at just the right moment,' said the vicar. 'I understand that you two ladies need help with the decorating.'

'No, we're fine, thank you,' I said.

'That's not what Dr Croucher told me.'

'Things have changed since I spoke to Dr Croucher.'

'Well, we're here now,' said the vicar. He nodded to the man beside him. 'This is Dafydd. He's a painter and decorator by trade and he owes the doctor a favour so we've persuaded him to give up an afternoon for you. Isn't that right, Dafydd?'

The man nodded. 'That's right,' he said.

'That's very kind,' I said, 'but we don't need any help.'

The vicar's expression had become decidedly less jolly. He adjusted his dog collar. 'Can't we at least come in and talk about it?'

'Amy? Who is it?' Julia appeared at my shoulder. 'Oh, hello, Vicar.'

'Mrs Laurent, I was just telling young Amy here—'

'The vicar was just leaving,' I interrupted. 'We appreciate you coming round, but we can manage the work ourselves. Thank you.'

I shut the door, turned my back to it and leaned on it. We could hear gruff voices on the other side, the vicar disgruntled, the other man annoyed.

'Oh, go away, you fussy, interfering old chauvinist,' I hissed.

Julia, in the gloom of the hallway, said, 'Amy, you just shut the door in the vicar's face! That was a terribly naughty thing to do.'

She widened her eyes and bit her lip. I stared back at her for a second, and then the two of us began to laugh. We covered our mouths with our hands to stifle the laughter but it bubbled up behind. The more I tried to contain it, the more I laughed until I was weeping with laughter, and Julia was too. I slid down the wall and crumpled on the floor with my head on my knees and I laughed and laughed until my sides ached. Our laughter spread through the old cottage. It echoed down from upstairs. It was only the echo, but it seemed to me that the laughter was coming from the empty bedroom too.

CHAPTER FORTY-EIGHT

By chance, Daniel drove by in his jeep while I was waiting to meet Viviane off the school bus that afternoon. I waved him down, and when he stopped and wound down the window I said, 'I'm sorry about this morning. I shouldn't have been short with you.'

'No,' Daniel smiled, 'you shouldn't have. That kind of behaviour doesn't bode well for our future happiness.'

'I'll do my best to ensure it doesn't happen again,' I laughed.

'I would appreciate that.' He leaned his elbow on the vehicle's doorframe and poked his head out. I reached up to kiss him. I kissed him for a long time and, when I had done so, he said: 'What did I do to deserve that?'

'You never told me the whole truth about your mother's death. You never told me that Caroline was involved.'

'I knew you would find out sooner or later.'

'You were right, I did. And Julia knows that I know and she is afraid that you will hate her.'

'How could I hate her? I've never even met her. And I

don't blame her for her sister's actions. I never have and I never will.'

'Then you must be acquainted as soon as possible. I think you would both like one another very much. And perhaps it will be better now that the truth is out in the open.'

'No more secrets between us.'

Only the pendant in the satchel under the bed. I would find a way to tell him. I would think of something. But in the meantime I wanted an excuse to invite him round to the cottage. I wanted him to meet Julia.

I told him about the shed, and how it had been padlocked shut and that we needed to open and clear it and that I didn't know how to set about doing so.

'How thick is the chain that holds the padlock?' he asked.

'About this wide.' I showed him with my fingers.

'Would bolt-cutters do the trick?'

'I'd imagine so.'

'Then I'm your man. Is there anything else?'

I glanced past him down the hill. The school bus was chugging up towards us. 'Could you get me some emulsion paint, just ordinary white paint, the thicker the better? I'll need a lot, at least a gallon.'

'What for?'

'To paint one of the bedrooms.'

'I'll do it for you.'

I thought of the words on the wall that I'd bleached, but which were still faintly visible: *I hate Jean Aldridge, I wish she was dead.* No matter that we all knew the truth now, I still could not let Daniel see those words. I couldn't hurt him like that and neither could I expose Julia to the shame.

'No, Daniel. I just need the paint, that's all.' I looked back to the bus. It was labouring around towards the stop. 'I'll give you the money.'

'You know I don't need the money. Why won't you let me help you?'

'It's just something I have to do myself.'

The school bus pulled up behind the jeep. The door opened and Viviane climbed off, dragging her bag behind her. I could tell at once from her demeanour that she was not in a good mood.

'I'd better go,' I said. 'It looks like there may be trouble ahead.'

'I'll come by with the cutters later,' Daniel said.

'Thank you.' I kissed my fingers and put them to his cheek.

Viviane sidled up as the jeep drove away.

'Hello, sweetheart.' I put my arm around her, but she shrugged me off. 'Are you tired, darling?'

'No.'

'Then what's the matter?'

'Nothing.'

'Did something happen at school?'

Viviane looked at me sideways from under her fringe. 'I had some extra coaching with Mr Leeson at lunchtime.'

'Singing coaching?'

'Maths. To make up for the lessons I missed.'

'That's good of him to help you.'

'I don't want to do the coaching.'

301

'But darling, you need to catch up with everyone else.'

'I hate maths.'

'You'll like it better when you understand it more.'

'I'm no good at it.'

'I'm sure that's not true but even if it is, it doesn't matter. You can't be good at everything. And I bet you're way ahead of everyone else in French.'

Vivi kicked a pebble. 'Also I don't want to be in the choir any more.'

'Why ever not?'

'I just don't. I've got to do the extra coaching and it's not fair that I have to do choir as well.'

'I thought you liked the choir. And it's your concert at Sunnyvale tomorrow. Oh, that's what it is! You're nervous about performing in public. But you mustn't be, darling, really you mustn't; I heard you singing during your practice in the church and you were wonderful. You sounded like an angel. Honestly, you'll be the star of the show.'

'I don't want to do it,' Vivi said. There was a tremble in her voice. 'Please don't say I have to.'

'Let's see what Mummy says.' I pulled Viviane close, tipped back her hat and kissed her forehead. 'Remember that you are very loved,' I said. 'Always remember that.'

I put Viviane's mood down to tiredness. Back at the cottage, she went upstairs to change, and when I checked on her a few moments later, she was asleep, sprawled across the bed. I went back downstairs and recounted the conversation about the concert to Julia while I prepared supper.

'She's adamant she doesn't want to sing for the old people.'

'Well, I shan't make her do it if she really doesn't want to,' Julia said. 'But I feel that she ought to do it, not least because that school has been so accommodating with her.'

'It might be good for her confidence too. She has such a lovely voice, and she doesn't realize how talented she is.'

'I'll telephone the school in the morning and have a word with Mr Leeson,' Julia decided. 'I'll see what he says about it. In his time he must have dealt with a thousand cases of first-night nerves.'

CHAPTER FORTY-NINE

D aniel was as good as his word. He came to the cottage later, just after dusk. Julia came out to say hello and they shook hands. It seemed enough to start with. After that I took the torch and led him down to the shed, past the old swing and the winter-dead shrubs, past the old washing-line. Daniel looked at the bolt, and the padlock securing the shed door. 'It's like Fort Knox,' he said. 'Someone wanted to make sure nobody got in there.'

He lifted the chain, felt its weight, dropped it and then he took out his cutters.

'Turn your face away, Amy,' he said, 'in case it splinters.' And then he squinted to protect his own eyes and held the two blades of the cutters over the thick chain.

It took a while but eventually I heard the grating sound as the cutter blades finally made contact with one another and then the clank and slither as the chain slipped through its housing and clattered to the ground. I turned to see Daniel leaning on the bolt, putting all his weight on to it. It would not budge.

'It's stuck solid,' he said. 'I need a hammer.'

He took the torch and disappeared back up the garden and I stood there, on my own, by the shed watching the swing of the beam of light from his torch until I lost sight of it behind the house. I looked up, sensing that someone was watching me. Viviane's face was at her bedroom window. I waved, but although she seemed to be looking directly at me, she did not wave back. Her light was on and I must have been invisible. Her chin was in her hands, her elbows resting on the window ledge. She tilted her head as if she were listening to something, and then her lips moved. Julia was in the back room; Viviane was not talking to her mother, she was talking to Caroline.

When Daniel returned, he asked me to hold the torch and I took it in both hands, directing the beam of light at the rusted bolt while he banged at it with the hammer. The noise was terrible, a tremendous reverberation through the quiet night air, so loud I imagined it making ripples on the surface of the lake. He hit the bolt a dozen times then pushed it with the flat of his hand, rocking it from side to side . . . and finally it slid open.

It took both of us, using all our strength, to pull the door open wide enough to look inside. The old hinges protested and did their best to hold the door back, but we persisted. A puff of air, slightly warmer than the outside air and smelling foul, of smoke and age, came from inside. Daniel picked up the torch and shone the beam into the shed. I was almost sick with anticipation. I told myself to buck up. What was the worst that could be in there? Mice, perhaps? Spiders?

I made myself look. In the beam of light I saw there was a small concrete step down into the shed, old, water-stained lino on the floor, a square of carpet wet and foul-smelling and almost completely disintegrated. The inside walls were black, sooted. The shed was full of junk. There was furniture, the criss-cross metal springs of the base of a single bed, an old mattress, horribly stained, boxes made of wood, a suitcase, a dressing-table mirror, a small stool and a table, a water-colour paintbox, splayed open. Cardboard boxes left on the floor had disintegrated, their contents ruined, but there were other things; clothes had been bundled together and thrown inside, and there were books, and toys. I picked up a small bottle from the floor. *Ashes of Roses* was inscribed on the glass. It looked as if Dr Croucher and Mr Cummings had simply gathered all of Caroline's possessions and thrown them into the shed before they sealed it shut.

I took a step forward.

'Don't let the door close on me, Daniel,' I said.

The beam of the torch swayed madly from the floor to the roof and back again.

'There's something written on the wall – there,' Daniel said. He pointed to scratches on the wall, four short vertical lines struck through with a single horizontal one. The scratches disappeared back into the darkness behind the clutter. 'Someone was counting something.'

'Julia used to play house in here. Maybe it was her.'

'And there's writing.'

'What does it say?'

306

'I can't tell. The brickwork is scorched.'

I pulled the metal bedframe away from the rest of the clutter and tried to make sense of what Daniel was showing me, but I could not. Behind me on the floor was a large trunk, secured by heavy-duty leather straps. I tugged at the straps but I could not move the trunk. Daniel tried to help me, but it was wedged solid. He put his hand on my shoulder.

'There's too much weight on top,' he said. 'We can try again in daylight. There's no hurry, is there?'

There was not, but I felt compelled to move the trunk.

'I just want to get all this stuff out, get it out into the open and sort it out and then get rid of it. I won't be happy until that's done,' I said.

'It must have been like this for decades, Amy. A few more hours won't make any difference. We'll come back to it tomorrow, in the daylight.'

'Can't we just move the trunk?'

'Tomorrow,' Daniel said. 'I'll come and help you tomorrow.'

CHAPTER FIFTY

Viviane and her friend Anaïs were standing in the sunshine by the pool at the back of Les Aubépines; they were in their swimsuits, their wet hair making rats' tails down their skinny little backs, playing a clapping game. Julia and Alain were sitting together at the table, beneath the shade of the umbrella. A half-empty bottle of wine was on the table between them. Alain was smoking, he was reading the newspaper, one hand on Julia's knee. I felt a rush of love and relief. *Alain!* I called and Alain looked towards me and smiled; he raised his other hand, the cigarette between the second and third fingers.

'I thought you were dead!' I called.

Alain looked down at himself, gave his stomach a poke, raised his eyebrows and shook his head.

'No, it seems I'm perfectly alive.'

'Oh, thank goodness!'

Julia pushed her sunglasses up on to the top of her head and smiled. 'Oh Amy, you are funny,' she said. 'You must have dreamed it and believed it was true!' She tipped back her head and laughed and Alain laughed too. The relief made me giddy and now I was closer to the edge of the pool. I was watching the girls and I was holding somebody else's hand and the hand I was holding was merging with mine, the skin between our fingers fusing, the nerves and capillaries weaving together, the bones splicing. The hand that was holding mine was like marble and my fingers were calcifying too. I tried to pull my hand away but I couldn't, it had become part of the other hand. My eyes travelled from the marble hand to a marble wrist, an elbow, a shoulder, a face; grape-coloured lips, dark hair. And all the beauty of the place turned ugly; the warmth turned cold. My relief turned to horror.

I was joined to Caroline and Caroline was dead.

I tried to scream, but I could not scream. I tried to run away, but I could not run. I was paralysed, turned to stone, and I was panicking, subsumed by panic like a mouse caught by its tail in a trap, like a moth in an upturned jar. I was helpless, melded to the dead murderess with her cold, dead eyes, her black nails, the awful soft rottenness of her.

Caroline held a finger to her lips. 'Shhh,' she said. 'Watch the children.'

The girls were oblivious; they stood clapping, water running down their bodies and darkening the dry paving beneath their bare feet. The blue mosaic tiles that lined the swimming pool sparkled bright in the sunlight and there was the usual jumble of coloured towels heaped at the end of the sunbeds, the orange bottle of Ambre Solaire oil tipped on its side; the red airbed bobbing on the water. Everything was as it should be. Everything was exactly as it always was, except that Caroline was there too.

I looked at her again and I saw that she had no eyes, that there were dark holes in her skull where her eyes should have been; her lips were dust, blown away by her breath, and her teeth were loose, falling from her mouth and bouncing on the paving like tiny white pearls, like beads from a broken necklace.

'Why are you here?' I asked her.

'Because of Viviane.' Caroline tightened her cold fingers over mine and her hair drifted away on the breeze like dandelion seeds. The skin was falling like ashes from her body; bone, glossy as paint, was exposed in her wrist, at her shoulder; the muscle of her heart was dry beneath the cage of her ribs. 'They're watching. They never went away.'

I woke in a cold sweat, a stillborn scream in my throat.

There was no chance of sleep after that. I turned on the light and tried to read but the nightmare was still too fresh in my mind. I slipped out of bed and pulled out the satchel from under it. I took out the matchbox, and the pendant. The pendant sat in the palm of my hand, the ruby dark red, like blood.

I wanted rid of the thing that Caroline, the murderess, had stolen. It was like a bad omen, a cursed talisman; she was the last person to have touched it before me and it was my secret under my bed. I didn't want it anywhere near me.

I decided I would throw it into the lake. I would drown it just as Caroline had drowned Mrs Aldridge. It would sink through that green water, down to the darkness at the bottom, and it would lie there, in the silt, with the silvery trout weaving above it, the light shining dimly in the deep. It would be one more secret, and when I was gone, even that secret would be forgotten.

CHAPTER FIFTY-ONE

Viviane dressed herself and came down for breakfast on time the next morning. She ate her porridge and drank her milk politely and neatly. She sat very still, with the heels of her shoes hooked over the wooden bar between the two front legs of her chair. I brushed her hair for her, and fastened it with a grip to keep the fringe out of her eyes.

'How are you feeling, sweetheart?' Julia asked.

'All right.'

'Are you nervous about the concert?'

She shook her head.

'You're going to be fine,' her mother promised. 'You're going to be the best of them all.'

Later, after Viviane had left for school, I went back to work alone on the wallpaper. I found more writing beneath the window – neat, unhurried letters decorated with tiny drawings of birds and flowers and floating musical notes.

'Bye bye, blackbird,' I whispered and I remembered how I knew that song. My mother used to sing it to me as we sat together in the bomb shelter in the back yard of the house in Sheffield, two inches of water on the ground and the candlelight flickering. It must have been cold and uncomfortable, frightening even, but I only remembered my mother's voice, and the song, the feeling of being safe and warm and loved, in her arms.

I blew my hair off my face, sat back on my heels and considered Caroline's transcription of the song lyrics. The words were so different, so gently written, in comparison to the hatred that had been scratched into the adjoining walls. I chipped away at another piece of paper and I found a drawing of a heart, a heart enclosed by two clasped hands. Inside the heart were two names: *Caroline and Robert*. Beneath was written, in very tiny letters: *Mrs Caroline Aldridge*.

'Oh Caroline,' I breathed. I leaned back against the wall.

And suddenly everything made complete sense; in fact, it all seemed quite simple to me. Caroline wasn't mad or evil or out of control; she was simply a teenager in love.

She had gone to work as Jean Aldridge's housemaid. While she was there at Fairlawn, she had fallen for Robert, a good-looking, charismatic man who would have been closer in age to Caroline than to Jean. Perhaps the Aldridge marriage had seemed wrong to Caroline. Perhaps Jean had seemed, to young Caroline, not enough for Robert. Either way, the girl was jealous and Jean was the obstacle in the way of her perceived happiness. Did Caroline steal the pendant, to make herself feel closer to Robert? Did Jean suspect her of the theft? Did Jean confront Caroline when the two women met, that sunny August day as Jean pushed her son along the dam in his pram? Did they fight? Jean had had a baby a few days earlier. She would have been weak. She wouldn't have stood a chance.

'But did you have to kill her, Caroline?' I asked quietly. 'Just because she was in your way?'

I carried on working and the room seemed to be vindicating my version of events. The vile yellow wallpaper was coming away from the walls more easily than before. It was as if the room was relieved now that the secrets were being exposed.

That morning, I cleared the rest of the window wall; now the only wallpaper that remained was a small patch on the chimney breast that had been so thoroughly glued on, it was impossible to remove. I had found one more message from Caroline: a single line of writing about twelve inches from the bottom of the wall. Smaller letters now, the writing very faint and shaky.

They are watching Julia.

I sat down and leaned my back against the wall, resting my elbows on my knees. I looked about the room. If Caroline's bed had been placed at right angles to the wall facing the door, then she could have written these words while she was in the bed. She might have written them in her last hours, as she lay dying. But that didn't help me. I didn't know what they meant, or why they had been written. I didn't know who was watching Julia, or why Caroline had felt it so important to write the words down.

Was it a warning?

Did she know she was dying?

314

The pattering of rain on the windowpane reminded me that time was passing. I stood, and went downstairs to find Julia. A draught was blowing in from the back door. I looked outside and saw her in the garden, leaning over a large object: the trunk. Somehow or other she had dragged it out of the shed, on her own.

CHAPTER FIFTY-TWO

I put on my boots and ran out through the rain. 'What are you doing, Julia? It's pelting down. Aren't you frozen?'

Julia wiped the rain from her nose with her wrist, leaning on her thigh, resting her hip.

'This trunk used to be in my parents' bedroom. It was where they kept all their special things. My father's war mementoes were in there, his medals, and Mother's best linen, my silver christening mug. Why did they put the trunk in the shed, Amy?'

'I don't know, but leave it now and come inside. You're soaked through, you'll catch your death.'

'I can't leave it here. Help me get it up to the house.'

'We'll never move it. It weighs a ton.'

'If you help me we'll move it together.'

'Julia!'

'Oh, come on. Don't give up before you've even tried.'

Julia leaned over the trunk and heaved at it. The rain fell on her back and shoulders, dripping from the ends of her hair, and her shirt was so wet that I could see her skin through it – the ridges of her spine, her shoulder-blades, even her ribs.

I puffed out my breath and took hold of the other handle.

It took the two of us working together to manhandle the trunk up the slope to the level part of the garden, me doing most of the donkey work. After that we dragged it to the back door. Its weight and bulkiness alarmed me. I was afraid of what might be inside.

We manoeuvred the trunk up the step and into the kitchen. By now we were both soaked to the skin and my back and arms were aching.

'Right!' Julia said. 'Now all we have to do is get it open,' and she set to hacking at the leather straps with a pair of upholstery scissors.

'It'll take you forever with those,' I panted.

Julia ignored me. She drove the point of the scissors into the old leather strap and twisted it, trying to make a hole. The trunk groaned and she grunted with the exertion.

'Julia, please, I'm afraid the scissors will slip. Let me call Daniel. He'll have the tools to open it in a jiffy.'

'I can't wait. I need to know what's inside.'

'Why is it so important that you open the trunk at once?' I asked. 'Why can't it wait?' Although I knew the answer to that question. I had felt the same compulsion the day before, when I was in the shed. I watched Julia helplessly for a few moments, and then my eyes were drawn to the clock on the wall.

'Did you remember to call the school?' I asked.

317

'Yes. I spoke to Mr Leeson. He said it's best that Vivi sings at the concert.'

'Oh.'

'He said he understands that she's feeling apprehensive but if she doesn't face up to her fears now, she'll only find it harder next time she faces a challenge.'

'That makes sense.'

'Anyway, he's going to arrange for her to have tea at the school, so she doesn't have to come home in between. That way, she can go straight to the concert with her friends and she won't have time to start worrying.'

'That's a good idea.'

Julia pushed the wet hair from her face. 'Yes, I thought so too. He's a good man, Eric Leeson. Did I tell you I used to be at school with him?'

'Yes, you mentioned it.'

'He was a bright boy. He had all these big ideas about becoming a scientist and going to work for the Space Agency in America, but all that went out of the window when his father died. He had to stay in Blackwater and look after his mother. Teaching was the most academic career he could pursue around here. And I suppose it was nice that he followed in his father's footsteps.'

'Eric's father was the old schoolteacher?'

'Yes, that's right. Frank, he was called.'

'And Frank was the one who was on the village committee?'

'Yes.'

'What was he like? As a teacher, I mean.'

'I owe a great deal to him. Without his help and

encouragement, I never would have got the scholarship into dance school.'

Julia laid down the scissors and sat back on her heels. 'He wasn't nice to everyone, though.'

'No?'

'Once he'd taken against someone, he used to humiliate them awfully.'

'Someone like Caroline?'

'Yes. Exactly.'

'What did he do?' I asked.

'Oh . . . He used to compare the two of us, always in ways that were disparaging to her. He did it in front of other people, in front of her too so she had to listen while he was running her down.'

'What kind of things did he say?'

'That I had inherited the looks *and* the brains in our family. That he had always known I would go a long way and that she would never amount to anything. That it was remarkable how different two sisters could be, one so precious and one so . . .' She trailed off for a moment as she remembered '. . . worthless.' Julia looked towards the window, at the rain running down the glass. I followed her eyes. The raindrops were like tears, endless tears, millions of them falling over the valley.

'That's so cruel,' I said.

'Yes, but that was all we knew at the time. School was a meritocracy. Diligent, well-behaved children like me and Eric were rewarded. And those who didn't behave were punished.'

'Beaten with the slipper?'

'The slipper . . . yes. I had forgotten. Mr Leeson made

them bend over a chair in his office.' The tiny shadows of the raindrops running down the windowpane dappled Julia's face so it seemed as if she were crying shadowy tears of light, echoing those outside. 'Some children were beaten every Friday.'

'Caroline?'

Julia nodded.

'Didn't she ever complain to your parents?'

'No, she would never have done that. She wouldn't have received any sympathy! They'd have told her that she must have done something to deserve the punishment, that it was for her own good. She was terribly proud, you know, Amy. When she came out of Mr Leeson's office she would hold her head up and she wouldn't cry. She always said that she didn't care that he beat her; she said he could hit her every day if he wanted, she would never care.'

The wind blew the rainclouds along the valley. For a moment a ray of sunshine beamed through and lit up the rain on the window, illuminated Julia's face. She smiled. Then the smile faded.

'When I was in London, I once met somebody who went to Blackwater village school,' she said. 'It was an old friend, Martha Clarke. We went for coffee together and we talked about the school. She was one of those Mr Leeson didn't rate, but she had become a lawyer. She told me that he used to make the children take down their underwear when he was punishing them, boys and girls. None of them ever said anything, of course, because they knew they'd be accused of lying, of being rude and vulgar.'

'Good God. Do you think it was true?'

'I don't know. At the time I thought it was a ridiculous accusation to make but later I wondered about it. What reason did she have to lie?'

Julia stood up. She went across to the window and rested her forehead against the glass.

'I couldn't ask Caroline, she was long dead and so was Frank Leeson. There was nothing I could do about it. I put it from my mind.'

She traced the progress of a raindrop down the windowpane with her finger.

'No, of course it wasn't true,' she said. 'How could it have been? It's unthinkable that a person of authority would really do something like that. Mr Leeson was the headmaster, for goodness' sake! He was on the village committee. He was a member of the local education board. He used to give inspirational talks to the Women's Institute. He was treasurer of the Church of England Headmasters' Association. He wouldn't . . . he would never . . . oh dear God, Amy, a person like him simply would not conceive such a thing!'

We looked at one another. I could see the exact pale colour of Julia's eyes, the tiny dark rim around her pupils, the flecking of the bluey colour over the pale aquamarine. I could see the colour and I could see my doubt reflected in Julia. For a few moments neither of us spoke; I am sure the same thoughts were going through our separate minds.

'I can't bear to think of it,' Julia said eventually. 'Caroline was *always* in trouble. She was *always* sitting outside that man's office, she and her sidekick, Susan

Pettigrew. What if it *was* true? If he made her do that, if he humiliated her like that, might that not explain some of her subsequent confusion? Her hatred of authority?'

I took hold of her hand.

'If it was true,' Julia whispered, 'then it went on for years and nobody did anything to protect her, or the others. Nobody helped her; she had nobody to turn to. Nobody.'

The two of us sat together, in silence. The rain fell outside. It fell into the reservoir and it fell on to the hills. It streamed down the windows of Reservoir Cottage. It fell on to the church, on to the churchyard. It soaked into the earth that lay above the lonely grave of Caroline Cummings and through the white marble chippings that covered the final resting-place of Jean Aldridge. It ran down the windows of the village school and was carried away by the guttering into the drains, and the drains took it down to the lake and all the new water became part of the old, part of the reservoir, part of the valley.

'Fetch Daniel,' Julia said. 'Fetch him now, Amy. Tell him to open the trunk. We need to know what's inside.'

CHAPTER FIFTY-THREE

I put on my coat and went to find Daniel. I saw him, from a distance, on the other side of the upper field. He was blurred by the rain and at least a hundred sheep were between us, the animals streaming towards me like a force of nature, like water running downhill. The tricolour collie was herding them. I stepped sideways, to be out of their way, and I waited as they ran past and were funnelled through the gate. The collie's ears were flat back against her head; she was panting, stressed – she did not seem to notice me.

Daniel followed after the sheep. He came straight over to me, took my face in his hands and kissed me deeply.

'What's wrong?' he asked. 'Why are you here and all out of breath?'

'I've been running. I needed to find you. Can you come to the cottage?'

'I was going to pick up the paint this afternoon and drop it by later.'

'Julia wants you to come now. She's desperate to open the trunk that was in the shed.'

'I need to get the ewes penned, Amy. If I'm not ready when the wagon comes we'll end up sending the wrong sheep away.'

'I know, but—'

'I'll come as soon as I can, as soon as I've finished this. That's the quickest I can be. The wagon will be here in an hour. I'll come straight after that.'

'OK.'

'Will that do?'

'Yes, that'll be fine. Thank you.'

Daniel put his arm around my shoulders. 'Walk back up the hill with me. I'll show you something.'

We trudged up together towards the sheep, which were huddling together, eyeing us suspiciously from the higher ground. When we reached a rocky outcrop, Daniel turned me around so I was looking back towards the valley. From where we stood, there was an excellent view of Fairlawn, the house standing proud in its gardens. The lodge, behind, was obscured by the skeleton trees.

'It's beautiful,' I said.

'I always loved this view.'

'I love it too.'

'And one day,' Daniel said, 'all of this will be ours.'

'Ours?'

'We could live there, you and I, if you'd like to.'

'I think I would like to.'

'There would be room for plenty of children.'

'Then we should make sure plenty of children lived there.'

We smiled at one another.

'What about your father?' I asked.

'He'll come round to the idea,' Daniel said.

I lifted my face up and Daniel leaned down to kiss me. I closed my eyes so that the rain would not fall into them. While we were kissing there was a call from the direction of the lane. Daniel's father and another man were standing by the pens at the top of the field, by the gate.

Daniel acknowledged the men with a wave.

'Amy, my darling, I've got to go. I'll be round at the cottage later, as soon as I can.'

'OK.'

I turned and walked away from him, back to the entrance of the field and then on through the village. And that's when I saw Susan Pettigrew. She was carrying a shopping basket and she was heading towards the vicarage.

I didn't stop to think about what I was doing. I went after her.

CHAPTER FIFTY-FOUR

I had never been to the vicarage before. It was a tidy house of modest size. There was nothing grand or ostentatious about it and the exterior, at least, was masculine in its austerity – a concreted front garden, a couple of ugly pots with equally ugly, spiky bushes growing out of them. I had seen Susan go inside only a few minutes earlier, but she took a long time opening the door to me. When she did, she peered around the edge with suspicion.

'My father is out,' she said.

'Good. It's you I want to see.'

'I haven't done nothing wrong,' Susan said.

'I know you haven't,' I said. 'I just want to talk to you.'

'What about?'

'About your friend Caroline.'

'I'm not supposed to let anyone in when my father isn't here. Especially not strangers.'

'But you know me,' I said. 'I'm not a stranger.'

Susan hesitated still. I should have stuck up for her the last time I saw her, I thought. She doesn't trust me.

'Where is your father?' I asked gently.

'At Sunnyvale. They're getting ready for the concert this evening. But he'll be back soon.'

'Please, Susan, let me in. I'll be ever so quick. And if your father comes back while I'm here I'll tell him it was my fault.'

'He'll say it was mine for letting you in.'

'Then I'll make sure he doesn't see me. I promise I won't let you get into trouble again.'

She bit her lip.

'Please,' I said.

She opened the door reluctantly and I stepped into a gloomy hallway lined with bookcases and dark, religious images. The inside of the vicarage smelled of cauliflower and Vim scouring powder.

'We'd best go into the kitchen,' Susan said, 'then we'll see him coming.'

She was not, I realized, as simple as she made out.

She showed me into a square, joyless room. The cupboards, the cooker and the sink were old and shabby and there was no colour in the room, but everything was clean. The shopping basket was on the counter and ingredients were laid out beside the cooker for a meal: bread, potatoes, onions, a packet of meat. A huge twin-tub washing machine was rattling in one corner, and there was a mangle beside it. Susan shuffled forward and picked a bundle of parish newsletters off one of the chairs, gesturing that I should sit there. She sat in the opposite chair and looked at her lap and twisted the fingers of her hands together, as if she were waiting for an accusation. I didn't know how to start to ask her the questions I wanted to ask. I didn't want to alarm her by being too direct and I didn't want to upset her by bringing back memories she'd probably spent a lifetime suppressing. So I dithered and she waited and the silence became uncomfortable.

'I have heard some things about Caroline,' I said finally, 'and I don't know what to believe.'

Susan's cheeks coloured slightly, but she did not move.

'You've tried to tell me about her, haven't you?' I asked. 'You've tried but other people keep stopping you.'

The woman shrugged. She was wearing a housecoat over an awful, beige-brown jumper with sweat stains under the arms, and those same ugly trousers I'd seen her in before.

'It's the past. It's best forgotten,' she mumbled.

'Well, that's what everyone says, even Julia, but I'm not sure that that's right. What do you think, Susan?'

She shrugged again. The washing machine slowed and began a rhythmic sloshing. The smell of detergent in the room was making it hard to think straight.

I looked at my watch. The minutes were going by.

'I know what the schoolteacher made you do,' I said, 'when he was punishing you.'

In a heartbeat a deep red flush spread from Susan's neckline to her jaw and her cheeks. She coloured so violently that I was afraid for her. The flush had told me everything I needed to know. What Julia had heard was true. Anger rushed up through me like boiling water through a geyser. I had to fight to contain it. Carefully,

I breathed, counting the breaths in and out, and when I could trust my voice to be calm, I asked, 'Have you ever mentioned this to anyone?'

Susan moved her head very slightly to the left, and then back to the right.

'Frank Leeson was a wicked man,' I said. 'You were not bad children – *he* was the one who should have been punished.'

Still Susan looked down. She would not meet my eye.

'The thing is,' I went on, 'the other things I've heard about Caroline – most of them are bad. Perhaps some are true. I don't know. You are the only person in this village I can trust to tell the truth.'

Susan twisted her hands together. The washing machine rattled and clanked.

'My father will be home in a minute,' she whispered.

'You're afraid to speak out, aren't you? Well then, how about I tell you what I know about Caroline and you tell me if I get anything wrong.'

She said nothing. I took that as acquiescence.

'OK then. I know that Caroline was your friend.'

Silence.

'Your best friend. And that you two were inseparable. You did everything together.'

'Inseparable,' Susan repeated softly.

'And that people – adults – weren't always kind to you.'

Silence.

'So you grew up, and after you left school I assume you went to work at the asylum, as it was then.'

'Yes.'

'And Caroline found a job working as a maid for Mrs Aldridge at Fairlawn House.'

'Yes. The committee found the jobs for us.'

'The committee?'

'Yes.' Susan nodded more emphatically.

I thought about this for the briefest moment and of course it made sense. The teacher, the doctor, the vicar and the politician – between them they would have the authority to slot the village's difficult-to-employ young people into available roles.

'Did you know Mr and Mrs Aldridge?' I asked Susan.

Silence again.

'Robert was an awful lot younger than his wife, wasn't he? Some people thought it was a marriage of convenience. Mrs Aldridge needed a husband from a respectable family and Mr Aldridge needed money.'

'And Sir George Debeger was going to help Mr Aldridge get into politics,' Susan added.

'Did he want to be a politician?'

'Honour thy father and mother.'

'He was told that's what he had to do?'

Silence. A bird flew across the window, casting a shadow into the room. The movement made Susan glance towards the back door. I looked too, but there was nobody out there. The washing machine sloshed. I tried to get to the point.

'Caroline didn't get on with Mrs Aldridge, did she?'

'She said she was mean.'

'But Caroline would say that, wouldn't she?'

Susan looked up then. 'It wasn't just Caroline who

330

didn't like Mrs Aldridge. Hardly anyone minded when she died. They all came to the funeral and stood around the grave, but it was only her parents as was crying, Sir George and Lady Debeger. And the baby. The baby cried the whole time. Poor little mite.' She looked again towards the door and then up at the clock. 'You have to go now.'

I leaned towards her, made her look at me.

'Tell me one more thing, Susan. Tell me what happened on the dam the day Jean Aldridge died. You said it was an accident.'

'Father will be home any minute.'

'What happened on the dam, Susan?'

'It's a secret.'

'I was told Mrs Pettigrew saw Caroline push Jean Aldridge into the lake, deliberately.'

'Whoever goes about slandering reveals secrets, but he who is trustworthy in spirit keeps a thing covered.'

I stared at her, confused. 'Is that the Bible?'

'If you don't keep a secret when you promised you would, everyone you love will burn in hell.'

'Please, Susan, just tell me what happened on the dam.'

We both heard the click of a gate opening. Susan jumped to her feet and looked through the window.

'It's him!' she cried, her hands clasped over her mouth.

'I'll go out the front.'

'Quick!' she squealed.

I scuttled towards the dark hall. She stood in the kitchen doorway, blocking me from her father's view as he approached the back door. And as I fumbled with the front door, she called something out to me in a low, urgent whisper.

'What's that?' I called back.

'Sam knows,' she replied. 'Ask Sam Shrubsole!'

CHAPTER FIFTY-FIVE

I asked in the shop and was directed to Sam Shrubsole's home, a small, neat bungalow right at the top of the hill, a good mile out of the village.

I walked up a narrow path, paving stones bordered on either side by parallel strips of bare soil interspersed with a few tidy pansy plants, not yet flowering. I prayed that Mr Shrubsole would be in, and he was. He was a small man in early middle age with large ears that stuck out at right angles from the side of his head. His hair was oiled back, he wore gaiters on his arms and his shirt was tucked into his trousers which were supported both by braces, and a sturdy belt. There was a gentleness about his demeanour which I found reassuring.

'Yes, miss?' he asked from the gloom of the hallway. 'Can I help you?'

I told him the bones of how I had come to be knocking on his door. When I explained that Susan had sent me, his face softened.

'Bless her,' he said. 'Her grandmother would turn in her grave if she knew the way that poor girl is treated. What is it that you want to know?'

I cleared my throat. 'I need to know about something that happened thirty years ago. I daresay it's not something you'll want to talk about, but I would so appreciate your help.'

'When you say "something that happened . . ."?'

'I mean a drowning.'

'You mean Jean Aldridge's death?'

I nodded apologetically. 'Susan told me to ask you.'

'Ahh.'

'She knows something, I know she does, but she's too afraid to talk to me. So she nominated you.' I smiled with as much charm as I could muster.

Mr Shrubsole rubbed his chin. 'I made a promise that I would never speak about that day.'

'I'm not here to cause trouble, Mr Shrubsole, really I'm not. I only want to know the truth.'

Still the man hesitated.

'Please,' I asked.

He held open the door for me. 'You'd better come in,' he said.

I followed him into the living room. There was a television set in one corner with a blown-glass fish arched on a crocheted doily on top of it, two easy chairs, two live goldfish swimming peaceably around a large bowl. We sat in the chairs. Dance music was playing from a transistor radio on the sideboard.

Mr Shrubsole sat back in his chair and considered his thoughts for a moment. When he spoke again, he spoke softly. He said: 'Secrets make you lonely, did you know that?'

'I never thought about it.'

'Oh, they do. It's their nature to isolate a person. Making someone keep a secret is the same as building a wall around them. Sooner or later the person behind that wall wants to set themselves free. Susan Pettigrew is trapped behind a wall of fear.'

'Yes.'

'And me, I'm trapped behind a wall of guilt.'

He stood up. He wandered over to the window and looked out. He patted his pocket, found a packet of cigarettes. He tipped the packet upside down, took out a Woodbine and put it between his lips. He offered the box to me and I shook my head.

'I was at school with Caroline,' he said. 'I liked the girl.'

He shook a match from a metal box on the sideboard, struck it on the serrated edge of the box, lit the cigarette and then blew out the flame.

'She knew about the reservoir,' he said, 'same as all the Blackwater children know, then and now. They know how dangerous it is below the dam. It's the deepest part of the lake and impossible to climb out – there's nothing to hold on to. And of course there's the pumps to contend with, the pressure of the water draining through the sluice-gates creating a downward current. You fall in there, and unless someone drags you out pronto, you're a goner. Caroline knew all that and everyone knew that she knew. If she *was* going to push Jean Aldridge in the reservoir, that was the place to do it.'

I said nothing. Mr Shrubsole's face was in shadow. Dust-motes danced in the light from the window behind him and in the cigarette smoke rising blue-grey towards the ceiling.

'I was fishing,' he said. 'I'd taken a rowing boat out on to the lake. I was supposed to be catching trout that my father could sell in the village but the fish weren't biting. It was hot and I was sleepy. The boat was hardly moving, the sun was beating down. I was lying across the seat with my hat pulled down over my eyes, half-dozing. I wasn't far from the dam, fifty yards or so, and it was a clear day. I didn't see Jean Aldridge arrive, but I saw her on the slope, with her binoculars, and the pram was up on the dam behind her. The hood was up on the pram, to keep the sun off the baby. It was a big pram, the kind they used to call a baby carriage, you know? Wheels the size of bicycle wheels and the frame like the hull of a boat. I wasn't much interested in Jean, to be honest. Didn't like the woman, she'd upset my mother once or twice. Mother was a seamstress. Nothing she ever did for Jean Aldridge was good enough and Jean could be funny about paying. But then I saw Caroline walking along the dam. Susan was with her, but a long way away, hanging back. I knew Caroline. I sat up when I saw her, called out to her and waved but she didn't see me and just at that moment, I got a bite on the line. So I was only half-watching Caroline because the other half of my mind was on the fish.'

'But you saw what happened?'

'Oh, I saw all right. She went over to the pram and looked down into it. Then she peered over the dam and saw Jean sitting on the slope below her. Everything Caroline did was very slow. It was like watching someone on the screen at the cinema. Slow. Not real. She picked the baby out of the pram and she held it up to her cheek, cuddled it. I was reeling in the fish. I thought she was just going to put the baby back. But then the pram started moving.'

'Caroline pushed it?'

'No, no. Maybe Jean hadn't put the brake on, or maybe the brake was faulty, I don't know. Caroline never touched it. The pram started to roll down the grassy slope. It soon picked up speed, bumping down the hill.' He drew on the cigarette. 'It reached the rim of the reservoir and it bounced right off the edge, into the water. There wasn't much of a splash, no noise or anything; the pram bounced into the water and it floated. It was all quite slow and dreamlike. That's what it was like.' A second pause while he took another drag of his cigarette. 'Caroline was standing on the dam with the baby in her arms but Jean, down below, didn't know she was there. She thought the baby was still in the pram. She was on her feet in an instant, took off her glasses, jumped straight into the water – plop – like that. Then she disappeared . . . and never came back up. She was gone and the pram was still floating. The whole thing was over in the blink of an eye. One moment she was there, and the next she was gone.'

He tapped the end of his cigarette and ash fell into the ashtray. 'I dropped the fishing line, lost it overboard because I was in such a hurry to get back to the shore. I rowed as fast as I could. When I got to the dam, Susan was with Caroline and Caroline was just standing there, holding the baby. She had a kind of faraway look in her eyes, and tears were running down her face. She said: "It wasn't meant to be like this." That was all she said: "It wasn't meant to be like this." Those words haunted me. They've haunted me ever since.'

I looked beyond the man, past the room, back down the valley . . . and I was there, on the dam, thirty years earlier. I was looking down into the water and the sun was hot on my skin and the surface of the lake was flat calm and the fish were jumping for the flies that dipped and floated just above the surface. And the baby was in my arms, tiny, warm, his hard little head bumping against my shoulder and I could smell the baby smell of him, the smell of the skin behind his tiny ear, the smell of his neck beneath the white cotton sun-bonnet.

And now I was looking through the water, through the greeny clearness of it, watching as the pram floated on the lake's surface, bobbing, the momentum it had gathered as it rolled downhill moving it further from the shore. I watched, and it was peaceful. My eyes were at water-level; it was as if I were a fly floating on the water's surface. On the bank, I saw Jean Aldridge push herself to her feet, saw the horror in her face, saw her take off her spectacles and drop them on the grass and then I watched as she jumped into the water clumsily, like the middle-aged woman she was, arms and legs flailing. Her jumping rippled the water and the ripple unsteadied the pram. It tilted and filled and then it began to sink, slowly, down into the water. Close to the dam wall, Jean sank more quickly, sank like a stone. She plunged down, to the sluice-gate, and was trapped there, pressed against the railings by the weight of the water, her skirt forced up around her body.

'It *was* an accident then,' I said. Sam did not hear me, he was not listening.

'I told Caroline and Susan to stay put while I went to Fairlawn to get help, and off I ran.'

'And did they stay put?'

He shook his head. 'No. They set off across the dam. They didn't get far though. Caroline collapsed halfway over, still holding the baby. I didn't see her fall. I went straight to Fairlawn and I could hear a right row going on inside, raised voices and that, and I had to bang on the door and yell until someone came. Dr Croucher was there with the vicar and Jean Aldridge's parents, Sir George and Lady Debeger, right posh folk. I took them back down to the dam and we saw Caroline all collapsed in a heap, with the baby in her arms and Susan sitting beside her, stroking her hair. The doctor went and fetched Caroline back home in his car and her ladyship took the littl'un. That was the last time I ever saw Caroline.'

'What about Jean?'

'They had to bring in professional divers from Bristol to retrieve the body. I was watching when they brought her up. I'll never forget it. She was like a mermaid, like something that lived in the lake, all the water streaming from her, and her arms and legs trailing. She was wearing a good tweed skirt and a white blouse. It was still buttoned. The thing that got me, though, the oddest thing, was that she still had one shoe on. Her stocking had come loose and it was down by her ankle, but her shoe was still on her foot.'

'But I don't understand, Mr Shrubsole. If Jean's death was an accident, like you said, why did it need to be covered up? Why the secrecy? Why weren't you allowed to talk about it?'

Mr Shrubsole put the cigarette to his lips and narrowed his eyes as he sucked on it. 'Sir George Debeger took me home that evening in his Jaguar. I almost got a clip round the ear, because my dad thought I was in trouble. But Sir George had a word and it all went quiet until a few days later. My father had me up and dressed in my Sunday best, gave me a lick and a spit, made me smart and he took me down to the village club. They were all there, the four big cheeses, the vicar, the doctor, the headmaster and Sir George. Anyroad, they made me stand in front of them as if I was up before the court and they told me Caroline had died of fever. They said it was a good job and all, because now she was dead, they wouldn't have to say anything to the police about her pushing Jean Aldridge in the lake. And I said she hadn't pushed Jean in the lake, Jean jumped in all by herself and Caroline was nowhere near her at the time. And they said that I couldn't possibly be sure of that because the sun would have been in my eyes and I'd been too far away to see clearly. They asked if I'd been dozing on the boat and I said that I had and they said, well then! As if that proved that I couldn't possibly have seen what I knew I *had* seen. They said I was mistaken. They told me I was wrong that many times that I started to believe their version myself.' He inhaled again. 'Anyway, they said it would be best if I didn't say anything at all to anyone about what I *thought* I'd seen.'

'They told you to keep quiet?'

'There was an incentive.'

'What kind of incentive?'

'My sister had been proper poorly, she had a dreadful

chest – TB. Mother was worried sick about her. Dr Croucher said if I promised to keep my mouth shut, they'd arrange for her to go to the hospital in Bristol and they'd pay for her medicine and everything. They were as good as their word. Mother was happy, my sister eventually came home right as rain and my old man was pleased with the outcome. I reckon they slipped him a bob or two as well. Life seemed to get a bit easier for us afterwards; wheels were oiled.'

'What about Mrs Pettigrew?'

'What about her?'

'I heard she was walking back from the asylum and witnessed the murder.'

'Nobody else was on the dam.'

'So the vicar's wife lied?'

'I don't suppose she had to say anything much. Word soon got around that Caroline had killed Jean Aldridge. It was the kind of thing people whisper about amongst themselves. The whole village knew they had to keep it quiet to stop the police poking their noses in. People told the story without any help from Mrs Pettigrew. It wasn't as if she ever had to stand up in court and say she'd seen something she hadn't. It was the same as me. I didn't have to lie. I just had to not say anything.'

'But...' I trailed off, overwhelmed with the unfairness of the situation, the injustice. 'Daniel Aldridge thinks Caroline killed his mother, Caroline's own sister thinks she was a murderer. Her parents went to the grave believing the worst of their daughter. It's so awfully wrong.'

'I was fifteen years old. My sister was at death's door. What else was I to do?'

'Oh, I don't blame you, Mr Shrubsole. It must have been terribly intimidating for you to be held up in front of all those important men. I just don't understand why any of this had to happen in the first place.'

The man stubbed out his cigarette. He ground it down into the ashtray.

'If it's any consolation,' he said, 'I've always felt bad about it. Always. But whichever way I look at it, it wasn't my fault people blamed Caroline. I never said a word about that day, one way or another. That girl had a terrible reputation, she'd done some bad things. It didn't take long for the story to go round and soon other people were putting in their three-penn'orth. They said they'd seen the two women arguing, Caroline attacking Jean, Jean trying to defend her baby. Once the story took hold, it stuck. I didn't like it, but I couldn't do anything, could I? I was trapped because as far as anyone knew, I wasn't there that day, I didn't see anything. I'd promised to keep the secret for ever. I'd promised on my sister's life.'

'It's not a secret any more,' I said.

'No.'

'You're free.'

'Have you told Susan Pettigrew that she's free?' he asked. 'Do you think her life will get better if her father knows she's been blabbing? No, of course it won't. Don't you think she's suffered enough? You can't do anything about the dead, miss. It's the living you need to look out for now.'

CHAPTER FIFTY-SIX

Julia was asleep in the living room when I got back to the cottage. I was dead tired too. All the way down the hill I had wondered what I should do. I didn't know how to present Julia with this new version of events. I was afraid of somehow making things worse. If I told her, the first thing she would want to know was how I had come by the truth – and that would mean implicating Sam Shrubsole, who I wasn't worried about, and Susan, who I was. The second thing Julia would want to do would be to confront Dr Croucher and Reverend Pettigrew, and while I knew a confrontation was necessary, I also knew that it would, without a shadow of a doubt, cause huge problems for Susan, who had nobody to stick up for her. What would she do if she lost her job at Sunnyvale and her father threw her out of the vicarage? What would become of her then?

But every moment I didn't tell Julia, the secret was mine too; I was trapped inside its wall, just like the others were.

I had two secrets now, the pendant and the truth:

two walls. Any more and I would find myself completely imprisoned.

I ran a bath. The water was lukewarm and did nothing to comfort me, and every time I closed my eyes I felt a chill as if I were reliving the moment when Jean Aldridge plunged into the reservoir. I turned the story over in my mind. Caroline loved Robert Aldridge and hated Jean, but she hadn't set out to hurt Jean that day. She had simply walked down to the dam with Susan, and she'd seen the baby in the pram and picked him up. And after Jean drowned, she carried the baby in her arms until she collapsed. Why did she collapse? Was it fear? Panic? The realization of what had happened? What was this fever that had killed her? And where was Robert when all this was happening? *Where was he?*

When the water was cold, I drained the bath, dried myself and dressed again. I then went into the empty bedroom. The only part of the walls still covered by paper was the patch on the chimney breast. The paper had been so thoroughly glued over an area roughly two feet square that water and elbow grease would never be sufficient to dislodge it. I looked at the area and considered. Then I went downstairs. Julia lay on the sofa, covered over by a blanket. I picked up the telephone and took it into the hall, as far away from Julia as the wire would allow me to carry it. I sat down with my back against the wall and dialled my father's number. Eileen answered. We exchanged small talk for a few moments. My father was doing fine, he had a bit of colour back in his cheeks, he'd had sausage and mash for his tea and he'd polished off the lot. And the dog, bless her, was keeping him company. Bess, she told me, was a godsend. They didn't want to give her back.

'Eileen, would you ask him something?' I said. 'Would you ask him what he'd suggest using to get some wallpaper off a wall when the paper's been so well glued that nothing seems to lift it.'

Eileen duly disappeared away from the telephone receiver to consult my father. As I waited, I closed my eyes and imagined I was there, in my father's house. I pictured him sitting in his chair with his feet on Granny's footstool, a cigarette burning in the ashtray at the side and the newspaper on his lap, Bess lying at his feet. I had a pang of missing that old house and my father so much that it hurt.

Eileen returned. 'He says have you tried white spirit? He reckons that will shift most things. He said to dab it on carefully, bit at a time, with an old rag.'

'Thank you,' I said. 'I'll give that a go.'

I could hear Julia stirring in the living room.

'I have to go now, Eileen,' I said. 'I'll be in touch soon.'

'Make sure you are,' Eileen said. 'Ta ta, pet. Take care.'

I took the telephone back into the front room. Julia was stretching in the corner of the settee.

'How are you feeling?' I asked her.

'I'm OK.'

'Daniel will be here soon to open the trunk. He's bringing the paint. There's only one patch of wallpaper left in the empty bedroom. I'll have it off by lunchtime tomorrow and then I'll start painting over the walls.'

Julia smiled sleepily. 'That's good.'

'I'll ask if he can give us a hand emptying the shed too.'

'We'll burn what we can and the rag and bone man can take the rest. Where's Viviane?'

'Didn't you say she was staying on at school for her tea?'

'Ah, yes, of course. It's the concert.'

'I'll make a start on our dinner, shall I, while we're waiting for Daniel?'

'Yes. Yes, you do that.'

I went into the kitchen, half-filled the sink with cold water. I tipped potatoes and carrots into the water and swirled them around to wash away the mud. Outside, darkness was falling and the air was cold. The lake was slate-grey, reflecting a bank of threatening cloud, and the branches of the naked trees were black, delicate as filigree against the sky. A mist was forming over the lower fields. It was fragile for now but as the mist rose, and the cloud descended, I knew there would be another thick fog; another masking of the lake. I thought of the black tide running through the sluice-gate; Jean Aldridge pressed against the grille by the weight of those millions of gallons of water and Caroline standing above, in the sunshine, holding the baby. I thought of Jean's lost shoe, lying in the silt at the foot of the dam. I thought of the pendant that I planned to throw in beside it. All these dark thoughts weighed me down.

I was so relieved when I heard the jeep drawing up outside. I dropped the carrot I was peeling into the sink, wiped my hands on a tea-towel and went out to meet my darling. I could see, as soon as he stepped out of the vehicle, that the side of his forehead, above his left eye, was swollen. This time I was in no mood to pretend I had not noticed. I was also relieved because concern for Daniel pushed the secret I was keeping from him to the back of my mind.

'Your father again?' I asked, reaching up to touch his sore face.

'I'm OK,' said Daniel.

'You're not OK! You're going to have a terrible black eye and that must sting like anything.'

'It's not that bad.'

'He can't carry on like this,' I said. 'Someone needs to stand up to him.'

'Standing up to him is what led to this,' said Daniel.

'Come in,' I said. 'Come in and let me see what he's done to you.'

I stepped back and Daniel followed me in, down the narrow hallway, past the awful old paintwork, beneath the yellowing lampshade that swung from the ceiling. I sensed a scuttling, a myriad tiny creatures moving, a change in the density of the air.

In the kitchen, Julia looked up and smiled.

'Hello,' she said to Daniel, 'have you been in a fight?'

Daniel propped the cutters against the wall and joked, 'You should see the state of the other fellow.'

'Sit there,' I said, 'under the light. Let me look at your face.' I tipped Daniel's head back, inspected the wound. 'I'll clean it for you.'

'There's no need.'

'There is.' I wanted to cover over the violence that had been inflicted on Daniel with tenderness. I wanted,

347

somehow, to prepare him for the news I was going to break. And at the back of my mind I was thinking: This is good news. His mother wasn't murdered, she died in an accident. But I knew it wouldn't be as straightforward as that. When somebody has believed something all their lives, it becomes part of them, and learning that that part is false is always difficult.

I went to the sink, held a bowl under the tap, filled it with warm water. There was a sound from upstairs. Julia looked up. I found some lint in the cupboard, cut off a piece. I went back to the table and began to bathe Daniel's forehead.

'Is that Viviane up there?' Daniel asked.

'No,' Julia replied. 'It's a draughty old house. The doors are always opening and closing by themselves.'

'Would you like me to take a look? I might be able to sort it out for you.'

'No, thanks,' I said. I had scrubbed and scrubbed at Caroline's words on the wall of the empty bedroom, soaked them in bleach, but the ghost of the letters remained. *I hate Jean Aldridge. I wish she was dead.* Daniel must not see those words, or he would never believe me when I told him the truth. Tomorrow they would be painted over. Tomorrow it would be safe to let him upstairs and then, perhaps, we could talk – he, Julia and I – about a past that none of us remembered. I dabbed the lint as gently as I could around the bruise. It would be difficult to know where to start to talk to them, how to begin. Secret was layered upon secret, lie upon lie, the truth so well hidden that it was almost unreachable. And still I did not understand why.

'Nearly done,' I said. I kissed the top of Daniel's head gently.

There was a crash from upstairs, the sound of something being dropped or broken.

All three of us looked up. Julia stood, picked up her stick, crossed to the door.

'What *was* that?' Daniel asked.

'Perhaps one of us left a window open.'

Julia went into the hallway, the stick tapping on the floorboards. I stood still with the lint in one hand and a bottle of ointment in the other. I felt as if the life were draining from me, running away through my capillaries, down into the ground. I felt weightless, lifeless, empty.

Through the half-open door, I saw Julia at the foot of the stairs, looking upwards. I saw her place a hand on the banister rail and start to climb the stairs with her awkward, painful motion.

I put my hands on Daniel's shoulders and examined his face. 'That's better now.' I smoothed his hair tenderly.

'It sounds as if something has got in upstairs. Shouldn't I go and have a look?'

'It's always like that in this house. It's a noisy house. It has a peculiar energy to it.'

'One of us should go up to Julia.'

'No, no. Julia is fine. Open the trunk, Daniel. That's the best thing you could do for her.'

He looked at me, unconvinced.

'Really,' I said. 'Julia's been waiting all day to get into that trunk. She's been desperate.'

'Are you sure?'

I nodded.

Daniel picked up the cutters and went over to the trunk, prodded it with the toe of his boot.

'Where do you want me to cut the straps?'

'It doesn't matter. It's not like anyone will ever use it again. We're going to burn it in the morning.'

Daniel walked around the trunk, considering.

I watched him and I remembered the dead weight of the trunk, how hard it had been to move it and I lost my nerve.

'No, wait, perhaps we should leave it,' I said. 'What if there's something awful inside?'

'Like what?'

'I don't know, but . . .'

He leaned over the trunk and put all his weight behind the handles of the cutters. I bit at a fingernail. He cut the straps.

'Piece of cake,' he said.

'Don't open it!'

'What's the matter with you?' Daniel laughed. 'Whatever's inside has been there for years and years. It can't hurt you now.'

He pressed the catches with his thumbs. They snapped open. Then he put his hand beneath the lid and he pushed. It opened wide, like the mouth of some giant creature; it exhaled a puff of foul air and what was inside was revealed.

CHAPTER FIFTY-SEVEN

The first thing we saw, on the very top beneath the huge old lid, was a picture, a little watercolour painting. It was such a pretty, innocuous thing and I was filled with relief.

'It's Fairlawn,' said Daniel, and he picked it up and looked at it closely. 'It's lovely,' he said. 'Whoever painted this must have known the house very well. See how they've caught the sunlight falling on the facade.' He held the picture up to see better. 'Oh. It's signed: *Caroline.*'

He moved the picture away then, as if it horrified him.

You're wrong about her, I thought, and I knew I wouldn't be able to keep the secret to myself for long.

'Can I see?' I asked.

Daniel passed me the picture and I held it between the palms of my hands by the frame. It was very cold, and surprisingly light. The colours of the paint had been perfectly preserved. In Caroline's picture, Fairlawn seemed a brighter house than it did now, a happier house; a house with potential. It was almost as if the facade were smiling; the greens of the garden were interspersed with pinks and yellows, light dapples. A man was standing in the shade of one of the trees, leaning against it, smoking. He was only sketched into the painting, but I was certain it was the young Robert Aldridge. He was looking out of the picture, at Caroline herself.

'She was such a good artist,' I said.

Daniel didn't reply.

'What else is in there?' I asked.

'Mostly clothes, I think.'

He took out a couple of old dresses, a green cardigan, an apron and then a tiny white knitted garment.

'Look,' he said, 'a baby jacket.'

'Isn't that gorgeous! It's so beautifully made; such tiny little stitches.'

'It looks like new.'

'How strange that it's in the trunk with all the old clothes.'

I sensed Caroline behind me. Her hand was on my shoulder, her breath on my neck. I almost realized something then, almost understood what it was that had been eluding me, but the thought slipped away again.

Julia was coming back down the stairs, the clump of the foot on her good leg, the drag of the other. I glanced at the clock. Viviane would be on her way to Sunnyvale by now. She would be sitting in the back of the minibus with the other girls, all of them wearing their choir gowns, whispering and giggling, sitting on their hands, nervous and excited.

'There's more,' Daniel said, 'look.'

'All those dear little clothes. Why hide them away? Somebody could have made good use of these.'

Now I had the sense of something close, something strong and real and physical, as vivid as my pulse. I felt a pull at my hand, a pull at my heart, a tugging deep inside; a pain. The only baby who had been born around the time of Caroline's death was Daniel. But surely Caroline wouldn't have knitted anything for Mrs Aldridge's baby? Why would she take so much care making gifts for the child of the woman she hated? The woman whose husband she wanted for herself? Had she wanted the baby for herself too?

Julia came back into the room.

'You've opened it!' she cried, shocked. 'Oh my goodness, what have you found?' She looked over Daniel's shoulder.

'Clothes, mainly,' said Daniel, 'and here's an old blanket, and . . . oh!'

'What's that?' Julia asked. Her voice was just a whisper. 'What is it?' The three of us stared into the trunk. Bundled inside was bedlinen, screwed up, terribly stained, dark brown, black.

'Is it blood?'

'I think so.'

I pulled at a corner of a sheet and it unfolded; the staining was awful – flakes of dried matter fell back into the trunk and on to the back of my hands. I shuddered, then pushed myself up to my feet, stumbled to the sink to wash the stuff away. As the water hydrated them, the brown flakes turned red again, liquefied, turned back to blood. The blood circled the perimeter of the drain, turned the base of the sink red and was rinsed away. I was shaking. I felt sick.

'It looks like somebody was murdered in those sheets,' Daniel managed to say.

'Or slit their own wrists.'

Julia touched the baby clothes on the table. 'Or they gave birth and haemorrhaged,' she said. She sat down heavily on a chair.

We were all silent for a moment.

Of course, I thought. Of course!

Julia said sadly, 'My sister didn't die of fever, she died in childbirth. And they hid the blood-stained bedding so nobody would know she'd been pregnant.' She covered her face with her hands. 'God,' she choked out, 'it just gets worse!'

Daniel was holding the sheets in his hand; the staining was so great that more of the old fabric was dark brown than was the original pale pink stripe. 'What happened to the baby?' he asked.

There was another silence.

'Perhaps it was stillborn,' Julia said. 'Something was wrong. There shouldn't have been so much blood.'

Daniel looked down into the trunk, the bundled old fabric, the quilted, bloodstained coverlet.

'Oh no,' I whispered. 'No, don't look!'

'Take everything out,' Julia said in a voice quiet and cold as ice. 'Make sure there's nothing in there.'

Daniel blanched, but he set his lips in a line and he pulled the sheets out of the trunk, the old quilt, the bedspread at the bottom. I stood behind Julia's chair, holding her hand. I watched but my eyes were unfocused so that if Daniel were to find anything worse than what he'd found already, I would not see it. Julia sat before me, still as a statue, hardly breathing. We were both dreading Daniel saying something, for some expression of horror, but in the end all he said was: 'It's all right. There's nothing else in here.'

'Where is it then?' Julia asked. 'Where is Caroline's baby?'

'Did they bury it with her?'

Of course. That's what they would have done – put it in the same coffin, in the same grave: *the last day of August 1931*. Out of sight, out of mind, far away from the other graves, the unnamed, unchristened child of the wicked, unmarried girl whom everyone in the village believed to be a murderer.

'It seems so cruel,' Julia said. 'Even for Caroline, it seems cruel for it to have ended like that.'

Daniel stood, went to the sink and washed his hands. His face was blank, shocked.

'Least said, soonest mended,' Julia said bitterly. 'Everyone knew my sister was a murderer, but they kept quiet about what else she was.'

I was thinking of Caroline's mother, sitting next door with Mrs Croucher, inconsolable throughout the long night while Caroline's father and Dr Croucher cleaned up the mess, the two women listening to the footsteps going up and down the stairs. In one night, they got rid of everything: the bodies of Caroline and her stillborn child to the undertaker, the soiled bedding and furniture into the shed, Caroline's story, the hopeless love affair, her hatred for Jean Aldridge, her picture of the hanging doctor all papered over.

The whole thing, her whole life, swept under the carpet, made to disappear, as if she had never existed.

CHAPTER FIFTY-EIGHT

We put everything but the picture and the baby clothes back into the trunk, closed it and dragged it outside, bumping it down the steps. The fog had come in; the garden was swathed in it, so thick that the rest of the world had disappeared completely. Daniel and I pulled the trunk as far away from the door as we could, into the middle of the lawn where we could douse it in petrol and burn it in the morning. I looked down towards the lake, trying to make out the lights of Sunnyvale but the fog was too dense. They would be there by now, the choir. They would be preparing for their first song and the old people would be getting ready to listen to them. I thought of Vivi, a bundle of nerves and excitement, and Dr Croucher in his wheel-chair, and his friend the vicar oiling back his hair ready to do the introductions. Did those two men ever think about Caroline Cummings? Were they haunted by the thought of what had become of her and her child? And what of the Debegers? They had been at Fairlawn the day their daughter died. They must have been part of the conspiracy. Had they ever wondered what became of poor pregnant Caroline? Had they known about her death?

Susan must have known Caroline was pregnant.

She would be there now, at Sunnyvale, nervous and shy in her too-small cardigan, Susan who used to have to pull down her pants and bend over a chair to be beaten by Frank Leeson's slipper, Susan who had been terrified by her own father into colluding in the lies about her only friend.

So much for the past being a better place, a more honourable place. It was not.

Daniel went back inside the cottage and I heard him talking to Julia. I stood in the fog and listened to the to and fro of their voices although I could not make out the words. I felt nothing but tenderness towards them both, but even that did not match the anger I was feeling on behalf of Susan and Caroline; it did not come close. I fetched the torch and went back down to the shed. I shone the torch into its furthest recesses. I shone it on the smudged writing on the wall. *Something something something smudge smudge smudge.* Caroline had done that, I was sure of it. She was the one with the propensity for writing on walls. What had she written? What had she been counting? Why had she set fire to the shed? What had she wanted the fire to destroy? All that was in there were blankets and cushions, Julia's toys. I crouched down, spat on my fingers and rubbed at the smudging, but the rubbing made it worse, less clear. I smacked the wall with frustration.

I went back into the cottage. Julia and Daniel were sitting in the kitchen. The gin bottle was open on the table between them. I went to Daniel and put my hand on his arm. 'Thank you for coming and for opening the trunk. Thank you for everything you've done. I know this must have been hard for you. Only I think it would be best if you went now. Julia and I need to talk.'

'Will you be OK?'

'Of course.'

'I'm so sorry you had to see that, Daniel,' Julia said. 'After all you've gone through already because of my sister.'

'Caroline didn't do anything to hurt Daniel,' I said.

Julia frowned at me.

'Caroline didn't kill your mother, Daniel,' I said. 'She didn't kill anybody. What happened on the dam was an accident.'

'Amy, please!' Julia put her hand on my arm. 'You don't know anything about it.'

'I can't let this go on. It's not fair. It's wrong. Caroline was there, on the dam, but she never laid a finger on Jean Aldridge.'

'Stop,' Julia said. 'Stop now.'

'Jean's death was an accident,' I said, 'for which Caroline was blamed.'

There was a silence. Daniel and Julia were both looking at me with shock, and something else – a kind of revulsion. I felt the weight of their confusion: it was crushing, but also I felt a lightness. After all these years of lying dormant, the seed of the truth had been exposed and there was an exhilaration that came with that.

'How can you know?' Julia asked.

'I spoke to someone who was there.'

'Nobody was there,' Daniel said coldly. 'Only Mrs Pettigrew saw what happened.'

I shook my head. 'It's all a lie.'

'A lie?'

'Yes. Mrs Pettigrew wasn't even there.'

Julia gave a brittle laugh. 'I'm sorry, Daniel, I don't know what's come over Amy.' She scowled at me. *Shut up!* she mouthed.

'I don't understand,' Daniel said, frowning. 'Why would the vicar's wife lie?'

'Why would anyone lie?' Julia asked, throwing her hands up in the air. 'Why would anyone say it was murder if it was an accident?'

'I don't know!' I said.

Daniel took hold of my arms. 'Who was it?' he asked. 'Who told you all this?'

I could not mention Sam Shrubsole without mentioning Susan Pettigrew. I stood hopelessly silent while they both gazed at me with the same expression, shock, confusion, horror. Then Daniel let go of my arms and turned from me. He picked up the cutters. 'I'll be off then,' he said.

I reached out for him. 'I'll come with you to the door.'

'No,' he said, 'I'll see myself out.'

'Daniel . . .'

He shrugged off my hand and walked away from me.

'Daniel, please . . .'

'You should have talked to me first,' he said. 'You had no right . . . It wasn't your mother, it's not your family. This has nothing to do with you.'

'I thought you'd want to know the truth.'

He turned. His face was suddenly furious. 'Do you think my father would have lied to me about something like that?' he said. 'Do you really think he would have lied about my mother's death? It's not the kind of thing anyone lies about, Amy!'

'What if they lied to him too?'

'They? Who were *they*?'

Mrs Pettigrew, I thought, and the others who were at Fairlawn that day. The vicar, the doctor, Jean's parents.

'Leave it, Amy. Just leave it.'

I followed him to the front door. He pushed it open violently. 'I'll leave the paint by the gate,' he said, and he was gone.

I leaned against the wall and caught my breath. The fog came in through the open door and dissipated in the hallway. I heard Daniel banging about for a few moments and then the sound of the engine of the jeep starting and being driven angrily away. I dug my fingernails into my palms.

I wanted to cry but I was too angry, still, for tears.

I went back into the kitchen. Julia was pale. She was staring down at one of the perfect little matinée jackets, running her fingernail along the ribboned seam.

'Oh congratulations, Amy,' she said, without looking at me. 'Well done. Ten out of ten. You timed that perfectly. Couldn't you have dropped that bombshell on him at a different time? When he hadn't just been rummaging through a trunk full of bloody sheets? When he wasn't still recovering from being battered by his father?'

'I thought you of all people would want to know the truth about Caroline.'

'I don't know what to think any more. I feel sorry for Daniel.' She pushed away the baby clothes and raked her fingers through her hair. 'At least that's the end of it.'

'No, that's not the end of it,' I said. 'It's worse than you think.'

'For God's sake, how can it be worse?'

'Robert Aldridge was the father of Caroline's baby.'

Silence. I could feel Julia's anger. The tension in the room was white-hot.

'I don't know for sure,' I said, tentative now, afraid that Julia might explode, 'but she definitely had a crush on Robert. She definitely liked him. She drew a heart on the bedroom wall with both their names inside.'

'Robert Aldridge took advantage of my sister?' Julia demanded.

'I think so. Daniel showed me the room where she used to stay when she was working at Fairlawn. I imagine . . . well, it would have been possible for the two of them to meet there. Robert and Jean had separate bed-rooms, you see. Or perhaps they met in the hollow by the lake. I don't know. But it could have happened easily enough.'

'God.' Julia shook her head. 'I always thought he hated us because Caroline killed his wife. Yet, if what you're telling me is true, she didn't. Are you sure, Amy? Are you sure that my sister didn't kill Jean Aldridge?'

'I'm as sure as I can be.'

'Does Robert Aldridge know the truth?'

'It's possible that he doesn't.'

Julia was silent for a moment. 'All these years,' she said softly. 'It's taken all these years for me to find out what really happened.' She held her hand to her cheek. 'All those years of shame for my family: my father going early to his grave and my mother sending me to ballet school, keeping me distant because she wanted me to be free of the weight of being a Cummings, of having a sister who murdered. And I've done what my mother did, haven't I, Amy? I've come back and hidden myself away because I didn't have the courage to face the villagers. Thirty years have gone by but I still didn't want to see the looks on their faces, to know what was going through their minds.'

Julia slid her fingers down the side of her face. 'And then there's Caroline,' she said. 'Imagine how she must have suffered. Imagine how frightened she must have been, seventeen, pregnant, living in Blackwater.'

'I've thought of little else.'

She smiled at me ruefully.

'And now you're seeing Robert's son?'

'Do you mind?'

'It would be unfair to blame him for any of this. But it's frightening, Amy, isn't it, once the stone is thrown into the water, how far the ripples spread.'

There was white spirit in the cupboard beneath the sink. I left Julia with the gin bottle and her thoughts and took the white spirit upstairs to the empty bedroom. It had been difficult before, but now it was impossible to see it merely as an abandoned room. Now I could slip back through time, back into the room as Caroline lay on the bed, a terrified seventeen year old, sweat sticking her hair to her skull, the terrible pain deep down in her belly, blood soaking through the sheets and the windows closed despite the August heat in case Caroline should scream and somebody walking down the lane might wonder what was going on. And who was with her? Her mother? Was her mother holding her hand, pressing a cool flannel to her brow, reassuring her? Dr Croucher had been there. Mrs Croucher had told me he'd stayed with Caroline after he'd brought her back from the dam. He would have been at the foot of the bed, his sleeves rolled up to the elbows, a basin of hot water at his side, towels, disinfectant, the smell of blood. Caroline hated the doctor and yet, when she was at her weakest, her most vulnerable, he was there with her, examining her, pressing her thighs apart.

There would have been no pain relief for Caroline. No sympathy for the girl. No consideration of her feelings or her modesty.

Was the doctor's the last face she saw?

Was his the last voice she heard?

I shuddered.

So Caroline had died in childbirth and the doctor had agreed to say it was a fever, to preserve what little was left of her reputation, to make things easier for her parents – or perhaps to protect Robert Aldridge. Yes, that was more likely. It was to keep Sir George and Lady Debeger's widowed son-in-law out of the limelight. The bastard.

I understood now that the history of the room accounted for all the odd things that had happened inside it. All the sadness and fear that had seeped into the brickwork was gradually being released as the paper that had sealed it in the fabric of the building, like a secret, was peeled away. Tomorrow I would open the window wide and give the room a proper airing. And I'd paint the walls, paint over the past and then I'd scrub the floorboards and fill the room with light and flowers. Once that was done, then Daniel could come in and open up the fireplace. We could put an electric fire in the opening, that would make the room feel more modern. The estate agent could come and take his photographs. And I'd carry some flowers to Caroline's grave, flowers for Caroline and the baby.

I tied my apron about my waist, unscrewed the cap and poured white spirit on to my cloth. I dabbed it in the middle of the last patch of wallpaper. The smell was awful and my eyes stung but I persisted, dabbing a wider area. And as I did so, so the wallpaper lost its opacity. It became transparent.

I watched as the vile yellow faded and the pattern disappeared; the paper became like tracing paper, and what was beneath it suddenly, after thirty years, became visible. The writing appeared, faint at first but then clearer.

At last I saw what Caroline had written on the wall behind the chimney breast.

Dear baby, I read. *You were born in this room on the 23rd of August 1931.*

My first thought was that that couldn't be right.

Caroline had died on the 31st of August. How could her baby have been born more than a week earlier?

I read on.

Dr Croucher told me you were stillborn but I heard you cry outside my window as he took you away. I will find you. And in the meantime wherever I am and whatever . . .

My heart was thumping. I tipped more liquid on to the cloth, put it on to the paper, waited for the paper to become invisible.

. . . becomes of me, even if I am in the asylum, know that I am your mother and I . . .

I poured some more liquid on to the paper, directly from the bottle.

. . . am not the wicked person they tell you I am. I wanted to keep you, I tried, but I was . . .

Dab, dab, dab on the paper.

. . . not strong enough to hold on to you.

I love you.

Though we are apart, I will be beside you, always.

I stepped back.

'Oh Caroline!' I said.

I closed my eyes.

I was in the same place as she had been.

We were separated only by time.

I am Caroline now. I am lying in the bed. The mattress is soaked, with sweat and blood and with the waters that broke when I went into labour. I'm so hot, the room is like a furnace. I'd begged to have the window open but the doctor had refused. If I cry out, or make any kind of noise, he threatens me with his pad of chloroform. There is such pain inside me, pain as if the bottom half of me has been macerated, ripped to shreds. And I feel empty. For weeks I've had the company of the secret baby growing inside me, I've felt its movements, day and night, the little flutters and kicks, the tapping of its fingers, the push against my abdomen as it turned in the womb. People had started to notice I was growing thicker round the waist. Madam knew. I overheard her talking to the doctor. She told her parents too, Sir George and Lady Debeger. I was all ready for the questions, all ready to be given my marching orders, but nothing happened. I thought everything was going to plan for me and Robert and our precious baby. I thought we were going to be fine. But now the doctor has taken the baby and I am alone. My nightdress is stuck to me, plastered to my sore, heavy breasts and my stomach. The bloody sheets are kicked off all over the floor. It wasn't meant to be like this. Robert has gone to Scotland. He has rented a little house where we can live together, in a place where nobody knows us. He will work on the estate, managing the fish, and I will stay at home with our baby. We are going to be happy. Everything is going to be fine.

Only it wasn't supposed to happen like this. Our baby came early. It should have been born the second week of September, and by then we would have been in Scotland, but I couldn't help the labour. I couldn't stop it. And now the baby is born and I've heard Dr Croucher talking to my parents: I've heard him say the best place for me is the asylum. He said I can go there for a few years until I am rehabilitated. I shall refuse to go. I shall put up such a fight. I shall run away. Robert will be back soon and he will save me, he will sort out this mess. Somehow. He will make everything all right.

What is it? I ask. *Is it a boy or a girl? Where is it? Where's my baby?*

My mother is here now, beside me, wiping my face with a flannel, holding my hand. She is talking about blood, about the tears in my flesh, about the afterbirth. My mother is crying.

Where is my baby? I plead with her. *Mother, dear Mother, tell me, where is my baby?*

The doctor is in the room. He has a basin in his hand. The basin is covered over with a cloth. His wicked face is severe, serious. He is speaking but I don't hear him.

Caroline, listen to me. You are a very lucky young woman. The baby is deformed. He was stillborn and it's a blessing.

No!

It wasn't supposed to be like this. I was supposed to have the baby in hospital. Robert was going to pay for me to have a private room in a hospital in Scotland, a room with its own private nurse. The room was going to be full of flowers and sunshine.

'It will be all right, my love,' he had told me. 'You'll have the best room and I'll make sure you have the best doctors, the best care. I want everything in our child's life to be perfect from the moment it opens its eyes and takes its first breath.'

He promised he would wait outside while the baby was being born, and the moment he heard its cry he would come into the room straight away, and be with me. He was never going to leave me. We were going to be a family – together, always.

The doctor is speaking again. He's talking to my mother.

It often happens when a young woman has a baby out of wedlock that the baby's development is corrupted and it is born deformed. It is nature's way. It's kinder in the long run for the mother and the child.

My mother is crying.

I am screaming. *Where is my baby?*

And there's that sickening sweet smell again, those ice-cold vapours, and the doctor's pad is over my mouth and nose and the pain is receding and the room is spinning.

I'm so hot.

I am burning up.

I open my eyes. I am alone in the room. I am so hot.

I climb out of the bed and throw open the window. I gulp in the cool air, great lungfuls of it, the fresh August air, the smell of hay from the meadows and a yellowy evening falling – and down below there is the doctor, putting something on the back seat of his car: a small, swaddled bundle, a bundle that is waving tiny pink fists, a bundle that is crying its little heart out.

I went back downstairs. Julia looked at my face.

'What now?' she asked.

'Caroline's baby wasn't stillborn,' I said. 'And it wasn't born the day she died but eight days earlier. They took him from her and they gave him to Jean Aldridge.'

Julia sat perfectly still and silent for a moment while she considered this.

Then: 'No,' she said. 'No. That would have been too cruel! My mother would *never* have agreed to that.'

'Your mother didn't know about it. She was told the baby was stillborn.'

Julia sighed lengthily. 'But Amy, it's all conjecture. We will never know the truth. Caroline is gone and we can hardly go demanding answers from Robert Aldridge. Nobody can tell us what happened all those years ago.'

I reached behind to untie my apron. 'One person can,' I said. 'Dr Croucher. He was there. He knows exactly what happened.'

CHAPTER FIFTY-NINE

I put on my shoes and coat and went out into the fog, but I had only taken a few steps when Julia called out to me: 'Wait! I'm coming with you.'

'What about Vivi?' I asked.

'She's at Sunnyvale,' Julia replied. 'We can collect her and she can come back with us.'

'Are you sure? It's quite a way.'

Julia was pulling on her coat awkwardly, balancing on her stick. Her breathing was quick.

'I want to hear every word the doctor has to say,' she said. 'I want to hear it from his own mouth.'

I put my arm around Julia's waist and she held on to the back of my coat and the two of us set off along the lane in the direction of the lake. Within moments we were enclosed by the fog, and we could see nothing but the bony fingers of leafless trees reaching out through the gloom. Julia was soon out of breath and every few steps she slipped on the damp surface. She slowed me down yet I was so glad we were together. Julia's weight leaning on me did not feel like a burden, rather the opposite.

'What if we get there,' she panted, 'and the doctor refuses to say anything?'

'He'll tell us.'

'How can you be so sure?'

'Because if he won't tell us, then we will make a commotion at Sunnyvale, in front of all his peers, all those respectable old men and women. He will tell us the truth to keep us quiet. His reputation is all that is left to him now.'

'Amy, you have become positively Machiavellian! Whatever happened to the meek little thing you used to be?'

'Caroline happened,' I said.

The fog became thicker the closer we descended towards the lake. We walked slowly, holding on to one another. I could feel Julia's heart pumping through the damp fabric of her coat. I could feel her fear and her determination and I thought: We will get to the truth this time, we will get to the bottom of this.

We reached the bottom of the hill and the walking became easier but Julia was becoming more tired with every footfall. It was so long since she'd taken any real exercise. We had to stop every few paces so she could catch her breath. I wanted to run – to hurry and confront the doctor, but Julia was really slowing me now. I was somehow afraid that he might know we were coming, and avoid the confrontation. I was afraid that if he slipped away from us now, we would never know the truth.

As we passed the entrance to Fairlawn, a man rode past on a motorbike, going in the opposite direction.

He seemed familiar to me, although I couldn't place him. I paid him little attention, although he was the only person we saw out that evening, and the noise of the bike engine going up the hill rang out over the foggy valley.

We crossed the dam without meeting anyone else or seeing a single vehicle. When we reached the spot above where Jean had drowned, my blood ran cold and I felt the hairs stand up on my neck. Our feet were walking over the exact place where Caroline had stood holding her baby. She had tried to take him back home but she had collapsed. Was that when the fatal haemorrhage started? Here, on the dam?

I imagined her lying on the ground, her face pressed against the earth, the baby still in her arms. She must have held him in such a way as to protect him as she fell. Did she know she was dying? Did she look out over the water and see the reflection of the summer sky and know that she only had a little time left?

The night was quiet and still; unearthly. The fog opened up only a few yards in front of us, and closed again behind us. It would be easy enough to fall into the reservoir on a night like this. Easy enough for anyone to go the same way as Jean Aldridge.

'Oh Amy,' Julia gasped, leaning heavily on me, 'this is so hard.'

'It's just a little further,' I replied. 'We're almost there.'

'I'm slowing you down.'

'Not really. Only another few yards, then you can rest.'

'You're very good to me,' Julia said.

'It's mutual.'

We turned right beneath the illuminated archway and the sign that said: *Sunnyvale: First-class Residential Nursing Care for Gentlefolk*, although the sign was blurred by the fog, the light smudged into the air. We walked along the drive, past the Hailswood School minibus, past a handful of parked cars. By now I was half-carrying Julia; she was wheezing and heaving at her breath. She was not difficult to carry, she was so thin and frail in my arms, little more than a bag of bones, yet I could feel her resilience. I could feel her old energy and fight returning. She was looking forward to this meeting. She was hungry for the truth.

Before we went into the reception I smoothed Julia's damp hair around her face and passed her her stick, so she could walk independently. 'Will you be OK?' I asked.

'I'll be fine.'

We went inside. The air was dry and very warm. A middle-aged nurse was sitting behind the desk transcribing figures into a ledger. From beyond, the sound of children singing came along the corridor – a pure, clear sound. I picked out Viviane's voice and was reassured.

The nurse's smile faded when she saw Julia, wheezing and white, with her wild hair, her mismatched clothes. The woman touched her earlobe nervously and her eyes swung from left to right, looking for support, but nobody else was around. Everyone was in the day room, listening to the choir.

'Can I help you?' she asked. She looked pointedly at

the clock, so that we would realize it was an inconvenient time to visit.

'We've come to see Dr Croucher,' Julia said.

'He's busy at the moment. We have a children's choir in to entertain the residents.'

'We'll wait in his room then.'

'Are you family?'

'Yes,' Julia said. 'We've come to surprise him.'

The nurse hesitated. 'I'm not sure . . .'

'We won't stay long,' Julia said. 'Come on, Amy.' And she walked down the corridor with her head held high, and although she was wearing shabby boots, although she looked like a bag lady and was relying heavily on her stick, she had regained her old elegance, her old charisma, her old confidence. I smiled at the nurse, and trotted after her.

We found the doctor's room easily enough at the far end of a carpeted hallway. His name was inscribed on a brass plaque, *Dr Gerard Croucher OBE*. I turned the handle, expecting the door to be locked, but it was not and I pushed it open. In the day room, distantly, the singing reached a crescendo and there was the sound of genteel applause.

Julia and I went into the doctor's bedroom. I had a feeling of excited dread in my stomach, like a child who knows it is doing something forbidden. Julia shut the door behind us.

'Well,' she said, 'here we are.'

It was a large, pleasant room, with predominantly dark wood and deep-coloured fabrics; a bed, a wardrobe, a commode, a bathroom to one side, emergency help buttons, handrails, hoists. There were a few antique pieces that had clearly been brought from Dr Croucher's home; a polished oak grandmother clock, an ornate plant-stand, a fancy coat-rack and a folding card-table with a green baize top. The curtains had not been drawn across French windows that opened out over the lake, and although, in darkness, we could not see the water through the fog, in daylight Dr Croucher must have had a wonderful view of the water, and the birds, the changing colours. I supposed in the summer months he could open the windows and sit outside.

Julia wandered around the room, touching the objects. There were decanters on the chest of drawers, a heavy ashtray, a cigarette-lighter mounted on to a brass stand, a television set.

'He doesn't want for any home comforts, does he?' she asked.

I crossed to the window and gazed through the glass at the blank whiteness beyond. My leg grazed something tucked behind the base of the curtain; the doctor's bag. I pulled it free, held it up. It was old, it had obviously seen good service – a black leather bag with two sturdy handles. I put it on the bed.

'It's the same bag,' Julia said.

'Hmm?'

'It's the same bag he always had. The one he emptied once on our kitchen table to prove he had not stolen Father's pocket-watch. Open it, Amy. Look inside.'

'I don't know if I should.'

'I'll open it then. What does he need his old bag for these days?' Julia came across to the bed and opened the clasp. The two halves of the top of the bag separated slowly. Inside was a silky lining, the fabric worn and faded from purple to a dull grey. Julia pulled out a stethoscope and tossed it on to the bed; an otoscope, a magnifying glass, a pair of surgical scissors, spatulae. 'What does he keep all this stuff for?' she asked. 'To relive his glory days? To remember how he used to be the most important man in the village, the one everyone turned to with their problems and their worries, the one who saw them into the world and out of it?'

'Julia, perhaps you shouldn't . . .'

Julia grabbed the bag and tipped it upside down. A clatter of pill boxes emptied on to the bed. Small bottles of God-knows-what. A bundle of photographs tied up with an elastic band.

'What are those?'

Julia picked up the bundle, picked at the band. The sensation of dread inside me had grown now so that it was hard inside me, pressing against my ribcage and my spine as if I had somehow swallowed a bowling ball.

'Don't look,' I said.

'I have to,' Julia said, and her voice was cold now and hard. She broke the band and discarded it. She looked at the first picture, dropped it, looked at the second, looked at the third . . . and then threw the whole bundle of photographs on to the floor. They scattered like leaves, or playing cards, covering the carpet, the bed, the seat of the chair. I picked up the image nearest to me. It was a photograph of a young boy, eight or nine years old. He was naked. He was holding the erect penis of an adult man. I dropped the picture, stepped away from it and wiped the fingers that had touched it on my skirt.

'Oh!' I cried. 'Oh God!'

Now Julia came to me. She put her arms around me. 'Shhh,' she whispered, and she held her cool hand against my cheek. 'It's all right, Amy. It's all right. It ends tonight.'

'The pictures, Julia . . .'

'Those were what Caroline wanted the police officer to find! That's why she went to so much trouble to make him look in the bag!'

Of course they were! The photograph I had seen danced before my eyes; the boy's awkward averted gaze, a scab on his knee, his pudding-basin haircut, the same as every other boy that age in Britain, the freckles on his nose. He looked like a perfectly ordinary boy, but what he was being made to do . . . Oh, I would never, now, be able to get the picture out of my mind. And there were so many photographs. So many of them.

And suddenly all Caroline's actions made sense. All those things she'd done that nobody understood, all of it became clear.

'If she knew of the pictures, Dr Croucher must have shown them to her,' Julia said.

'The shed. He took her into the shed and she counted the times off on the wall.' *Something something something smudge smudge smudge. Dr Croucher made me do it.* Did Dr Croucher make a game of it at first? Did Caroline have to pick a card and then copy the action it depicted, like a new twist on a game of charades? Was it something like that? Did she go willingly the first time, play along, and after that was she trapped? Did he take photographs of *her*?

If you don't do as I ask, then I'll tell your mother what you did. I'll tell her what you saw, what you touched, what a bad, unlovable, dreadful girl you are. There'll be no point denying it, I will show her the photographs.

'Frank Leeson and Gerard Croucher both with the same predilection for children,' Julia said quietly. 'Both of them acted out their fantasies on my sister. That's half of the village club committee.' She walked away from me and poked at the doctor's bed with her stick. 'Bloody Dr Croucher with his bloody brass plaque on the door, his bloody OBE for bloody services to the community.' She raised the stick and slammed it down hard on the doctor's pillow, making a massive dent. The photographs on the bed lifted into the air, and settled again. Julia stood and breathed deeply. She trembled on the exhale. She said, 'He must think he's untouchable. He must think he's unanswerable to anyone. Come on! Let's go and find him.'

CHAPTER SIXTY

We walked back along the corridor, out of the bedroom wing, towards the main hallway that would
take us back towards the communal rooms of Sunnyvale.
However, the geography of the place worked against us.
The concert had just finished and when we reached the
hallway, it was busy with traffic coming the other way
– old women who were unsteady on their legs being
helped by nurses, old men with sticks shuffling along
the carpet, the group of schoolchildren hurrying out
towards the exit. I looked for Viviane, but did not see
her. There was a niggling anxiety inside me but I ignored
it. I'd heard Vivi singing a few minutes earlier; I knew
she was safe. Some of the elderly people were humming
or singing; they all seemed happy. I heard murmurings,
snatches of conversations: *beautiful voices, sang like angels,
took me back, made me remember, made me forget.*

It took Julia and me a while to excuse our way through
the old people and get ourselves into the day room, and
when we reached it, the place was empty save for Susan
Pettigrew, who was stacking up the chairs that had been
arranged in a semi-circle around the central area, where

a microphone stood on a stand attached to a plug in the wall by a snaking cable. The lid of the piano was still open, sheet music still held in place on the stand above the keys. Empty sherry glasses were scattered about the surfaces of the room, and ashtrays; little bowls of crisps and nuts. Through the window, I saw the last child climb on board the Hailswood School minibus. Its engine was already running, smoke puffing out of the exhaust. I watched as it reversed, turned around, and then headed off into the fog.

I thought Viviane must be on the bus. There was nobody at home to meet her and we hadn't left a note, but the front door to the cottage was unlocked. The lights were on. She would be worried but she would be safe on her own for a short while.

I didn't have time to worry about Vivi now.

Susan was clearly alarmed to see me again. She put down the chair she was holding and stood with her arms at her side, a worn green cardigan stretched tight at the buttons over an ugly brown dress patterned with tiny sprigs of heather. She was wearing plastic house-shoes on her feet, thick tan stockings. Her feet were swollen and her ankles bulged over the tops of the shoes.

'Hello,' she said, her eyes flickering anxiously from me to Julia and back again.

'Hello, dear,' I said, and I went to Susan and embraced her. Susan felt warm and soft. She smelled of the harsh detergent I'd smelled in the vicarage kitchen and she stood tense in my arms as if she did not know how to respond to an affectionate touch. I stepped back and smiled, saying, 'It's nice to see you again.'

Susan would not look me in the eye.

I turned to Julia. 'Julia, this is Susan Pettigrew.'

'I remember you,' Julia said. 'You used to come to our house sometimes to play with Caroline. I was her younger sister, do you remember? I used to tag along after you. Caroline used to call me Goody Two Shoes.'

Susan nodded carefully, as if unsure whether this was the answer she was supposed to give. She twisted her fingers together anxiously. 'She only said that to tease,' she said, barely a whisper.

'What's that, dear?'

'She only called you Goody Two Shoes to tease. She was proud of you. She looked after you.'

'I didn't know, back then, that I needed looking after. I didn't know there were bad people in the village.'

Susan looked embarrassed. Her fingers wound together and then she remembered what she had been doing and returned to the stacking of the chairs.

Julia laid a hand on her arm. She tried again, gently: 'We know Frank Leeson was a bad man, Susan, and we know he wasn't the only one. We know about the pictures in the doctor's bag.'

Now Susan paled with fear. There was panic in her eyes. The feet of the chair she was holding hovered inches above the carpet.

'It's a secret,' she breathed.

Julia took the chair from Susan and slotted it on to the stack. Then she clasped Susan's hands in her own. 'Sit down with me for a moment, please,' she said.

'I have to finish clearing up.'

'This won't take long, dear.'

'I must clear up properly or I'll be in trouble.'

'You won't be in any trouble, Susan, I promise. Just sit with me for a moment. Sit here, beside me.'

Susan's eyes flicked backwards and forwards, to the door that opened out to the corridor, to the closed door that went into the dining room, but she sat, heavily, in the chair beside Julia and waited obediently for the questions, still twisting her fingers together on her lap, the smell of fear oozing from beneath her clothes.

'Are there any more secrets that we should know about?' Julia asked.

'Secrets aren't for telling,' Susan said. '"Whoever goes about slandering reveals secrets, but he who is trustworthy in spirit keeps a thing covered."'

'Someone told me that secrets make a person lonely,' I said. 'Anyone who makes you keep a secret doesn't want you to be happy. They don't really care for you.'

'But the Bible says . . .'

'What the Bible says is sometimes taken out of context.'

Susan continued to twist her fingers, making patterns with her hands. The clock on the mantel ticked. A long way away, a door clicked shut and she jumped.

'Susan, dear,' Julia said, 'you used to share your secrets with Caroline, didn't you? I remember how the two of you used to shut yourselves up in Caroline's bedroom. I could hear you inside, whispering, and I always wished I had a friend like you – someone I could talk to about anything.'

'I was going to live with Caroline,' Susan said suddenly. 'In Scotland.'

'Were you, dear?'

'She was going to run away with Robert Aldridge and live in a little house at the side of the loch and he was going to work as the gamekeeper and I was going to go and live with them. Caroline said as I could help with the baby. We were going to have to change our names and everything because Mrs Aldridge's father was very powerful. He could have had us all put in prison.'

'Was that the dream?'

'It was the plan. We had it all worked out. Robert had took some jewellery from his wife. Caroline was looking after it. They were going to sell it in Scotland.'

The truth, finally, was almost within reach; it was hovering on the periphery of the three of us, the three women sitting in the empty day room, the fire burning low in the grate. The truth was like a moth hovering around the flame of a candle. I knew it was there but I could not quite catch it.

'Caroline told you she was going to live with Mr Aldridge?' Julia asked.

'Yes. They would say they were married and nobody in Scotland would know any different.'

'But he already had a wife.'

'One he didn't love.'

'Are you sure he didn't love her, Susan? Or is that just what he told Caroline?'

'No, no, I'm sure!' Susan said, wide-eyed, anxious now to be believed. 'Mr Aldridge loved Caroline. He did! He had it all planned out. He had a friend, a lawyer who was going to help him sort things out. He had found somewhere for us all to live and he'd gone to Scotland to settle the arrangements. He was going to come back and collect Caroline and me the following week. But then the baby came early. It wasn't supposed to be born until September. It wasn't supposed to be like that.'

She paused, looked at Julia for approval.

'You're doing very well to remember all this, Susan,' Julia said.

'It's all I think about, all the time,' Susan said. 'Sometimes I pretend that everything went to plan, and that me and Caroline and Mr Aldridge and the child are all living in Scotland. I imagine that we are having a lovely time and that we are all happy.' Her face lit up as, for a moment, she imagined herself in this alternative life. Julia glanced at me and I could see, from her face, that the story was almost breaking her heart.

'But it didn't happen like that, did it?' she said gently.

'No.' Susan shook her head. 'The baby came early.'

'And then what?'

'I went to visit Caroline,' Susan said. 'She was in bed. She was very poorly. Her mum – sorry, miss, I know she was your mum too, and she was a nice lady – but she told me I must tell Caroline to forget about the baby. She said the baby was stillborn and that was the end of it. But Caroline had heard the baby crying. She knew the doctor had taken him away and she wanted him back.'

'Did she know where the baby had gone?'

'She guessed.'

'Ahh,' said Julia. She patted Susan's hand, but I saw that her own hand was shaking.

'Caroline knew they were going to put her in the asylum and that would be the end of everything. She would never see her baby again so she had to do something straight away. I helped her get up and I helped her get dressed and I helped her walk down to Fairlawn – but when we got close, we saw Mrs Aldridge on the dam. I was too scared to go on the dam, but Caroline went and she picked the baby up out of his pram. She didn't mean for the pram to go into the water. She never even noticed. She picked the baby up and she started walking back. I went to meet her. I said: "Let me take him for a while, Caroline," but she said: "No," and I said, "But you're ever so pale," and she said: "I am never going to let him go again." She was walking very slowly, very shaky and there was blood all down the back of her dress. I could see the blood but I didn't want to say anything to frighten her. She was holding the baby and she was saying: "Isn't he beautiful? Isn't he the most perfect thing ever?" And I said that he was. Then she said: "Oh Susan, I feel so strange!" And she sort of sat down and then she laid down. She was still holding on to the baby. I sat with her and I stroked her hair until the doctor came to fetch her. Lady Debeger took the baby and the doctor took Caroline. He told me I had to find a pail and clear up the blood that was on the road.'

A tear ran down Susan's face. She wiped it away with a handkerchief. 'I fetched a pail from the pumping station and I filled it up with water and I washed away the blood. And Sam Shrubsole helped me. And then the other people came to shut the sluice-gate and get Mrs Aldridge out of the lake.'

'And we know the rest,' Julia whispered.

'I don't know what they said to Mr Aldridge when he came back from Scotland,' Susan said, 'but he still loves Caroline.' She nodded her head for emphasis. 'He still goes up to her grave. I see him there, on his own, talking to her.'

'Thank you, Susan,' Julia said. Her voice was very calm. 'Thank you for explaining all this to Amy and me. There is only one more thing I want to ask. Can I ask you one more question? Would you mind terribly?'

Susan nodded. Julia breathed in deeply, and then exhaled shakily.

'We know about the teacher, and the doctor. What about your father, Susan? Is he a good man, or a bad one?'

The woman screwed the handkerchief up and stuffed it back up her sleeve. She said nothing. But she moved her head. She tilted it slightly towards the door that led to the dining room.

CHAPTER SIXTY-ONE

I reached the door first. I turned the handle and pushed the door open. It made no sound. There were two men in the room, Dr Croucher in his wheelchair and Reverend Pettigrew. The vicar was standing in the shadows, by the far wall. I could not see what he was doing. The doctor was sitting in his wheelchair in a circle of yellow lamplight cast by a tassel-fringed standard lamp. Kitty Dowler was sitting on his lap. The doctor had one arm around her waist, the other was hidden behind Kitty. His face was in her hair. He was groaning softly.

I had been angry before. I had been angry when my mother walked out on me, I had been angry when I'd caught street boys tormenting cats outside the Paris apartment, I'd been angry when I'd seen the wounds on Daniel Aldridge's face.

I'd been angry for Caroline and for Susan.

But I had never, *never*, been as angry as I was in that moment. And neither had Julia. Julia was across the room in an instant; in an instant she had grabbed Kitty's arm and snatched her away from the doctor, in the next she had hit the doctor across the shoulders with her stick and then, before he even realized what was happening, she walloped the vicar in the stomach.

'Fuck you both!' she cried. 'I'm going to make you pay for this!'

She pulled Kitty from the room, murmuring under her breath: 'Bastards, you bastards!' and I followed in her wake, shocked and horrified and full of admiration for her. After that, we acted as one. We collected Susan, and hurried her and Kitty back along the corridor to the reception desk where the middle-aged nurse was still sitting, yawning over a cup of Camp coffee. Kitty was sobbing as she stumbled along with us. She thought she was in trouble and so did Susan. We kept having to reassure them that the opposite was true.

The nurse looked up. 'What's happened?' she asked.

'You'll find out soon enough,' Julia said.

We hastened outside with Susan and Kitty. And afterwards, I could not understand why it took her so long to ask the question, but as we walked back along the drive, away from Sunnyvale, me holding Kitty safe, trying to comfort her, and Susan holding Julia's arm and helping her along, Julia suddenly asked: 'Where's Vivi?'

'The minibus will have dropped her at the cottage by now,' I said.

'No,' said Kitty. 'Mr Leeson's taking us both home in his car.'

'Mr Leeson? Then where is he?'

'He was going to come back and pick me up,' Kitty said, 'after . . .'

'After what?'

Kitty looked down at the ground.

'After what, Kitty?' I asked again, gently.

'After I'd had my special time with Dr Croucher.'

'Mr Leeson knows about the . . . the "special time"?'

'Yes.'

'Him too?' Julia asked. 'He is part of it too?'

'Like his father,' I whispered. I crouched down to Kitty's eye-level and wiped a tear from the child's cheek with the back of my finger. 'So where is Viviane?' I asked.

'With Mr Leeson.'

'With Mr Leeson where, sweetheart?' My voice trembled.

'In his car.' Kitty sniffed. 'They're having special time too.'

Julia screamed. Her scream disappeared into the fog and then it came back, an echo from the lake, another scream and then another behind it and another; myriad screams rushing across the water, through the mist, zithering this way and that, tiny zephyrs rippling the lake's surface, and the density of the millions of gallons of water beneath changing, an alchemy as the screams returned and ricocheted, bounced from the walls of the old asylum into the cold air, the bone-cracking cold of that night. The scream went back into time; it zig-zagged through the water as Jean Aldridge dropped down towards the sluice-gate; it pushed the base of the pram as the pram floated away from the dam. It cut through time.

I let go of Kitty's warm hand and I ran.

I felt the road beneath the soles of my shoes, I felt the earth beneath the road, I felt the world beneath the earth, and the night and the fog, and I heard my own heartbeat and the in and out of my breath, and I felt the strength in my bones and the contraction and extension of the muscles in my legs as I ran. I ran beneath the Sunnyvale archway and I turned left and ran along the dam and I saw the car's yellow headlights blurred by the fog in the middle of the dam, where I had known it would be, because the headmaster couldn't have stayed in the car park – and where else could he have taken the child? I ran towards the lights, and the closer I came to the car the brighter the lights were in my eyes, the more they blinded me. I tried to call out Vivi's name as I ran but I couldn't make a sound; my lungs were too full of the damp night air, too full of anger.

It was anger for Caroline and Susan, for Kitty and Viviane, for all the girls and boys, all the children who had been playthings for the village committee and those other people, those men and women who did things to children because the children had neither the vocabulary, nor the voice to tell what was being done to them. It was anger for the cynical way these children were chosen, the quiet ones, the damaged ones, the less loved, unloved, difficult to love ones, the vulnerable ones, those who were desperate for attention; those who craved affection and believed that was what they were being given.

I reached Mr Leeson's Jaguar and slammed my hand on the bonnet. The bonnet was still warm, the engine still running. I ran around the side of the car and only when I was out of the immediate glare of the headlights did I see that both the front doors were open, the driver's door and the passenger door. The radio was playing in the car, 'Moon River', and the heater was pumping out hot air; the key was still in the ignition, the front passenger seat had been pushed back but the car was empty.

I bent over double for a moment, put my arms around my stomach, panted, panted, caught my breath. Then I stood up and looked around but all I could see was the fog, weaving and twisting like thick currents of water, like weed caught in a slipstream, like hair blowing in the wind. 'Vivi!' I called, but my voice disappeared into the fog; it was muffled by it, as if the fog were a thick scarf pulled around the lake. To my left was the grassy slope leading down to the water; I was close to the spot where Jean Aldridge had drowned, close to the spot where Caroline had fallen. I could not see the water for the fog, but I knew it was there. And ahead, further on, was the spillway. I could not see that either, but I could hear the sound of the water falling, splashing over the wall, falling into the stone canal below. There had been so much rain recently, rain pouring down from the Mendip Hills, bubbling up through countless little springs in the fields and woodland, finding courses through the limestone, making its way downhill, down the valley, into the reservoir. The reservoir was holding all the water it could and what it could not hold was rushing through the sluice-gate and over the spillway, rushing back to the sea.

'Vivi!' I called again, frantic now, desperate, and I walked slowly towards the spillway. The fog was dense, dense as a nightmare. I held my hands out in front of me, feeling my way. I trod carefully, keeping to the road, afraid of tripping, of rolling down the grassy slope and tumbling into the water, into Jean Aldridge's grave.

'Vivi!' I called. 'I'm coming, darling, I'm coming.'

And the closer I came to the spillway the louder the sound of the water, until it was no longer a whisper but a tumultuous roar, until I could feel the icy spray of the displaced water in the air with the fog, so it was like walking through rain that was falling upwards, towards the sky, in contravention of the laws of nature. Dizzied by this sensation, deafened by the noise, I crept forward.

And then I saw them.

CHAPTER SIXTY-TWO

I saw two figures silhouetted against the fog – indistinct, but I knew the smaller figure was Viviane because I loved Viviane and I would have known her anywhere; in a crowd of a million people, I would have picked out my beloved girl. She was standing on the spillway wall, water rushing around her ankles, and her arms were outstretched for balance. She must have walked along the top of the wall, over mossy stones smoothed by a hundred years' worth of water-flow to the consistency of glass, walked along the wall to escape her teacher. And he was just a few feet along the wall, water rushing around his ankles too and the flaps of his jacket hanging loose as he called to her.

'Viviane, come back. Come back to me now and you won't be in any trouble.' He was holding on to the bank with one hand, too afraid to let go, too afraid to follow the child right out on to the wall. He stood there, hunched and spider-like with his long arms and his long, bent legs, and his back arched like a toad's back – and I wanted to kill him.

But I did nothing. I stood perfectly still. I was

terrified. I did not dare call to Viviane, did not dare do anything to distract the girl in case she lost her concentration and her balance. Vivi stood on the wall and the water gushed past her ankles, over her socks and shoes and she stood there, arms outstretched, swaying . . . and it would take the tiniest push, a puff of air, a fraction of a second's loss of concentration to tip her over, down with the gushing water on to the flat stone slab of the canal bed below.

Mr Leeson had not noticed me. He was scared and he was losing patience. 'Viviane!' he called. 'This is ridiculous! *You're* being ridiculous. Listen to me! You must come back to me now. Now, right this second! Walk towards me, Viviane – come towards me. There'll be no trouble if you come now. I won't tell your mother how badly you've behaved. I won't say anything to anyone if you come now.'

He took a tentative step sideways, closer to Viviane. His feet were bigger than hers. It was harder for him to balance. And he did not have Vivi's natural grace or athleticism. But he was still close to the edge, close enough to jump to safety if he needed to, his fingertips still touching the bank. He was in a far less precarious position than Viviane, who was yards away with the lake behind her and the canal deep down in front of her and the darkness and fog and the water spray all around her.

I began to cry. I did not know how to reach Viviane. I did not know how to help her. I started to walk towards the spillway, slowly, carefully, terrified to take my eyes from the girl, terrified to look at her in case I saw the fall, when it came. Even if I reached the spillway wall, even then I did not know if I had the strength, or the courage, to go forward or how I would get past the teacher. I did not know if I could save Viviane. Tears ran down my cheeks.

'Help her!' I cried. 'Oh please, please, somebody help her!'

And the water gushed and the fog closed in and the lake lay still and quiet behind.

And help came.

Afterwards I could not explain it.

I tried, but there are no words for what happened, no reference for me to use – but it was Caroline, I know it was Caroline who came.

She came out of the fog, like the wind, a rush of ice-cold air, a force of nature, so fast she came. She knocked past Mr Leeson, brushed past him and he lost his balance. He tipped backwards and his arms waved like windmills for a second or two as he struggled to regain his footing but his flat-soled shoes were useless and his jacket was too tight across the shoulders and he could not save himself. He fell backwards into the water, and he disappeared at once, dragged down towards the sluice-gates, following Jean Aldridge, separated only by time. And in the same instant, the same rush of wind seemed to snatch up Viviane from the spillway wall and whisk her back to the safety of the dam, back on to the roadway, and set her down beside me.

Afterwards, Viviane would say that it was me. She said I was the one who came down on to the spillway after Mr Leeson fell, I was the one who walked across the slippery stone and took hold of her hand and led her back to safety. But that wasn't how I remembered it. Not at all.

CHAPTER SIXTY-THREE

We walked back to the lodge, the five of us, a disparate little group of women and girls. I took them there because it was the nearest habitable building, because there was a telephone, because I knew where to find the key, because I wanted to be with Daniel . . . although he might still be angry with me, although there was so much to tell that I had no idea where I would start.

Only he wasn't there. I found the key and we went inside anyway. I lit the fire while Julia telephoned the police. After that, she telephoned Kitty's father – except he wasn't in. He had gone with the other local men to put out a fire in one of the cottages on the hill. I helped Viviane take off her wet clothes and she and Kitty sat on the bed, wrapped in blankets, while Susan boiled water for hot water bottles and heated milk for them to drink. Susan was happy to be useful, glad to have something to do. She looked more at ease than I'd ever seen her before.

I then took off my own wet skirt, shoes and stockings. I put on a pair of Daniel's trousers and a pair of his socks, slipped my feet into his huge boots and, while the others warmed themselves, I went outside to wait for him. I sat on the step and folded my arms about my knees. I waited.

The dog came first, the tricolour collie, running out of the fog. The dog recognized me and came creeping towards me, wagging her rear end, grunting with pleasure.

Daniel was behind, the beam of the torch in his hand reflected back by the fog, lighting the branches of the bare trees around the lodge, the door, me sitting on the step. He held the beam steady to pick me out, wearing his clothes, one of his hats pulled down low over my head, my hands deep in the collie's fur, scratching the ruff of the dog's neck.

'Oh, thank God,' Daniel said. 'I didn't know where you were.'

He was filthy. His face was covered in dirt, in soot. He came slowly towards me and I stood and went to him. He held me close. He breathed into my hair.

'Where have you been?' we both asked, together, and then we smiled at one another, touched by our mutual concern, by the fondness we each felt for the other.

I wiped the smuts from Daniel's cheek.

'I was here,' I said. 'Where were you?'

'In the village. Amy, Reservoir Cottage is on fire. I don't think it can be saved.'

The immediate shock I felt at this news was replaced almost at once by the realization that the burning down of the cottage was inevitable. The man I had seen on the motorbike was the vicar's friend, Dafydd. The doctor must have realized that we would, eventually, find everything that Caroline had written on the walls in the empty bedroom and must have paid Dafydd to set fire to the cottage, to cover up the evidence for ever. Only he was too late. We already knew everything there was to know. There were no more secrets in Reservoir Cottage; nothing else was hidden beneath the wallpaper in the empty bedroom. Everything was out in the open.

'The doctor's cottage is burning too,' Daniel said. 'We couldn't find Mrs Croucher.'

'She's in hospital. She's safe,' I told him. 'Both cottages are empty. Julia and Viviane are in the lodge.'

'Both of them?'

'Yes. And Susan Pettigrew and Vivi's friend Kitty.' I took his hand. 'I'm sorry, darling, we have completely taken over your home. A great deal has happened since I saw you.'

'Obviously it has.'

'I'll explain everything, only not here.'

'Then let's walk.'

He led me to the back of the lodge, across the grassland, down towards the lake. The fog drifted; there was a splash as a fish leaped, somewhere in the darkness. The fog was masking the other lights, the police cars that must surely be on their way towards Sunnyvale by now; the frogmen who would come with their powerful lights to search for Eric Leeson. The fog would mask the sounds, the commotion, everything. We walked down to the water's edge, into the grassy hollow, and we sat together, side by side, on the trunk of the fallen tree.

Daniel held my hand between his knees. 'You and your cold hands,' he said.

We were silent.

'I don't know where to start,' I said.

'That's OK,' said Daniel. 'Take your time. I will sit beside you for as long as it takes.'

I rested my head on his shoulder. The lake was stretched out before us, flat and calm and black beneath the drifting fog. Caroline had sketched the view from here. I was certain she had come with Robert. Perhaps the two of them had sat in this same spot and felt the peace of the lake. Perhaps they had sworn their love for one another here. Perhaps this was where Daniel had been conceived.

It would always be the same. Minutes would go by, days and weeks and months and years, centuries would change, but lovers would sit on this fallen tree and they would gaze out over the water and they would feel the agelessness of it, and the peace, and it would be the same for them all; they would be separated only by time.

'You told me your father has never stopped loving your mother,' I said softly to Daniel.

'That's right,' Daniel said, 'he never has.'

'Let me tell you about her,' I said.

CHAPTER SIXTY-FOUR

June 1962

I was in Fairlawn, upstairs, sitting in the bedroom where Caroline slept when she was housemaid here. We had had the room converted into an office, and with its new, primrose-yellow walls and its cream- and rose-coloured curtains, it felt warm and friendly. It was a room where I liked to sit.

I had pulled the table up to the window, so I could look out over the lake while I wrote to my father. The window was open and the sunshine came in, making warm spangles of light on the floorboards. Bess lay in one of the patches, her legs outstretched, soaking up the heat. Down in the house, I could hear the sound of banging, hammering, the workmen's voices as they put the finishing touches to the alterations. Outside, the only sound was birdsong.

Beyond the window, the lake lay calm and quiet, its reflective stillness only disturbed by dozens of small white gulls flashing like arrows above the shallows. It was a different place now the summer was here. Its dark shadows and sinister moods were gone; in their place were colour and beauty. Myriad wildflowers dotted the grassy perimeter with splashes of the sweetest pale yellow, pink and white, and the water was a gorgeous, azure blue. The trees, full of young leaves and flower candles, formed the softest border to the lake, no longer spiky and black, but different shades of green, round and kindly with lacy clouds of cow parsley below. If I leaned forward, I could see the shallow section of the lake, closest to the grassy hollow. Robert Aldridge was there, in his boat, checking the rope that connected the buoys segregating the area beside the hollow where it was safe for children to swim. Vivi was standing on the shore directing him, wearing shorts, an aertex blouse and Robert's fishing hat. Robert and Daniel had built a wooden pier reaching out into the lake. Robert planned to take children out on to the pier, and teach them how to fish. He had already started to teach Vivi and she was proving a good apprentice.

The dog sat up, scratched her ear, turned a circle, sighed and lay down again. I looked down at the letter I was writing.

Vivi and Julia are settled here. Susan Pettigrew is with us. Once we are properly up and running we will pay her a salary to work for us – if she still wants to. She is really blossoming, Dad, you wouldn't believe the difference in her! Julia has taken her under her wing. The two of them have become best friends. And Vivi is going to the local school and is doing terribly well. I've told her you and Eileen are going to come down for the wedding and she is very excited. My future husband and I are very much looking forward to seeing you both too. I hope you'll stay for a while. I can't wait to show you what we have done with this place.

I watched as Robert pulled the boat up to the pier and climbed out. He sat on the edge of the pier and Vivi went to sit beside him. The two of them gazed companionably out over the lake.

The last months had been hardest for Robert.

He had been the chief witness for the prosecution at the trial of the doctor and the vicar. They were part of the fabric of his life, and always had been. He had been brought up to believe they were good men, pillars of the community. It had taken him a long time to come to terms with the fact that everything he believed about them was false. Once he knew the truth, once it sank in, he had been willing to give evidence against them. He wanted them punished, as we all did. He wanted them to feel a fraction of the humiliation they had imposed on the children they had hurt. But still it was hard for him. It was hard having the role he had played in the events that led to the deaths of Jean and Caroline made public, but we had been there for him, Daniel and I. We had stood by him.

I picked up the pen.

Julia is writing a biography of Alain. His old editor is going to publish it for her. There is a great deal of excitement around the book and she has been back to France to discuss the publicity. She is almost back to her old self.

On the pier, Robert lit a cigarette. I watched the smoke drifting around him.

He had been a victim too.

He had returned from Scotland, all ready to pick up Caroline and elope with her, to find that both she and Jean were dead. His own father-in-law had told him Caroline had pushed Jean off the dam. Robert hadn't believed him, he knew Caroline was incapable of murder, but by then the story had circulated. Robert found himself trapped by the web of secrets and lies, some of them of his own making. If he tried to speak out and tell the truth about the girl he loved, then the son he adored would be branded, for ever, the child of an adulterer and his teenage mistress, the Blackwater Murderess.

Robert could not do that to Daniel.

So he'd done his best, living the lie to protect his son, covering over the picture of Jean, telling Daniel stories of his real mother, but never saying her name, struggling all the time with his contradictory feelings. Telling lies for thirty years was exhausting.

Now the truth had been uncovered, Daniel and his father had achieved a new closeness. They were free to talk about Caroline, about the plans she and Robert had made, the future they now envisaged. It was wonderful to see them together, father and son, working on the project to convert the house. They were so alike, really. They worked so well together with such enthusiasm, firing ideas at one another, teasing one another, laughing. And if, occasionally, Robert took himself off on to the lake with a bottle of apple brandy and his memories, then nobody minded. We watched him go and our hearts were out there, on the lake, with him.

Some things had been lost, but others had been gained. Julia had a beloved new nephew, Daniel an aunt and a cousin who adored him. Robert was part of a family again and he had found himself capable of showing Viviane the gentle affection he'd always denied his son.

I picked up the pen once more.

Anyway, Dad, I'm going to sign off because the children will be here soon and I want to be ready to welcome them when they arrive, and to settle them into their new home. Robert has moved into the lodge, did I tell you that? He likes it there, it's closer to the lake. Dan and I will continue to live here. We've converted all the spare bedrooms into little dormitories and hope, eventually, to make a home for a dozen foster-children. It will be strange for the newcomers at first when all they've known has been institutions, but I hope they'll soon come to be happy here.

I paused, looked around the room. The photograph that used to hang on the wall – the large, blown-up picture of Jean Aldridge's parents – was gone. It had been returned to Jean's family, the Debegers, together with Jean's portrait and certain items she had brought with her when she married. Her sister and nieces had accepted them graciously. They would, they said, pass them on to their children and grandchildren. Daniel and I had even gone back to the ruins of the cottage and searched through the wreckage for the pendant. We had found it, and had it cleaned. I was all for throwing it into the lake, as I'd planned, but Daniel insisted that was returned too. When they'd found out the truth about the village committee, and Sir George Debeger's role in the conspiracy, Jean's sisters had made a generous donation towards the refurbishment of Fairlawn and set up a trust fund to help pay for the care of the children who would eventually live there.

I finished the letter.

So goodbye for now, Dad. Give my fondest love to Eileen and I'll see you both soon.

All my love, Amy

I folded the sheet of paper and put it in the envelope I'd already addressed. I propped it on the desk, called Bess and left the room. I ran down the stairs, the dog following me, out of the front door, out into the bright sunshine. I walked into the garden, out among the flowerbeds, the roses just opening their buds, and the peonies, the valerian, the late blossom, the gorgeous, scented lilac. Susan was pegging laundry on the line that stretched across the lawn, and Julia sat close by, in the shade of the cherry tree, a book, face down, on the bench beside her. She lifted her head and smiled at me as I passed by. I lay back on the grass with my arms stretched above my head, enjoying the feeling of the warmth on my skin, enjoying being alive.

And I knew I was lucky to be alive, to be able to enjoy this beautiful day.

Nothing we did now would ever bring Caroline back, or put the past right. We had cleared Caroline's name. People knew now that she had been the victim, not the perpetrator, but we could not change the past, only view it from a different perspective.

One thing still troubled me and would always play on my mind. I wondered if the doctor had tried to save Caroline's life after her collapse on the dam, or if he had allowed her to bleed quietly to death. While she was alive, she would always pose a potential threat to the committee. Caroline was not the kind of person to go down without a fight, and if Robert knew she was in the asylum, he would have done everything in his power to have her released.

I would never know. The doctor was not entirely without conscience, as his defence lawyer had explained to the jury. It was he who had persuaded the committee to give money to Julia's parents so they could afford to fund her way through ballet school. He called it 'compensation'. It didn't stop the judge from sending him to prison for eight years. The bastard.

The Church of England had taken responsibility for the punishment and rehabilitation of Reverend Pettigrew. We did not know what had become of him. Julia, whose old cynicism had returned, was certain that he had merely been dispatched to some small, far-away parish where the local church was not attached to a school. There was nothing we could do. He was gone and we had turned our faces from the darkness of the past towards what we were certain would be a brighter future.

The sun beat down on my face. The grass was warm. Bess yawned and stretched herself out beside me. I tried to put the past from my mind. I didn't want thoughts of it to spoil this wonderful day.

There was lemonade in the fridge, a cake in the pantry. There would be sandwiches and sausage rolls and ice cream for tea. That afternoon, we would have a little party to welcome our new children. We would do the right thing by them.

The sun shone down on me, and down on the lake. White birds dipped and dived above the water, catching the little eddies and breezes that danced over its surface. Cloud shadows followed one another over the hills and fields, they swept over the lake and the wind disturbed the leaves in the trees and the wildflowers shook their pretty heads. The fish were feeding on the swarms of midges at the edges of the water, the waders stood amongst the reeds and iris, the ducks and moorhens swam in and out of the weeds, followed by their broods.

I heard the engine approaching and then I heard my darling call my name and I stood up and smoothed my skirt. I took a deep breath. This was it, the start of the new beginning.

'I'm coming,' I called.

I walked across the lawn towards the car that had pulled up on the drive. Daniel caught my eye as I approached. I could not keep the smile from my face, or the happiness from my heart. He reached out his hand and took hold of mine.

Three small, distrustful faces looked out at us from the back window of the car.

There was a great deal of work ahead; we would need patience and gentleness and courage. We would need to tread carefully with the children, to gain their trust and to convince them that we were worthy of it. We would need to be kind, always, no matter how they tried to test us, because that was what they would do; they would push us to the limit to make sure our promises were real and that we meant it when we said we would never reject them and always treasure them. And we would need to be vigilant, to make sure no harm came to them and that nobody ever hurt them.

We would need time, but no matter how long it took, that's what we would do.

We would do it for Caroline.

ACKNOWLEDGEMENTS

The biggest thank you goes to Bella Bosworth who has worked so patiently on this book in its several iterations and has been the most amazing editor. Thank you also to Harriet Bourton, Viv Thompson, Joan Deitch and everyone else at Transworld. I am so privileged to be part of such a great team.

Thank you and love to my agency family, Marianne Gunn O'Connor, Pat Lynch, Vicki Satlow and Sophie Wilson.

I am hugely grateful to the support of the online book community who make life and literature such fun: Kim Nash, Anne Cater, Lora Bingham and my other friends; you know who you are and that I enjoy every moment of your company.

The authors I know in real life and online are without exception talented, funny and hugely generous people and I still can't believe that I'm part of this amazing club! Special thanks and love to Tammy Cohen, Amanda Jennings, Rachel Brimble and Alison Knight.

To my family and friends, I love you with all my heart.

And a special mention to lovely Estelle Taylor, and gorgeous Katie Andrews.

Blackwater and all its residents are entirely fictitious, but they inhabit the exact area in North Somerset where Blagdon exists in the real world, and Blackwater reservoir is similar, although not identical, to Blagdon lake. Most of the other locations mentioned in the book, including the Mendip Hills and Blackdown, are real places and I've tried to describe them honestly. I walk the hills with our dogs Lil and Lola whenever I can, and Blackdown is where this story was conceived.

Finally, hello to my good-looking and clever friends at Airbus including Malin, Carolynne, Caroline and Maxine.